A DARK MIND

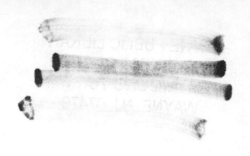

Also by T.R. Ragan

Abducted (Lizzy Gardner Series #1)
Dead Weight (Lizzy Gardner Series #2)

Also by Theresa Ragan

Return of the Rose
A Knight in Central Park
Taming Mad Max
Finding Kate Huntley
Having My Baby
An Offer He Can't Refuse

A DARK MIND

T.R. RAGAN

THOMAS & MERCER

Published by Thomas & Mercer
PO Box 400818
Las Vegas, NV 89140

ISBN-13: 9781611099850
ISBN-10: 1611099854
Library of Congress Control Number: 2012923474

DEDICATION

To Cathy Katz, my sister and best friend, thank you for the countless brainstorming sessions, and for taking the red pen to all my manuscripts, over and over again, and for doing it with enthusiasm and joy. Thank you for the long walks and endless talks, for the amazing trips and sisterly advice, and for making my life truly magical. Thank you, thank you, thank you.

CHAPTER 1

We serial killers are your sons, we are your husbands,
we are everywhere. And there will be more of your children
dead tomorrow.
—Ted Bundy

John and Rochelle
Sacramento
June 2007

John Robinson loved the way his fingers felt, entwined with hers. One year, three months, and two days. That's how long he'd known Rochelle. So many people never found someone to love, but he was one of the lucky ones. Rochelle was the best thing that had ever happened to him. He knew that better than most since he'd never known his father and his mother, who died when he was young. After living in a string of foster homes until he was adopted at the age of thirteen, John had learned that love was fleeting. That's why he appreciated his relationship with Rochelle all the more.

She squeezed his hand, and just that small gesture made his blood flow faster through his veins—made him feel alive. He'd asked her to marry him, and she had answered with an emphatic *YES!*

"Are you all right?" she asked.

Of course he was all right. Filled with joy, he wanted to reach for the sky and tell the world about his good fortune. They had seen a show not too far from his house and were now walking back to his car so he could drive her home. She had declined his invitation to come inside for a nightcap. Rochelle tended to be demure at times, but he didn't mind. He was in love.

"I'm fine," he told her. In the moonlight, he saw her eyes sparkling—hazel eyes, the color more gold than green. "Better than fine," he added. "You make me happy, Rochelle."

He stopped and pulled her close to his chest. "Let's elope."

"Tonight?"

He nodded. "Right now."

"Mom would never talk to me again."

"You've got a sister and a brother. One of them will get married soon. She'll get over it."

Rochelle laughed the sort of laugh that told him his grand plan was not going to happen. *No reason to rush things*, he thought, especially since his only goal was to make her happy. Not that he was a fool or anything. It was just that making Rochelle happy made him happy.

They started walking again, the clicking of her heels loud against the concrete walkway. She shivered, and his first thought was to offer her his jacket, but then he felt a tug on his hand. He looked at her and saw worry etched across her face. "What is it?"

"Do you know those people?"

His dark-blue Toyota Camry was still a block away, but sure enough, there were two guys up ahead. One man sat on the hood of John's car, and a big beefy guy leaned against the driver's side door. He heard laughter. "Looks like a couple of guys having a good time."

"I think we should be safe instead of sorry," Rochelle said. "Let's call the police."

"The police? Are you kidding me?"

She stopped walking and let go of his hand, clearly not happy with his tone. "OK," she said, crossing her arms. "I'm going to go back the way we came, and I'm calling a taxi. It sounds like they've been drinking."

He planted his hands on her shoulders. "You stay right here. I'll get the car and pick you up."

Her shoulders slumped. "You really think they're harmless?"

"I do, but I don't want you to come with me if you're uncomfortable."

She exhaled. "I'll go with you," she said. "Everyone is always telling me I need to grow a spine, so I might as well start now."

"You're the smartest, bravest woman I've ever met. Who said you needed to grow a spine?"

"My brother. He accuses me of being afraid of my own shadow."

He didn't know what to say to that since he still wasn't sure what to think of her brother. Whenever he went to her parents' house for dinner, he felt as if her brother was staring at him. It was like he was waiting for John to make a wrong move so he could pounce.

John forgot all about Rochelle's brother, though, when the guy leaning against his car saw them coming and straightened to his full height. He stood well over six feet. Even from here, John could see that the guy's hands were uncommonly massive—the size of small boulders. He found himself thinking that fifty dollars for a taxi might have been money well spent. Tightening his grip on Rochelle's hand, ready to make an about-face, he heard someone say, "Chuck, I think this car belongs to these people. Get off."

The guy sitting on the hood quickly obeyed and slid off. His feet made a clunking noise as he hit pavement.

There were only two guys. John figured he could handle them. As long as Rochelle didn't have to squeeze by either of them, they could climb into the car and quickly hit the lock button. His Camry was equipped with a smart key, which would make their getaway easier. No need to insert a key to start the ignition. Just one push of the button and they would be off.

As they approached his car, he could see pockmarked faces and bloodshot eyes. Rochelle was right again. These guys were definitely on something. He took a quick look around the neighborhood, at the chain-link fences and windows covered with plywood. The front yards consisted of dead trees and bushes, more weeds than grass. No wonder Rochelle had no interest in coming inside. Maybe it was time to move. The third house on the left had a light on, and he could see a silhouette of a person inside. It looked like his neighbor Claire Schultz was either peeking through the blinds or fiddling around in the kitchen—it was hard to tell.

"How's it going?" one of the guys asked just as John's fingers curled around the door handle. The car beeped, telling him that all the doors were unlocked. Out of the corner of his eye, he saw two more guys coming toward them. What the hell was going on?

The moment Rochelle climbed in on the other side and shut the door, he breathed easier.

It was then that he noticed his backpack was no longer in the back of his car. He enjoyed photography and had been taking a class at a local college.

How did they get inside? No broken windows as far as he could tell, and all the car doors were locked. The blood flowing through his veins thickened, but he decided not to confront them. He'd drive straight to the police station and fill out a report.

He opened the door, his jaw clenched.

"I asked you how it was going," one of the guys said again.

Ignoring the question, John climbed in behind the wheel, shut the door, and locked the doors.

He pressed the ignition button.

Nothing happened.

Shit.

He pressed it again.

Laughter erupted outside his door. He didn't bother to look at them.

The punks would pay.

If he had his way, each and every one of them would be held accountable for the anxiety they were causing, not to mention his stolen backpack and whatever else might be missing.

He reached into his jacket pocket, grabbed the smart key, and held it next to the ignition button. He'd had to do this once before. Only this time nothing happened. The car wouldn't start. *Shit.* He didn't have to get out, lift the hood, and look at the engine to know that the punks standing around were responsible.

Rochelle pulled her cell phone from her purse.

A giant fist slammed through her window. Shards of glass hit his face.

And it was all chaos, broken glass, and regret from there on.

CHAPTER 2

Look down on me, you will see a fool. Look up at me, you will see your Lord. Look straight at me, you will see yourself.
—Charles Manson

Sacramento
Monday, April 30, 2012

Lizzy looked up as her assistant, Jessica Pleiss, came through the front door of her office downtown. Lizzy was drowning in a mountain of work and needed all the help she could get. "Are you all moved in?"

"I am and I'm ready to get to work. What have you got for me?"

Jessica wore a pair of electric-blue fitted pants and a ribbed cardigan over a white blouse. Her brown hair hung in one long thick braid over her right shoulder. She wore little makeup and didn't bother trying to hide the freckles sprinkled across the bridge of her nose.

Jessica had recently switched from attending school full-time to taking a night class and two online courses. Now that she was living away from home, she needed to earn a full paycheck.

Lizzy scribbled a reminder on her calendar and said, "I've got plenty for you to do."

"Something not too dangerous would be great. I've already been shot at and I've been kidnapped," Jessica reminded her for the hundredth time. "I don't mind surveillance jobs. They bore me to tears, but I'll do it, of course, if that's all you've got." Jessica waggled a finger at Lizzy. "But that doesn't mean I'll follow some stranger on the highway for more than five miles. A few miles should give you and your boyfriend enough time to take over."

Lizzy tried to listen as Jessica rambled, but her cluttered thoughts made it difficult to concentrate. Two months ago she'd moved in with her boyfriend, FBI agent Jared Shayne. Things were going well between the two of them, but adjusting to her new environment was proving to be exhausting. Every movement she made in her old apartment had been instinctive. She could move around blindly and still know where everything was: scissors, pens and pencils, her gun. Nothing was the same at Jared's place, and it was getting to her. It was probably time for her to have a talk with her therapist.

"What's wrong? It's Hayley, isn't it?" Jessica asked. "Have you heard from the attorney?"

"Not yet. We should have a release date any day now." Lizzy shuffled through the papers on her desk, located a manila file, and handed it to Jessica. "I'd like you to get started on the Danielle Cartwright case today."

Jessica sat on the chair facing Lizzy's desk and skimmed through the file. "Danielle Cartwright is thirty-nine," she read aloud. "She's been married three times and she's—"

"In a nutshell," Lizzy cut in, "Danielle tends to fall for men who could easily be categorized as womanizers. It's left her with a sour taste in her mouth. Her past experiences have made her distrustful, but not enough to stop her from getting engaged to a man named Dominic Povo."

"She doesn't trust him?"

"She doesn't trust anyone. She's been burned too many times."

Jessica flipped through the pages. "So she wants us to do a basic search on this Povo guy. Makes sense."

"I'd like you to do an in-depth background check. The works: any criminal record, driving history, past addresses, credit reports, any and all phone numbers. His name, birth date, and Social Security number—it's all in there."

"OK," Jessica said. "Does Danielle know she'll be working with me?"

Lizzy nodded as she grabbed another file from the stack on her desk and handed it to Jessica. There was a list paper-clipped to the front.

Jessica mumbled under her breath as she looked over the list. "Five of these are workers' compensation cases. Looks like I'll be sitting in the car every day."

Lizzy nodded again.

"And the last name on the list is Adele Hampton," Jessica said. "Another adoption case—a mother is looking for Adele, the daughter she was forced to give up eighteen years ago."

"Do you think you can handle it all?"

Jessica stood. "I guess I better get started."

"That would be great." Lizzy read another e-mail, but her heart wasn't in it. She scratched her forehead, grabbed a rubber band from her top drawer, which she used to pull back her dirty-blonde hair, and then shoved the pencil back in her mouth.

It was no use.

Until she had a sit-down with Jared and told him she was thinking about moving back to her apartment, she wasn't going to get a whole hell of a lot of work done.

CHAPTER 3

I'm a sick person. I know that. How could a normal guy do what
I did? It was like another guy was inside me.
—Albert DeSalvo

Maureen and Charles Baker
Placer County
August 2011

Maureen brushed her fingers over the leather seats. She'd never
been in a limousine before, and she'd always wanted to take a ride
in one. She looked longingly at her husband, Charles. It wasn't
often in their fifty years of marriage that they were able to dress
up and go to dinner, but tonight was special. A friend and bridge
club member had written up a short article about their big anniversary. A man had called Maureen at home, telling her that an
anonymous donor had read about their love story in the local
paper. The mystery man wanted to treat Maureen and Charles
to a night out on the town. An anniversary extravaganza, he had
explained to her over the phone.

Although Charles didn't like the idea of allowing a stranger to
pay for their dinner, he would never deny her an opportunity of

a lifetime. You had to be somebody to get reservations at La Vue, a famous restaurant in the area. Maureen had been talking about going to La Vue since they first met. But they didn't have much money now that Charles was retired, and they couldn't afford such extravagance. She planned to order the bacon-wrapped king salmon and hoped to talk Charles into ordering the medium-rare Angus New York strip with a balsamic reduction sauce served on chard. Her stomach rumbled and her mouth watered at the thought.

She continued to admire the way Charles looked, all dressed up. There was nothing Charles disliked more than putting on his suit and going to a fancy dinner. Her husband had served many years in the Navy. In the late sixties and early seventies, he was part of a Navy SEAL team and was involved in unconventional guerilla-warfare situations. The proud recipient of the Purple Heart, Charles was also the suspicious sort, which is why he had called the restaurant to see if reservations had, in fact, been made in their names. They had.

Charles was her protector, and he made her feel safe.

Maureen was wearing her best dress, the one she had found on sale to wear to her neighbor's funeral, bless his soul.

The limo wasn't a stretch, but it was long enough to fit three more couples, Maureen figured. She was so eager she could barely contain her excitement.

Charles, on the other hand, was still apprehensive. He pulled his gaze from the view outside and looked at Maureen. "What is the driver's name?"

"Andy."

"Isn't La Vue located downtown?"

"Yes, but I don't know the exact address," she said with a dismissive wave of her hand. "The caller said that it was an anniversary extravaganza with more than a few surprises planned for us, so stop your worrying."

Charles sighed. "I've gone this route before. Unless he turns off this road soon, there's nothing but farmland and cows for miles."

"Oh, come on, Charles. Don't ruin this. How often do we get out of the house? Just go with it. You called the restaurant yourself."

Despite his tugging at his tie and staring out the window, she could see that Charles was trying to loosen up. Relaxing just wasn't in his genes.

A man's soothing voice came through a speaker at the back of the limo. "Help yourself to the champagne," he said. "It's chilled and ready to drink, compliments of La Vue."

The lights were dimmed, making it difficult for Maureen to see as she looked around until she saw the champagne bottle wrapped in a dark napkin and nestled in ice. Charles reached for the bottle, saw that it was open, and poured Maureen a glass.

Charles knew his wife would argue with him if he didn't pour himself a glass, too, so he did. "Cheers," he said, clinking his glass against Maureen's. "To the best fifty years of my life."

"I love you, Charles."

"I love you, too."

He tilted the glass against his lips, but didn't drink any since he'd never been fond of champagne. Maureen finished her glass in a few swallows. Although he was enjoying seeing his wife so happy, he couldn't rid himself of the feeling that something was not right with this picture. He tried to see through the tinted window separating him and his wife from the limo driver, but it was no use. The driver was nothing more than a dark shadow.

"Charles, what do you think Mitch and Carol will say when they find out about all of this?"

He grimaced. "Mitch will be thankful it was me instead of him."

Maureen laughed. Her laughter usually soothed him, but not tonight. He was definitely on edge. The farther they went, the more uptight he felt.

"If you prefer, Mr. Baker," the voice said, "there's some Woodford Reserve whiskey for you."

He and Maureen didn't get out much. They didn't have a lot of friends, but somehow La Vue had known that Woodford Reserve was his favorite whiskey. He turned his gaze away from the dark shadow that was their driver and looked at his wife instead. She finished off her second glass of champagne and then leaned her head back against the headrest and smiled.

"Who paid for our night out?" Charles asked her.

"I asked, but apparently whoever it is wants to remain anonymous."

"So you never talked to the actual person or people who set this all up?"

She shut her eyes. "Charles, please, we've been over this. You called the restaurant yourself. Someone read our story in the local paper. Evidently, the anonymous donors were married straight out of high school, just like us."

"That still doesn't explain why they would want to help us celebrate our anniversary."

"Doing nice things for people must make them feel"—her voice drifted off slightly before she finished her sentence—"better about themselves."

Charles moved closer to his wife. "How would they know that my favorite whiskey is Woodford Reserve?"

His wife didn't answer, prompting Charles to put his hand to her shoulder and give her a shake. "Maureen, are you falling asleep?" Maureen had never been one to take naps or doze off, especially for no good reason. "Maureen," he said again, surprised by the panic lining his voice. "Wake up."

Nothing.

He put his ear on her chest and listened. Her heart was beating. She was alive, but something was seriously wrong.

An idea struck him and he looked at the champagne bottle. He lifted it from the ice, took a whiff, and then dabbed a taste on his tongue—definitely a bitter taste.

Charles slid across the seat, moving closer to the window separating him from the driver, and drummed his knuckles against the glass. "Open this window right now!"

The dark shadow didn't flinch.

Charles slammed his fist hard against the glass. "Turn this vehicle around and take us home!" For the first time in his life, Charles wished he hadn't been so stubborn about owning a cell phone. He refused to purchase one of those modern gadgets. In his opinion, consumers were easily misled into wasting too much time on phones and computers.

"Did you know that your wife kept a diary?" the voice asked through the speaker.

"Take us home now," Charles repeated as he opened every cabinet and compartment, looking for something that might give him a fighting chance if the driver ever decided to stop the limo.

"For fifty years your wife dreamed about one man and one man only. And it wasn't you."

"Shut up, you crazy son of a bitch."

"Harry Thompson. That's the man she's been pining over for fifty years, the man she wishes she had married."

Charles stopped his frantic search and looked through the thick glass at the shadow. "How would you know anything about Harry Thompson?"

"*How* I know isn't important, but *what* I know about Harry and your wife is something I am sure you would find very interesting."

"There's nothing you could say about Harry Thompson that would interest me." Charles shook his head, wondering why he was even talking to the wacko. "Maureen didn't want anything to do with that stick-in-the-mud."

"Then why did she spend six weeks in Italy with him when you were involved in covert operations overseas?"

He refused to let the crazy driver get the best of him. "She went to Italy with her girlfriends," Charles stated calmly. "I've seen pictures. I know what you're trying to do."

"What am I trying to do, Charles?"

"You're just one more crazy who likes to spend his free time putting doubt in people's heads."

"And why would I do that?"

"Because putting doubt in people's minds makes you feel powerful in some way. You have low self-esteem, but you want to feel superior. I hate to break it to you, pal, but you're nothing more than pond scum." Charles eyed the champagne bottle and slid across the leather seat until he was closer to the bottle. "What's the plan?" Charles asked. "You do have a plan, don't you?"

Before the driver could answer, Charles took hold of the neck of the bottle and slammed it against the glass partition. The bottle broke in half. Champagne sprayed across his face, but the tinted glass didn't even crack.

"Your wife has been fucking Harry for fifty years," the voice said.

A kick of adrenaline soared through Charles's body, making his hands shake. He leaned back on the seat, and with all the strength he could muster he kicked both feet through the glass, shattering the partition to pieces.

The limo swerved and Charles fell hard to the floor. His wife's limp body rolled on top of him. Charles wiggled his way out from beneath her. On his knees, he caught a glimpse of the driver's eyes in the rearview mirror right before Charles shoved a hand through the frame of broken glass and wrapped his fingers around the scrawny man's neck. He might be in his seventies, he thought, but he was in tip-top shape. Back in the day, he could kill a man with one hand. He'd done it before and he'd do it again.

The driver yanked the wheel hard to the left, sending Charles flying. Charles used his forearms to protect his face from hitting the door. His gaze locked onto the broken champagne bottle, which had become lodged beneath the leather seat. Crawling that way, he grabbed hold of the neck of the bottle once more, came to his knees, shoved his hand through the broken window, and stabbed the jagged edge of glass into the driver's ear.

The limo swerved across the road, to the left and then to the right, before it careened down an uneven embankment. Charles was violently thrown around, his teeth biting into his tongue as he did his best to protect his wife from injury. At the same instant at which the vehicle made contact with something rigid and inflexible, he felt a jolt as his head made contact with the door. A searing pain jabbed through his skull and all went black.

CHAPTER 4

I thought, "God, what have I done?"...I realized I would be in serious trouble. I thought the best way out of the mess was to make sure she could not tell anybody.
—Peter Sutcliffe

Davis
Monday, April 30, 2012

After a long day at the office, Lizzy returned home, jumped in and out of the shower, combed the tangles out of her hair, and slid on a V-neck T-shirt and a pair of soft gray sweatpants that hung low on her hips.

A noise at the bedroom window caused a prickling down her spine.

She stood there for a moment...staring...watching...waiting.

She took a step toward the window. Her legs felt like heavy weights, her heart racing and her palms clammy and shaky as she reached for the blinds. Fear could be such a subtle yet sinister emotion. It clogged her throat and scraped its tiny fingernails across the back of her neck.

"Dinner's ready," Jared said, stepping into the room.

She put a hand to her chest and let out the breath she'd been holding.

She'd hoped that moving in with Jared would help in some way, but she'd been wrong.

The fear she'd been working so hard to control was back with a vengeance, eagerly spreading terror with every noise, and pumping panic through her veins. Only this time it had no name, just an evil, shapeless face covered in blackness and despair. It was influencing her daily activities: her dreams, her thoughts, her relationship with Jared.

"I scared you. I'm sorry."

"Don't be," she said, surprised by the normalcy of her voice. "I'm fine."

He came up next to her and drew her into his arms. "You're shaking."

"I'm fine. Really," she said again as she stepped out of his arms and headed out of the room.

He followed her down the stairs and to the kitchen. He stood close as he watched her open a cupboard and pull out a wineglass. "Wine?" she asked.

"Sure."

She found another glass and then found herself fixated on Jared's profile as he opened a bottle of Selene Cabernet. He had a strong jaw and a straight nose. His hair was dark and thick, curling a tiny bit around his ears. He looked handsome, as always, and tired.

Forgetting about the wine, Lizzy raked her fingers through her damp hair. She'd hardly said hello before running upstairs to the bedroom to take a shower. She couldn't remember the last time she'd asked him about his day. "How are you doing?"

He didn't look up, not a twitch of his eyes to serve as a clue that he'd even heard her. He remained focused on what he was doing. But she knew his mind was churning away as he carefully chose his words, probably afraid of saying the wrong thing. *What do you say to a crazy woman?*

She'd been living with him for two months, and nothing was working. The terror, the nightmares, and the constant feeling of alarm were all there, worse than ever, thick and tangible, beckoning her with their familiarity. It was no use. She'd been fooling herself into believing the anxiety and panic would magically vanish.

A sigh escaped his lips as he turned toward her, his dark eyes searching, probably hoping to find something worth fighting for—a pinch of optimism, a dash of hope, anything that might stop them from tumbling down another muddy hill. Rolling about in the mud for a while wasn't so bad. It was the climb back up that could be a real bitch.

"Are you sorry you asked me to move in with you?" she asked.

"Never," he said, forcing a smile. "I like having you around."

"I work late most nights," she said. "I come home and hardly say two words to you before hopping into the shower. I find it difficult to focus, and I jump when you enter a room. I'm not getting any better. It's getting worse."

"You just need time to adjust to your new surroundings."

"It's been two months."

He shrugged. "Two months, two years, there's no time limit, Lizzy."

"Linda Gates said the same thing."

"She's a smart woman."

Her therapist was right. Jared was right. She needed time to adjust.

He poured the wine. She took the glass he handed her and followed him to the couch. The news was on and a reporter announced that the Lovebird Killer had struck again. In a distressed tone, the reporter delivered fear through the screen and across the airwaves, no doubt sending more than one million people in Sacramento County into a panic as she talked about two more bodies found.

Lizzy sat on the couch next to Jared and tucked her feet under her. "Another double homicide?"

"Two bodies found miles apart, one strangled, one stabbed. Too soon for the media to assume it's the work of the Lovebird Killer. These two were not married, but they were childhood sweethearts who recently reunited. They were also living together. The man reported the woman missing a week before their bodies were found. If these killings are the acts of LK, then we have our work cut out for us. Every couple found has been killed in a different manner. No pattern, no particular style of murder. The only consistent factor is that the victims were in relationships."

"So you don't think this is the work of the Lovebird Killer?"

"It's too soon to tell. The task force is on it. We'll be able to compare preliminary reports in a few days, but it's highly unlikely that the string of homicides in the past few years were the acts of one single psychopath."

"What about the older couple who went missing last year? Were they ever found?"

He shook his head. "Maureen and Charles Baker are still considered missing persons."

As Lizzy sipped her wine, she looked at him over the rim of her glass. Jared had been assigned to the Lovebird Killer task force nine months ago. He was working closely with a National Center for Analysis of Violent Crimes coordinator in Virginia.

Working with the NCAVC meant a lot of traveling, yet the stress and fatigue rarely showed.

"How do you do it?"

"Do what?"

"Work on some of the most horrific murder cases in the country and still keep your upbeat, encouraging attitude?"

"It gets to me at times, if that's what you're wondering."

"Yes, that's exactly it. How do you stay sane in an insane world?"

"When I come home, I try to leave it all behind. I do the best I can. That's all anybody can do."

"That's the difference between people like me and people like you," Lizzy said. "I can't seem to let it go. Logically, I understand that's what I need to do, but all of those horrid memories pop into my mind when I least expect it."

"I try to find criminals and stop them before they find another victim. You were a victim. It's not the same. You're too hard on yourself. You know what I hate most? Offenders get caught and they go to jail. Perhaps they die," Jared said. "But even in death they are still inflicting pain on their victims."

She knew he was talking about her, but there was nothing she could say to make either of them feel better, so she said nothing.

"I'm not telling you to let it go or get over it, Lizzy. It makes me sad that one evil man has the ability to continue to hurt someone I love from his grave, but you're the only person who can fix whatever it is that's broken inside you. I'm here for you, though. I can lend an ear. I can hold you during the night and tell you everything will be all right, but only you and you alone can fight the demons within."

Setting her glass on the coffee table, she slipped her arms around his waist. She wasn't ready to talk to him about moving back to her apartment. In fact, she might never be ready. She wasn't sure what their future held, and she had no idea how long she could live in his house or sleep in his bed without crying out in the middle of the night. She knew he would find a way to deal with whatever life brought their way, but she didn't know how she would…or if she could.

CHAPTER 5

My first murder was thrilling because I had embarked on the
career I had chosen for myself, the career of murder.
—John Christie

Rene and Harold Lofland
Sacramento
March 2012

Sometimes he hid within fields of tall grass, stayed low behind
the wheel of a stolen vehicle, or—as he was doing now—tried to
get comfortable amid thick shrubbery. Sharp branches kept biting into his arms.

As he watched and waited, his thoughts drifted from one
thing to another, from the past to the present and on to some
of the people he'd met along the way. He liked to think about
the people he'd killed and the gravesites he'd visited. He loved
to rewatch the videos he'd made. He especially enjoyed reading
books about behavioral profiling and stories about other serial
killers. He collected famous killer quotes and watched true-crime
shows.

He did get annoyed by the ex-agents who considered themselves experts on profiling a killer. The idea was absurd. These guys talked about facing some of the most notoriously mad criminals. But they sat in a room with murderers who were chained and cuffed while security guards lined up at the door, waiting to pounce if the killer so much as lifted his hand.

Big deal.

These so-called profiling experts didn't have a clue. It was the everyday people like Mr. and Mrs. Lofland, the couple he was watching right now and had been watching for months, who got to truly look into the eyes of madness. They were the ones who saw evil firsthand. Not some pansy-fuck investigator or profiler sitting behind a desk, talking to a guy in cuffs.

He shook his head at the silliness of it all. Those guys probably made a lot of money from their books. He should know, since he'd bought and read most of them. What a joke.

One of the reasons the FBI would never catch him was because he knew how to change things up every once in a while. He killed young and old, married and not married. He shot, stabbed, and strangled. And yet, despite the fact that he considered himself a man of many names, the media had managed to label him with just one: the Lovebird Killer. He shrugged. In the beginning, he had killed randomly, but as his skills improved, so did his reasoning for doing what he did. He now chose his victims more carefully. It wasn't just about choosing couples in relationships, but more about love itself.

If he couldn't love and be loved, why should anyone else?

He'd thought about sending a letter to the media explaining why he did what he did, but the killers who sent clues and letters always got caught. Although the idea of teasing the police force did hold a certain appeal—especially since he enjoyed screwing with people's minds—he had ultimately decided against it. He dealt with them enough already.

How, he wondered, would he be described after he was dead? Although he didn't plan on getting caught, there was no getting around dying since everybody died eventually. Would they perform an autopsy? If so, would the report be straightforward or exceedingly complex? Perhaps he would be reduced to a physical description: five foot ten, 150 pounds of gangly limbs. Big round hollow eyes—blue, the same color as a robin's egg—and humongous feet. When he was much younger, the girls in school used to dance around him on the playground and call him names like Pick-Up Stick or Skinny Freak or Big Foot. The girls always looked happy when they held hands and skipped in circles around him, which made him happy. He didn't care what they called him as long as they kept hopping up and down. He liked to watch their newly blossoming bodies forming beneath their shirts. Not too many girls in sixth grade wore bras, which had been a definite plus. *Call me any name you want, girls, just keep dancing.* That's what went through his mind. He couldn't help but wonder, if they'd known how much he enjoyed the show, would they have kept the gig going day after day?

He exhaled and focused on the house in front of him. He'd been watching Rene and Harold Lofland for six months now, along with a few other potential couples.

He'd never gone that long without killing before. Most people, including the "experts," had no idea how much patience and skill it took to do what he did. Many believed that killers suddenly snapped one day, grabbed their gun, and shot the first random person on the street. Hell, what fun would that be? People who went ballistic for a minute and then regretted it later were not killers. They were just stupid.

His only worry was that Rene Lofland was a big lady. It would take at least two doses of his usual tranquilizer to get her down, but it would be worth it. He'd knocked out and beheaded a cow before and then raped the carcass. He figured it would be sort of like that.

Thunder boomed, making him shiver and giving him an adrenaline boost. He wouldn't have come out tonight if he'd known it was going to rain. And he might have left if two bright headlights hadn't lit up the driveway.

He knew the house as if it were his own. But he also knew that the cleaning ladies had been there today. Rene Lofland was anal about the carpet, and there would be no moving around inside without her knowing someone had been in the house.

He had chosen the Loflands because a) he always selected complete strangers, and b) the Loflands were so damn syrupy with each other. When he'd first noticed them at the nursery all those months ago, he'd known right away that Rene wore the pants in the family. The whole idea of Rene being the boss caused him to pass them right by. But thirty minutes later, fate stepped in when Harold had a heart attack right there in the middle of a path next to a bunch of fruit trees. Harold went down like a newly cut pine, and Rene fell to her knees and wept like an infant before coming to her senses and shouting orders like "Call 911!" and "Somebody do something!" and "HELP!"

Not only did he follow the ambulance to the hospital, he made sure he ran into Rene every chance he got while Harold was being cared for. Rene figured he was at the hospital visiting a relative. She didn't really care what he was doing there, which made everything perfect. He helped her and she helped him. She just hadn't questioned his motives yet. But she would understand his intentions very soon. He couldn't wait to see her face when he told her who he was and why he was there.

Her expression, no doubt, would be priceless.

Sacramento
Tuesday, May 1, 2012

Lizzy had meant to leave the office before 5:00 p.m. to deliver papers to Michael and Jennifer Dalton, the owners of J&M Realty. It was almost seven when she pulled up next to the curb. J&M Realty was lodged between a dry cleaner and a boutique on a quiet street located in downtown Sacramento. She planned to leave the envelope in their drop box and call it a day. She turned off the engine and got a whiff of new-car smell. After her last car died, she'd picked out a brand-new Ford Escape. It was a brown four-door, environmentally conscious, with aerodynamic design.

After catching a glimpse of someone inside the office, she grabbed the envelope sitting on the passenger seat and climbed out of the car.

The door to the realty office was unlocked. Jennifer Dalton was on the phone, but she waved Lizzy inside. Not wanting to rush her, Lizzy went ahead and took a seat in the leather chair positioned in front of Jennifer's desk.

Jennifer was a beautiful woman. She had a perfect figure, brown eyes, and thick auburn hair that swept past her shoulders in soft waves. Cindy Crawford's twin sister, Lizzy decided. And as if that weren't enough, her smile was bright enough to light up the entire room. When Jennifer and Michael had first come to her seeking help with a workers' compensation case, Lizzy had been mesmerized by the couple's outward affection for each other. It had surprised her to learn that they had been married for nearly fifteen years. With the way they couldn't keep their hands off each other, she would have guessed they were newlyweds.

"I do appreciate that someone has gone out of their way to make plans for Michael and me on our special day, but it's not going to work out," Jennifer said into the receiver. "No, that won't be necessary. Yes, I understand feelings might be hurt, but I'm sure whoever called you will understand." There was silence while Jennifer listened to whatever the caller was telling her. "My husband and I have already made arrangements. I'm sorry, but my answer is still no. I really need to go. I'm sorry."

Jennifer sounded beyond annoyed. More silence followed as she listened to the caller.

"If you could give me the name of the people who called you to set this up, I'll give them a call and take care of it myself."

An open folder sat on the middle of Jennifer's desk, invitations and lists spread out from one end to the other.

Jennifer looked at Lizzy as she listened to the caller and rolled her eyes, clearly perturbed. She used her pen to make notes on a sticky pad. "Yes, that's very kind of you," Jennifer said into the receiver. "I really do have to go now."

Jennifer hung up the phone. She looked at Lizzy and her shoulders slumped forward. "Wow. That guy would not take no for an answer."

Lizzy said nothing. She'd met the woman only once before, but she felt her pain—nothing worse than a stubborn caller who wouldn't listen.

"As you can see," Jennifer went on, gesturing at all the papers on her desk, "Michael and I are planning a party." She began stuffing half-finished notes and invitations into the open file. She crumpled up the sticky note and tossed it toward the garbage behind her, missing by a few feet.

Lizzy nodded. "I remember Michael mentioning that your anniversary was coming up."

"That's right." Jennifer smiled, but she was obviously still upset by the phone call. She rubbed her temple. "The man on the phone was adamant about picking Michael and me up before the party, but I have already made arrangements with another couple. If he told me who was behind the idea of this 'special ride,' I would have been able to clear it all up with one quick phone call. With the economy spiraling downward, I think he was just desperate not to lose the job, which makes me sad."

"Understandable," Lizzy agreed.

"I'm sorry," Jennifer said. "I'm rambling on while I'm sure you have better things to do than sit here listening to me worry and gripe." She took a breath. "What have you brought me?"

"It's the contract for the Simpson case. As soon as it's signed, I can get started."

Jennifer took the envelope Lizzy handed her, pulled out the papers, and read them over.

The contract was short, basically stating that Lizzy would initially charge up to, but not more than, fifteen hours of surveillance over the next few weeks. She would use video and photographs to keep track of Simpson's activities. Eli Simpson, an employee of J&M Realty, was claiming he slipped and fell while showing one of their foreclosed properties. According to his claim, there was little he could do without pain, and he was therefore housebound. The insurance company wasn't working on the claim fast enough, so the Daltons had hired Lizzy to get proof to help them speed things along. If Simpson raised any red flags while Lizzy was watching him, she would meet with Jennifer and Michael again in a few weeks to view videos and pictures. At that time, they would decide whether they had enough evidence.

"Everything looks great," Jennifer said as she signed the contract. "Michael and I would like you to get started on this right away." She stood and went to make copies. The moment she disappeared, her phone rang.

The answering machine picked up after two rings. "Office hours are from eight a.m. to five p.m. Please leave a message and we'll get back to you shortly."

After the beep, a man's voice came on the line. "I'm calling about your property off Guadalupe Drive in El Dorado Hills." There was a long pause as the caller waited for someone to pick up. Lizzy heard a noise in the background, a tinkling of bells, like someone had just walked through the front door of an antiques shop. "It's late," the caller said. "I'll try again tomorrow."

Jennifer came rushing back into the room. She picked up the phone, but it was too late. "Damn. We've had that place on the market for over a year. He didn't leave a number, did he?"

Lizzy shook her head. "I don't believe he did."

"It's not usually so crazy around here," Jennifer said as she sorted through the copies she had made. "Too many weird things happening to me lately."

"What's going on?"

She waved a well-manicured hand through the air. "Hang-up calls, dead bugs, bumps in the night, you get the drift."

Lizzy didn't get the drift at all. "Are you being harassed?"

Jennifer stopped what she was doing and shook her head. Her shoulders slumped a tiny bit. "My mother passed away six months ago. It seems every little thing is upsetting me lately. I need to take a deep breath and settle down. Everything is fine. I bet you're regretting that you stopped by."

"Of course not," Lizzy assured her. "I'm sorry about your mom."

"Thanks." Jennifer did her best to sort the copies from the original, making sure not to include any of her party-planning papers. She restapled the original contract and handed it to Lizzy along with a check. "The deposit is attached. That should do it."

Lizzy put the envelope in her bag, and then stood and shook Jennifer's hand. "I'll get to work on this right away and call you in a week or two with an update."

"Thank you," Jennifer said as she followed Lizzy to the door. "Looks like it's going to rain."

Lizzy looked out at the sky. Dark gray clouds were huddling together, up to no good. Before she had a chance to open the door, a man's face appeared on the other side of the glass.

Jennifer shrieked and jumped back.

Lizzy instinctively reached toward her shoulder holster for her gun.

Jennifer put a hand on her chest. "It's Michael." She opened the door. "You scared the daylights out of us."

Michael Dalton stood well over six feet. He was in his late thirties, but with blond windswept hair, broad shoulders, and a healthy tan, he didn't look a day over twenty-nine. He gave his wife a sheepish grin. "Sorry about that. I was surprised to see your car still parked at the curb. I wanted to make sure you were OK."

Jennifer gave him a forgiving smile before she gestured toward Lizzy. "You remember Lizzy Gardner. She stopped by to bring us the contract for the Simpson case. I already signed it, made copies, and gave her a deposit. She's going to get started right away."

"Great. Nice to see you again," Michael said, offering his hand. "Nice to see you, too."

Stepping inside, he held the door open for Lizzy and said, "Let me know if there's anything I can do to help you snag Simpson. Nothing worse than a freeloader."

"I will," Lizzy said. "I'll be in touch."

A couple of raindrops dotted the sidewalk as Lizzy unlocked the car door. Once she had her seatbelt on, she turned on the ignition and glanced over her shoulder at the realty office. Michael Dalton was staring out the window at her. Shivers coursed over her body. She gave him a quick wave, but he didn't wave back. As she drove away, a strange sense of foreboding rose up around her.

CHAPTER 6

It was an urge…a strong urge, and the longer I let it go the stronger it got, to where I was taking risks to go out and kill people—risks that normally, according to my little rules of operation, I wouldn't take because they could lead to arrest.
—Edmund Kemper

Antelope
Wednesday, May 2, 2012

Dominic Povo took the boring out of surveillance work, Jessica decided as she watched him work. The man was sizzling hot, a Greek god in the flesh. A couple of his coworkers weren't too bad either. No wonder Danielle Cartwright was considering throwing caution to the wind and marrying for a fourth time. According to the research she had done on Povo, he was the foreman on this particular construction site in Antelope, California, a flat area with few hills and no major bodies of water.

Povo grew up in Pittsburg, California. When he was eighteen, he moved to Las Vegas and went to culinary school. He never earned a degree, and it was still a mystery to Jessica as to how or why he detoured from culinary to construction. Extracurricular activities included hanging out with his pals and making regular treks to Las Vegas, something she intended to ask Danielle about.

From what Jessica had seen so far, the man spent most of each day inside the trailer parked on the site—a lot of meetings were held in that trailer. He would appear in the morning dressed in khakis and a collared shirt. He usually carried building plans under his arm and did a lot of pointing as he gave his men instructions. He appeared to have a temper, although she was basing that solely on his expressions seen through Lizzy's expensive HD binoculars. It was easy to see every bit of strain on Povo's face when he became annoyed and angry.

Povo had surprised her a few hours ago when he stripped his shirt off, grabbed a hammer, and began working right along with the rest of the guys. He had rock-hard abs and biceps that wouldn't quit. He had a strong jaw and a pretty face, too.

It wasn't exactly hot outside, but obviously Povo didn't want to mess up his fitted dress shirt. She'd been following him for three days now. Last night he'd gone out with a few of the guys, drunk a few beers, and ended up at his apartment alone. The night before that, he'd slept at Danielle's house.

After leaving Povo, Jessica always returned to her apartment. There was little furniture, but she liked having a place to call her own. Although she worried about her mom, she didn't think she was doing Mom any good by living with her and lecturing her day after day about drinking too much. After Jessica's brother moved to New Jersey, she decided it was time to grow up, move on, and get a life.

Last night, Jessica did what she usually did when she got home: she heated up some Top Ramen, studied for a bit, and then watched television. She also spent too long feeling sorry for herself. Pathetic. Her last boyfriend, Casey, had broken up with her after she refused to sleep with him. She hadn't been ready to take their relationship to the next level, but now she regretted holding back. Although everybody mistook her for a teenager, she would be twenty-one soon. And she was still a virgin. But that didn't mean she didn't think about sex. She thought about it a lot. She just hadn't met the right guy yet.

Jessica looked at the clock on the console. It was almost three in the afternoon. She needed to take off soon and meet Danielle at the coffee shop in Rocklin. Danielle did a lot of traveling, so she wanted an update before her upcoming trip.

As Jessica watched Povo, a large white van backed up onto the smooth flat dirt that would later be the backyard of what was now a shell of a house. Her stomach grumbled. She was starved. And she was also broke. Hopefully Danielle would offer to buy her lunch. Ever since she'd moved into her own apartment, she couldn't afford luxuries like food. Lizzy had finally given her a raise, but that extra seventy-five dollars a month barely covered utilities.

She took a long gulp from her stainless-steel water bottle and watched a construction worker push an empty wheelbarrow toward the van. He opened the double doors at the back and then looked about, first to his left and then to his right.

Jessica looked around, too. What was the problem?

There was nothing but a few model homes and more than fifty acres of semismooth soil.

The driver climbed out and the two men made quick work of tossing bulky garbage bags from the van to the wheelbarrow.

Strange.

The man with the wheelbarrow disappeared behind the house, while the driver shut the van doors, hopped behind the wheel, and took off. Jessica stayed low as he passed by.

Once the van was out of sight, she straightened and looked at the clock again. Time to go. She turned the key.

A *rap tap tap* on the passenger window made her jump. She put a hand to her chest when she saw a young man looking inside her car. *Shit!* It was one of the construction workers.

Stay calm, she told herself. *Pretend nothing's wrong...just looking at a few model homes, trying to get a feel for the neighborhood.*

The engine was running. She could take off, but what good would that do besides confirm that she was guilty of spying? She needed to play it cool. Her car was an older model, and she had to lean over the passenger seat and manually roll the window down a few inches, leaving enough room so she could talk to him, but not enough so that he could get his arm inside and unlock the door.

"I was wondering if there was something I could help you with."

"No," she said, shaking her head for good measure. "Everything's fine."

"You're sure?"

She nodded.

He took a closer look at the neighborhood, which consisted of a labyrinth of empty lots and three finished model homes surrounded by a colorful string of flags. In the distance, she could see a few homes under construction.

When his gaze returned to her, she held up a folder filled with pamphlets and detailed plans of the three-thousand-square-foot homes with two and three bathrooms. "I like the Tuscon home the best," she said.

"Yeah?"

"Yeah," she said, trying not to stare at his broad shoulders or well-built arms. "I like the large kitchen and the three-car garage."

He looked at her old beat-up Volvo with its dented fender and bald tires.

"A girl can dream, can't she?"

"Yeah," he agreed, "a girl can dream."

She found herself smiling at him. The way he was looking into her eyes made her wonder if he was coming on to her. He was definitely cute, and the idea of him noticing her at all made her feel good. After Casey broke up with her, she'd lost her confidence.

"I know why you're here," he said.

Her heart skipped a couple of beats. "You do?"

His smile reached his expressive eyes as he slipped his card through the opening in the window.

The card landed on the passenger seat. She picked it up and read it. "Magnus Vitalis, handyman, there isn't anything I can't fix."

His smile widened, revealing straight white teeth, making her take a closer look. Not only was he charming, he had no idea what she was doing parked across the street. He was definitely coming on to her, and she liked it. "I have to go," she said, wishing she could stay and talk to him. There was something about him that made her insides do funny things. "It was nice meeting you."

"The pleasure was all mine…"

He was waiting for her to tell him her name.

"Kat," she said, inwardly groaning. "Kat Sylvester." She would have told him her real name if Lizzy's number one rule was *not* to give anyone a name while on surveillance duty.

"If you come back tomorrow, Kat, I'll give you a private tour of one of the finished homes."

"I wish I could, but I'm busy tomorrow," she said. "It was nice meeting you, Magnus. I better go."

He stepped away from her window, and she put her foot on the gas, already regretting not giving him her number. He was super hot and extremely personable. What harm would it do to have lunch or a cup of coffee with him?

Damn.

Kat Sylvester? She rolled her eyes, and then took in a deep breath as she concentrated on the stretch of road ahead of her. She thought about the van and the garbage bags and decided she was being paranoid. If she kept it up, she'd end up with stomach ulcers. More often than not, she wondered why she was in this business at all. Ever since her sister, Mary, had disappeared, she'd imagined herself as a criminal profiler. She preferred to look at the crimes *after* they were committed—not before, and certainly not during. She wanted to analyze information from the crime scene: blood splatters and ballistic reports. The idea of working with criminal investigators and detectives appealed to her. She would gather information, make lists, and check them twice. Hard facts along with deductive reasoning would give her a clear and logical list of suspects.

She exhaled. She'd been working with Lizzy Gardner for nearly two years. If not for Lizzy, she might never have found out what had happened to her sister. Finding the truth had given her closure, and yet knowing Mary was gone forever hadn't helped fill the hole in her heart. Maybe because Mary wasn't the only one she'd lost. In a way, she'd lost her entire family. Her dad had left home and her mom had begun to drink. Jessica had tried clinging to her brother, but he hadn't been able to take the pressure, and now lived across the country. Nothing had been the same since. Nothing would ever be the same again. But still, the idea of quitting her job didn't feel right. She looked up to Lizzy, thought of her as an older sister. Once she had her degree, Jessica thought, she would move on. Until then, she would just have to deal.

Sacramento
Wednesday, May 2, 2012

Lizzy sat on the edge of Brittany's bed and watched her niece as Brittany typed what appeared to be a hundred words per minute on the keyboard. A self-portrait Brittany had drawn in her art class hung on the wall, tilted to one side. Brittany didn't look anything like her mother or her aunt. Green cat eyes, a small nose, and high cheekbones gave her an exotic look.

Movie and boy-band posters had been taken down, Lizzy noticed. The walls of Brittany's bedroom were now painted a dark maroon. The floor was covered with clothes, binders, and CDs. Jewelry, mostly pendants dangling off long chains, hung from wooden pegs screwed into one of the walls. Dirty clothes filled the hamper, spilling out onto the floor. A large whiteboard covered the wall directly in front of Brittany's computer. Lyrics from a song she didn't recognize were scribbled across the board in different colors of dry-erase markers, along with cryptic messages only another teenager would be able to decipher. There used to be a framed picture of the two of them on the dresser next to the bed. It was gone. Or maybe it was hidden beneath the magazines and empty bag of chips. It was hard to tell.

"How's cheerleading going?"

"I quit," Brittany said, her fingers not missing a beat on the keyboard.

"Why? I thought being a cheerleader was all you ever dreamed about?"

"Dumb little-kid dreams."

"You're not even sixteen."

The keyboard noises stopped. Brittany swiveled around in her desk chair and pinned Lizzy with a serious look. "Why are you here?"

"Is there something wrong with my wanting to visit my favorite niece?"

"Mom called you, didn't she?"

"What's going on, Brittany?"

"What do you mean?"

"You quit cheerleading. Your room looks like the local dump. Your grades are slipping. And look at your hair, for God's sake. Don't play dumb with me, and I won't play dumb with you."

Brittany swiveled another quarter of a turn so that she could look at herself in the mirrored closet door. "What's wrong with my hair?"

"Nothing. I just wanted to make sure you were listening."

Brittany released a frustrated breath and then said, "Can you handle the truth?"

"That's why I'm here."

"I'm trying to forget everything that happened with that sicko Spiderman. I really am, but I can't. One minute I'll be doing my own thing, enjoying my friends, and then suddenly his face will pop into my mind when I least expect it and BAM! It's over. I can't think. I can't concentrate. I followed the therapist's advice. I really did. I became more involved at school. I filled my time with activities I enjoy doing. I write my feelings down in a journal. But it's not working." Brittany's eyes glistened, but her resolve not to cry was apparent in the firm set of her jaw. "I can't get his face or his voice out of my mind."

Lizzy's head fell, her chin nearly touching her chest. She felt responsible. She *was* responsible. Samuel Jones/Spiderman had gone after Brittany to get to Lizzy, and it had worked. But she would never say as much to her niece because that would serve only to make Brittany feel guilty for speaking up. And that's not why she was here.

"I'm not blaming you," Brittany said.

"I know you're not." Lizzy picked up her head and met her niece's gaze straight on. "You're the best thing that ever happened to me and my sister." She swallowed a knot in her throat, thankful that her niece was alive and in one piece after all she'd been through. "You know that, right?"

Brittany nodded.

"Don't ever forget that. You're doing everything right, Brittany. Just promise me one thing."

Brittany waited for Lizzy to elaborate.

"Promise me you'll call me if you ever need someone to talk to, all right?"

Brittany nodded again. "When is Hayley getting out of jail?"

"Any day now."

"You said that same thing three weeks ago."

"You're right. I thought we would be able to get her out by now. Jared is working on it. We both are."

"I have a savings account," Brittany said. "How much do you need for bail money?"

"It's not that easy."

"It's OK," Brittany said. "I know you're trying. Did Mom tell you that she's seeing Dad?"

"No, she didn't." Lizzy marveled at how her niece could change the subject within the blink of an eye. "How do you feel about that?"

Brittany shrugged. "He's my dad. I love him. I was angry with him for a while, but then I realized Mom is no angel either, and there are two sides to every story."

Lizzy was not a fan of her ex-brother-in-law, but the kid had a point. He was Brittany's dad and she loved him, which meant Lizzy needed to try to like him, too. Lizzy held up her keys and jingled them in the air. "Want to go for a drive?"

Brittany's eyes lit up, reminding Lizzy of better days.

"You're going to let me drive your new car?"

"Yep."

"What about Mom?"

"Before running to the grocery store, she gave me her blessing and wished us luck."

Brittany swiveled back around, shut down her computer, and said, "Let's go."

Davis
Friday, May 4, 2012

Lizzy couldn't remember the last time she'd felt so relaxed. Seeing Brittany this week had definitely helped her mood. She sat on the couch in her usual position: feet tucked under her as she sipped her wine and listened to Jared talk about his day. It was good to see him opening up. He was the strong one in their relationship, the listener, the composed FBI agent. But as soon as the conversation turned to his work on the Lovebird Killer case, he became tense and withdrew slightly.

"Talk to me," she said. "Tell me what's going on."

He looked at her, his eyes probing hers, no doubt trying to determine how much she could handle, but his phone rang before he could continue.

Lizzy went to the kitchen to give him some privacy. When Jared finished with the call, she returned with a large bowl of popcorn.

"Looks like I'll be leaving again tomorrow," he said. His brows slanted inward. "No Rice Krispies Treats?" he asked.

"I thought we should stay away from sugar for a while," Lizzy said. When she'd stopped working out with the late Anthony Melbourne, she'd taken up running. What had started out as a jog through the neighborhood every once in a while had turned into a five-mile run at the park near her office. She ran at least four days a week and she was in the best shape of her life. The other thing Melbourne had lectured his clients about was his disgust with sugar, which he referred to as white poison. Exactly why she had decided to give up her beloved Rice Krispies. She took a seat on the couch and told Jared it was his turn to pick the movie.

While he examined the endless rows of DVDs for something to watch, Hannah jumped onto Lizzy's lap, purring and begging for attention.

Jared rubbed his hands together, pulled three DVDs from the movie rack, and held them up for her to see. "*Crank, Commando*, or *The Big Lebowski*."

"That's easy," she said.

"*Commando*, huh?"

She shook her head. "*Crank*."

"Really? I thought you were more of a Schwarzenegger than a Statham kind of gal."

"You don't even know me," she said, marveling at how there was always something new to learn about Jared, despite the fact that they had dated in high school and shared a long history.

He set the movies on the table, and then moved the cat out of his way so he could sit next to Lizzy and wrap her in his arms. "You're right," he said. "Tell me something about you that I don't already know."

His serious tone took her by surprise. "I hate pickles," she told him.

"Tell me it isn't so."

"I'm scared to death of earthquakes," she added.

"Hmmm," he said, before nibbling on her earlobe.

"When I was twelve," she went on, "I went to an ice-skating party. Hours later, they had to drag me off the ice. For years, I dreamed of being a figure skater."

He pulled away slightly and gazed lovingly at her. "I bet you would have been an Olympian by now."

"Your turn," she said with a smile. "Tell me something I don't know."

He thought for a moment. "I like apple juice on my Cheerios."

Her nose wrinkled. "That's disgusting."

"I'm pretty good at skipping stones. Fifteen skips is my record."

"Nice."

"I couldn't tie my shoelaces until I was seven years old."

"Oh, no," she said, complete with a seriously worried face. "I'm sorry."

It was Jared's turn to smile.

After a long week and another long day at the office today, it felt good to unwind, especially wrapped within Jared's arms. "Want to know something else?" she asked.

"I do."

"I'd rather make love than watch a movie."

Without hesitating, Jared stood, scooped her into his arms, and carried her to the closest bedroom. "I have a lot to learn about you, Lizzy Gardner."

With her arms wrapped around his neck, she laid her head against his shoulder and said, "No worries. We have plenty of time."

CHAPTER 7

The first good-looking girl I see tonight is going to die.
—Edmund Kemper

Sacramento
Monday, May 7, 2012

Lizzy sat in her Ford Escape and watched the Simpson house from less than a block away. The street was quiet. No children playing outside. No dogs barking. Just Lizzy all alone with her thoughts. The funny thing about surveillance work, Lizzy thought, was that although she was the one doing the watching, she often felt as if *she* were the one being watched.

Her car doors were locked. There were no thick hedges or dark alleyways for someone to hide in. She had nothing to worry about, she told herself, but somebody needed to tell that to her rapidly beating heart. She drew in a deep breath and tried to collect herself.

Next, she counted to five.

Breathe. Think about the weather. Despite the continuous rain of the past week, there was only a light sprinkle today. Spring was definitely in the air, she decided as she watched a wild rabbit scurry across the empty lot next to Simpson's place.

She fiddled with the camera in her lap. Holding it at eye level, she looked through the lens and played with the shutter speed and the aperture until she could see every detail of the brass handle on Simpson's door. As she made a few adjustments, she moved the lens across the front of the house. Through the front window, she saw movement and decided to keep her lens focused there, hoping Eli Simpson would make an appearance.

He was not married, but somebody was definitely moving around inside the house. *Come on, Simpson...move closer to the window.*

When her phone rang, she looked down and saw that it was a number she didn't recognize. She held her camera with her right hand and her cell with her left and pushed the Talk button.

"Hello," the caller said, "is this Lizzy Gardner?"

"Yes, it is." She was about to put the camera down, when Simpson's front door opened.

"Hayley Hanson is ready to be picked up," the caller said. "She's been cleared to leave. If you can get here before three o'clock and fill out all the necessary paperwork, she'll be released to you today. If not, we'll have to wait until Wednesday afternoon."

Lizzy had been praying this day would come, but she'd begun to lose hope that they would be able to get Hayley out before her first year was served. "Hayley can come home?" she asked, trying to concentrate, unable to believe what she was hearing, her voice shaky with emotion.

"She'll be wearing an ankle monitor, but yes, she can be picked up."

Lizzy gave up trying to talk and take pictures at the same time and set the camera aside.

"By the time Hayley's situated," the caller said, "the monitor will have been activated. The rules are strict. At timed intervals, the monitor sends a radio frequency signal with location to a receiver. If the offender has moved outside a permitted range, the police will be notified. The monitor cannot be tampered with in any way. Removal attempts will cause authorities to be alerted and she'll end up right back where she started."

Lizzy looked at the clock. If she left now, she could make it in time. She couldn't let Hayley spend another night in that place. "I'll be there by three. Thank you."

Simpson walked like an old man as he reached into his mailbox, but then he grabbed his mail and ran up the path and into his house.

Damn.

"I'll be back," Lizzy told him, inwardly cursing as she pulled away from the curb and drove off.

Juvenile Detention Center
Sacramento
Monday, May 7, 2012

After filling out ridiculous amounts of paperwork, Lizzy returned to her car and drove to the other side of the California Division of Juvenile Justice building, where she parked at the curb, climbed out of the car, and waited, her eyes focused on the steel double doors.

It wasn't long before the blocks of steel came open and Hayley stepped outside.

Lizzy closed her eyes, inhaled some cool afternoon air, and let the moment wash over her before she pushed herself from the car and headed toward her. For the first few months after Hayley's incarceration, Lizzy and Jared had spent every waking moment discussing possibilities of how they were going to go about get-ting Hayley released before her term was served. Lizzy had gath-ered documentation about the men who had hurt Hayley over the years, while Jared had worked on the legalities of Hayley's release. They had met with the judge three times before they had finally been allowed a hearing. At the moment, though, none of that mattered. Their persistence had paid off. Hayley was free.

Lizzy crossed the street and waited outside the gate as she watched Hayley get closer and closer to freedom. In the nine months that Hayley had been incarcerated, her dark auburn hair had grown well past her shoulders. Lizzy had visited less than two weeks ago, but today Hayley looked paler and thin-ner. Her hair was unbrushed and stringy. She wore loose jeans, a dark T-shirt decorated with a symbol Lizzy didn't recognize, and black tennis shoes with white lace. Her piercings had been removed upon her arrival at the detention center, and had yet to be replaced.

The guard and Hayley did not exchange words as he opened the chain-link door surrounded by barbwire fencing.

As the gate was locked behind them, Lizzy took Hayley into her arms. Although she had been planning for this moment for months, and she knew Hayley wasn't the touchy-feely type, she couldn't help herself. She wrapped her arms around Hayley and held her tight. Hayley felt stiff and rigid, but Lizzy didn't care. She didn't want to let go, but she finally released her hold, and they walked toward the car without speaking.

Lizzy held her keys toward her new car and pushed a button. A beep sounded and the trunk popped open.

"Movin' on up, I see."

"I also replaced the carpet with wood flooring in the office."

"Nice."

"Faux wood, not real wood," Lizzy said, "since I don't want my clients thinking that they're overpaying me."

Hayley shoved the few things she had in the trunk, clicked it shut, and then climbed into the passenger seat. Lizzy was already strapped in. As soon as Hayley had her seatbelt on, Lizzy merged onto the street and headed for home.

"How bad was it?" Lizzy asked after a few quiet moments passed between them.

"It could have been worse. I met some interesting characters."

Lizzy wasn't sure if that was a good thing or a bad thing.

"Have you seen my mom?"

Lizzy nodded. She figured Hayley would have preferred to move in with her mom so that she could protect her, but the judicial order stated that Lizzy was her guardian, and therefore Hayley had no choice but to live with her and Jared—at least for now. "I've been watching your mom, just as I promised I would," Lizzy said. "A few days ago, I followed her downtown. She went to the grocery store and then dropped an envelope in a drop box outside the post office. She was wearing jeans and a T-shirt and her hair was pulled back in a ponytail. She looked good."

"Any sign of Brian?"

"No. According to county records, he sold his house a few months ago. I have yet to find out where he moved to." Lizzy knew Hayley had reason to worry about Brian's whereabouts. Because of him, Hayley had spent the past nine months in the juvenile detention center. After Hayley had cut off his penis and burned "child rapist" across his chest, Brian had promised her he would kill her mother, which was why Hayley had asked Lizzy to keep an eye on her. Brian's penis was reattached, and the day after he left the hospital, he was brought in for questioning. Unfortunately,

Hayley's mom was strung out and unwilling to speak out against the man she believed loved her and cared about her. Despite the years of abuse she and her daughter had been subjected to, Brian was released within twenty-four hours, and there was nothing Lizzy could do about it.

Hayley picked up her right leg and settled it on her left knee so she could examine the monitor covering her ankle.

"Is it too tight?"

"It's OK. I just need to get used to it."

Lizzy noticed that Hayley couldn't fit a finger beneath the plastic. "I think we should turn around and make them loosen it."

"No. It's fine." She let her foot drop to the floor and kept her gaze straight ahead.

Hayley was still the same stubborn girl she'd always been, so Lizzy let it go. "To keep you from going stir crazy, I was hoping you would be willing to work for me from home."

"You know how I love paperwork."

Lizzy smiled at her sarcasm, glad to know Hayley still sounded like Hayley.

"What's my radius on this thing?" Hayley asked, gesturing toward her foot.

"You can go anywhere within a mile of the house. Any farther than that, and the receiver transmits your new location to authorities and you could end up right back in jail."

Hayley exhaled. "I bet Jared's excited about having a new roommate."

"He's fine with it," Lizzy said, which was the truth. Jared was easygoing and flexible. "He's been traveling a lot. He's gone right now, but he'll be home for a few days before he has to take off again."

"What's he working on?"

"He's meeting with the NCAVC coordinator to determine whether he can get some assistance from the Behavioral Analysis Unit on a case he's working on here in Sacramento."

"A lot of psychos in the world to keep him busy, I guess."

"Sad, but true," Lizzy said before changing the subject. "I'm going to take you home and then run to the grocery store. What can I get for you?"

"I'm fine. I'll eat whatever you have at the house."

"Come on," Lizzy pressed, "there must be something you crave after all these months."

"I'll never eat bologna or beans again. Other than that, I've got nothing."

"I was thinking you might want to call Tommy in a few days, since he keeps asking about you."

"Tommy who?"

"The boy you met at the high school where we talked—"

"Are you talking about the Karate Kid?"

Lizzy chuckled. "Sure, yeah, I guess I am."

"Lizzy."

"Yes?"

"I know you mean well, but can you just not worry about me? I mean, if we're going to live together for a while, I'd rather you not mother-hen me. No cooking me meals, and I'd prefer to choose my own friends. From what you've been telling me when you visit, you're busier than ever. I don't want to organize a youth club or write my feelings in a journal every day. No offense. I'd rather just keep busy organizing your files, doing basic searches, reading my books, stuff like that."

Lizzy sighed.

"I'll clean my own dishes and make my bed every day. Thanks to this ankle monitor, you won't have to give me a curfew. If you can't find me, I'll be in the backyard. Will that work? Do we have a deal?"

Lizzy nodded. "Yeah, sure, we have a deal."

"Good. Now tell me about Jessica. Has she quit yet?"

"Jessica? Quit? No. Jessica recently moved into her new apartment. She's still taking classes and going for a degree in criminology."

"Still dating that nerd?"

"Casey?"

Hayley nodded.

"No, they broke up a while ago."

"Probably for the best."

"Why is that?"

Hayley shrugged. "I don't know. I guess I just didn't like his face."

Maureen and Charles Baker
Placer County
August 2011

Maureen awoke with a migraine. She could feel the blood vessels literally getting smaller, restricting much-needed blood and oxygen to her brain, which in turn caused other blood vessels to expand and throb. Usually too much caffeine or eating the wrong foods caused her to get a migraine, but this time it was definitely caused by stress.

She pushed herself upward and glass cut into her palm. A few seconds passed before her mind cleared and she remembered bits and pieces of what had happened. She was inside the limousine, sprawled across the floor. There was glass everywhere.

Charles. Where was Charles?

Crawling to the open door, she saw two shadowy figures. She squinted, concentrated, tried to wait until her eyesight was no longer blurry, but it was no use. There was a man lying in an open field…Charles. Someone else, most likely the driver, was huddled over him. There were no buildings in the area, only cows grazing in the distance. She slid both legs out the door, careful not to cut herself further, and then held on to the doorframe until her feet hit solid ground. There was a narrow dirt road nearby, but she could not see the main road from where she stood.

Her legs wobbled as she made her way over uneven dirt clods toward the two men. She fell to the ground. It took her a moment to get up. Her vision grew worse, hazier than before. The two people were blurry shadows. The sun was setting. It would be dark soon.

"Oh, Mrs. Baker," the driver said, "thank God you've come to."

At closer view, it looked as if the man was holding a razor in one hand and a clear plastic tube, narrow like the inside of a pen, in the other.

"What's going on?" She stepped up her pace, frantic to be by Charles's side. "What are you doing to him?"

Charles's face was pale, his eyes wide with fear. His chest rose and fell more rapidly with each breath. His breathing sounded ragged and wet. His clothes were torn and there was blood everywhere.

"I've called 911," the driver said. "They're on their way."

Thank God. She grabbed hold of Charles's hand and squeezed. "What happened?"

"There were two deer," the driver explained. "I swerved and lost control. It was an accident."

She looked at the razor in his hand. "What are you doing with that?"

"As I carried your husband from the car, he told me he used to be a SEAL and that he couldn't breathe. He said I needed to perform a tracheotomy."

"No," she said. "Absolutely not. Charles," she said as tears rolled down her cheeks, "did you say that? Is that what you need him to do?"

A weird gurgling noise came out of his mouth, but he couldn't seem to form any words. His eyes twitched as if he were trying to look toward the driver, pleading with her to understand what was going on. "Where's the ambulance?" she asked. "Why aren't they here?"

More gurgling noises erupted. She put her ear closer to his mouth. "What are you trying to tell me, Charles?"

"If you don't perform a tracheotomy," the driver interrupted, "he's never going to make it."

She looked at the man with disgust. "Are you saying you want *me* to cut into his throat?"

"It's the only way. Look at him. He's turning blue. He doesn't have much time."

She shook her head. "You do it," she said.

"I can't," he said. "I thought I could, I really did, but I could never be responsible if something went wrong."

"I can't do it." She pushed curly gray hair out of her face and looked Charles over. His breathing had grown much worse, much more ragged than before. He was struggling for each breath he took.

"He's going to die," the man said calmly.

Nothing made sense. Maureen looked from one end of the field to the other. "If you swerved to miss the deer, then where's the main road?"

He waved a frustrated hand toward the dirt road. "It's right there, Maureen. For God's sake, are you going to let your husband die?"

No sounds of an approaching ambulance could be heard. What was taking them so long? She looked at Charles. She couldn't sit here and watch her husband die. She needed to help him. She held out her hand.

The driver placed the razor in her palm. "You better hurry."

As she brought the razor to her husband's throat, tears clouded her already hazy vision. "I can't do this."

"You must. If you want to save his life, you're going to need to find his thyroid cartilage."

She wiped her eyes. "His what?"

"His Adam's apple. Do you see his Adam's apple?"

"Yes."

"Move your finger over his neck until you feel another bulge." She did as he said, but her hands were shaking. "OK, I feel it."

"That's the cricoid cartilage."

"How do you know that?"

"Your husband told me before he lost his ability to speak. You need to make a half-inch horizontal cut between that bulge and the Adam's apple."

Her hands shook even more as she lowered the razor to her husband's throat.

"You better hurry."

She looked at Charles. She couldn't stop sobbing. His eyes were bulging. His mouth was moving but still no words came forth. And then it hit her. "He's not moving. Why isn't he moving?" It was as if Charles were paralyzed.

"I'm not a doctor," the man said, holding up his hands in surrender. "I'm merely repeating what your husband told me before you awoke."

"Oh, Charles," she cried as she put her head to his chest.

"Make the cut or he dies."

She straightened, used her sleeve to wipe her eyes once again, and then examined Charles's throat. He was turning purple now. He would never make it if she didn't do something fast. The gasping and gurgling continued as she located the area where she would need to make a small cut. She could do this. Charles often said she would have made a good army nurse. She couldn't let him die. She would never be able to live with herself knowing that she could have saved him.

She placed the razor on his throat again and this time began to make a cut. His skin was much thicker than she thought it would be. She swallowed hard, pushing harder and deeper, trying not to think of what she was cutting into. When that was finally done, she asked the man to hand her the tube.

The annoying man began to crawl about in the high grass.

"What are you doing? Hand me the tube. Now!"

"I can't find it. It was right here a minute ago."

She used her fingers to pinch the incision closed as she watched the man crawl on all fours. He appeared to be moving in slow motion, as if he didn't have a care in the world. She didn't want to look into Charles's eyes and allow him to see the fear etched across her face, but she couldn't let him die alone. And he would die if she didn't insert a breathing tube into the hole. Now. Blood oozed from Charles's throat, and there was nothing she could do to help him. She remembered her purse in the limo. Maybe there was something in her purse that she could use to save her husband.

"Hold this shut," she shouted at the man.

He did as she said as she ran to the limo, tripping and falling along the way, but never stopping until she reached the vehicle.

T.R. RAGAN

Frantically, she scrambled on all fours across glass, feeling no pain as pieces of bottle and window cut into her skin. She found her purse and dumped the contents onto the floor: a comb, lipstick, ID, and a pen. She took the pen apart. Ink spilled onto the seats and floor. She grabbed the brandy, unscrewed the lid, and poured alcohol into the small tube until the liquid coming through the bottom was no longer blue. Then she scrambled out of the limo and ran through the high weeds back to Charles.

The driver was no longer holding her husband's throat. His eyes were focused intently on her face as if he welcomed the pain he saw there when he told her Charles had died without her at his side.

"You killed him," he told her.

"Charles," she wept.

"You cut too deep."

"I didn't. There was hardly any blood."

She knelt down next to Charles, propped his neck in such a way that she could stick the tube into his trachea, but there was much more blood now and he was no longer breathing. She put her fingers to his wrist. No pulse. Nothing. He was dead.

"The good news is that your husband knew the truth before he died."

She pulled her gaze from Charles and forced herself to look into the man's icy blue eyes.

"I told him about Harry Thompson."

Her breathing felt irregular as blood raged faster through her veins. "What are you talking about?"

"You know…Italy…Carlton Hotel Baglioni."

One mistake, she thought. In fifty years of marriage, she'd made one mistake—one night with Harry Thompson. She'd never thought of Harry after that night. Only Charles. If she hadn't

56

taken Harry up on his offer, she would have spent the rest of her life wondering what could have been. But being with Harry for twenty-four hours had been anticlimactic in so many ways, and yet that night had taught her so much. By morning, she'd known without a doubt that Charles was the only man for her. But she wasn't going to give this lunatic the satisfaction of knowing any of that. Charles knew she loved him. In his heart, no matter what this man might have told him, Charles knew.

The man was insane, she realized too late.

She curled up next to Charles, wanting to be with him, knowing that more than likely she would be soon.

CHAPTER 8

I would go home and watch what I done on the television.
Then I would cry and cry like a baby.
—Albert DeSalvo

John and Rochelle
Sacramento
June 2007

As John lifted his head, blood pulsed inside his ears and made a loud swooshing noise. Both of his eyes were swollen shut, but he could see murky shadows through the corner of his left eye. He tried to lift his hands to his face before he remembered they were tied behind his back with thick, scratchy twine. The same twine had been used to tie both of his ankles to the front legs of the heavy metal chair he was sitting on.

He moved his head at every angle possible, trying to see where he was.

The room was dark and had a musty smell. The floors were concrete. He was in a basement. Not moving, he listened. All was quiet. After a moment, he tried to rock the chair, but either it was too solid or he was too weak, because the chair didn't budge.

How long had he been here? A few hours? Twenty-four hours?

Rochelle. Where was Rochelle?

He remembered her screams as glass sprayed, cutting them both. A baseball bat was the last thing he had seen before everything went dark. Out of the corner of his left eye, he saw something move across the room.

"Rochelle," he whispered. "Is that you? Can you hear me?"

He heard a moan and then recognized her voice when she said his name.

She was alive.

"Did they hurt you?" he asked.

"I want out of here," she said between sobs.

What had they done to her?

"Listen to me, Rochelle. I don't know how many men there are upstairs, but I'm going to find a way out of here. I swear to you, I'll get us out of here." He paused, waited, and listened. If only he could see her. "Did they touch you? If they so much as laid one finger on you, I'll kill them."

More sobbing.

"Are you tied up?"

This time when she moved, he heard the rattling of chains.

Chains? What was going on? Had those punks planned this? Nothing made sense. Tears quickly gathered, blocking what little vision he had left, blinding him.

"I want to go home," Rochelle cried. "I just want to go home."

Davis
Tuesday, May 8, 2012

Lizzy heard a car pull up in front of the house and went to the window to peek outside. "Jessica is here," she told Hayley, before realizing she might as well be talking to herself. Hayley was engrossed in a book.

Tonight would be the first time Hayley and Jessica had seen each other since Hayley had been incarcerated nine months ago. The two didn't always get along, but whether they were willing to admit it or not, there was an undeniable connection between them.

Hayley was more reserved than ever. Not sad. Not happy. Just quiet—keeping her feelings to herself.

Before Jessica had a chance to knock, Lizzy opened the door. Jessica blew past her and headed straight for Hayley. She leaned low and held Hayley tightly in a bear hug.

The contrast between the two was startling. Jessica was tall and healthy, with a pinkish complexion, while Hayley appeared pasty white and much too thin. Long seconds passed before Jessica finally released her and straightened. "I'm so glad you're back."

"Thanks," Hayley managed, squirming in her seat.

Lizzy kept her eyes on them as she headed for the kitchen.

Jessica set her backpack on the floor and took a seat next to Hayley. "So, you're OK?"

"I'm fine."

"You're sure?"

"Yep."

Jessica gestured toward Hayley's ankle. "How long do you have to wear that thing?"

"Six months to a year."

Lizzy brought a tray of cheese and crackers from the kitchen and set it on the coffee table in front of the couch. While Jessica made idle chitchat and Hayley did her best to feign interest, Lizzy picked up the remote and pointed it at the television. Before she hit the Off button, a picture of Michael and Jennifer Dalton flashed across the screen.

She moved closer to the television and increased the volume.

"Woman brutally murdered in a truly bizarre chain of events. Husband is in custody. More at eleven."

"Unbelievable," Lizzy said.

"What is it?" Hayley asked.

"That's the same couple who recently hired me to watch one of their employees. Jennifer and Michael Dalton own J&M Realty in Sacramento."

"How well did you know them?" Jessica asked.

Lizzy turned off the television, figuring she'd watch more at eleven. "I met them twice. They were very loving toward each other, and they were planning to throw a big party to celebrate their fifteenth anniversary." She shook her head. "There's no way Michael Dalton would harm his wife."

"Maybe it was all an act," Hayley said with a shrug.

"That makes sense," Jessica added. "Who would pay more attention to all of the little details than a private investigator? Maybe that man hired you on purpose and then put on a big act."

"But they were *both* kissy and huggy," Lizzy explained. "What you're suggesting would make sense if it had been just one of them being affectionate."

"Well, you know how women are," Hayley said without elaborating.

Both Lizzy and Jessica stared at Hayley and waited. They knew the drill. If you stared at her long enough, she would eventually come around and finish her thought, which she did.

"Let's pretend this couple is like most couples out there in the world. Lizzy arrives at their initial meeting. The husband knows

Lizzy is coming, and he's ready. He knows he's going to kill his wife, but he doesn't know when he's going to do it, so he wants to make it look like he and his wife are getting along. Days before their scheduled meeting with a private investigator, he tells his wife that they should throw a big anniversary party to demonstrate how in love they are after all these years. The wife, who has been waiting years for her husband to show her some affection, is thrilled beyond words. Husband continues to woo his wife up until the day the private investigator arrives, making it look as if the two of them are madly in love and have been all along." Hayley leaned against the cushions behind her. "Women can be so naïve when it comes to men."

"You don't look convinced," Jessica said to Lizzy.

"I'm not. Jennifer was a sweet woman, but she wasn't a pushover. I don't think he did it."

"Statistics will likely prove otherwise," Hayley said.

Davis
Wednesday, May 9, 2012

Lizzy stood at the kitchen sink, rinsing dishes as she talked to Jared on the speakerphone.

"Looks like I'll be staying in Virginia longer than I thought," he told her.

"OK," Lizzy said, feeling the same unease she'd been feeling more often than not. She felt safer with Jared here, but she had Hayley to keep her company. Besides, she didn't like the idea of becoming too dependent on him.

"Is anything wrong?"

"No, just a lot on my mind."

"You're working too hard."

"I think that's what most would say is calling the kettle black."

"You've been awful quiet lately," Jared said. "What's going on?"

Lizzy was still looking out the window when a dark Mercedes drove up and parked at the curb across the street. Their neighbor Charlee had a guest, and Lizzy now had an opportunity to change the subject. "Looks like your neighbor might have found herself a man."

"Don't tell me you have your binoculars out again," he teased. She laughed.

"It's good to hear you laugh."

After a short pause, she said, "I'm going to meet with Lieutenant Greer in the morning. After I file a report, he wants to talk to me privately. I'm hoping he'll take me to Jennifer Dalton's office, where I talked with her last."

"Are you sure you want to get involved?"

"I have to get involved," she said, but even as she said the words she knew it wasn't completely true. She had no proof Michael hadn't killed his wife. She believed that Michael was innocent based solely on intuition. In fact, she had yet to tell anyone about the strange look Michael Dalton had given her when she left the realty office that day. Something had been bothering him. More than anything, Lizzy wanted a chance to talk to Michael herself, but she wasn't ready to tell Jared that bit of news, since it would only worry him. She would talk to the lieutenant tomorrow and see what he had to say about the matter.

"Are you still there?"

"I'm here," Lizzy said.

"What are the neighbors doing now?"

Lizzy smiled. "It looks like her new boyfriend drives a big, shiny Mercedes. He carried a large bouquet of roses to the door. He's inside the house now, so I have no idea what's going on."

"Sounds like I need to step up my game."

She laughed again. It felt good to laugh. "I like you just the way you are."

"I'm glad," he said. "How's Hayley?"

"She's bored stiff. She already reorganized my files, and so she's on to doing all of my paperwork. I ran out of books to give her to read, so now she has my Kindle. I have hundreds of books on there. That should keep her busy for a few weeks."

"If you run out of things for her to do, I'm sure I can find something to help keep her busy."

"That would be great. I miss you."

"I miss you, too."

Lizzy didn't like battling all the conflicting emotions within. She loved Jared. There was no denying that. Although living in a new house in a new area was proving to be a challenge, having Jared in her life was anything but challenging. He was flexible and easygoing and, at moments like this, she wondered how she'd ever managed without him.

Sacramento
Thursday, May 10, 2012

At eight o'clock sharp the next morning, Lizzy walked toward the entrance of the Sacramento police department. Less than a block away, she saw the Channel 10 News van. With any luck, she would be able to avoid the media altogether.

Hours later, Lizzy was sitting in Lieutenant Greer's office. The lieutenant was a close friend of both Jared and his father. Lizzy had the good fortune to have met the lieutenant on more than one occasion. He was a giant of a man—six foot six, with big broad shoulders. If not for his charming smile, his size might be intimidating. His eyes were the same shade of gray as his hair. His misshapen nose made him look as if he might have been a boxer in his younger days.

She had spent most of her morning writing a detailed report about everything she'd seen the last time she met with Michael and Jennifer Dalton. Now she was repeating, word for word, what she'd just spent over an hour writing down. It was redundant, repetitive, and ultimately a waste of time, since nobody really seemed to care what she had to say about Michael Dalton. But she knew the drill, and she knew if she pushed long and hard enough, she might get a chance to talk to Michael in person. And that's all that mattered. She needed to talk to him, look him in the eye. Five minutes with the man, that's all she needed.

Lizzy sighed. "I'm telling you, Dalton didn't kill his wife."

"I hope you're right, because some of the things that were done to Jennifer Dalton go beyond the human imagination. It's hard to believe she could be married to someone for fifteen years and never know her spouse was capable of such peculiar and horrifying devastation."

Since arriving at the station, Lizzy had picked up pieces here and there of the mutilation Jennifer had been subjected to. Her eyes had been glued shut and organs had been not only removed, but replaced with undisclosed objects. Jennifer had not been granted a quick death; instead, rumors had it that her killer had kept her alive for hours after the horror began.

"Tell me more about the phone call, if you don't mind. You mentioned that while you were at Michael and Jennifer's office downtown, Jennifer was talking to someone on the phone." Greer skimmed over the report. "A man, it says here. Could you hear his voice?"

"No, but I remember Jennifer referring to the caller as a 'him' or a 'he' after she had finished with the call." Lizzy sighed. "I didn't hear her mention a name. She hung up the phone and told me the *guy* would not take no for an answer."

"Was she crying?"

"No, she wasn't sad. She was frustrated. She was busy and she had work to do, but she also felt sorry for the caller because she figured he must be desperate for work. The call had something to do with a car picking her and Michael up on the day of their anniversary party. There was a yellow sticky pad in front of her and she was doodling on it while she was listening to the man talk." While Lieutenant Greer made additional notes, Lizzy couldn't help but wonder what had been on that sticky note that Jennifer had tossed.

"Is there anything else?"

"Everything I know is in the report, but I do have a question." He waited.

"The more I learn about the Michael Dalton case, the more I find myself wondering why the FBI isn't looking at it more closely."

"Why would they? Hundreds of women are killed every year by their husbands. How is this case any different?"

"Jennifer's body was mutilated. That sounds like the work of a sadistic killer to me."

"The Lovebird Killer?" he asked.

"Precisely."

"I haven't requested assistance because there is absolutely nothing to connect Jennifer's murder with the cases currently attributed to the Lovebird Killer."

"For starters, Michael and Jennifer were a couple," she reminded him.

"And Michael Dalton is alive and well."

It was quiet for a moment before Greer added, "I would love to hand the Dalton case over to the feds. I have plenty of other work to keep me busy, but as things stand, there is too much evidence against Michael Dalton. Fingerprints on the knife used to cut her body. Fingerprints on the needle plunged into her heart. Tire tracks outside belonging only to Jennifer and Michael's vehicles. Nobody else. Same can be said for footprints and fingerprints inside the home. The same superglue used to glue her eyes closed was found in Michael's glove compartment. Neighbors saw Michael arrive. According to witnesses, nobody else came or left. Should I go on?"

Lizzy sighed as she shook her head. "Is there any way I could talk to Michael?"

Greer rubbed his chin thoughtfully for a moment. "There's nothing I would like more than to get that man to talk to someone, but since his arrest, he's pleaded the Fifth."

"Maybe if Michael knows I think he's innocent—if he knows I'm on his side—he'll agree to talk to me."

"It wouldn't be a private affair," Greer said matter-of-factly. "Your conversation would be taped…and that, of course, is only if he agrees to talk to you in the first place."

"I understand."

"I'll see what I can do." He stood and offered her his hand.

She stood too. "Aren't we going to the Daltons' realty office?"

His hands fell to his sides. "I don't know if that's a good idea, Lizzy."

"Come on, Greer, let me in the office for five minutes so I can show you exactly what she was doing the last time I saw Jennifer alive."

"Channel 10 News has been camped outside for days," he said. "If they see you here, they may become even more disruptive."

She angled her head. "The media? Disruptive?"

"It's been known to happen," he said with a sparkle in his eye.

"I know you don't eat well," she said, glancing at his half-eaten pastry, "but worrying about things you can't control isn't going to help your insomnia and—"

He shook his head. "Your boyfriend has been talking too much, I see."

"Jared's worried about you, that's all."

Greer gestured a hand toward the door.

"Does that mean we're going to the realty office?"

"Do you think I would dare say no and risk having an ex-judge and the FBI snapping at my throat?"

Before he changed his mind, she grabbed her bag and followed Greer out of his office and through a sea of desks and cubicles. They stepped through the double doors and outside onto the wet sidewalks and into a media frenzy. Scores of reporters and photographers swarmed the area, making it difficult for Lizzy and Greer to get to their vehicles.

Two news stations followed Greer to the right, while the rest stayed glued to Lizzy as she tried to cut a path across the parking lot.

Reporter Stacey Whitmore was one of the new gals anchoring for Channel 10 News, which meant she was hungry...like a shark. Stacey's assistant held an umbrella over her head while Stacey shoved a microphone toward Lizzy. "Is it true that you knew Jennifer and Michael Dalton?"

"No comment," Lizzy said as she pushed through the crowd toward her car.

The woman stayed glued to her side. "Rumor has it you met them both weeks ago when they hired you to investigate a workers' compensation claim."

"Whether I knew the Daltons or not has no bearing on this case."

"You believe Michael Dalton is innocent, don't you?"

Lizzy flinched and immediately regretted it. How could Stacey Whitmore or anyone else know she had her doubts about Michael Dalton's guilt? William Greer was the only person, other than Jared, who knew any of her private thoughts about the case. Reporters weren't only like sharks, they were like flies. Always somewhere…waiting, watching, spreading their germs.

By the time Lizzy was within a few feet of her car, every media crew with the exception of Stacey's had disappeared. Lizzy pulled out her keys and pushed the Unlock button. She climbed in behind the wheel, but before she could shut her car door, Stacey handed her a card and said, "If there's something, anything at all, that you know about this case and want to get off your chest, give me a call."

"And why would I do that?"

Stacey ordered her crew to back off. They did as she asked, dispersing like ducks in a pond after the bread runs out.

Lizzy shut her door but rolled down her window, curious to hear what Stacey had to say, because obviously she had something on her mind.

"Michael Dalton and I both attended UC Berkeley," Stacey confided.

"So, you and Michael are friends?"

Stacey sighed. "We dated for a few years before he met Jennifer."

Ahh, it's starting to make sense. Jilted reporter wants to make sure ex-boyfriend burns in hell, or at least in prison. "So, you think he's guilty?"

"On the contrary. I know with one hundred percent surety that Michael Dalton is innocent. If you agree, which I think you do, we need to talk."

"How do I know you're not just saying all of this to use me? You know, to find out what I'm thinking so you can be the first to tell the people of Sacramento that Lizzy Gardner is once again involved in a murder case?"

Stacey waved that thought away with a hand through the air. "That's old news, Ms. Gardner."

"Please, call me Lizzy."

"We weren't the only news station that caught wind that you were talking to Greer this morning. Everyone knows Lieutenant Greer is focused on the Dalton case right now, but that's beside the point. I'm not using you. I know Michael's innocent. My husband and two kids will tell you the same thing."

"You and Michael remained friends after he left you for another woman?"

She smiled. "You met Jennifer. She's beautiful and she's a wonderful person. Who could blame him?"

Lizzy looked intently at Stacey as she realized the shark might not be the great white she'd first imagined.

"Jennifer and Michael babysat my two kids for a week while my husband and I were in Hawaii. Would I let a killer babysit my kids?"

Lizzy saw that Greer's car was gone. "I have to go," Lizzy said as she turned the key and started the engine.

"Come to my house tomorrow night. Anytime after six p.m.," Stacey added as she moved away from the car. "I wrote my address on the back of my card."

Thursday, May 10, 2012

Whenever he looked into a mirror, he saw his mother. They both had small, straight noses. They also had the same round blue eyes, which according to Mom were their best feature. Although they were both small boned, he was a smidgeon over five foot ten, while Mom had been five foot three inches at most.

His mother's image disappeared, prompting him to step away from the mirror and take a seat on the lone chair in the room. After all these years, it amazed him that he could still look into the mirror and see her face as clearly as if he'd seen her yesterday. She'd been so beautiful. "You're my sweet little boy and nobody else's," she would say to him as she pulled the covers up tight around his shoulders before kissing him on the cheek every night. Sometimes she would hum a little tune, a sweet lullaby she'd made up.

He closed his eyes and imagined breathing in the scent of her. She often smelled like a field of newly blossomed flowers. She had been named after a flower, too. He'd never met his father. He learned early on that it wouldn't do any good to ask about him, either. It just made his mom sad when he did.

His mom was a hard worker. Like most people, she had her bad days, and she didn't always have enough time for him, but he didn't like to think about those days. He preferred to concentrate on the good days. His mother had inherited a small farm in California from her grandfather. It took a lot of hard work to keep the farm running. Every morning, he would help his mom collect eggs. Afterward, he was in charge of making sure the straw lining was clean and free of broken shells and bird poop. He would chase the roosters and then feed the pigs. The mother he remembered was always smiling and laughing. She was the happiest person he'd ever met. Sometimes she would chase him and tickle his sides when she caught him. Good times on the farm—at least until the day he found his mom in the barn with a shovel in her hand and dirt on her face. He'd never forgotten the way she'd looked at him when he entered the barn. She'd looked angry and sad all at once. That was the day she'd accused him of all sorts of transgressions, and even decided to tell him about his long-lost father and how they were more alike than she'd ever dared to imagine.

His mom disappeared soon after. Nobody knew what happened to her, but one thing for sure, his life hadn't been the same since.

From age eleven to thirteen he lived with a total of four different families. He never understood why the first three foster families didn't like him enough to keep him for very long. He behaved and did as he was asked. He ate his vegetables and made his bed. He was a good boy.

The first family he stayed with was the King family. Mr. and Mrs. King didn't like him wetting the bed. He didn't like wetting the bed either, but they never really seemed to get that, and they would yell longer and louder every time it happened. He tried his very best not to wet the bed. One day, he didn't drink water all day, but in the morning the thin mattress was soaked clean through.

He had yet to turn twelve when he moved in with the Platt family, family number two. The Platts had a lot of kids, and he remembered how much he liked it there. He'd never had friends before, but living with the Platt kids was like having a half dozen built-in friends. After Mrs. Platt found all of her children playing doctor—he was the patient and her biological kids were the doctors and nurses—*he* was the one who was sent away to live somewhere else. That was the first time he could remember crying since his mom left him.

His new foster parents, his third family, had picked him up straight from school the next day. He never even got to say good-bye to the Platt children. His new foster parents were the Hargroves. Mr. and Mrs. Hargrove had two other foster kids. Both boys. All three of them walked to and from school every single day. Everybody made their own meals, mostly peanut butter and jelly sandwiches. Nobody ever asked him if he did his homework. Nobody cared. On two separate occasions, one of his teachers, Mrs. Trumble, walked him home early so she could talk to Mrs. Hargrove. On the first occasion, he didn't pay them any mind. The second time, though, he listened from the kitchen and was surprised to hear them talking about one of the boys having a dark mind.

A dark mind.

To this day, he wondered which of the Hargrove boys they had been talking about.

He never found out because two days after his twelfth birthday, he was taken to live with the Becks. He liked Mr. and Mrs. Beck straight off. They were hard workers. They ran their family business right out of their home. The Becks loved their work and it wasn't long before they told him they loved him, too.

They made sure he did his homework. They praised him when he received good grades, and they scolded him when he dragged mud into the house or forgot to feed the dog or the cat. If he complained about being bullied at school, Mr. Beck met with the principal and made sure appropriate actions were taken to see that the bullies were punished.

The best part was when Mrs. Beck tucked him in bed at night. It was the strangest thing, because no matter how many dead bodies she embalmed during the day, she always smelled as sweet as a rose at night.

CHAPTER 9

I didn't want to hurt them, I only wanted to kill them.
—David Berkowitz

Davis
Friday, May 11, 2012

On the third knock, Hayley set the Kindle to the side, removed the cat from her lap, and went to the door. Lizzy had made her promise she would look through the peephole before opening the door, so she did it out of respect more than anything else. She released a heavy sigh when she saw that it was Jessica. She opened the door and Jessica stepped inside without waiting for an invitation. Hayley had almost forgotten how pushy she could be. She shut the door and bolted it, as Lizzy had instructed.

"Well, hello to you, too," Jessica said, a big sappy grin plastered across her always-happy face. "Where's Lizzy?"

"She had a meeting tonight."

"With who?"

"I didn't ask."

"Why not?"

"Because if Lizzy had wanted to tell me, she would have."

Jessica rolled her eyes and then leaned over and rubbed her fingers through Hannah's soft fur. "You're getting so big, kitty cat."

Hayley took her seat on the couch and picked up the Kindle again.

"What are you doing?" Jessica asked.

"What does it look like?"

Jessica left the cat alone and grabbed the leather satchel hanging from her shoulder. She pulled out a pile of mail along with a half dozen manila folders and placed it all on the coffee table in front of Hayley. "Turn your Kindle off. We have work to do."

"I thought you were working on the Cartwright case."

"I'm working on at least six different cases at once. But I'm keeping a few hours every day open for you."

"Wonderful."

Jessica ignored her sarcasm and rambled on some more. "I figured the two of us could work together while you're trapped here. I'll stop at the office every chance I get, grab any work Lizzy has for us, and bring it here."

Hayley nodded, hoping she had finished.

"I would have come earlier, but I was watching one of the claimants today. He was doing all sorts of heavy lifting. I got some great pictures. I think I might be finally getting the hang of this whole surveillance thing."

A quick learner. It only took her two years, Hayley thought. "What about school?"

"Since when do you care about my schooling?"

"You're right. I don't care. Forget I asked."

Jessica waved a hand through the air. "No, I'm going to tell you, because the truth is I like that you care about me. I care about you, too."

Hayley wanted to shoot herself, wondering why she'd asked her about school in the first place.

"I'm taking a night class and a couple of online courses," Jessica began. "But I've moved out of my mom's house and into my own apartment and I need money, which is why I figured I'll squeeze in all the overtime I can." She stopped talking long enough to point a finger at Hayley. "If you ever get that monitor off your leg, I'd love to show you my place."

"Yeah," Hayley said, "I'd like that, too." She meant she would like to get the monitor off her ankle, not the part about seeing Jessica's place. The two of them were sweet and sour, oil and water… there was no reason to pretend they were buds. But, of course, Jessica took it the wrong way.

She smiled again and her eyes lit up excitedly. "I don't think Lizzy has ever been this busy," Jessica went on. "She has at least a dozen workers' compensation cases, and now that you're out of the gray-bar hotel, she wants you and me to work together on finding an eighteen-year-old girl."

"What's the deal?" Hayley asked, ignoring the reference to jail as the gray-bar hotel. Jessica was by far the weirdest person she'd ever met.

"A woman living in New York has asked Lizzy to find her daughter. The woman was forced by her parents to give her up eighteen years ago. Lizzy would like this case solved pronto." Jessica handed Hayley a file.

"What's the urgency?"

"The woman recently married a politician. I'm assuming she wants to bring everything out into the open before her husband runs for office. She wants Lizzy to find her quickly and discreetly, and she's willing to pay more for faster service."

"If she lives back East, why would she hire Lizzy?"

"An investigator in Manhattan already located the adoptive parents. According to the report, their adopted daughter, Adele Hampton, who is also our client's daughter, ran away from home when she was sixteen. Although her adoptive parents haven't seen her since, Adele took a few things that didn't belong to her when she left, including their credit card. The charges that went through before they closed the account were all made in the Sacramento area. The statements and receipts are all in the file. The investigator in New York referred her client to Lizzy since they worked together before."

"I'll read through the file, do a search, and then make a few calls if I need to," Hayley said. "What else do you have?"

Jessica grabbed another file, but before she opened it, she said, "Has Lizzy told you much about the Danielle Cartwright case I'm working on?"

Haley shook her head.

"Danielle Cartwright is thirty-nine, but she's been married and divorced three times. I've met with Danielle once already and I've read the files. If what Danielle says is true, all three husbands were douche bags. The last husband was into pornography; he even did some of the filming himself. After she found videos with his name as director and producer, she kicked him out of her house."

"Where was she when he was making movies?"

"Danielle is a personal shopper. Her business is booming. She spends half her time in New York City, London, and Paris."

"So it makes sense that she might not know everything these guys are doing."

Jessica nodded. "She also tends to go for flashy, good-looking guys."

"Men who easily attract the attention of beautiful women."

"Right again."

"So what's the story?" Hayley asked. "I'm assuming you brought her up for a reason."

Jessica nodded. "Dominic Povo, her newest fiancé, is up to something, but I have no idea what. He works in construction and he has a crew of guys working for him."

"So, you're sitting in the car watching these guys hammer nails all day?"

"Yes, because that's what they do," Jessica said, using her hands for emphasis. "They're in construction. Dominic Povo is good-looking, too, easy on the eyes, but that's not the problem—"

"Jessica, get to the point. What do you think Povo is up to?"

"I don't know, but during my last visit to the construction site, I saw a van pull up to the side of the house they were working on. Two men transferred big bulky garbage bags from the van to a wheelbarrow. If they had loaded the wheelbarrow with bricks or paint, I wouldn't have looked twice, but big bulky garbage bags?"

"Are you insinuating that they were getting rid of bodies?"

Jessica looked behind her as if to make sure the construction workers weren't standing in Lizzy's kitchen. "I don't know, maybe," she whispered as she turned toward Hayley again. "Crazy, huh? Do you think I'm being paranoid because of everything that's happened in the past?"

"Yes, that's exactly what I think."

"That's not all…before I could drive away, one of Povo's guys knocked on the passenger window of my car. He asked me if I needed any help."

"What did you do?"

"I told him I was looking at model homes and getting a feel for the neighborhood."

"You didn't give him your name, did you?"

Jessica winced. "I told him my name was Kat Sylvester."

"That's the stupidest name I've ever heard."

"I know."

Hayley sighed.

Jessica pulled a business card from her pocket and handed it to Hayley.

"Magnus Vitalis, a handyman," Hayley read aloud.

"He gave me his card and told me he'd be happy to give me a private tour of any of the homes I might be interested in."

"Do you think he knew you were watching them?"

"I don't think so."

"So what have you learned about Danielle's fiancé so far?"

"Not much."

"Other than the dead bodies being delivered in garbage bags," Hayley reminded her.

"Povo moved to Las Vegas when he was eighteen," Jessica said, ignoring the sarcastic comment. "He went to culinary school, but he never graduated. Now he's a foreman. He makes a couple hundred thousand dollars a year."

"That sounds high to me, you know, for a construction foreman. It would make sense if this was some crazy-ass twenty-story building, but it's not."

"Povo is clean. He's never even gotten a speeding ticket."

"What else?"

"What do you mean?"

"You've been working on the case for a while now, right? What else do you have?"

Jessica frowned. "This isn't my only case. I can't afford a hundred dollars a month to have portable Wi-Fi or whatever it takes to bring my computer with me and have Internet capabilities. I certainly can't afford to drive to and from the office with the cost of gas what it is right now. And Lizzy doesn't have the money to fly me to Vegas on the weekends to see what he's up to."

"You can't just sit in the car all day. You need to get social and start talking to people. Do *something. Anything.*"

"I'm working my ass off," Jessica said.

"But you're not getting anywhere, are you? You're working for a private investigator. You can't wait for everyone to hold your hand and tell you what to do."

"You don't have to get so snippy," Jessica said.

Hayley picked up her Kindle and started reading where she had left off.

"I guess jail time didn't change your disposition any."

Hayley ignored her and kept reading.

"That was uncalled for," Jessica said. "I'm sorry. Was it bad in there?"

"It was a fucking tea party."

"Oh."

Hayley sighed. She didn't want to take her frustrations out on Jessica, so she set the Kindle aside once again and said, "Listen, Jessica. Lizzy wouldn't have given you the job if she didn't think you could handle it. Focus. Try to think outside the box and do what you were hired to do."

Jessica seemed more apprehensive than usual, and that's when Hayley realized she was seriously concerned. "Nobody's going to kidnap you or shoot you, if that's what you're worried about."

"How do you know? What if those bags were actually filled with dead bodies?"

"What are the odds?" Hayley asked. "Use your instincts, Jessica. If something feels wrong to you, then something is probably very wrong; it's how the universe works. The people who don't listen to their instincts are the ones who end up in trouble...or worse."

Granite Bay
Friday, May 11, 2012

No matter how hard Lizzy worked on not allowing her thoughts to get the best of her, it was as if a dark sense of foreboding continuously floated close overhead. She'd talked to her therapist about it on many occasions, but the darkness was something she still needed to work on.

The navigator told Lizzy in its robotic voice to make a right onto East Roseville Parkway and then another right after that. A private security guard greeted and allowed her through the decorative iron gates after she told him Stacey Whitmore was expecting her. Lizzy drove to the front of a sprawling mansion at the top of the hill and shut off the engine. As she made her way to the front entry, she admired the healthy green palm trees surrounding the property.

Stacey opened the door, thanked her for coming, and ushered her inside before Lizzy had a chance to rap her knuckles against the solid oak door.

The house was enormous. They passed by a large kitchen with impressive cabinetry and beautiful granite countertops. The living room was filled with Victorian furniture: heavy chairs with dark finishes and elaborate carvings. Every piece looked as if it belonged in a museum. The views outside the floor-to-ceiling windows were stunning: endless manicured lawns, a small lake in the distance, and the sky painted lavender and peach. It made her feel like she was looking at a painting.

Stacey gestured for Lizzy to take a seat on the couch while sat in a green velvet chair close by. "I'm really not sure why I'm here," Lizzy said. "I hardly knew Jennifer or Michael before she was killed, but I'm going to be forthright with you because, strangely, I felt your pain when you spoke to me about Michael. You were right. My gut feeling is that the man is innocent, but gut feelings are never enough when it comes to murder."

Lizzy sipped her tea, hoping Stacey would chime in, but she didn't. Stacey was a great listener, a professional, and it was clear the woman wasn't going to say a word until she was certain Lizzy had finished talking. Lizzy had no reason to withhold information, so she told Stacey everything. "Jennifer and Michael hired me to check out a workers' compensation claimant. I met with them twice. The first time I met Michael and Jennifer was at their house. I liked them both straight off. They were friendly, and I was especially impressed with the way Michael and Jennifer treated each other with love and respect. Since they didn't have children and they tended to hold hands and gaze into one another's eyes—"

Stacey shifted in her seat, her eyes downcast.

"Is something wrong?"

"No, not at all. I was thinking of Jennifer. Please continue."

"I was saying that their loving gestures made me think they were newlyweds, which is why I was surprised to learn they had been married for so long. The second time I met them was when I dropped a contract off at their office downtown. Jennifer was on the phone and she was more than annoyed by the caller, especially agitated when the man refused to take no for an answer... something to do with someone hiring a limo driver for their anniversary party. Before I left, Michael showed up to check on Jennifer and take her to dinner." Lizzy let out a sharp breath. "That would have been it, except Lieutenant Greer allowed me inside the realty office yesterday." Lizzy opened her purse, pulled out a piece of paper, and handed it to Stacey. It was a copy of a picture she'd taken on her cell phone.

"After Jennifer hung up the phone, she crumpled up a yellow sticky note and threw it toward the garbage bin, only she missed. On a hunch, I waited until Greer was in the other room before I looked to see if the note was still there. Of course, I couldn't take anything that might be considered evidence, but that didn't mean I couldn't take a picture of the note. It's all scribbles and hard to read."

"Best Limousines," Stacey said, squinting to make out the letters.

Lizzy nodded. "That's it. That's all I've got. A gut feeling that Michael is innocent and a picture of a sticky note."

"Thank you," Stacey said. She picked up a photo album and handed it to Lizzy, asking her to take a look. As Lizzy flipped through page after page of Stacey and her family sharing many happy moments with Jennifer and Michael, it was her turn to listen.

"Although I'm new to Channel 10 News, I come from a long line of reporters. My father and I have had endless talks about trusting our gut feelings. Between my father and me, we've talked to dozens of criminals, cold-blooded killers included. Of course, I recognize that you were forced to live with one of the worst kinds of lunatics for months. Neither of us is being naïve, Lizzy. Michael is innocent."

After a while, Lizzy set the photo album aside and said, "I told Lieutenant Greer I wanted to talk to Michael."

"Why? What would you say to him?"

"I'm not sure at this point. I want to ask him a few questions, see his reaction, I guess."

Stacey nodded as she processed Lizzy's plan. "You'll let me know if you get to talk to Michael?"

"Of course."

They both stood.

Lizzy offered her hand, and Stacey clasped it between hers. In that moment, she noticed a look of desperation in Stacey's eyes. *Why?* Something told her there was more to this story than Stacey was letting on. But for now, she decided to keep that thought to herself. Instincts were great, but there was a lot to be said for patience, too.

CHAPTER 10

I talked to her, saying I was sorry for what I had done. It was the
first time I had apologized to someone I had killed.
—Peter Sutcliffe

Saturday, May 12, 2012

The wooden stairs creaked as he descended, each step deliberate,
his hand brushing against the cold wall in the dark until his right
foot landed on the concrete surface below. Reaching outward and
upward, he grasped onto the end of the chain and gave it a tug.

Click.

And then there was light.

Everything was immaculate, just the way he liked it. The
room smelled of disinfectant. Both cages at the far end of the
room contained a twin mattress, a blanket, granola bars, water
bottles, and even a porta potty. He was ready for the next hurrah.

He'd spent countless hours working on his special room,
making sure everything was in its place. Every time he came
down the steep wooden stairs, which was not nearly as often as
he would have liked, he felt overwhelmed with pride at what he'd
created. One smoothly plastered wall was covered with memorabilia, including handcrafted necklaces adorned with rings, tufts

of hair, gold teeth, driver's licenses, a thumb, fingers, and five beautiful toes.

Breathing in, he felt dizzy with satisfaction as he summoned the smell of fear and relived the terror of days and nights long past.

His favorite bit of décor was the amazing heart-shaped design he'd made out of Susan and Raymond Fenster's dried skin, which had been framed years ago. Susan made up the left side of the heart and Raymond the right. He'd taken special care in preserving the skin before letting it dry by using a mixture of formaldehyde and solvents. The tiny stitches he'd used to bind the two halves were hardly noticeable.

Susan and Raymond may have suffered the longest of all his victims, but they were the only pair of all his couples who had willingly died in the name of love. Neither had been able to bear seeing the other suffer and so they had made a pact. If the opportunity arose, Raymond would kill Susan somehow and then take his own life immediately afterward. Although they had been in separate cages at the time, the cages were close enough that they were able to reach out of one and into the other if they wanted to touch each other.

After listening to the two of them talk about starving to death in order to end their nightmare, he'd handed Susan a hunting knife, giving her the option to kill herself fast and efficiently. He'd been surprised when, more excitedly than ever, they continued their suicidal talk. He even tried to talk them out of it, but their minds were made up. Within an hour after Susan had gotten the knife, Raymond had sliced his wife's throat clean through.

Despite his promise to let Raymond go if he followed through in killing his wife, Raymond didn't hesitate to cut his own throat after killing his wife, but not before reaching through the bars and clasping onto the hand of his beloved.

Susan and Raymond, as far as he was concerned, were the epitome of true love.

For all eternity.

As he stared longingly at his wall of memorabilia and relived many of his best moments, his thoughts wandered. The room was windowless, and, more importantly, it was also soundproof. The small hidden door leading into his hideout was made of galvanized steel. Nothing escaped, including the eerie sounds made by thousands of beetles and their young as they burrowed through the wood inside a six foot–by–six foot box with wire mesh sidings.

He'd avoided bugs when he was small: worms, spiders, mosquitoes, you name it. It didn't matter what kind of bug, he'd kept his distance. He could handle rats and frogs, but bugs…bugs had too many legs and weird-looking eyes. They clicked and buzzed and they were practically invisible—now you see them, now you don't. He never knew when a bug was going to end up in his soup or drop from the ceiling while he slept. They were quiet, creeping up on him when he was unaware.

But it was the pine sawyer beetle that really made his skin crawl. They were large, cylindrical, hard-shelled insects with long wriggly antennae, and yet they could squeeze into any crevice, no matter how thin or small. Beetles were stealth.

Years ago, surrounded by darkness as he slept, he had no way of telling how many beetles were under his bed or clinging to the walls, waiting and watching. He'd discovered the pine sawyer beetle after the Becks had adopted him. He had just turned thirteen. The pine sawyer beetle, he'd realized after moving into their home, made him feel things he never thought he was capable of feeling. They frightened him.

At night, when the windows were left open, he'd hear the peculiar, unnatural hum of the fleshy, round-bodied larvae as they burrowed their way through the soft center of the many trees surrounding the property, and he would wonder if they were planning an attack. His heart would beat faster and his hands would grow clammy. Maybe it had been the beetle's indifference to his existence that had enthralled him back then.

His gaze left the cage and instead focused on the jar sitting next to the television. He couldn't help but shake his head every time he looked at the preserved heart inside. Betsy Weaver had been by far the loudest, most obnoxious person he'd ever had the pleasure to slaughter. Although it didn't always happen, he liked to keep the clients he brought to his special hideout for as long as possible before and after their death. But within hours of abducting Betsy Weaver, he'd recognized his mistake. She didn't love anyone but herself. She had been married for nearly thirty years, but she'd been willing to throw her poor husband under the bus within minutes of arriving.

To this day, Stan Weaver had no idea how close he'd come to losing his life.

Before he could even give Stan a call and put his well-laid plans into action, he'd taken care of Betsy himself, saving Stan the bother. Betsy's death had been a painful one. And yet he still wasn't sure if she'd learned anything from the experience. He certainly hadn't taken any joy in killing the woman. She was the most heartless bitch he'd ever met. *Literally*, he thought with a smile as he stared at the contents of the jar.

Exhaling, he moved toward the television sitting atop a tall, narrow dresser and turned it on. He also kept a small desk in the room, along with a computer. He took a seat at his desk, picked up the remote, and then pushed the buttons until he was watching the nightly news.

As he waited for the computer to boot up, he looked at the list of names on his notebook. At the top of his list were Kassie and Drew Scott. Kassie and Drew could very well be the next couple to take up residence in his dual cages, but, contrary to popular belief, his victims were *not* just couples. Sometimes—exactly three times in the past ten years—he had killed on the spur of the moment without any preplanning whatsoever. For instance, after he'd discovered that a couple he'd been watching for a long while had moved to Europe due to an unexpected job opportunity, his frustrations had gotten the best of him. And Felicia Potter happened to be the unlucky recipient of his aggravation.

Getting killed by a serial killer was like winning the lottery, at least when it came to odds, but that night, a cold windy night when even most dogs were let inside, Felicia had made the mistake of leaving pruning shears and a ladder in her front yard next to a decaying tree. The circumstances were too good to pass up, and it ended up being the first time he'd ever made love to a corpse.

He'd spent the entire night making passionate love to the dead Felicia. The cold dank smell of death only added to his pleasure. Blood had oozed from her mouth when he mounted her. Just holding her hand made him feel loved, and he had to drag himself away from her the next morning. For days afterward, he drove by her home on 14th Street, wishing he could check up on her and pay her another visit. It was a week before her body was discovered.

The police had been baffled.

And that was when he understood that it was to his benefit to change things up every once in a while to throw off the police and the feds. Every time a body was discovered, the media sent the people of Sacramento into a panic.

After Felicia, he began to spend his cooling-off periods reading about other serial killers. He became obsessed with books written by profilers and federal agents. He read about criminal profiling and motive, sociopathic behavior, and the gripping stories of other killers: his mentors, his idols, all innovative pioneers of evil. He studied, he examined, interpreted, and learned. If his last victim had been mutilated, his next victim would be strangled, and so on.

Smiling at his cleverness, he scratched his chin as he studied his notebook, staring specifically at number two on the list: Ken and Barbie. No kidding. Kenneth and Barbara Garbes. As he made a few notes about new information he'd garnered regarding the couple, he listened to the weather report.

More rain was expected. That was good. He liked the rain. He hoped the rain would last into the beginning of summer as it had last year. Out of the corner of his eye, he caught a glimpse of Michael Dalton's picture when it filled the screen.

Michael's arrest had been the top news story for days now, but Michael Dalton was nobody. What was the big deal? Husbands killed their wives every day in America. The next picture to flash across the screen showed Lieutenant William Greer exiting the Sacramento police department. A petite blonde woman, five foot two, followed close behind.

He turned up the volume. Lizzy Gardner, a private investigator, had reason to believe Michael Dalton had not killed his wife, Jennifer.

Skimming through the channels, he noticed more of the same: every local news station talking about Lizzy Gardner's belief that Michael Dalton was innocent. All speculation, of course, but still, it bothered him. What could that woman possibly have to say to the lieutenant? Michael Dalton was in custody for the murder of his wife. The evidence against him was overwhelming.

He turned to his computer and did a quick search on Lizzy Gardner.

Ahh, now he remembered. He'd thought she looked familiar, and now he knew why. She was the private investigator who had been kidnapped when she was a teenager, the one who got away. Lizzy Gardner had spent a few months with Spiderman, a notorious serial killer who liked to torture young girls he considered to be menaces to society, which made perfect sense. No big loss to society. But what made Lizzy Gardner special was that she had lived to tell about it.

He scanned the articles, skipping some, reading others more than once. Her business was booming and she was still located right here in Sacramento. He laughed for no particular reason. Maybe because private investigations seemed like such a silly business to be in; anyone could slap a sign on her door and call herself a private eye.

Jake Gittes, Jim Rockford, Sam Spade. Those guys were the real deal.

He laughed again and then continued reading.

Many locals considered Lizzy Gardner a hero for helping to take down a killer who had spread fear across Sacramento for too many years. A few saw her as someone who went looking for trouble, leaving chaos in her wake. At the moment, he tended to agree with the latter crowd.

Movement in the corner of the room caught his attention. He turned toward the woman sitting on the wood chair.

She looked tense.

Although in the beginning he'd used a heavy rope to secure her slim ankles to the front chair legs, he no longer felt the need to strap her down. She was allowed to walk around if she wanted to, but she never did, at least not when he was around. She had snatched the granola bar he'd left by her feet and was now munching away.

"Hungry?"

She didn't respond. In fact, she looked as if she might have gained a few pounds.

"I thought you said your family loved you," he said. "If they really loved you, they would have found you by now."

He shook his head. She was ignoring him again. If she wasn't talking his ear off, trying to convince him to let her go or telling him what to do, she was pretending he didn't exist. More than once he'd considered letting her go—he really had—but whenever he felt the urge, another thought took over his brain waves and prevented him from doing so. They both knew she would go straight to the police. Sure, he'd taken precautions—blindfolds, sleeping pills, yada yada yada—to make sure she didn't know their location, but the truth was, as much as he tried to deny it, he was in love with her. Madly so, and had been for many years.

He could never let her go.

CHAPTER 11

You'll never get me. I'll kill again. Then you'll have another
long trial. And then I'll do it again.
—Henry Brisbon

Davis
Monday, May 14, 2012

Hayley opened another file, did a search on the Internet, and
took some notes, but it was difficult to concentrate with Lizzy
and Jared snuggling in the kitchen. Jared had returned last night,
making Lizzy a little too saccharine for her liking. Jessica should
be the one living with the two lovebirds, not her.

Kitally, a girl she'd met in the detention center, would be
stopping by in an hour. Lizzy and Jared should have left for work
already, but they were too busy catching up after being apart.
She'd had enough. "Could you two take it to the bedroom, or do
I need to put on my headphones?"

Jared laughed and said, "I'm just glad to be home."

"I never would have guessed."

He gave Lizzy one last kiss and then picked up his briefcase at the door. He turned to Hayley and said, "If you ever need anything, my number is on the fridge."

"Thanks, Dad."

He shook his head at her as he headed out the door.

After he was gone, she could feel Lizzy's eyes on her.

"What?" Hayley asked.

"Are you OK?"

"I'm fine," she said as she picked up a business card for Lily's Flower Shop and held it in the air for Lizzy to see. "I've been updating the electronic spreadsheets on all of the open cases. I found this card for a flower shop in the Simpson/Dalton file. I don't think it belongs in here."

Lizzy took it and examined it closer. "Are you sure this was in the Simpson file?"

"Yep. It was stuck between the pages of the signed agreement between your agency and J&M Realty."

"Jennifer must have accidentally scooped it up and put it in the envelope before she handed it to me."

"Is this the same Jennifer that was killed recently?"

"It is," Lizzy said as she gathered her purse and tucked the card inside. "Do you have the Simpson file or did Jessica return it to the office?"

"It's right here."

Lizzy took the file and then headed for the door. Hand on the doorknob, ready to leave, she looked back at Hayley. "You're sure you're OK?"

Hayley looked her in the eyes. "I'm fine. Really."

"OK. Lock up after I leave, all right?"

"Will do."

Lizzy shut the door behind her.

Figuring Lizzy was probably standing on the other side wait-ing to hear the click of the lock, Hayley got up and slid the dead bolt into place. Then she leaned her forehead against the door and wondered if Lizzy would ever feel safe again.

Her next thought was about her mom. She couldn't stop thinking about her. Already this morning, she'd called the house more than once, but nobody had answered. Hayley wondered if Brian was really out of her mom's life. She looked at her phone. Maybe she could call Jessica and ask her to stop by her mom's house.

Before she decided whether to make the call or not, there was a knock on the door. Hayley jumped up, looked out the peephole, and saw Kitally. She let the girl inside and then shut and locked the door behind her.

"Hey," Kitally said. "How's it going?"

"Not too bad. Thanks for coming."

Kitally was seventeen, Asian, and stood about five foot five. She wore a retro couture red strapless dress that would never work on anyone but Kitally. The girl had strong cheekbones and a sharp, well-defined jawline. Her eyes were brown and framed with thick colorful eyeliner. Her head was shaved, leaving noth-ing but a soft downy layer of black fuzz.

Despite the fact that the girl reminded Hayley of a hyper puppy dog, she had liked Kitally straight off. Kitally was brilliant, but most people might not notice since she hid her intelligence behind an odd personality. Sweet one moment, tactless and gross the next. She could be blunt with her words as well as with her actions, which is why many of the kids in the detention center had steered clear of her.

She first noticed Kitally during her second week of incar-ceration when she was eating lunch. All the inmates ate their meals together. Hayley, like everyone else, looked up when Abby, the biggest bitch in the place, began shouting at the lunch lady. The woman serving the food didn't decide what food to serve; she was just doing her job. But Abby didn't care. Abby needed to screech and holler at someone, and the woman serving the food just happened to be in the wrong place at the wrong time.

While Abby held her plate to her side and cussed the woman out, Kitally strolled by and shot a snot rocket right into Abby's plate of spaghetti. Nobody said a word before or after Abby sat down and munched down her spaghetti. But the lunch lady had a smile on her face for the rest of that day.

Rumor had it that Kitally was also part of a gang. She had broken a few legs, arms, even blinded a kid with a plastic fork. There were usually guards in the room, but everyone knew they didn't carry guns. What good was a guard without a gun? Besides, the guards liked it when an inmate stirred the pot a little and added some excitement to their shift.

The day Hayley and Kitally became friends was the same day one of the security guards decided to pick on Hayley. He called her names and poked her with his stick. To this day she had no idea why, but he wouldn't stop.

Kitally happened to be sitting nearby when Hayley glanced at the metal tongs in the salad bowl that had been left on the table. Kitally scooted closer to Hayley and advised her against using the tongs as a weapon. She then proceeded to give Hayley a mathematical equation that summed up the results of what her actions would be were she to follow through with her plan, a plan she had yet to verbalize.

The kid had fucking read her mind.

For the next six months, they sat together at every meal, until Kitally was released. She never did tell Hayley why she was in the place.

"Want something to eat?" Hayley asked.

"No," she said. "I'm good."

Before Hayley could reach the couch to take a seat, there was another knock on the door. Eyes narrowed, Hayley headed back that way.

What the hell was he doing here?

It was the boy who had helped Lizzy with her defense class months ago. Tommy. The same boy Lizzy had made a point of talking about when she came to visit Hayley at the detention center and then again when she picked her up to take her home. She'd been set up. "Shit."

"What is it?"

"The lady I live with has a bad habit of trying to set me up."

Kitally took a peek out the peephole. "Looks like the geek squad sent him. Does he use gel in his hair?"

Hayley agreed. Tommy Ellis was in a league of his own. His hair was neatly combed to the side. His lime-green shirt had zero wrinkles and a stiff collar. His pants weren't exactly skintight, but they weren't loose either. The only thing he was missing was a colorful sweater hanging loosely around his shoulders. She unlatched the dead bolt and opened the door before he could knock again. "What do you want?"

"Hey there," he said. "How's it going?"

"Fine."

"Did Lizzy tell you I was coming?"

"Nope."

"Ahh, I see. Well, she thought you could use some company."

"Well, she was wrong." She started to close the door, but he stopped her.

"Can I at least come in for a few minutes?"

"What's your name again?" Hayley asked, not wanting to give him false hope of someday being her friend.

"Tommy Ellis. I teach kids self-defense at the Self-Defense Institute in Roseville."

Hayley was about to send him away for the second time, when Kitally opened the door wider and said hello.

Tommy offered his hand, but Kitally ignored it.

Now Hayley was really worried. Just because she didn't want to be his friend or let him inside the house didn't mean she wanted to crush him like a bug before sending him away. And that's exactly what Kitally would do. She didn't like too many people.

Kitally was still looking him over, her gaze focused on his shoes, her expression filled with disgust, when suddenly her gaze shot past him and her eyes widened. "Is that your motorcycle?" She pushed past him and headed for his bike.

Tommy followed her.

Hayley crossed her arms and watched them both get all animated and weird over the thing. "I'll be in here when you guys are done talking shop."

Nobody responded. Hayley left the door open and headed for the couch.

They returned a few minutes later.

Hayley had already taken a seat, but after Tommy shut the door, she placed her foot on the coffee table and pulled the right pant leg to her knee so Kitally could take a closer look at her ankle monitor. She wanted the thing off—the sooner, the better. She refused to let Karate Kid get in the way. If he didn't like it, he could leave.

Kitally took a seat on the couch next to her and examined the anklet.

"It's a GPS ankle monitor—" Hayley began.

"Yeah," Kitally said, cutting her off. "It's passively receiving information from global positioning satellites that give the ankle bracelet the satellites' position and time. When there are at least four active satellites, the GPS receiver can mathematically determine its own three-dimensional location. The in-home unit will poll the bracelet wirelessly and ask for its coordinates. The bracelet will then encrypt its information and send it to the in-home unit. This is where it gets a little complicated and very appealing to people like me. This 'packet' of information holds a few items in order to communicate effectively, one of which is a MAC address—Media Access Control address—which is unique for *every* device that communicates via an IP."

Hayley didn't like Tommy hovering over them, since she didn't want him mentioning any of this to Lizzy or Jared, but she figured she could talk to him about that later. Threaten to break his leg if she had to. She glanced at Kitally. "Can you do it?"

Kitally turned Hayley's ankle to the right. After a long moment, she shook her head and said, "I don't know. This isn't like the tracking devices I've seen before."

"What are you trying to do?" Tommy asked.

Hayley sighed. "I'd rather not say."

"A five-year-old could get that thing off you, but if you're planning on leaving during the day, you don't want to have to take it off and on. Too risky."

"Thanks," Hayley said. She looked at Kitally. "What do you suggest?"

Kitally looked at Tommy. "What do you think, Geek Boy?"

Hayley angled her head, waiting to see what Tommy would say next, figuring it was time for her to stop worrying about him. If he wanted to come over uninvited, then he would have to learn to fend for himself.

Tommy pulled out his iPhone and took at least a dozen pictures of the device. "I think I could do a MAC address clone on another device. Then you could just leave the real device at home."

Hayley looked at him. "You're shittin' me."

He took two more pictures before putting his phone away.

"You could do that?" Hayley asked.

He blew air out of his nose and said, "This is kindergarten stuff."

Hayley didn't trust what she was hearing. If Tommy could clone her monitor, she would have some freedom over the next six months or however long they made her wear the device. More importantly, she could keep an eye on her mom and make sure she was safe. She would be free to roam. "When can you get started?"

"Today."

Kitally rubbed her hands together. "Well, that was easy." She headed for the door.

"You're leaving?"

Her smile looked more like a smirk. "Places to go, people to see."

"What do I owe you?" Hayley asked.

Kitally laughed, a funny squeaky noise that sounded more like a sneeze, before she said, "My dad has more money than he knows what to do with, and I'm his princess. If you need me for anything else, give me a call."

Tommy and Hayley both followed her outside.

She did a skip and a hop down the pathway, stopping at Tommy's bike again. "If either of you ever wants a ride on a real bike, let me know." She laughed and then climbed behind the wheel of a shiny silver Porsche and took off.

"She's great," Tommy said.

"Yeah."

"She's driving a Porsche Carrera GT. They don't make those cars any longer. Her dad must have some real money, since there were only six hundred sold in the US."

"Fascinating," Hayley said. *Not*. When she glanced his way, she didn't like the way he was smiling at her, as if he found her humorous or friendly or anything at all.

He followed her back to the house, which was equally annoying. Stopping at the door, she turned to face him. "So, I guess you're going to go work on cloning my ankle bracelet, right?"

He laughed. "Yeah, sure, I can take a hint."

"Oh, good, because I didn't want to have to spell it out for you."

"What? You don't want to be my friend?"

She peered into his eyes. "I thought you were some big important businessman with a company to run."

"Is that the impression I gave you last time we met?"

He looked away from her, toward the street.

Damn. Now she felt bad. "I'm sorry. I didn't mean anything by it."

He lifted his hands in surrender as he headed for his bike. "No problem. You don't want to be my friend. I can handle it."

Hayley bent her head forward and then backward to get the kinks out. "What about the ankle bracelet?"

He hopped on his motorcycle, even looked sort of cool for a geek. "What about it?"

"You're still going to help me out?"

"I don't know," he said with a stupid twinkle in his eye. "I'll have to think about it."

"You're really pissing me off."

"OK, OK. But you have to promise me that if I do it, once you're free again, you'll take a ride on the back of my Suzuki."

She didn't like to play games or make promises, but she wanted the ankle monitor off, so she said, "Sure, fine, whatever."

"Just so you know," he said, his tone in serious mode, "I don't break the law for just anyone."

Oh, God. He definitely had a major crush on her. And judging by the stupid-ass grin on his face as he slipped his helmet over his head, he knew she'd just figured it out.

She exhaled as she headed back inside, locking the door behind her.

Sacramento
Monday, May 14, 2012

It was well after midnight. Water drizzled off his hood and into his face. His coat had a double-front storm seal with inside and outside snap closures. Overall, he was reasonably dry, even in this downpour.

He stood across the street on the curb and watched the same house he'd been watching for the past five years: a single-family residence. The house was small, with few regular windows, and painted brown. Nothing to write home about. Not really. Not unless you knew the monster who lived inside.

He wasn't the same imaginary monster who hid in closets and frightened kids in the middle of the night. Nor was he the grunting, green-skinned giant whom millions liked to call Frankenstein. This guy was the real deal—a man with ten fingers and ten toes, muscles, and arteries.

Most people who looked at him or bothered to talk to him might think he was just a regular guy, but they would be wrong. The man inside the house on Bunker Street was missing an essential ingredient: a soul. And unlike the imaginary bogeyman, this monster had a name: John Robinson.

As raindrops dripped off his nose, he took a closer look at his surroundings. The neighborhood hadn't changed much over the past five years. Two houses down, somebody had planted a row of rosebushes with long thorny stems. A fence made of thorns. Not a bad idea. The house behind him was boarded up. A piece of paper taped to the door read: Do Not Enter. Plywood covered the broken windows. The entire house was infested with rats.

The house he was watching, though, the house across the street, had a light on in the kitchen, which meant the man who lived there was probably washing dishes after eating his evening meal.

Eli looked at his watch. The backlight glowed. It was fifteen minutes past nine. The monster ate at about the same time every night, at least when he was home. Some nights, he never came home, which made sense since he was a fucking monster. No wife and no kids. Made sense since murderers weren't usually the marrying type.

He was tidy for a madman, though.

Eli Simpson knew this because he'd been inside the house twice already.

Five years ago, the cops had gone inside the house, too, and found nothing. No evidence of any kind. No blood. No fingerprints. Nothing at all to prove that John Robinson, the man who lived inside that house, had ever known his sister, Rochelle.

But Robinson *had* known Rochelle, and Robinson had killed her. Eli was sure of it, but he had no proof. Not even a body to bury and lay to rest. According to the police reports, John Robinson and Rochelle had been accosted by four men and then held captive for days. There were pictures in the file, and John Robinson had the black eyes and bumps and bruises to show for his ordeal, but Rochelle was never found. Not one hair, not one bit of forensic evidence, to prove or disprove Robinson's story.

The police had made it clear from the start that they didn't like Eli's attitude, which was why they hadn't listened to Eli when he told them that John was the culprit, the man who was responsible for Rochelle's demise. Eli hadn't trusted the cops to do their job, so he'd found a way to get inside John Robinson's house. But Robinson was one step ahead of him; he'd called the cops and Eli had been arrested.

Jaw clenched, Eli rolled his fingers into fists at his sides. Eli had no choice but to watch and wait. This wasn't the only place he visited regularly. Every month he also visited the Sacramento police station and talked to the guys working Rochelle's case. He would walk into the station and all eyes would be averted. He would pick an officer's desk and proceed to sit there for most of the day, making sure they were doing everything possible to find Rochelle. Now, everybody in the police department knew him, and when Eli showed up, they all had the motions down to a science. Whoever happened to draw the short stick would retrieve Rochelle's case file from the cabinet and then tell Eli what they had done since his last visit, which was never much: a few phone calls usually, nothing more. Now when Eli walked into the police station, he liked to do the whole eeny, meeny, miny, moe thing and take a seat wherever that little rhyme led him.

They all knew his name and he knew theirs.

He was pretty sure that every uniformed officer and every detective in the place thought he was crazier than the guy who had killed his sister. When John Robinson managed to get a restraining order against him, the guys in blue actually stuck up for the crazy man! His sister was dead, but *he* was the one named in a restraining order?

Life was sort of strange that way.

His parents didn't talk to him for years. Not until his mom died and his dad needed somewhere to go. He shook his head.

He was the only one who seemed to care about finding Rochelle. And in the process, he'd somehow become the bad guy. His parents, his ex-girlfriend, everyone he met begged him to drop it. Let it go. Move on. But he couldn't. There was no doubt in his mind. John Robinson had killed his sister. He'd known there was something wrong with the guy within five minutes of meeting him.

He knew John Robinson was responsible for his sister's disappearance. He knew it as surely as he knew the sun would rise tomorrow. He would gladly snap the asshole's neck tonight if that would help him find Rochelle's body. Until he found her, the monster was safe.

And he knew it.

CHAPTER 12

Big deal. Death always went with the territory.
I'll see you in Disneyland.
—Richard Ramirez

Davis
Tuesday, May 15, 2012

After watching Jared and Lizzy leave for work, he waited fifteen minutes before checking windows and doors to see if any were unlocked. No such luck, but he was surprised to find a flimsy lock on the garage door on the side of the house. He was glad about that because one way or another, he was going to find a way to get inside Lizzy Gardner's house. His plan was to search through her things, get a feel for the woman, and find out what she was up to. Not only did he want to see if he could give her a nudge into the darkness she was trying to distance herself from, he suddenly found himself beyond curious about Lizzy Gardner. Who was this woman who had somehow taken out Spiderman, his champion, his idol?

With a gloved hand and a thin steel tool, he opened the door, smiling at the ease with which the lock popped loose.

Once inside the house, he stood in the kitchen and inhaled. He could smell air freshener and a hint of breakfast. Somebody had eaten eggs and bacon. Stopping, listening, he heard a noise upstairs. Usually he took his time, working his way methodically from one end of the house to the other, but instead he followed the noise up the stairs and into what appeared to be the master bedroom. A cat rolled around, playing with some wire that made a tinny noise whenever it hit the door to the bedroom. Using the toe of his boot, he nudged the cat out of his way so he had a clear path to the king-sized bed. He picked up the framed picture on the bedside table, smiling when he recognized the two people as Lizzy Gardner and Jared Shayne.

He lay down on the bed, flat on his back, and stared at the ceiling. He found himself wishing Spiderman could see him now, wondering where Samuel Jones had gone wrong. Spiderman had terrorized Sacramento for decades, but somehow Lizzy Gardner had gotten the best of him. He didn't like her putting her nose where it didn't belong; nobody had hired Lizzy Gardner to prove Michael Dalton's innocence. She needed to learn a lesson or two, and he figured he was the perfect guy for the job.

When he'd first seen her on the news, he'd considered ignoring her actions, pretending she didn't exist. He had options, including watching quietly from afar while Lizzy Gardner stirred up trouble. But twenty-four hours later, he was still thinking about her…wondering if the little blonde private eye was getting closer. Thinking about her was messing with his mind, causing him to lose focus.

Unacceptable.

And that was why he was here today. It hadn't taken much research to figure out she wasn't all there. Lizzy Gardner was a ticking time bomb waiting to explode and lose it for good. He figured he'd just speed the process along.

Welcome to the world of insanity!

The private eye seemed to have a thing for killers, maybe even for serial killers specifically. She had befriended Spiderman and had gotten away in the end. He thought about that for a moment as he released a ponderous sigh. Just because he thought she should mind her own business didn't mean he didn't understand. He definitely understood her keen interest in the Dalton case. Everybody had crazy fantasies that involved one evil deed or another. Why else would people give serial killers names like Son of Sam, Spiderman, Angel of Death, or the Lovebird Killer?

The name the media and the citizens of Sacramento had given him was interesting. The Lovebird Killer had a nice ring to it.

The world's fascination with evil was understandable. Not only were regular everyday citizens mesmerized by killers—the more pictures, the better—killers were also fascinated by killers.

He should know.

Not only were destroyers of life charming, they were intelligent beings. They easily fit into society and were impossible to recognize, difficult to distinguish from anyone else. How else would it have been possible for Jack the Ripper to walk the streets of London without getting caught? He struck and then he was gone. Many speculated that the man was well educated, possibly an aristocrat.

Jack the Ripper was a brutal character. His work inspired many, but still, the man had received way too much print time over the years. The intriguing thing about Jack, though, was that he was never identified. Everything else about Jack the Ripper was rubbish. You didn't need surgical knowledge to figure out how to mutilate a corpse. No Reference 101 tutorial necessary.

Henry Holmes or Joseph Vacher, now those were some blood-thirsty sons of bitches. And nobody ever talked about Vacher.

Richard Ramirez liked to talk about Lucifer dwelling within all people. It was true. Serial killers were doctors and lawyers, nurses and priests. Nobody was safe.

He read that Lizzy Gardner suffered from recurring nightmares. If anyone knew about nightmares, it was him. He wasn't a bad person.

He deserved to be loved.

Squeezing his eyes shut, stopping the onslaught of emotions that followed when he allowed his mind to travel to the past, he quickly opened his eyes, then pushed himself off the bed and slid his feet to the floor.

Time to get to work.

He walked out into the hallway and peered into the first room to the right. It was an office. There were two desks, two chairs, two computers. He opened drawers and sifted through files, scattering pens and papers across the floor. He wanted Lizzy to know someone had been inside her house. He wanted her to understand that she would never be safe.

Deep inside the file cabinet, he found dozens of notebooks bound together with rubber bands. He cut the bands and opened one notebook, then another. Notes and journals of Lizzy Gardner's life; it was like finding treasure, and he felt giddy with excitement.

She wasn't the only one who liked to cause trouble and stir the pot a little.

Seeing Lizzy Gardner's face on every news station across America had not only perturbed but also made him curious. What was she up to and why? And what was the deal with her and FBI agent Jared Shayne? They had dated in high school, and according to an in-depth interview with her father, an interview he'd found on the Internet, the man's daughter had been out tramping it up with Shayne the night she was abducted all those years ago. Now the lovebirds were back together again and he, for one, wanted to know why. Was guilt the underlying reason Jared had come back into her life? Did they love each other or were they in love with the idea of love? Could someone as fucked up as Lizzy Gardner ever trust anyone enough to feel true love?

For the next ten minutes, he found himself absorbed in Lizzy's journals. He pictured her walking into her office right now. If that happened, what would he do to her? He was no Jeffrey Dahmer. He didn't have a crazed, maniacal side to him. He didn't eat people and he didn't want anything to do with little boys. With him, it was more—

A noise coming from downstairs stopped him cold. Had Lizzy forgotten something and returned to the house, or was it her boyfriend? Adrenaline kicked in, making his heart race. Straightening, he headed for the hallway; he wasn't worried or afraid, he was excited.

Hayley sat at her desk in her bedroom going through a thick pile of case files. She logged in each case number and made a checklist of things that still needed to be done before she could stamp the file: CASE CLOSED.

Thinking she heard the phone, she pulled off her headset. All was quiet as she left her bedroom and made her way to the kitchen to get some cereal. She grabbed a clean bowl and a spoon from the dishwasher and then went to the pantry to see what they had. It looked like someone had picked up some fiber cereal. She opened the lid, reached inside, pulled out a piece of fiber, and stuck it in her mouth. It tasted like cardboard. Disgusting. She tried the bran next. Not much better.

A weird bumping noise sounded from another part of the house. She put the cereal down and listened for a minute. Leaving the cramped area of the pantry, she stepped quietly into the kitchen, still listening.

Was somebody here?

Leaning over the counter, she grabbed a knife from the butcher block and headed for the front door. Before she reached the coffee table, she saw a booted foot and then another as it hit the landing.

What the fuck?

An unfamiliar man was inside the house. The dark cap on his head covered his ears and eyebrows, but no hat in the world could cover those vibrant blue eyes as their gazes locked.

They both lunged forward. She went for him while he went for the door, but he seemed better prepared for the unexpected. He shoved her to the ground. The knife flew from her hand and hit the wall. He was quick and he had the locks undone and the door opened before she could get to her feet.

Tommy stood on the other side of the door, ready to knock, surprising both Hayley and the burglar.

She scrambled to her feet and ran after the man.

Tommy had fallen into the hydrangea bush, his legs tangled, his feet sticking out. Hayley didn't stop to see if he was OK; she ran at full speed across the lawn and down the street. The asshole was getting away and he was fast. By the time she made a right on the main cross street, he had disappeared.

Winded, she plunked her hands on her hips and watched closely, eyes narrowed. After a few minutes, she turned and headed back, pissed at herself for not realizing someone had been inside the house to begin with.

As she approached the house, Tommy greeted her. His face was scratched up pretty badly, his nose bleeding. "Which way did he go?"

"I have no fucking idea."

He followed her as she limped inside.

Tommy locked the door and grabbed the phone.

"What are you doing?"

"Calling the police."

"Call Lizzy first."

He released a frustrated breath, but then did as she said. While he talked to Lizzy, Hayley headed upstairs. "Hannah," she called out, suddenly worried about the stupid cat. "Here, kitty, kitty. Come on, kitty." If that cat got hurt while she was in charge, she would never allow herself to get close to another animal for as long as she lived. This was the very reason that she didn't like animals. They made people worry and then they died way too soon.

"Come on, kitty," she said again, her voice angry.

Her shoulders fell at the sight of Lizzy and Jared's shared office. Papers and files were scattered about, spread across the floor. Hannah's food and water dishes had been knocked over and Hannah's bed was upside down.

The carpet near the door leading into Lizzy's bedroom was covered with bloody little paw prints. Hayley closed her eyes, took in a deep breath, and headed that way.

No. No. No.

She followed the prints into Lizzy and Jared's bedroom. She'd never had any reason to enter their bedroom until now. The prints disappeared under the bed. Swallowing a knot in her throat, she got down on all fours and continued to call Hannah's name. She could see a little ball of black-and-white fur with big round eyes.

Hannah wasn't a kitten any longer, but as far as cats went, she was on the small side. "Come here, Hannah. Come on. It's OK." Pressing her face against the wood base of the bed, she reached as far as she could until she was finally able to reach the cat and pull her out from under the bed.

"Hannah," she said as she cradled the animal in her arms. For a moment, she merely held the cat close to her chest. Then she began to look her over.

"That's not blood, is it?" Hannah didn't have a single scrape on her. It wasn't blood. It was ink. With the cat tucked in her arms, she walked into the office. A red pen had been stepped on and crushed, leaving a puddle of red ink on the floor near the desk.

"Meow."

Hayley looked at the cat and shook her head before setting her on the floor in front of her.

When Tommy appeared, Hayley realized she was actually thankful that he was here with her.

"Are you all right?"

"Yeah."

"Is that blood?"

She shook her head. "Red ink."

"No, I mean on your leg." He pointed to her calf.

Hayley looked down at her leg. It was bleeding. She must have been cut with the knife when she was pushed to the ground.

"Come on," he said, ushering her out of the room. "Let's get your leg cleaned up."

Lizzy stood inside the house and watched the flurry of activity, relieved that Tommy's and Hayley's wounds were only superficial and would not require stitches. Lizzy had already spent an hour talking to the neighbors, a few of whom still stood outside, huddled in the middle of the street, watching and discussing the burglary and what they could do to protect themselves in the future.

Response to the break-in had been quick. Because their house belonged to a federal agent, Lizzy figured, the break-in was being treated like a homicide investigation. Never mind that there was no body and little blood. One uniformed officer was stationed outside the front door while another was across the street, talking to the woman next door, who had seen the man run down the street. The upstairs had been established as a crime scene. A technician collected evidence: footprints, fingerprints, hairs, fibers, any physical evidence possibly left behind.

In the living room downstairs, Lizzy stood off to the side as an officer questioned Hayley and Tommy. Hayley described the intruder as under six feet tall. A dark cap, she said, covered most of his head, so she had no idea what color his hair was or if he had any hair at all. He was on the thin side. He wore a long-sleeved dark shirt and dark pants. She described him as having a regular nose, thin lips, and big eyes.

Lizzy focused on the dust motes floating about as the ceiling fan twirled above their heads. Her eyes darted to the window above the kitchen sink. Somebody was there, looking in. She couldn't see anyone, but she could feel it. He was out there, watching. She knew the drill.

She headed that way, reached for the cord on the blinds, and pulled.

Nobody there. She could breathe again.

"Is everything all right?" an officer asked from the other room.

Stay calm, she told herself. *You can do this.* She turned, planted a smile on her face, and returned to the living room. "Everything's fine. I thought I saw something, that's all."

Tommy continued to answer questions while Hayley stared at her.

The cut on Hayley's leg had stopped bleeding. Hayley would be fine.

They were all fine.

But something niggled at the back of Lizzy's mind, reminding her that life could change in an instant. Spiderman was dead, but evil was not; it was alive and well, and it was pointing its thin, crooked finger at her, and there was nothing she could do about it.

John and Rochelle
Sacramento
June 2007

"Why are you doing this?" Rochelle asked.

John woke to the sound of rattling chains and Rochelle's voice. His neck was stiff and every muscle in his body cried out in pain. Out of the corner of his left eye, he could see two guys hovering over Rochelle. He wasn't sure whether it was night or day. There were no windows in the place. What little light there was came from the opening at the top of the stairs.

"Fuck!" one guy said, jumping away from Rochelle. "The bitch bit me."

The other guy laughed so hard he failed to see Rochelle grab onto the length of chain. She wrapped the chain around his neck and yanked as hard as she could. He fell backward on top of her. She was determined and didn't loosen her hold. Judging from the gasping sounds coming from the guy's mouth, he wouldn't last long.

John struggled with the ropes tied around his wrist. He'd been rubbing the ties against a jagged edge on the metal chair for two days now. The rope was frayed. He couldn't see it, but he could feel it loosening.

The guy who'd been bitten scrambled around in the dark for something to use to protect himself. Whatever he found was long and solid and John couldn't tell if it was a bat or a two-by-four as the man stalked toward Rochelle with the object raised above his head.

"Watch out!" John shouted.

It was too late. He swung, hitting her in the back of the head. The chain fell limp around the other man's neck, and he choked and gagged until he was able to breathe again.

"Let her go," John cried. "I'm begging you to let her go. I have money in my bank account. You can have it all if you let her go. Anything. I'll sign over my house, my car, whatever you want. Just let her go."

It was quiet, and for a moment John thought they were considering his offer, but then laughter rang out and bounced off the walls.

John closed his eyes and saw a kaleidoscope of colors. His mouth tightened and a piercing, stabbing pain shot through his skull until the laughter finally subsided. When he opened his eyes again, he felt his stomach turn. "What are you doing to her?"

"What does it look like? The bitch tried to kill me. I'm going to fuck her until she wakes up, and then my friend is going to fuck her until she loses consciousness. And then I'm going to drag her ass upstairs to see if the other guys want a turn. Got a problem with that?"

The beat of his heart spiraled out of control. "Get away from her."

The man who'd almost been choked to death minutes before hiked up Rochelle's dress and slid her underwear down to her knees. Rochelle hadn't moved or made a sound. John wasn't sure whether she was alive. "If you touch her, I'll kill you."

The threat worried them enough that the other guy came to check his ropes.

John felt a tug on his arms and then his legs.

"He's secure."

"Get off her," John warned, his voice deepening. "If you touch her, you're going to die." John angled his head so that he could see the man's shadow against the concrete wall, the man who had hit Rochelle over the head. "You're going to die, too. Both of you."

And the strangest part was that John knew it was true. They were as good as dead. The two men standing before him would not die a natural death. Their deaths would be long and painful and they would spend their last days wishing they had never touched Rochelle.

"Maybe we should take her upstairs," one of them said.

"No. I want John here to watch. He's all talk."

"I know where you live," John lied. "I know your neighbors and I know where you work. Best of all, I know where your families live: your sisters, your brothers, and your mothers. They're all as good as dead."

"Come on," the guy who'd hit Rochelle said. "Let's go upstairs."

"If you want to go, then go, you little pansy-fuck. I'm going to take what I have coming to me."

As the minutes wore on, the scene before him would not compute. John could only see shadows of the man moving back and forth, grunting and groaning, but he couldn't see or hear Rochelle, and he couldn't imagine, or maybe wouldn't allow himself to imagine, that she was there at all.

John felt his vessels expand, every vein in his body ready to explode. Blood surged, popping and sizzling through him until the shapes and shadows before him turned a hazy red. He opened his mouth and released a high-pitched guttural cry that pierced the air and made the walls move.

Seconds later, endless footsteps fell on the stairs, booted feet like the low bass beat of a hundred conga drums. John imagined the feet belonging to a dozen military men, coming to save the day. But it wasn't the military at all. It was the big guy with the massive hands. The same man he and Rochelle had seen leaning against his car days ago…back when they'd still had a chance to get away…back when he'd forced Rochelle to be brave. And she'd been so courageous, too: her spine stiffened, her resolve scrawled across her face for all to see as she followed him unknowingly into Hell.

The massive hands ripped the bat from the other guy's hold, and before anyone knew what was happening, he turned toward John and swung swiftly and concisely, hitting a home run on the first swing.

CHAPTER 13

I don't believe in man, God nor Devil. I hate the whole damned
human race, including myself...I preyed upon the weak, the
harmless and the unsuspecting. This lesson I was taught by
others: might makes right.
—Carl Panzram

Sacramento State Prison
Wednesday, May 16, 2012

Lizzy was subjected to a thorough search before she was allowed
to enter the ten-by-ten room. The room was painted white from
floor to ceiling. The wall to her right was completely bare; the
wall to her left had a large two-way mirror. A uniformed security
guard stood at the door.

Michael Dalton sat at a long rectangular table. His attorney, a
big-boned woman with shoulder-length gray hair, sat next to him.

Dark shadows circled Michael's eyes, making him look ten
years older than the last time she'd seen him. Lizzy met his gaze
and said, "Thank you for meeting with me."

"Why are you here?" he asked without greeting her first.

"She wants to help you," his attorney said.

Michael's eyes bored into Lizzy's. "Is that true?"

For the first time since Lizzy had heard about Jennifer Dalton's death, she felt unsure of Michael's innocence. His dark emotionless eyes made her question her reason for being here. She hardly knew the man. He seemed depressed and ill-tempered. "I needed to talk to you, face-to-face."

"So you're really not sure why you're here, are you?"

That much was certainly true. She refused to let him get the best of her, though, and refused to look away. He was angry and he was going to take his anger out on anyone who came near him. "I'm here because when I met you and your wife, I was struck by the love and devotion the two of you shared. I thought you two were newlyweds. When Jennifer told me you were celebrating your fifteenth anniversary, I was surprised."

"And now you're wondering if it was all an act?"

"The media has said as much. They think I'm a paranoid schizophrenic who believes a serial killer hides behind every bush in Sacramento, and they think you're a nut job."

He smiled.

"Why is that funny?"

"It's not. It's just that I appreciate your honesty. That's what Jennifer and I both liked about you from the moment we met you."

Within the blink of an eye, Michael Dalton's expression went from despairing to hopeful.

Lizzy exhaled a breath she hadn't realized she was holding and said, "Can you tell me what happened?"

His lawyer reached over and touched his forearm.

"It's OK," he told her. "The truth will set me free. It has to. It's all I've got."

Lizzy reached inside her purse and retrieved a notebook and pen. "Is it all right if I take notes?"

Michael nodded.

His lawyer whispered something into his ear.

He disagreed with whatever she had told him and said, "I received a voice mail on my cell from Jennifer to meet her at 134 Deer Valley in El Dorado Hills."

"So you have proof, then."

He shook his head. "They've been unable to locate my cell."

"But there should be a phone record of some sort."

He glanced at his lawyer before saying, "They're working on it. Anyhow, I tried calling Jennifer on my way to the house in El Dorado Hills. As you know, we specialize in foreclosures, auctions, and bank-owned homes. This particular foreclosure has been on the market for two years. It's a monstrosity of a house that sits on top of a hill overlooking Folsom Lake."

Lizzy nodded, taking notes as he talked.

"When Jennifer called me that day, she said the man who was showing interest was the same guy who had called the day you were in the office, the day you brought the contract for us to sign. She was unable to get to the phone before the caller hung up. She was excited at the prospect of selling this house. I was, too." He raked his fingers through his thick head of hair. "When I got to the property, her car was the only vehicle parked in the area as far as I could see."

"But she wasn't alone when you went inside?"

"No. She wasn't alone."

Lizzy could see the pain etched across his face.

"The door was unlocked. I walked inside, didn't see or hear anyone. I called out for Jennifer, but she didn't answer. I've been inside the house dozens of times. I know my way around. There were no strange sounds. Nothing unusual. Nothing out of place."

Lizzy watched him swallow a knot in his throat. He was struggling to continue. She wasn't sure how much time she would be allowed with Michael, but she refused to rush him or push him into saying anything he wasn't ready to divulge. She didn't have to wait long for him to find his voice again.

"The people who designed the house spared no expense. There were two laundry rooms, a theatre room, and a wine cellar. I found her downstairs, lying on the floor in the cellar. She was on her back and I could see her breathing. Her eyes were closed tight, and she didn't open them. I thought it was because she was scared. Hell, I know she was scared—I was scared. She kept mumbling. Her speech was slurred and it was difficult to understand her. It turned out she was trying to warn me. By the time I turned toward the door, someone had shut and locked it. I couldn't get out. More importantly, I couldn't get Jennifer the help she needed."

His shoulders slumped forward in defeat.

"What was wrong with her?" Lizzy asked.

"I have no idea," he said. He lifted his head and met Lizzy's gaze. "I'm sure she was drugged. She was also chained to the built-in wine rack."

"She was chained?"

"Handcuffed," he amended. "Her right wrist was handcuffed to the wine rack."

"So, her speech was slurred," Lizzy said, trying to keep him talking.

He nodded. "After she'd made more than a few attempts at speaking, I understood some of what she was trying to tell me. Somebody had injected her multiple times with a needle. She kept saying the word *heroin,* but that didn't compute because she'd never done drugs before and it never entered my mind that somebody would give her drugs against her wishes. Nothing made sense. Neither one of us was ever into drugs."

"What did you do next?" she asked.

"I couldn't understand why she wouldn't open her eyes, so I tried to open them for her. That's when I noticed that there was a hard, crusty substance on her eyelashes. Both of her eyes had been glued shut."

He took a moment to breathe as he relived the nightmare.

Lizzy found herself thinking about the glue found in his glove compartment.

"Her lips were turning blue and her breathing was slowing with every passing moment. Then I heard a voice."

Lizzy narrowed her eyes. "As in a heavenly voice?"

"No, not even close. Satan's voice. The real deal."

Lizzy waited for him to go on.

Michael lifted his hands to the sides of his face and rubbed his temples. "I never saw him, but I'll never forget his voice. He was talking to me from the other side of the door. He spoke slowly and calmly."

"What did he say?"

"He said Jennifer was going to die unless I did something. He told me there was a hypodermic needle in the room to my left. I turned that way and there it was on the bottom shelf, where a wine bottle should have been."

Michael looked downward, visibly upset. For a moment, Lizzy wondered whether or not he'd be able to continue, but then he said, "He then asked me if I'd ever seen the movie *Pulp Fiction*. I told him I had."

"And then what?"

"He said, 'That's good because you're going to have to do exactly what they did in the movie. You're going to have to stab her in the heart.'"

Michael's hands were on the table and his fingers curled into fists. "Why would he do such a thing?"

Lizzy didn't have an answer for him, so she merely shook her head.

"Jennifer was losing consciousness," Michael continued, his voice cracking.

Lizzy gave him time to pull himself together.

"The voice told me to thrust the needle directly into her heart if I wanted to save her. I reached for the needle, picked it up, and held it high above my wife's chest."

Michael was staring at Lizzy, his eyes pleading for answers, but all she had were more questions. "What happened after that?"

"I asked him what was in the needle. He told me it was adrenaline." Michael's mouth turned down and his eyes drooped in sadness. "I knew then that it was all just a game to him."

"Did you have your cell phone in the cellar?"

"Yes."

"Did you try to call 911?"

He nodded. "More than once, but I couldn't get a signal. A knife had been left in the cellar, too. I used it on the door, hoping I could unlock it."

"Did you know that the knife was from your house?"

His shoulders sagged. "No."

"So did you use the needle as instructed?"

"I lifted the needle high above her chest, aimed and ready to go, but I couldn't do it."

"Why not?"

"Because nothing the voice said made any sense. My wife was having trouble breathing…she was having respiratory problems. Shooting adrenaline into her heart wouldn't help her. It wasn't her heart that was the problem."

"You're not a doctor. How would you know that?"

"Talk to my friend Stacey Whitmore. Jennifer and I have spent a lot of time with Stacey and her husband, Dan. One of our longest-running arguments has been about the scene in *Pulp Fiction*. I think this guy…the voice…he knew that."

"You think he researched your life that thoroughly? He would have had to bug your house or theirs."

"That's right. Definitely. Anyhow, adrenaline wouldn't sober up someone who had overdosed. If the guy had truly followed the movie to a tee and given her heroin, then I needed something else."

"What do you mean?"

"To neutralize heroin you'd administer a drug"—he snapped his fingers—"I forget the name of the drug, but you would give the person a drug that would block the receptors in the brain. That's the drug that might bring a junkie back to life in minutes."

"OK," Lizzy said. "What happened after you decided not to use the needle on your wife?"

"I started noticing other things on her body. There were bruises on her arms and blood on her shirt, so I lifted her shirt." He squeezed his eyes shut. "There were sutures everywhere. She'd been dissected and sewn up in several places."

The anguish on his face was heartbreaking.

"I asked her why he would do such a thing, but by then she couldn't talk any longer. I was losing her fast. That's when the voice told me that I didn't know Jennifer as well as I thought I did. He told me that although she had never cheated on me physically with another man, she had lied to me on many occasions. He told me that Jennifer had been putting money into a private account."

"Is that true?"

He nodded. "Jennifer had no idea that I knew about the account. There's no more than five thousand dollars there. I believe having the money stashed away gave her a feeling of independence. Either way, I didn't care. The only thing I cared about at that moment was getting my hands on that man's neck and squeezing the life out of him."

Lizzy wanted to reach over the table for his hand, but she wasn't allowed to touch him.

"Even if I had thought the adrenaline would work, I never would have plunged the needle into my wife's heart. I could never have risked killing her. The main thought running through my mind the entire time I was in that room was that I needed to escape. I knew that if I could escape, I could get Jennifer help before it was too late."

"According to the reports, you *did* plunge the needle into her heart. Your fingerprints were on the syringe."

"Of course they were."

Lizzy sighed. "It wasn't adrenaline in the syringe."

"That doesn't surprise me."

"How did you escape?"

He shook his head. "The killer must have understood that I wasn't going to do what he said, so he decided to let me go." Michael shrugged. "Maybe that was his plan all along. Suddenly, I heard a *click*. I checked the door and, sure enough, it was unlocked. I didn't see anyone, so I ran."

"Did you look for the man?"

He shook his head. "There wasn't time. Jennifer needed help."

"You left Jennifer?"

"She was handcuffed to the wine rack. I had no choice but to try to get her help before it was too late."

"You could have taken the needle with you."

"I guess I could have done a lot of things differently, but I did the first thing that made sense to me. I ran to get help."

"And it took you five minutes to get to the neighbor's house?"

"Two or three minutes at the most. The woman who answered the door looked frightened, but she let me use her phone. I called 911. I returned to the house moments later. Jennifer was dead. He'd killed her."

"I read the report, but why don't you tell me what you saw."

"A hypodermic needle was protruding from her chest." His voice quavered, but he closed his eyes for a moment and composed himself. "I pulled the needle out," he went on. "I'm not sure how long I held her in my arms after that, but I know it wasn't long enough. The ambulance came. The police came, too, and they took her from me."

"What about the handcuffs?"

"Wasn't that in the report?" he asked.

Lizzy shook her head.

"When I returned, the handcuffs were gone."

"You never heard the voice or saw the man after you returned to the house?"

"No, but I believe Jennifer tried to give me a clue."

It took all the restraint Lizzy had not to look over her shoulder at the two-way mirror. "What clue?"

"When Jennifer was trying to talk to me, she kept repeating the word *limo*."

"Why wasn't that in the report?"

He shrugged. "You might ask Greer, because I told them everything I've told you. Seems they're withholding information from you."

Lizzy stiffened, but she kept her thoughts to herself. "I have two more questions for you, if you don't mind."

He waited.

"Do you recall my being at the realty office when you showed up to take Jennifer to dinner?"

"Like it was yesterday."

"Before you arrived, Jennifer said something to me about dead bugs, hang-up calls, and bumps in the night."

"Yeah," he said without hesitating, "we had been receiving quite a few hang-up calls."

"Did you do anything about it?"

He shook his head. "We were both busy. If it didn't stop soon, one of us would have taken care of it. That's how we handled things."

"How about the dead bugs?"

He rubbed his temples again. "I do remember her complaining about bugs, but I don't recall where she had seen or found them, maybe in her car. That was long before we called you about the workers' compensation claim."

"And the bumps in the night?"

He shook his head again. "I'm a sound sleeper. She never mentioned bumps in the night."

"Time's up," the guard said.

Lizzy held up a hand and asked the last question. "When I was leaving J&M Realty the last time I saw you and Jennifer, you were staring at me. I was in my car. Your eyes narrowed, and the look on your face was what I would call intense."

"There's a pub across the street," he said. "The windows are tinted, but I saw a man sitting at the table by the door. He was watching us. I wasn't looking at you. I was watching him watch us. I thought it was odd."

Fifteen minutes later, two security guards escorted Lizzy out of the prison. She followed them with Stacey on her right and Lieutenant Greer on her left. She had called Stacey on her way to the prison, and Stacey had not come as a reporter. She had come as a friend of Michael's and now Lizzy's.

"Why didn't you tell me about dead bugs and hang-up calls, not to mention the strange look he was giving you that day?" Lieutenant Greer asked Lizzy.

"Because Jennifer told me it was no big deal and that she was upset because of her mother's recent passing. Why didn't you tell me about the cuffs or Jennifer saying the word *limo*?"

They were approaching the exit.

"We'll talk about this later," Greer said.

"Looks like we've got some ambulance chasers outside," one of Greer's men told him.

"Just a bunch of greenies," Stacey said as she stepped outside, greeting the paparazzi and the cub reporters with composure that only someone with her experience could pull off with such ease.

CHAPTER 14

I'm sorry I killed five people, OK?
—Gary Alan Walker

Antelope
Wednesday, May 16, 2012

Jessica parked her car at the curb and headed for the trailer where she knew Dominic Povo spent much of his day. It was early. She looked around. The site looked clean, no garbage bags to be seen. She needed to stop being so paranoid.

Whenever she watched Povo's trailer and his house, people always seemed to be coming and going, which was why she'd driven to the site early today. The crew wouldn't arrive for another hour, at least. She wanted to get a quick look around the inside of Povo's trailer and see if anything popped out at her—any sign that might tell her Povo was trouble. Maybe there would be a lady inside, bras and panties scattered around.

She pulled the collar of her coat up, closer to her ears. It was cold and each breath came out in puffs of white fog. As she made her way up the unpaved driveway, her boots crunched over gravel. Last night, as she sat alone in her empty apartment, she had decided she needed an attitude adjustment. She was being paid to do a job, and she needed to do it well. Danielle Cartwright was a nice lady. She deserved to know if the man she was going to marry was a decent guy.

Hayley had been right when she told her she needed to knock on some doors and talk to people. Jessica had her speech prepared. She was ready. When Povo opened the door, she would feign interest in the house he was building.

She would have preferred to come later in the day, when Magnus would be working, but her instincts told her he was probably a player, the kind of guy who dated a different girl every month. And that was that last thing she needed. Sure, going out with a guy like Magnus might be a confidence booster, but he was beyond handsome, and the chances of his sticking around for very long were a million to one. She shook her head at her wayward thoughts as she approached the trailer. She knew she was being foolish. She'd met Magnus one time and yet she couldn't stop thinking about him.

As she raised her knuckles to the door, she heard men talking inside. When she leaned her ear closer to the door, she noticed mud on the side of the trailer.

"We delivered the goods as promised. This is your last chance, Povo. Where's the money?"

There was a scuffle accompanied by a couple of loud grunts. Something shattered against the wall. Jessica's eyes widened and her heart rate soared. Her gaze kept connecting with the mud splattered against the side of the trailer. She examined it closer. It wasn't mud at all. It was blood splatter. She stood frozen in place, knowing she should run, but unable to move.

A hand clamped over her mouth.

Her screams were muffled as she struggled to get away, but then she saw that it was Magnus. "Quiet," he said as he took hold of her arm and ushered her down the driveway and toward her car.

He opened her car door. "You need to go, Jessica."

"You know my name?"

"Where are your keys?" he asked, ignoring her question.

Jessica shuffled around inside her bag for her keys, then started the engine. "What's going on?"

"Go! I mean it!"

Sacramento
Thursday, May 17, 2012

Lizzy and Brittany had been driving through the streets of Sacramento for thirty minutes when Lizzy said, "I think you're ready to drive on the freeway."

"Really?"

"Yep. Let's do it. Take a right at the light and then take I-80 East toward Reno."

This was Lizzy's third time driving with her niece at the wheel, but Brittany was a natural, so Lizzy wasn't worried. It was noon on a weekday and there was hardly any traffic.

A silver Toyota Tundra appeared out of nowhere and swerved into their lane.

Brittany slammed on the brakes. They both jerked forward.

Tires squealed and Lizzy braced herself, but the car behind them didn't make contact. The truck sped through the red light.

"Did you see that guy? What an idiot," Brittany said. "He almost hit us and then went through a red light!"

"Are you fine to drive?"

"I'm good. Are you OK?" The light turned green and Brittany took off again, a little slower than before but still confident in her abilities.

Lizzy took a breath. "I'm fine. Crazy bastard," she muttered.

A few minutes later, Brittany merged onto the freeway without any problem. The sky was gloomy and gray, but rain wasn't in the forecast. Lizzy was about to show Brittany how to use cruise control when she spotted the same truck in her side-view mirror. She decided not to mention it to Brittany. No reason to needlessly scare her. In fact, it was difficult to tell if it was the same truck, since she hadn't been able to see the driver through the tinted windows. Leaning forward, she peered into the side mirror and tried to make out the driver's features. It was no use.

"Looks like he's back," Brittany said. "Do you recognize him?"

"I can't see a thing. He's too far away and the windows are dark. Stay in this lane and keep going the speed limit. He can go around us if he's in a hurry."

To minimize distractions, Lizzy had insisted they drive with the windows up and the radio off, so the only sound was the steady beat of her heart. Lizzy silently counted to ten. Hoping to keep Brittany's mind off the truck, Lizzy decided to strike up a conversation. "How's your mom these days?"

"You talk to her every day. It's not going to work."

"What's not going to work?"

"You're trying to make me forget about the crazy person tailing us."

Lizzy sighed. "It was worth a shot."

Brittany put on her blinker, sped up, and then merged into the fast lane. She got up to eighty miles per hour before Lizzy told her to slow down.

Brittany returned to the middle lane and slowed to the speed limit again. Not more than five seconds later, the truck was back on their tail.

This was not amusing.

"When it's safe to do so, get into the far-right lane," Lizzy said. "I'm going to see if I can get the license plate number."

Brittany moved into the slow lane. The truck did, too.

"It's a Toyota Tundra, four doors. The license plate had a number six and then maybe an *M* and a *B*."

Lizzy nodded. "Did you get a look at the driver?"

"No. Sorry." Brittany glanced at the rearview mirror. "The last three digits are zero-zero-two."

"You're doing great. Remain calm, keep your eyes on the road, and we'll be fine."

"You're the one who's worrying."

"OK, you're right, I'm worrying," Lizzy agreed. She pulled out her cell phone and called the police. When she had finished, she said, "Take the next exit."

"Are you sure? What if he has a gun or something?"

Lizzy tried to think. "I don't want to get too far from home. We'll get off at the next exit and I'll drive."

"Great." Brittany put on her blinkers and did as she said.

The truck followed them off the ramp.

The light was red. Brittany stopped at the intersection, where a massive blur of cars passed by at high speeds in both directions. Across the street, Lizzy saw a mall. "When the light turns green, go straight and then pull into the parking lot in front of the shopping center."

Brittany tapped her fingers on the wheel as she waited for the light to change colors. Lizzy kept her gaze on the side mirror, still hoping to see what the driver looked like. Probably male, over five feet nine inches tall, and thin. She opened the door.

"What are you doing?"

"Just stay where you are."

Lizzy got out of the car, reached under her sweater, and unsnapped her gun from its holster. Tires squealed as the truck reversed, hitting a white SUV behind him. The SUV honked—one long continuous blare. Before she could catch up to him, she grasped what he was about to do. "No!"

He revved the gas, sped forward, and slammed into the back of Lizzy's car.

Fear clogged Lizzy's throat when she heard Brittany screaming as the maniac held his foot on the gas, pushing Lizzy's car—with her niece still inside—into the speeding cross traffic in front of them.

Lizzy shouted for Brittany to keep her foot on the brake and hit the emergency brake. The smell of burnt tires filled the air.

The driver of the damaged SUV climbed out, but then he saw Lizzy aim her gun at the front tires of the truck and he ran back to his car, yelling for his passengers to get down.

The silver truck backed up again, preparing for another run. This time he came after Lizzy.

She whipped around, running for her life. She jumped high above the curb and over a ditch, digging her fingers into clumpy dirt, climbing as high and as fast as she could up a small hill. The earth rattled when the truck hit, missing her left leg by a few inches.

Tires squealed as he reversed.

Her feet slid on damp grass as she scrambled upward, gritting her teeth when her hand grasped a clump of thorny brush. *Shit!*

Back on her feet, she turned and saw that the asshole had reversed far enough that he could make another move on her car. Lizzy locked gazes with Brittany just as the truck hit again, harder this time. Brittany's body jerked to the side, but the car was sturdy and well built.

Lizzy could see the determination in her niece's expression. That girl wasn't going anywhere, which scared her all the more.

135

The driver of the SUV was on his cell, talking to the police, no doubt. She could see children in the backseat of his car. He was a big guy, and if the kids hadn't been with him, she had a feeling he would have taken care of the maniac himself.

She heard the sound of approaching sirens. Traffic had stopped all around them. The light had turned green a while ago. The truck reversed again, clipping her back bumper once more before speeding off.

Groups of people huddled together across the street, watching.

Lizzy ran for her car and opened the passenger door. Brittany was shaking, but she wasn't injured.

The driver of the SUV got out of his car again. "Did you know that guy?"

"No," Lizzy said. "Did you happen to get a look at him?"

He shook his head. "Afraid not. If my kids weren't with me, that guy would have been toast."

Lizzy nodded.

"What's with the gun?"

"Private investigator. Everybody's safe." She never should have pulled out her gun. If they had been on a private road somewhere without any innocent bystanders, she would have shot first and thought about it later. But this wasn't the place, and perhaps the driver of the truck had been counting on that.

Brittany opened the door on her side, but Lizzy told her to stay where she was.

Two police cars pulled up. One of the officers directed traffic while the other officer greeted Lizzy and the driver of the SUV. For the next hour, the officers took reports. There were plenty of witnesses, but nobody could give a good description of the driver. Lizzy's car had more dents than a crash-dummy car, but it was still drivable. They were two blocks away from Brittany's house when Lizzy said, "You did good today. I'm proud of you."

"I didn't do anything."

"That's not true," Lizzy said. "You never once lost your cool."

"I talked to Mom while you were talking to the cops. She's freaked out. Who was that guy, Lizzy?"

"I have no idea."

"Why do all the lunatics in the world go after you?"

"That's a good question, but I don't have an answer."

"Mom's never going to let me drive with you again. She doesn't want me to see Hayley either."

"Why not?"

"She thinks Hayley is a bad influence."

Lizzy sighed. "It'll take some time, but she'll get over it. I'll talk to her. Until then, maybe I can come over and we can watch movies together like we used to when you were small."

"Maybe Mom's right. Maybe you should find another way to earn a living."

Lizzy made a left. A few houses down, she saw her sister Cathy standing in the driveway, arms crossed. Richard was there, too. *Damn.*

"This is not going to be pretty," Brittany said.

"Let me handle your parents."

Lizzy pulled to the curb and turned off the engine. The moment Brittany climbed out of Lizzy's beat-up car, both of her parents hovered over their daughter, glad to see she was unharmed. They weren't the only ones.

Before Lizzy could get out and join them, Richard was in her face, pointing his index finger at her nose and raising his voice. "Who do you think you are? Taking our daughter whenever and wherever you want."

"I had Cathy's permission. This isn't the first time I've taken Brittany out to practice driving."

"I had no idea you were going to let her drive on the freeway," Cathy cut in. "What were you thinking?"

Lizzy shook her head. "She's a very good driver. I never questioned for a second that she couldn't handle it. There isn't anything Brittany can't do exceptionally well."

Brittany smiled at Lizzy and then headed for the house.

Lizzy stayed where she was until Brittany disappeared inside and shut the door. Then she grabbed hold of Richard's pointy finger and twisted it backward until he cried out and yanked his finger from her grasp.

"Your sister is a fucking nutcase!"

Cathy stormed to where Richard and Lizzy stood and wedged her way between them. "Don't you dare cause a scene in front of our neighbors," Cathy said to her ex-husband under her breath, her face red.

"She tried to break my finger and you're going to take her side?"

"I'm not taking any sides," Cathy said.

"Are you two back together?" Lizzy asked her sister.

"We're dating again, taking it slow. That's all."

"What do you mean that's all? I'm moving back in." Richard looked down his nose at Lizzy. "She wasn't ready to tell you because you tend to be judgmental and closed-minded."

Lizzy looked at Cathy. "Is that true? Is that what you said?"

Cathy shifted her weight from one foot to the other. "Not exactly. I wasn't ready to tell you yet because I knew you wouldn't like it."

"I don't. He doesn't deserve you, Cathy. He's an asshole."

Richard's hands balled into fists at his sides as he came at her.

"What are you going to do, Richard, hit me?" Lizzy asked.

"You're an insufferable bitch."

Spittle hit her cheek, and Lizzy used her sleeve to wipe her face. She wanted nothing more than to dare him to make a move. Jared would be on his scrawny ass so fast he would find himself behind bars before the end of the day. But the look on Cathy's face prevented Lizzy from provoking him. Richard's face was a maze of angry lines, the cords of his neck swelling in anger. But the minute Cathy moved to his side, he managed to restrain himself from saying anything more.

"Could you give us a few minutes alone?" Cathy asked him. "You drove all this way to see your daughter. She's in the house."

Richard headed for the house, but he was not happy about being asked to leave.

"I don't like that man."

"Believe me, his feelings for you are mutual."

A million responses begged to be put into words, but Lizzy gritted her teeth and kept quiet.

"I will tell you this," Cathy said. "What you did today, taking Brittany driving on the freeway, was unacceptable."

"Are you kidding me? Taking that abusive, disgusting man back into your life…that's unacceptable."

"How many times have we had this conversation? Why do you always have to push the limits?"

Lizzy stiffened. "Meaning?"

"We agreed that you would take Brittany driving every week, but never once did we talk about you taking her on the freeway."

"You can't expect her to get her license and then stay off—"

"You know what I mean. I would have taken her on the free-way myself."

"When? You're working full-time, and now that you're dating that clown, you're never home."

Cathy sighed. "Brittany told you that?"

"She mentioned you two were seeing one another."

"Does she know how you feel about Richard?"

"She's a smart girl and it's pretty obvious, but if you mean do I call him a clown or an asshole in front of her—no, I do not. That clown is her father. I have to respect that."

"I was once married to the man."

"It's like a bad dream. It's over now."

Cathy sighed. "It wouldn't hurt you to give me the same respect."

Lizzy chuckled and headed for her car.

"What?"

"That's so typical of you," Lizzy said, "I've had to listen to you rant on about Jared Shayne and how much you despise him, and you don't even know him. He's never said a bad word about you. He treats me right. He doesn't have a mistress hidden in every hotel in Sacramento. He's a decent man. And yet I'm supposed to respect you enough to call that asshole in there a decent, respectable man." Lizzy shook her head again. "I won't do it. I love you, I really do, but I will never, for as long as I live, understand why you would take that man back."

"I'm lonely."

"What about that lawyer you were dating?"

"He met another woman and dropped me faster than you could say hot potato."

Damn. "What about simply being single for a little while? What's wrong with that?"

"I'm not like you, Lizzy."

"I'm not the only woman in the world who was fine with being single for a while."

"I don't like being alone," Cathy said. "I need a man in my life."

"You don't even love him, do you?"

"He's my daughter's father."

"That's not good enough," Lizzy said. "You're stronger than you think." She was about to climb into her car when she glanced back at Cathy. "Don't do it. For Brittany's sake, don't let him back into your lives. He's selfish and verbally abusive. He doesn't deserve either of you, and you know it."

Sacramento
Thursday, May 17, 2012

He watched the stolen Toyota Tundra sink into the irrigation canal, which happened to be about 117 miles of prime dumping grounds. It wasn't the first stolen vehicle to be dumped here and it wouldn't be the last. He'd been dumping a lot of interesting things in the canal for years. He scratched his collarbone and headed for the thick underbrush where he'd left a bike, also stolen. He'd ride the bike to the nearest bus station, and then bus home to Sacramento.

He was born and raised in Sacramento. The city was known for many things, including its colorful government bureaucrats, allergies, and, most recently, its abundance of housing foreclosures. He laughed to himself as he jumped on the bike and began to pedal. The sky was filled with dark clouds that looked ready to burst. He hadn't ridden a bike in years. He felt like a kid again, which prompted his thoughts to become darker than the clouds hovering overhead.

Mother, Mother, Mother.

Everything had been perfect until the day he found her in the barn.

He pedaled faster, hoping to outrun the memories. His eyes stung.

He refused to cry.

Nothing that had happened to him was his fault. Rarely did he feel guilt or remorse; only when he thought of his mother. He didn't like to think about her because he knew he should have tried harder to make her understand. He told her he hadn't done it. But then she had called him names, all sorts of horrible things, and even told him that his therapist had said he was delusional, which meant he twisted the truth until lies became reality. That was rubbish.

He pedaled faster. He knew that if he pedaled long enough and hard enough, the darkness would pass. And it did.

With two miles left to go, he thought of Lizzy Gardner instead and his mood lifted. He'd thought that a break-in would throw her off balance, take her out of the game for a bit, but he'd been wrong about Lizzy. The police had gone to the house, she filled out a report, and that was the end of it. She was back on the news the very next day! He couldn't believe it when he turned on the television and saw Lizzy Gardner exiting the California State Prison. Once again, the media was all over it. The woman didn't know when to quit.

It wasn't good enough that she talked to Lieutenant Greer about Dalton's supposed innocence. The bitch needed to talk to Michael Dalton, too? Who did she think she was, anyhow? The goddamn mayor of Sacramento?

His insides began to quiver with anger.

The idea of Lizzy Gardner, a nobody, getting deeply involved in his business was too much. Perhaps she wasn't teetering as close to the edge as he'd first thought. But she would be soon. Nobody was safe in this cow town…especially Lizzy Gardner. It was hard to believe she'd gotten the best of Spiderman. The woman was a pale, tiny thing—five foot four inches at most. She liked to wear her dirty-blonde hair tied back in a ponytail. She had a decent mouth. Not full pouty lips, but soft pretty ones. He wasn't sure of the color of her eyes yet, but he was in no hurry. There was time.

She enjoyed sushi and she liked to run at the park most mornings. Other than that, she didn't seem to have a set schedule. Every day was random. He liked watching her do surveillance because he could tell by her movements that she didn't like sitting in her car for too long. It made her antsy. He had to admit he was enjoying waking up every morning, wondering what Lizzy would do that day.

She spent a good amount of time in her office on J Street. According to articles he'd read, she used to live in an apartment with her cat, but not any longer. Spiderman had taken care of the poor little feline. Unlike Spiderman, he would never kill a poor defenseless creature.

The fact that Lizzy lived with an FBI agent really made things interesting. Getting an FBI agent into his cage was not going to be easy, but nothing was impossible, and he was certainly up to the challenge.

Since breaking into the house, he'd learned more about the crazy girl who lived with them, the one who'd come after him. He prided himself on his research, and it bothered him that he hadn't known about the girl before he entered the house. Her name was Hayley Hansen. She was damaged goods. Who wasn't? This particular young woman had recently done time for cutting off a man's penis.

Ouch.

He made a mental note to stay away from that one.

CHAPTER 15

I haven't blocked out the past. I wouldn't trade the person I am,
or what I've done—or the people I've known—
for anything. So I do think about it.
And at times it's a rather mellow trip to lay back and remember.
—Ted Bundy

Davis
Friday, May 18, 2012

Hayley called her mom. Still no answer. She looked at her ankle.
If she could get the damn thing off, she could check on her mom
herself.

To hell with it. She picked up her cell and dialed Jessica's
number.

Jessica answered on the first ring.

"It's Hayley. Where are you?"

"More surveillance. Same-o, same-o."

"Povo?"

"No, some other loser."

"Can you do me a favor?"

"Of course, anything."

"I need you to check on my mom. Lizzy was driving by and keeping tabs on her while I was away, but I'm worried. Mom hasn't been answering her phone. I was hoping you wouldn't mind going to her house and knocking on the door or peeking through a window. If nobody answers, she keeps a spare key under a decorative concrete rabbit near the front door."

There was a long pause before Jessica said, "If she doesn't answer the door, you want me to go inside the house?"

"Yeah, that would be great."

"If she doesn't answer, shouldn't I call the police?"

"I'd rather not."

Hayley heard Jessica sigh.

"Never mind," Hayley said. "It's probably not a good idea for you to go there alone. Forget I asked."

"No, I'll do it tomorrow…Saturday."

"Cool. Thanks."

"Not a problem," Jessica said, but they both knew that was a lie.

Hayley clicked her cell shut and began to pace. Tommy was supposed to have come over days ago with her new monitor, but he was a no-show. What if he couldn't figure out a way to make it work? What would she do? She needed to get out of the house once in a while. How much longer could she sit in her room doing nothing but filing and reading?

She might as well be at the detention center. Ever since someone had broken into the house, Lizzy wanted the curtains and blinds shut tight. Hayley found herself spending a lot of time staring out her bedroom window. Freedom was right there for the taking, and yet she couldn't walk more than a mile without the light on her monitor flickering and beeping.

The sound of a car outside drew her attention. She went to the front window and peeked through the curtains. It was Jared and Lizzy—at two o'clock on a Friday. *What are they doing home?*

She returned to the couch, opened a file, and pretended to be working when they walked through the door. Raising a brow, she feigned surprise. "What are you two doing home so early?"

Lizzy headed for the kitchen and set her purse on the kitchen counter. "I had to drop my car off at the shop. Jared picked me up and brought me home."

She'd forgotten all about Lizzy's mangled car. "How bad was the damage?"

"Over five thousand dollars' worth of damage."

"That sucks."

"Insurance will cover it, but I'm sure they'll raise my premium."

Jared was already upstairs, checking windows. Every window throughout the house had been hooked up to a cool new device. If anyone so much as touched the latch, inside or outside, an alarm sounded, a barely perceptible beep that would send a text message to Jared's and Lizzy's phones.

The ring of the doorbell caused Hayley to hold in a groan. *Shit. It better not be—*

"It's Tommy," Lizzy said as she looked through the peephole, her face brightening. Lizzy opened the door and let him in.

Hayley shut the file and stood up. "Hey, Tommy."

"Hey."

Of course, Jared strode downstairs to see what all the commotion was about.

Lizzy introduced Tommy to Jared and that should have been that, but Jared and Lizzy were acting like nervous parents who wanted to make sure everybody was getting along. Lizzy knew Tommy and liked him, so she was fine.

Jared, on the other hand, was staring at Tommy, sizing the poor guy up with one long, hard stare. If Tommy wasn't here bearing gifts of freedom, she would have enjoyed the scene. But he was and so she wasn't.

Hayley massaged her neck as she waited for the awkward moment to pass.

"Can I get you two something to eat?" Lizzy asked as if she'd suddenly turned into June Cleaver. "Crackers and cheese? Cookies and milk?"

Jared locked the front door and made his way upstairs again without another word. Clearly, he was not impressed.

"Cookies and milk sounds great," Tommy said as he followed Lizzy to the kitchen. Hayley hovered over Tommy and watched him eat cookies and wash it all down with a glass of cold milk. The entire process felt like an hour but in reality lasted only ten minutes. "Come to my room," she said the minute he finished the last cookie. "I want to show you something."

Lizzy was trying to busy herself around the house, but Hayley could tell she was all ears. She was acting weird, making Hayley think she had a problem with Hayley taking a boy into her room, but that was too bad.

The moment Tommy stepped inside her bedroom, Hayley locked the door and then turned on some music just in case Lizzy decided to try to listen in on their conversation.

"Did you bring it with you?"

One corner of his mouth turned upward, a cross between a smirk and a smile, as he pulled a black plastic strap out of his pant pocket.

"We can't possibly do this with Jared upstairs," Hayley said. "That's Lizzy's boyfriend and he works for the FBI."

"Awesome."

"No, not awesome. If the alarm goes off, he'll find out what we're up to."

"Chill. My little brother could do this blindfolded."

"Can you come back tomorrow?"

"I can't. I would if I could," he assured her, "but I'm leaving town for a few days."

"When?"

"Tonight."

Hayley's arms dropped to her sides. *Screw it*. There was no way she had the patience to wait any longer. "OK, then, let's just do this." She took a seat on the edge of the bed and pulled up her jeans so he could get the monitor off her ankle.

He looked around the room.

"What do you need?"

"My tools. I left my backpack by the stool in the kitchen."

Great. Just great. Hayley pulled her pant leg down, and then stood. "Stay right there," she said before she headed out the door.

Lizzy was folding laundry on the couch.

Jared had reappeared and was in the kitchen, fixing a sandwich.

Hayley picked up Tommy's backpack and headed for her room.

"What are you two doing in there?" Jared asked.

God, I really hate living with the guy. Hayley lifted the backpack. "He made me a CD and we're going to listen to it. Lizzy's the one who forced the guy on me. She likes to play matchmaker, so if you have any questions about Tommy, ask her."

"Go," Jared said. "Have fun."

Hayley returned to her room and locked the door behind her. Tommy must have figured out her password, because he was sitting at her desk, playing on her computer. Hayley took a seat on her bed with her back resting against the headboard. She pulled up her pant leg again. "Let's hurry up and do this before June and Ward Cleaver decide to kick you out of here."

"Why would they do that?"

"Let's just say they're not very trusting."

"Lizzy likes me," he said.

"But her boyfriend doesn't."

"Is that why you want this thing off? Are you going to run away?"

"I'm not going to run away. I simply need to visit a few people, that's all."

He laid out his tools on her bed next to her foot. "We could have used a thirty-dollar plastic box to jam the GPS, but that would have been chaos: air-traffic controllers would be peering at malfunctioning monitors, emergency pagers would stop working, people would find that they had no signal on their cell phones, and ATMs could even stop giving out cash. The feds would be on to us within a few days, especially with your FBI friend upstairs. Instead, we're going to do this a little differently. It'll still be easy, just not as fun."

"Yes, please, let's keep the military and the feds out of this."

He didn't waste any time getting to work. Using pliers and another tool she didn't recognize, he had the bracelet off her ankle in less than two minutes. She stretched her leg and wiggled her ankle. "Excellent."

He held up a hand to stop her from saying anything more.

"Stay right where you are and don't move. We've got to work fast. I have no idea how often the GPS tracks the coordinates."

She remained silent after that and watched him examine the box and reconnect the band he'd just taken off. Then he placed the new and improved fake band around her ankle and used metal rivets he'd brought with him to connect it. It looked identical.

Impressive.

Once he was done with her leg, he carried the original ankle bracelet to the computer and began to click away on her keyboard.

"What are you doing now?"

"I still need to assign your monitor an IP address." He pulled a device out of his backpack. "This Ethernet switch supports IP multicast. The switch will use the IP addresses and the IGMP for controlling of the multicast routing but will use the MAC addresses for the actual routing."

"Oh," Hayley said, although not one word of what he'd said made much sense. And she had a feeling he knew that.

He continued to work as he talked. "If they had used checksums in lieu of faster routing, we might have had a few problems. Nothing I couldn't handle, but there are so many issues of reliability that I could talk about it all day."

"Please don't. My head would explode."

He hit a couple of keys and then signed off. The screen went blank. "It's simple," he went on as he collected his tools. "The IP has two functions. Addressing hosts and—"

She tossed a pillow at his head. "OK, well, now you've asked for it." He stood.

She pointed a finger at him. "Stay away from me."

He picked up the pillow and tossed it back at her, but she was too quick. She rolled over and the pillow missed her completely and knocked over a picture frame instead.

She laughed. "Lizzy is not going to be happy with you if you break her lamp."

He was staring at her.

"What are you looking at?"

"I don't think I've ever seen you laugh before."

She looked away from him and slid off the bed. "Yeah, well, it's been known to happen."

He scratched his head.

That they were experiencing an awkward moment would be putting it mildly.

He began to pack up his tools.

Once he was done with that, she followed him out of the room, glad to see that Lizzy and Jared had disappeared upstairs.

Shutting the door behind her, she followed Tommy to the curb and watched him climb on his motorcycle.

The perky neighbor, Charlee, was watering her flowers and she waved.

Hayley waved back.

"So, it's all taken care of?" she asked Tommy.

"Well, you do owe me a ride on the back of my motorcycle."

"Yeah, yeah, we'll do that later, but what about my monitor? Am I free to roam?"

"The bracelet with the packet needs to stay in your room at all times. It's in your top drawer. I suggest you hide it somewhere."

She nodded. "I can go anywhere I want without any alarms going off?"

"I guess you'll find out."

"You're not sure?"

His laugh was a low rumble under his breath.

She shook her head at him. "Have fun on your trip," she said as she headed for the front door. "And thanks for the CD," she shouted in case anyone in the house was listening.

Sacramento
Saturday, May 19, 2012

The house where Hayley's mom lived was one of the smallest homes Jessica had ever seen. It was literally a pinkish stucco box with tiny square windows. She'd been sitting there staring for ten minutes now and she had to force herself to get moving.

There were no cars parked in the driveway or at the curb. No neighbors were out walking their dogs or enjoying the fresh air. It had been raining for most of the day, but at the moment, it was more of a light drizzle. It was by far the gloomiest springtime Jessica could ever remember experiencing. Where were all the May flowers and sunshine?

With a sigh, she climbed out of the car and shut the door behind her. As she headed up the cracked walkway, she tried to imagine growing up in the neighborhood. The thought of all that Hayley had been through saddened her. She peeked through the garage window. The place was filled to the brim with boxes and plastic bags. There were rusty old bike parts, a twin-sized mattress with the stuffing coming out, a stack of tires, and a broken chair. An endless assortment of crap stuffed into every crevice.

She pulled away from the window and inhaled.

Standing before the front door, she counted to three, collected herself, and then knocked. *Get this over with and get out of here.*

As she waited for someone to answer the door, she took inventory of the mess. It was hard to miss. There were beer cans scattered around the walkway and a zillion cigarette butts. A dark sheet was hung from the inside, covering the front window, preventing her from seeing through to the main part of the house.

Jessica shifted her weight from one foot to the other as she prayed Hayley's mom would answer the door soon, because she was quickly losing her nerve. But nobody came to the door, not even after Jessica's third attempt at knocking as hard as she could. *Damn.*

She tried opening the door, but it was locked. She looked around for the decorative rabbit Hayley had mentioned. For a brief moment, she thought luck was with her because there was no rabbit to be found. But then she spotted it—its grayish concrete ears peeking out from behind a clump of high weeds. The rabbit wasn't exactly ornamental. She headed that way and tried her best to avoid disturbing all of the gigantic, intricately made spiderwebs. She squealed when a lizard raced out from under the rabbit and found a new hiding spot beneath the house.

"Please don't be there," she said aloud. But the key was there, just as Hayley said it would be. *Damnation.*

Jessica knew she should call the police regardless of Hayley's instructions, but she also knew she could never do that to Hayley. Obviously, Hayley was worried about what the police might find if they entered the house—some sort of illegal substance, no doubt.

The door was unlocked now, leaving Jessica no choice but to head inside. As she stepped over the threshold, she pinched her nose because of the horrible stench. She gave the room a quick once-over before she shut the door quietly behind her. The filth and the smell were nearly unbearable as she tiptoed her way through dirty clothes and what looked like rotting garbage. She wanted to cry at the notion that Hayley had once lived here. No wonder Hayley had chosen to live on the streets. Jessica had never in her life seen anything like it. The television screen was cracked. The kitchen didn't look any better than the living room, the counters covered with junk and the sink overfilled with dirty dishes and God knows what else.

The dark sheets over the windows made for a poorly lit trip down the narrow hallway.

Stay calm, she told herself. She would check each room, make sure nobody was there. If, God forbid, she found a dead body, she would call the police immediately.

The first room to the left wasn't nearly as unkempt as the rest of the house. The bed looked like somebody had even attempted to make it. *Thank God. A sign of life.*

For the first time since she'd arrived, she felt as if she could breathe normally. This had to be the master bedroom since there was a connected bathroom. Judging by the damp towel and the makeup scattered across the tile counter between the two sinks, the bathroom had been used recently…by a woman.

She had one more room to check and then she could leave, but before she stepped out of the bathroom, she heard the front door open. Her body tensed. *Shit.*

It took her only a few seconds to figure out what she needed to do. She needed to walk out there and introduce herself—tell Hayley's mom the truth about why she was here. She made it past the bed and was about to step out of the bedroom, when she heard a man's voice.

"I told you to lock the fucking door."

"I did lock it."

The door slammed shut.

"Brian! No!"

There was a horrible cracking sound right before Hayley's mom cried out in pain.

"Look at this place!" he shouted. "All these months away, and the house still looks like shit."

Jessica's heart lodged in her throat. Eyes wide and unblinking, she looked for a place to hide. She quickly headed back to the bathroom. Footsteps sounded, loud footsteps pounding across worn carpet. He passed the master bedroom and went to the room at the end of the hall.

Jessica moved the shower curtain aside, climbed in and sank down inside the bathtub, and then tried to think. As she pulled out her cell phone from her pant pocket, somebody entered the bathroom. She didn't dare breathe.

The water faucet came on.

And then Jessica's phone vibrated.

The shower curtain came open and Jessica found herself staring up into familiar-looking eyes. Beneath the bruises and the bloodied lip, the woman looked exactly like Hayley.

"My name is Jessica," she whispered. "I'm Hayley's friend. She—"

Hayley's mom put a finger over her mouth, telling Jessica to remain silent, and then gestured at her phone, letting Jessica know now would be a good time to turn it off. She shut the curtain, but before Hayley's mom could leave the bathroom, Brian returned.

"What the hell are you doing?"

"Just fixing my face."

"You're lucky nothing was stolen. Why are you so fucking stupid?"

"I'm trying to change."

"Yeah, whatever. Come on. I got my shit. Let's blow."

As they headed out of the room and their voices grew quieter, Jessica could hear Brian telling Hayley's mom what to say if anybody asked about the bruises on her face.

Jessica shivered.

She heard the door close. She needed to get the hell out of there, but her body refused to budge.

Sacramento
Monday, May 21, 2012

Lily's Flower Shop was on the corner of 11th and T Street. Dried yellow leaves covered the ground. There was a tea shop across the street. A biker zipped past her and she could see two women a few blocks down pointing at something in a shop window. Overall the street was quiet. No rain today, but the gusty winds were stirring up pollen and making for itchy and watery eyes. Sacramento tended to be like a giant bowl with a lot of pollen sources.

Lizzy entered the shop and was greeted by tinkling bells and the sweet scent of daylilies and tuberoses. She'd never seen a flower shop like it before. A small winding walkway lined with every color and size of flower imaginable led her to an antique desk where customers could pay. Behind the desk with the old-fashioned cashbox, there was a refrigerator with a glass door filled with premade bouquets.

She hit the little bell on the desk and waited.

A tall woman with wavy blonde hair poked her head out of a back room. She held up a finger and said, "Someone will be right there."

"Take your time," Lizzy called out.

A young teenage girl appeared a few minutes later, wiping her hands on a well-used apron. Her hair was dark with strips of red and purple on one side.

Lizzy usually attempted to strike up a casual conversation about the weather or the neighborhood before she began asking questions, but not today. "Hi," she said. "I'm Lizzy Gardner, private investigator. I was hoping you wouldn't mind answering a few questions."

The moment Lizzy said that she was an investigator, the girl's demeanor changed. She looked stiff and nervous. "If this is about my DUI, I really don't think—"

"My visit has nothing to do with you," Lizzy assured her. "Not unless you're the person who signed her name on this business card." Lizzy handed it to her.

"Belle Gunness," the girl said aloud. "I've never heard of her. Want me to get Jane?"

"Is she the owner?"

The girl nodded. "I'm not allowed to bother her when she's in her office, but we just received a large shipment of flowers and she's working in the back. Should I see if she can spare a few minutes?"

Lizzy nodded. "I would appreciate it."

A few minutes later, Jane appeared. It was the same woman she'd seen when she first walked in. She was dressed in a long black skirt and a purple blouse. Her long wavy hair was tucked behind her ears. Black-rimmed eyeglasses hung from a chain around her neck. Lizzy guessed the woman was in her late thirties. Her skin was flawless, her cheekbones high and pronounced. Her coral lipstick accentuated thin lips, but it was the large eyes that captured Lizzy's full attention.

"What can I do for you?" the woman asked.

"I was hoping you could tell me if you ever made any flower arrangements for Jennifer Dalton."

The woman's expression became thoughtful, her nose dutifully scrunched as if she were thinking hard, before she shook her head and said, "Sorry, the name doesn't sound familiar."

Hard to believe, Lizzy thought, considering Jennifer Dalton's name had been all over the news. She handed Jane the same business card she'd shown the younger girl. "Jennifer Dalton was murdered. She was given this business card before she was killed. Somebody signed it. I need to know if Jennifer came here to order flowers for a party she was planning."

Jane took the card and turned it over in her hand. Her nails had a yellow tint to them, brittle looking and cut short. "Ahh, Belle," she said as she handed the card back to Lizzy. "She's the one you would need to talk to."

"Can you tell me when she'll be in next?"

She scrunched her nose again. "Sorry, but that might be a problem," she said as if she were *so* not sorry.

"Why would that be a problem?" Lizzy asked.

"Mrs. Gunness is visiting family back East. She won't return until November, hopefully before Thanksgiving. If you want to leave me your name and number, I can ask her to call you."

"Do you think you could give me a number where I could reach her?"

"No. It wouldn't be right."

Lizzy was tempted to threaten Jane with a warrant, which would force her to produce the number. Instead, she grabbed one of Jane's business cards from the holder on the cashier's table in front of her and wrote her name and number on the card and then handed it to the woman. "Thanks for your help." Lizzy angled her head. "What was your name again?"

"Jane," she said. "Jane Toppan."

"Who's Lily?"

"My dear, dear mother," Jane said with a smile. "She passed away when I was small."

"I'm sorry."

Uncomfortable silence followed.

"Did you make that bouquet behind you—the one with the yellow flowers?"

This question made Jane smile and brought a sparkle to her big blue eyes. "Those are sandersonia," she told Lizzy. "The flower originated in South Africa. Beautiful, aren't they?"

"Yes," Lizzy agreed, hoping to befriend the woman since Jane Toppan would definitely be going on her watch list. "I'd like to buy that arrangement for my sister. She's not happy with me at the moment, but those flowers might do the trick and change all of that."

CHAPTER 16

I've killed twenty people, man. I love all that blood.
　　　　　　　　　　　　　—Richard Ramirez

Monday, May 21, 2012

He fastened his newest piece to the growing collection on his special wall and then stepped away so he could better admire his latest keepsake. For a few seconds, he closed his eyes and relived the moment when he was inside Lizzy Gardner's home, lying on her bed and smelling and touching her things. The experience had been thrilling. For his wall, he'd torn a page from her journal: a very special page that she'd written years ago when she was sure she was being watched and was afraid of her own shadow.

As his gaze focused on one piece after another, each item giving him goose bumps, he could feel his lover's eyes burning a hole through the back of his head. He twirled around and abruptly stopped so he could see what she was up to. "What are you looking at?" he asked.

With her head angled just so, she sat in her chair and stared at him, unabashedly and unafraid. She knew she had him right where she wanted him. God, he hated that. Without losing eye contact, he took a seat in the chair by his desk. "Not talking again, I see. Up to your old tricks?"

He scratched his neck as he looked at her, hoping to get a rise out of her. Better that she toss her shoe or yell at him than say nothing at all. Although her actions infuriated him every so often, he couldn't get angry with her.

She was all he had—she was his everything.

Still, after all these years together, she was the most beautiful woman in the world. Flawless skin and expressive eyes. Her hair hung past her shoulders and was a beautiful shade of copper blonde. Today she wore red. She looked dazzling in red and she knew it.

"I love you," he said, and then he turned his chair until it faced his desk and all of the work he had piling up.

As he lifted his pen and began to write out a check to pay the electric bill, he heard her whisper the words "I love you, too."

Swallowing the knot in his throat, he closed his eyes and tried not to cry.

Sacramento
Tuesday, May 22, 2012

For the past two hours, Lizzy had been sitting in the car, watching the Simpson house from half a block away. A variety of trees shaded the section of the road where she was parked. The rental car she was driving didn't have navigation, satellite radio, or a new-car smell.

Her camera was in her lap, ready to go. She had already stopped by her sister's house early this morning and used the key Cathy had given her years ago to get inside. Glad to see that

Cathy's ex-husband was nowhere in sight, she'd left the flowers with a note on the dining room table.

She picked up the camera and looked through the lens at Eli Simpson's front window. She had yet to see any movement at all and she was beginning to wonder if Simpson was even home.

Michael Dalton was in jail and Jennifer was dead, but Lizzy had already been paid a deposit for the Simpson job. If Michael was innocent, Lizzy liked to believe justice would prevail and he would be released. Either way, there was no reason for Lizzy not to finish the work she'd been paid to do. If Simpson had not been injured on the job, then he shouldn't be collecting benefits. End of story.

Lizzy set the camera down and reached for the file on the passenger seat. She skimmed through the contents. Before he worked for J&M Realty, Eli Simpson had worked for Crawford Pools in Roseville. Before that, he had worked for Sunset Realty in Elk Grove. Lizzy picked up her phone and dialed the number for Crawford Pools. They were no longer in business, and the phone had been disconnected. Next, she called Sunset Realty. A woman answered. After Lizzy explained why she was calling, she was put on hold.

As she waited, Lizzy watched a white Honda pull into the driveway next to Simpson's house. A young woman climbed out of her car, opened the back door, then herded three little boys from the car to the house, which was no easy feat. They kept tickling one another and laughing.

By the time the woman came back on the line, Lizzy was smiling.

"I'm sorry," the woman said, "we've never had an Eli Simpson work for us, but a man by that same name did apply for a job here."

"So he never worked for Sunset Realty?"

"No, but Eli Simpson is the sort of man you don't forget. While being interviewed, the man wouldn't make eye contact.

When my husband called him the next day to tell him the position had been filled, he laughed."

"That is strange," Lizzy said. She watched a large white truck pull into Simpson's driveway. A man climbed out and disappeared through the gate at the side of the house.

"Are you thinking of hiring him?" the woman asked.

"Actually, he applied for workers' compensation and I was hired by the company to check him out."

"I would be careful if I were you."

"Why is that?"

"Well, I probably shouldn't say too much, but ever since that man stepped into our office, strange things have been happening around here."

"For instance?"

"For instance, our office was broken into within days of our interviewing the man. Strange things were taken: a wedding picture, my husband's fishing hat, of all things, and a sympathy card from my mother. I had an envelope of cash, five hundred dollars, at least, in my drawer, and it was still there, untouched."

"Did you call the police?"

"Yes. They even paid Eli Simpson a visit, but he denied everything, including ever applying for the job. The police said that he allowed them to search his house and none of my missing things were found. There was nothing else they could do. But it didn't stop there."

Lizzy waited for her to elaborate, which she did.

"Since then, my husband and I have received strange calls at the office at least once a week. You can hear him breathing, but he won't talk. Sometimes the caller lets the phone ring once or twice and hangs up. We've tried everything, even had our numbers changed, but he still calls."

"You think it's Eli Simpson?"

"I do." Another short pause before the woman said, "I should get back to work. Is there anything else I can do for you?"

"Could you give me a description of the man?"

"My husband is six feet tall and he says Eli was a few inches shorter. He also remembers him being thin, with no muscle tone—not a big man. Thin and lanky would be a good description overall."

"Hair color?"

"He wore a hat, so he's not sure about that. He could have been bald for all he knows."

"Can I get your names in case I need to talk to you again?"

"Sure. Barbara and Ken Garbes. Call this number and ask for either one of us."

"Thank you, Barbara. You've been a great help." Lizzy said goodbye and ended the conversation. As she mulled over what she'd learned, she knew what she needed to do.

She climbed out of her car and headed for Eli Simpson's house.

A breeze rustled the leaves of the trees lining the street. It was chillier than it looked. The only sound was the click of her boots hitting the pavement as she walked.

The truck parked in the driveway was filled with tools and a ladder. The lawn had been mowed recently. She knocked on the door and waited. Nobody came. She moved to the front window and pressed her face close against the glass.

"Can I help you?"

Her heart skipped a few beats. She turned around. The man standing behind her was tall and brawny. He wore a button-up plaid shirt, Levi's, and a tool belt. "I'm looking for Eli Simpson."

"That would be me. What can I do for you?"

Her eyes narrowed. This was not the same man she'd seen running to his mailbox. And neither was it the same man who had just been described to her over the phone. "My name is Lizzy Gardner. I was hired by Jennifer and Michael Dalton to check on a workers' compensation claim you filed."

"You most definitely have the wrong Eli Simpson."

"Are you saying you never heard of Jennifer and Michael Dalton?"

He nodded. "I guess that's what I'm saying."

"I want to grab the file and show you something. Please stay right where you are."

He didn't answer, but Lizzy headed for her car anyhow and grabbed the file from the passenger seat. When she returned, she found him standing at the rear of his truck.

She pulled out a copy of Simpson's claim and handed it to him. "Is that your name, address, and signature?"

He looked the paper over, frowned, and then handed it back to her. "That's my name and address, but that's not my signature."

"Did you ever apply for a job at Sunset Realty?"

"Never." He slapped a hand on the tailgate. "I've been running my own construction business for over ten years. Must be another Eli Simpson."

"Who happens to live at this very same address?"

"Are you calling me a liar?"

"No, I'm simply trying to straighten this all out. I was here a few weeks ago. I saw somebody run out to collect your mail. Can you explain that?"

He scratched his chin. "You know, under different circumstances, being that you've just admitted that you've been stalking me and getting into my business, I might feel inclined to call the police instead of answering your questions. But there's something about you that tells me you're just trying to do your job."

"Well, thank you," she said. "I think."

"The man you saw running to get the mail must have been my dad."

"He lives with you?"

"He does. He's taking a nap; otherwise I would invite you inside to meet with him."

She knew that wasn't true. She'd seen movement inside the house before he'd showed up, but if she said as much he'd only accuse her of calling him a liar again, which could well be the case.

Without warning, Eli Simpson flipped open his toolbox and reached inside, his movements hurried.

Instinctively, she reached under her sweater.

He pulled out a screwdriver.

She unsnapped her holster.

"Whoa there," he said, putting both hands in the air. "Is that a gun you have under there?"

She dropped her hand to her side. "Sorry, didn't mean to frighten you."

"I came out here to get a screwdriver to fix the cupboard door in the kitchen, and that's when I saw you standing at the window, peering inside."

"I'm sorry," she said again. "I thought you were going for the hammer." Actually, she didn't know what the hell he'd been going for, but his hurried movements had caught her off guard. One thing for sure, she was on edge.

His brow furrowed. "And what if I was going for my hammer? You thought I was going to hit you over the head with it?"

"Yes."

"Well, at least you're honest. But I'm glad I didn't bring you inside with me. I don't think it would have been fair to Dad if I invited an anxious gun-toting private eye into the house."

Now he was just being an ass. She wanted to point out that his dad was not asleep, but instead she said, "I guess you've heard my name, then?"

"Yeah, you could say that, but I didn't want to believe all the gossip."

"What? That I'm jumpy and tense and a little quick on the draw?"

"That about sums it up."

She reached into her pocket, pulled out a business card, and handed it to him. "Do you mind giving me a call if your dad knows anything about Sunset Realty?"

He took the card. "He's in his seventies, but sure, if he's applied for a job without telling me or heard anything about Sunset Realty, I'll give you a call."

"Thanks."

"Sure."

"Sorry about the gun."

"Sorry about the screwdriver."

His sarcasm was clear, but the man had a sense of humor, and she couldn't help but smile as she walked off.

Sacramento
Tuesday, May 22, 2012

As Jessica drove down J Street toward Lizzy's office, the gloomy damp weather matched her mood. The truth was she felt sick to her stomach. About everything: her job, her nonexistent love life, the Povo case, and especially Hayley's mom.

She was in no hurry to get to the office and pick up work, because as soon as she did that she would have to drive to Lizzy's house and talk to Hayley about her visit with her mom. Hayley had called her yesterday, even left a message, which was something she rarely did. Hayley was a girl of few words and knew better than most that life wasn't fair, but this was ridiculous.

Jessica exhaled. She was a coward. How could she possibly tell Hayley what had happened? "Hayley, I don't want you to worry, but Brian is definitely back in your mom's life. I happened to be hiding in the bathroom when he gave your mom a bloody lip and a black eye, but don't worry because it could have been much worse."

Yeah, that would go over just great. Hayley would go straight to her mom's house. And then the alarm on her ankle monitor would go off and the police would come and lock her up again. And it would be all Jessica's fault.

After Jessica found a parking spot, she climbed out of the car and spotted Lizzy crossing the street. She called out her name.

Lizzy turned and waited for her to catch up. "Are you just now getting here?"

"Sorry. I'm a little late getting started today."

"That makes two of us."

"If you have time, I need to talk to you about a few things."

Lizzy nodded as she searched through her purse for her keys. She unlocked the door to the office and then held it open, allowing Jessica to enter first.

Jessica screamed and jumped away.

"What is it?"

"Gross." Jessica pointed at the insects on the ground. "Are those bugs? I don't think they're moving. Are they dead?"

Lizzy moved closer to get a better look.

One of the bugs twitched slightly, causing Jessica to jump again.

Lizzy looked at her. "Stop it. You're going to give me a heart attack."

"I'm sorry, but those things are huge. The antennae are longer than their bodies. What are they doing in here?"

"I don't know," Lizzy said. "Those are the biggest beetles I've ever seen." Lizzy pointed at her. "Stay where you are. I'm going to get the broom and a dustpan and something to put them in."

"Good idea. There's an empty box in the file room."

Lizzy disappeared.

Jessica examined the bugs from where she stood. Lizzy was right. They looked like gigantic beetles. She'd never seen anything so ugly in her life. She scanned the floor, making sure there weren't any more creepy crawlers exploring the office.

Getting the monstrous bugs into the box was uneventful. They were dead or at least dying.

"The poor ugly things," Jessica said. "What are you going to do with them?"

"I'm not sure yet."

Lizzy set the box on her desk and went to the door. She opened it and checked the lock not once, but twice. She was obviously worried, Jessica thought, but she was trying to act like it was no big deal.

Jessica had worked with her long enough to know the drill. "You don't always need to be so calm under fire, you know."

"What are you talking about?"

"It's not good for you to hold all the bad feelings inside you... keep all the dark scary feelings of despair deep in the pit of your stomach. It's not healthy."

Lizzy looked at Jessica and smiled. "I appreciate your concern, Jessica, but those two beetles over there are just a couple of bugs...and they're dead."

Jessica exhaled. "You didn't even jump or gasp. Nothing. It's not healthy for a person to never show fear or apprehension."

"I jumped when you screamed."

"That doesn't count."

"Who told you that anyhow?"

"Psychology 101. Showing fear is normal."

Lizzy shut the door and locked it.

Now that the bugs were out of the way, Jessica followed Lizzy around the office. There was a small bathroom with a window in the back. Lizzy checked the locks even though there were iron bars on the outside and there was no way anybody could get in through the bathroom window.

"I need to take some work over to Hayley," Jessica said, already bored with the search. "She's probably wondering what's taking me so long."

"Go ahead and get what you need and go. You don't need to worry about me."

"Well, OK, but there's something I need to talk to you about."

Lizzy stopped what she was doing and turned toward her. "What is it? What happened?"

"Can we go in the other room? It stinks in here."

"Go," Lizzy said, ushering her out with both hands.

Jessica eyed the box, making sure the beetles were still inside before she took a seat in the chair facing Lizzy's desk.

Lizzy sat, looked at Jessica, and waited.

Jessica sighed and decided to forget about the Povo case for now. "It's about Hayley."

"OK."

"Well, it's really about Hayley's mom, which I guess makes this about Hayley."

"Spit it out, Jessica."

"Last week, Hayley asked me to check on her mom since she hadn't been answering her phone. She wanted me to knock on the door, and if nobody answered I was to find the key that they kept under a decorative bunny and let myself in."

"Please tell me you did not enter the house alone."

"This past Saturday, I entered the house alone."

"Great."

"Yeah, it wasn't a good idea. I only wanted to make sure her mom wasn't injured or even dead."

"Why didn't you call the police? Or *me*? You could have called me."

"Hayley asked me not to."

Lizzy closed her eyes but kept her composure. "What happened, Jessica? Please don't make me put my hand down your throat and pull it out of you."

Jessica's eyes widened. "That's better. Let it all out."

Lizzy groaned.

"OK, OK. The place was a mess. I mean a real disgusting pigsty. It wasn't easy making my way through the trash and the moldy smell, but when I got to the master bedroom, I noticed that the bed had been slept in. That made me feel better because, first of all, there was no dead body, but, second of all, the attempted bedmaking and the makeup on the bathroom counter were enough to convince me that Hayley's mom was alive and probably out running errands. I should have left right then, but I knew I couldn't leave until I checked every room."

"What did you find?"

Jessica shrugged. "I never made it that far. Before I made my way out of the bathroom, I heard two people come through the front door. I knew it was Brian because I heard Hayley's mom say his name. He was angry with her for leaving the door unlocked. I heard him slapping her around. She was crying, but he slammed the door shut and kept on beating on her. It was awful."

"What did you do?"

"I hid in the bathtub. And then I heard Brian marching down the hall to the other room. Hayley's mom came into the bathroom where I was hiding. I guess she was cleaning up her face when my phone vibrated. It was my brother."

Lizzy looked impatient, so she quickly wrapped it all up, telling her how Hayley's mom found her hiding in the bathtub and told her to be quiet. The story ended with Hayley's mom leaving with Brian, which allowed Jessica to finally escape unharmed.

"It's only been a few days, but I haven't had the guts to tell Hayley about my visit," Jessica added. "She left a message on my cell, and I'm sure I'm going to get an earful the moment she sees me. I don't want to tell her the truth because I'm afraid she'll do something stupid, something crazy."

"We'll both tell her. Come on. Grab what you need and let's go."

"What about your cockroaches?"

"They're beetles. I'll deal with them later."

CHAPTER 17

I'm glad they caught me, because I'd do it again.
—Arthur Gary Bishop

Davis
Tuesday, May 22, 2012

Hayley could not contain her frustration. For four days, she'd been free to roam, but whenever Lizzy was gone, Jared would appear. If he wasn't having alarms installed, he was working from his office upstairs. And now she was being told that Brian was back in her mother's life and yet Jessica hadn't had the balls to tell her. "I can't believe you're both sitting there telling me that Brian is beating my mom to a pulp and yet you expect me to sit here and do nothing."

Lizzy shook her head. "We didn't say that. The only reason you can't do anything, Hayley, is because if you do, you'll end up behind bars again."

"But at least I will have tried to help her."

Lizzy crossed her arms. "How much help will you be to your mom if you're in jail?"

Hayley paced the living room, her body stiff, her expression grim.

"Go ahead and get angry," Lizzy said. "I get that. I'm angry, too. I never once saw Brian at your mom's house. Why he would show up now after all these months makes no sense."

"He probably heard that I was out of jail. He's probably waiting for me to show up at Mom's house."

Jessica shook her head. "I think Lizzy's right. I think he's been away."

"How do you know?"

"I don't, but when they first entered the house, I heard Brian yelling. He said something about the house still looking like shit after all these months. I got the feeling he's been away."

Hayley looked at Lizzy. "Just a big fucking coincidence, I guess."

Lizzy sighed. "I called Jared. He and I are going to visit your mom and have a talk with her."

"What good will that do?"

"We can take her to a women's shelter where she'll be safe."

"She won't go. She'll never leave Brian. I should have taken care of him when I had the chance."

"Let us talk to your mom," Lizzy said. "I'll invite her to dinner so you can see her, too. Just promise me you won't do anything to jeopardize your freedom before then."

"I don't call this freedom, and I don't make promises."

Davis
Tuesday, May 22, 2012

That same night Lizzy lay in bed next to Jared, her body pressed against his left side, her head against his chest. The soft rhythmic beat of his heart soothed her. He was the calm in her life, a stable force in a sea of chaos.

"You're tense," he said as he held her close, his thumb brushing over her arm. "I called a couple of home security businesses to get quotes. I was also considering something more comprehensive."

"As in hiring a security guard?"

He nodded. "Whoever attacked you with a truck had clear intent."

"No way. Not yet. Go ahead and set up additional alarms in the house, but no security guard, Jared, I mean it. I'm fine." Big lie. She'd already been treading on unsteady ground, but nothing had been the same since someone had broken into the house and gone through her journals. But why? And for what? As far as they could tell, the intruder hadn't taken anything. She'd been worrying more and sleeping less.

And she knew this wasn't the last she'd hear of Jared hiring a security guard.

She had taken the time to have a telephone conversation with her therapist, Linda Gates. She told Linda about the nightmares she'd been having again. For most of her life, she'd spent her nights running from someone—down alleyways and through narrow streets. Recently, she found herself rushing downward into a dark cave, nobody around to hear her screams.

Jared kissed the top of her head. "Tell me what's been going on. It seems like forever since we had a moment to catch up with each other."

"Yesterday," Lizzy said, "I visited a flower shop to question the owner about Jennifer Dalton and I learned absolutely nothing. But I did buy a nice flower arrangement for my sister. Today I was caught peering into the front window of a house where I'm working surveillance, and I almost pulled a gun on the owner of the place when he reached too quickly for a screwdriver in his toolbox."

Jared simply brushed her arm with his thumb and listened.

"I also learned from Jessica that Brian is back in Hayley's mom's life."

"Does Hayley know?"

"She does now. Hayley is the one who sent Jessica to her mom's home with instructions to enter the house if nobody answered the door. Jessica was inside when Hayley's mom returned with Brian. While hiding in the bathroom, Jessica heard Brian yelling and hitting Hayley's mom. Jessica didn't want to tell Hayley because she's afraid Hayley will go after Brian and end up in jail again."

"I can understand her reluctance."

"I agree, but if we're all going to work together, we need to trust one another. We had no choice but to tell Hayley the truth."

Jared gave her a squeeze. "Honesty is the best way to go."

"I was hoping that you would go with me to visit Hayley's mom; maybe we could convince her to move into a safe house for a while."

"I think that's a good idea," he said. "It won't hurt to try." He nuzzled her neck.

She sighed. "I also found two dead beetles in my office."

Suddenly tense, Jared sat up. "In your downtown office?"

She nodded. "The strange thing is that Jennifer Dalton mentioned dead bugs and bumps in the night and—"

She stopped talking and instead watched Jared run around the room like a crazy man.

He grabbed his iPhone and after a few minutes handed her the phone and said, "Did the beetles look anything like this?"

"Exactly like that. I put them in a box. I had planned to return to the office, but after I talked to Hayley, it was late and I decided not to bother."

Jared had already pulled on a pair of jeans and was now slipping a clean white T-shirt over his head. He grabbed his phone and punched in a few numbers.

Lizzy slid off the bed, too, and scrambled for her clothes. "What's going on? It's eleven o'clock at night."

"We're going to your office. I'm going to have my team meet us there. Meet me downstairs. I'll tell you more on the way."

Sacramento
Wednesday, May 23, 2012

It was past midnight. Two technicians were dusting for prints in Lizzy's downtown office when the door opened and a familiar face walked in.

"Well, if it isn't Jimmy Martin," Lizzy said. He looked thinner and grayer than the last time she'd seen him, but he had color in his face. "You look good, Jimmy."

"You look good yourself, sunshine."

"You're feeling OK?"

"Better than ever."

Jimmy was a special agent. Although she and Jimmy didn't always see eye to eye, it was good to see him up and moving again. She and Jimmy had worked together on the Spiderman case before he discovered he had cancer. Jared had been keeping her updated, and she knew Jimmy's wife had left him. The silver lining was that his illness had brought him closer to his daughters, and he now made a point of spending quality time with them. Lizzy smiled at him and said, "You're so mean you just kicked cancer right in the ass, didn't you?"

"That's right, kiddo." He used his chin to gesture at the box sitting on her desk. "I heard you might have made friends with another maniac."

"Apparently," she said. "What's the deal with the beetles?"

Jimmy shoved his hands into his pant pockets and jiggled his keys. "Some killers like to keep creepy souvenirs so they can relive their fantasies, and others like to leave little treasures like dead insects just for fun."

"What if it's merely a coincidence?"

"Let's hope," he said before he exchanged a few words with Jared and then headed across the room to talk to one of the technicians.

Lizzy glanced at the clock on her desk and watched the second hand go around and around. She didn't like the old familiar smell of fear causing shivers to course up her arms and make the hairs at her nape stand on end. Although she was playing it cool, she couldn't help but wonder if the media was right: she didn't let trouble find her, she went looking for it instead. Not purposely, of course, but she definitely seemed to have a knack for getting involved in other people's business.

She refused to beat herself up over it. When it came to wanting to help Michael Dalton, her heart was in the right place. And yet she couldn't help but wonder: Jessica, Hayley, Brittany, Michael Dalton, were they better off without her?

Jared was sitting in the chair behind her desk, wearing gloves and examining drawers, looking for any sign that someone who didn't belong had been there. On the way to her office, Jared had explained the significance of the beetles in relation to the Lovebird Killer. Although the people of Sacramento had been kept well informed of most things concerning the murders so far attributed to the Lovebird Killer, what they didn't know was the one oddity that tied many of the victims together: the pine sawyer beetle. The first couple, discovered by the American River, had been newlyweds; both had had a beetle shoved down their esophagus. There was another woman, Betsy Weaver, mutilated beyond recognition. Most of her organs had been removed, including her heart. Her teeth were used to identify her body, which was found dangling from a tree in Curtis Park. Her husband, Stan, had reported her missing weeks before her body was found. At first, the FBI had kept a close eye on Stan, but after months of surveillance, Stan Weaver was left alone to move on with his life. The people of Sacramento, Betsy's husband included, were not aware that the FBI considered Betsy's death to be linked to the Lovebird Killer due to the beetles found stuffed in her rectum. The most recent couple to be found both had a beetle squeezed with great care into their nostrils.

The problem with the pine sawyer beetle link was that the pesky bugs were easy to find in California.

Another detail that tied the potential Lovebird Killer victims together was that they were all childless. Due to the FBI's ability to keep a few of the particulars of the murders quiet, the media and the citizens of Sacramento were not aware of these details.

Lizzy knew that if and when the media picked up on the relationship between the beetle and the Lovebird Killer, her office would become a zoo overnight.

After Jared had filled her in, Lizzy had brought up Jennifer and Michael Dalton again. But just as Greer had told her, the evidence against Michael was solid. And no beetles, Jared assured her, had been left anywhere near or on Jennifer's body—nothing whatsoever to connect the Lovebird Killer to Jennifer's death.

Lizzy looked at the beetles in the box on her desk. Was this the killer's way of leaving her a message?

She caught Jared staring at her, and she knew what he was thinking. There was no way she was going to be able to stop him from hiring a security guard now.

Antelope
Thursday, May 24, 2012

"Hey, look there. She's back."

Magnus looked over his shoulder.

Shit.

He thought he'd made it clear to her that she should stay away. Obviously, he'd been wrong. She could ruin everything. He needed to get rid of her for good, and fast.

"We're going to have to tell the boss or take care of the problem ourselves."

"I don't think she's a problem," Magnus lied.

"You heard Dominic. His fiancée hired someone to trail him. He found a contract in her office. That girl over there works for a PI—a PI who happens to be living with an FBI agent. It doesn't get much more problematic than that. Who's going to take care of her? You or me?"

Magnus shoved his hammer into his belt and headed toward the most beat-up, faded red Volvo wagon he'd ever seen.

Damn.

He hated this part of the job. He should have made himself clear; he should have scared her off from the beginning. It was her face and those big expressive eyes and wild lips that had caught him completely off guard.

What a waste.

Jessica watched Magnus head her way. *Are you frickin' kidding me?*

He couldn't possibly have seen her that quickly. Not only had she waited more than a week before returning, she had parked two blocks away from the construction site, and had pulled up to the curb less than five minutes ago.

Jessica had told Danielle what she overheard, told her that is sounded as if Povo was being roughed up a bit and somebody wanted money, but Danielle's only concern was whether or not Jessica had seen Povo with another woman. The conversation had been awkward. After Jessica had told Danielle that she might have to lie low for a while, the woman had asked Jessica to please stop by the construction site once a week, while she was in Europe, and make sure Dominic was at work. Danielle didn't care what time of day Jessica showed up—she only wanted to be sure Dominic was on the site; she wanted to know firsthand that he wasn't lying to her. That seemed fair enough. Although Jessica's last visit had been intense, she still had no idea what Povo was up to, if anything.

She needed to chill. That wasn't blood splatter on the trailer and those weren't dead bodies being delivered in garbage bags. Nobody would leave blood splatter on the side of his trailer and not bother to clean it up, and the garbage bags could have been filled with supplies for all she knew.

Jessica's new plan was to visit the site once a week, wait for Povo to arrive at work, then leave. Easy-smeasy.

With a sigh, she watched Magnus head her way. He certainly knew how to walk with a swagger. She couldn't exactly speed off as he came toward her, looking all macho and cocky as hell.

Her window was already rolled down.

He put a hand on her door, his long tan fingers settling on the frame of her car door. His T-shirt was snug in all the right places, making it extremely difficult for her to find her voice. "You caught me," she managed to say.

He raked his fingers through his hair. "What's it going to take to make you see that you shouldn't be here?"

Her face heated. "I really am just checking out the neighborhood. The only reason I went to the trailer was to talk to your boss about the house you're working on. To tell you the truth, I really didn't appreciate you manhandling me that way."

"You don't get it. You shouldn't be here."

"This is my favorite street and I'm interested in—"

He raised a hand, stopping her from saying more. "My boss thinks you're spying on him. He said that if I didn't find a way to get you out of his hair, my job would be on the line. Do you want me to lose my job?"

She opened her mouth to speak, but he stopped her again by putting a hand on her shoulder, the brush of his fingers sending shivers up her spine. She really did need to get a life.

"I know you work for an investigative company."

"That's not true, I—"

"No more lies."

She lifted her chin. "It works both ways. What happened last week inside that trailer?"

"Nothing that concerns you."

"I need to know what's going on with Dominic Povo. Is he in trouble?"

"You need to leave now."

"Not before you tell me what's going on here."

"Tell me where you want to meet, and we'll talk."

Dominic Povo was obviously hiding something, and Magnus was the only one who might be able to tell her what was going on. "Why don't we meet for coffee next week," she said, hoping she could learn more about Povo, not to mention the bulky garbage bags that had been dropped off. Having coffee with Magnus could be considered work.

"You name the place and the time."

"Shady's Coffee and Tea in Roseville. Tuesday. Three o'clock." She was scheduled to do surveillance in Roseville earlier that day. Getting Magnus to come to her would be killing two birds with one stone.

His expression was much too serious as he said, "I'll meet you, but only if you promise to stay away from this place."

"And if I promise you I'll stay away, you'll tell me what's going on?"

"Yes. Now go."

As he walked away, her eyes locked on his backside and stayed there until he disappeared down the road. Maybe she and Danielle Cartwright were more alike than she ever would have imagined—they both liked bad boys. Magnus was probably in his late twenties, definitely an older man. He was arrogant, cocky, aggressive, and possibly dangerous.

And she liked him already.

John and Rochelle
Sacramento
June 2007

John opened his mouth for another spoonful of broth. He felt as if he'd been drifting in and out of consciousness for days. He remembered waking up when Rochelle wiped a cool rag over his forehead. Her fingers had felt like a soothing balm all their own. He must have passed out before she finished, because now she was spoon-feeding him. The warm liquid felt good against his raw throat.

He also recalled her using an empty coffee tin as a makeshift bedpan to help him relieve himself. She had helped him clean his pants and his undershorts, too, using a bucket of dingy water. He wondered how long they'd been here, but he didn't have to wonder for long.

"It's been two weeks," Rochelle said.

He had no family to speak of, but Rochelle had a mother and father who cared deeply for their daughter. She was also close to her sister and brother. Of course they would all be worried out of their minds by now. "I bet your family has sent out the cavalry. They'll come bursting in here at any moment," he told her, his voice weak. "I'm sure of it."

Her head fell forward and he felt her wet cheek brush against his hand.

"Don't cry," he said. "I'm sorry I've let you down. It's my fault we're here."

"I want to leave this place. I want to go home."

"I know you do. I'm going to get you out of here, I promise." When he looked downward, he noticed a long, jagged cut across the length of her calf. "What's that on your leg? What did they do to you?"

She was sobbing in earnest now, her shoulders quivering.

He leaned over far enough that he could kiss the top of her head. If it weren't for Rochelle, he'd be dead already. He couldn't stand to see her suffer. "Rochelle," he said as an idea came to him. "I need you to find something to help with these ropes. Before I was knocked out, I was able to loosen the ties by rubbing them against the jagged edge of the chair leg, but it will take too long without your help. I have a long way to go."

When she pushed herself to her feet, he got a better look at the cut. The monsters had cut an irregular line into her leg, like a lightning bolt, at least a foot long. They'd used crude stitching to sew her up. *Why would they do such a thing? It doesn't make sense. Nothing makes any sense. Why are they keeping us tied up as prisoners? Why would they do that to her?*

"I bet they keep tools of some sort over there," he said, gesturing with his chin.

She walked that way, the chain clinking as she went.

"No, John," he heard her say.

"You're almost there. You can do it, Rochelle. Just a little bit farther."

She maneuvered her body so that she had another inch or so of leeway. The tip of her finger touched the pointed end of a screwdriver. Her breathing was ragged as she pushed and pulled and miraculously managed to knock the screwdriver from the table. It clacked to the floor, and luck was on their side because it rolled in their direction.

She did it! Such a clever girl.

She picked up the screwdriver and held it up for him to see. Her eyes were filled with pain and suffering. He loved her so much.

"See if you can loosen the ropes," he whispered.

Her chains allowed her to reach the front of him, but she had to strain even further to reach his hands tied behind his chair. She managed to stick the screwdriver between the knots and push and prod. The ropes were loosening. He'd never felt such relief. Just a little longer and his hands would be free.

Hope.

For the first time since they'd been taken, he felt hope, a light ethereal feeling, almost tangible within a room so thick with despair.

"You think I'm weak, don't you?"

He could see that she was trying to be brave, but the tears wouldn't stop.

He closed his eyes, concentrated on breathing. He had never loved anyone as he loved Rochelle. Before he could comfort her, the cellar door creaked open.

"Rochelle," he said, his voice a frantic whisper now. "Somebody's coming. When he gets close enough, use every bit of strength you can summon to stab him with the screwdriver."

He let his head fall forward as if he was dead.

Judging by the footsteps, it was only one person. Perfect. He struggled to get his hand loose so that he'd be able to stab the man.

"What's going on down here?" the man asked.

"Please stop," Rochelle cried. "I can't take any more of this. Let me go!" Her forehead fell limp, her head resting on John's knees, her body shaking.

The man came closer, grabbed her arm, and yanked her away.

John's eyes were closed, but he could smell the man's sour breath as he leaned over him. *Now, Rochelle,* he thought. *Do it now.*

He heard the clink of her chains. He opened his eyes.

The man hovered over him as Rochelle brought her arm down hard, stabbing him with the screwdriver again and again. He'd never seen her look so angry. She must have gotten him good, because blood was everywhere.

John's pulse skyrocketed. He pulled with all the strength he had left inside him, twisting and yanking, shocked when his right hand came loose. He reached for the screwdriver and pulled it from the man's body, then used it to work the knots around his other wrist.

CHAPTER 18

It wasn't as dark and scary as it sounds. I had a lot of fun…
killing somebody's a funny experience.
—Albert DeSalvo

Davis
Friday, May 25, 2012

Hayley stood in front of her mirrored closet door. She didn't like
the jittery feeling inside. Her nerves were getting the best of her.
Jared and Lizzy had talked to her mom and somehow convinced
her to come to dinner. Hayley had been at Lizzy's for a few weeks
now, but this was the first time she'd gone out of her way to look
"presentable." She had on a pair of jeans and a mossy green top
with three-quarter-length sleeves that Lizzy had bought for her.
The clothes felt strange and too snug for her liking.

When she glanced in the mirror, she didn't recognize herself.
Her hair had grown long, a few inches past her shoulders. The
ends looked like shit, but whatever. She couldn't remember her
hair ever being so long. She hadn't bothered to have her piercings
redone, mostly because of the restrictions due to her ankle monitor. She had to admit, she was getting used to looking at her face
without all of the adornments.

An hour ago she'd thought it was a dumbass thing to do, primping and worrying over things like hair and clothes. But then she'd decided her mom wasn't the only one who needed to change if they wanted to turn things around. And that's exactly what Hayley wanted. She would do anything, including dressing up a bit, if it would help her mom stay sober and get the hell away from Brian.

The moment she heard the front door open, her heart pounded harder and faster against her chest. She straightened, took a deep breath, and headed for the other room. It had been almost ten months since she'd seen her mom last, but it felt like years. Jessica had said that her mom appeared to be free of drugs and alcohol, but that was hard to believe since Hayley could count on one hand the number of times she'd spoken to her mom when she was sober.

As Hayley entered the living room, she saw Lizzy come through the door first, followed by Mom. Her hair was now more gray than brown, but she'd combed it and fastened it with a clip. She wore blush and mascara, too.

Hayley was afraid to move, unsure of what to do next. They both stood there and sort of looked each other over. Hayley found her voice and said, "You look good, Mom."

Her mom stepped her way and reached out to gently brush the hair out of Hayley's face. "Your hair has gotten long." She sighed. "You're so grown up."

Jared came through the front door next, and he and Lizzy went to the kitchen and made themselves busy.

"Come on," Hayley said with a wave of her hand toward the couch, disappointed when she caught a whiff of alcohol on her mom's breath. "Let's sit down."

Mom wasn't drunk, Hayley decided, but she'd probably taken a swig or two from a bottle before coming. Her hands were shaking, and she looked nervous when she asked if she could see Hayley's room. The question threw Hayley off balance. She wasn't sure why the question would make her pause, but it did.

"It's your private space," Mom said, waving the request away as if it were an annoying gnat, nothing more. "I shouldn't have asked."

"No," Hayley said, snapping out of whatever craziness was going on inside her head. "Let's go to my room. I want you to see it."

"If you're sure."

Hayley led her mom to her room. Taking a seat on the edge of the bed, she watched her mom look at all of the knickknacks on the shelf above the desk. Her mom touched the computer monitor and then picked up a framed picture of the two of them. Lizzy had found the picture among her things when she'd moved Hayley's stuff from the apartment, and then had gone to all the bother of framing it. The photo was of Hayley and her mom outside, the wind blowing their hair to one side. Hayley figured she was thirteen at the time. She and her mom wore twin smiles.

Mom turned away.

Hayley couldn't see her face, but her shoulders were shaking. She was crying when she said, "We had some good times, didn't we?"

Hayley closed her eyes. She wanted to go to her and hold her tight, but she also felt a familiar stab of anxiety and anger. Suddenly, she regretted having her here at all.

Mom set the frame down and continued looking around. "Ms. Gardner and her boyfriend...they've been good to you?"

"They have."

"And you like it here?"

"It's fine."

"I'm sorry I never put you first."

"Don't worry about it."

"Shhh, no, listen," Mom said, her eyes unblinking as she finally got the nerve to look Hayley in the eyes again. "I'm sorry… about everything. When you were little, I told you that things were going to be different, but I turned out to be just like the rest of 'em."

Mom was talking about her own family: her parents, brothers, aunts, and uncles—all a bunch of crazy, selfish assholes. "You're not like them," Hayley tried to assure her.

Mom's gaze fell to the picture again. "I messed up." She moved to where Hayley was sitting and sat down next to her. She used her feet to bounce a little and then patted the mattress. "This is nice."

Hayley sucked in a breath and forced a smile. She could see bruises on her mom's neck and arms. She wanted to ask her about Brian, but the words wouldn't come and she knew why. She was afraid to ruin the moment, afraid her mom would get upset and the air would quickly fill up with bad feelings and resentment, clogging their lungs with past mistakes and making it feel as if they were breathing in secondhand smoke. Mom was trying to change, and that was all Hayley had ever wanted.

"Do you want to spend the night?" Hayley asked. "I'm sure Lizzy and Jared wouldn't mind."

"I can't," she said. "Jared is going to take me to a shelter after dinner."

Hayley's heart nearly stopped. "You're going to go?"

"You didn't think I would?"

"No," Hayley said, stunned. "I didn't think you would agree to it."

"It's time." She anchored a gray strand of hair behind her ear. "I've thought a lot about what you said when I saw you last." Her voice cracked. "I made bad choices. I've been selfish, always putting myself first. It's time for a change."

Hayley swallowed a knot in her throat.

Her mom's head fell forward. She was crying again.

This time Hayley reached over and pulled Mom closer so she had no choice but to rest her head on Hayley's shoulder. "It's OK. You didn't mean to hurt anybody."

Hayley wasn't a dreamer. She knew her mom had a long way to go. But that was OK. This could be the beginning of something good—a fresh start was what she needed. It was what they both needed.

Mom lifted her head and wiped her eyes. She patted Hayley on the knee. "We're gonna be fine."

"We are," Hayley agreed. "I really think we might be."

Marshall Park, Sacramento
Monday, May 28, 2012

Lizzy arrived at Marshall Park at exactly five minutes past 6:00 a.m. She climbed out of the car, breathed in a lungful of crisp morning air, and stretched before beginning her run. When she'd first started running nine months ago, getting her butt to the park consistently had been a constant battle. Now, regardless of weather, she looked forward to her daily run.

Lizzy never would have thought she had the patience to run one mile, let alone five. Running had become an important part of her life. It cleared her head and gave her energy. She'd grown accustomed to the other runners, paying less attention to her surroundings, at least until all of the recent events. A break-in. An incident with the truck. And the beetles, perfectly placed so that she wouldn't miss them. And yet no fingerprints had been found, no sign of a break-in at her office. Nothing made sense. She and Jared both knew that the beetles were not a mere coincidence. Lizzy also knew that her freedom, including morning runs like this one, would soon be put to the test. Jared was already in the process of hiring a security guard to watch over her. He would follow her to the office, et cetera. Wherever she would go, he would go.

All thanks to a couple of dead beetles. The Lovebird Killer liked to leave the pine sawyer beetles as some sort of horrifying calling card, letting the police know he'd been there. And yet he wasn't otherwise consistent. The Lovebird Killer knew exactly what he was doing. He was keeping everyone guessing, screwing with expectations.

As Jared and his crew had recovered evidence inside and outside her office and carefully documented the scene, she had feigned indifference, but felt anything but calm inside. Even this morning, her instincts had cried out, telling her to stay home and hide out for a while, but she refused to do anything of the sort.

Been there, done that.

Someone was playing with her. *One of Spiderman's friends, perhaps?* She had no idea why another asshole might be toying with her, but she refused to hide away and change her routine. She was done with sick bastards who had nothing better to do than fuck with her.

Up ahead, she saw one of the regular runners at the park sitting on a wood bench lining the parkway. The woman had taken a shoe off and was examining her bare foot.

Lizzy stopped. "Do you need some help?"

"I'm fine," the woman said. "New shoes, new blister."

Digging into her belt pack, Lizzy pulled out a Band-Aid. "This should help."

"Thanks." The woman took the Band-Aid and then offered her hand. "My name's Erica."

Lizzy shook her hand. "Lizzy."

"I've seen you here before. Have you been running for long?"

"Nine months now."

"Five years," Erica said as she took care of the blister and then slipped her shoe back on. She waved at a man as he passed by. "That was William. I tried using him the other day to challenge myself, but he's too fast for me. I need to pace myself."

Lizzy watched William disappear around the bend.

Erica stood and jogged in place. "Perfect." She pointed to the path ahead. "If you don't mind, I'll run with you to the next cutoff and then I have to get to work."

They ran together for two minutes before Erica took the path to the right. "It was nice meeting you," she called out. "Thanks again."

"No problem. See you later."

Lizzy continued on. It wasn't long before she could hear another runner coming up from behind. He passed and she followed behind. He wore a dark hooded sweatshirt and matching sweatpants. He was five foot ten, thin build. He slowed.

She slowed, too.

Her heart rate picked up a notch. Her gaze darted from one side of the path to the other. A copse of trees to her left—the woodsy center of the park—no cutoff path to the main street for another half of a mile. Reaching into her pocket, she grabbed a small can of Mace.

Her jog became a fast walk. She was about to turn and head the other way, when he suddenly twirled around and lunged for her. All she saw was a fist coming straight at her and smashing into her nose. Staggering backward, she hit the ground hard. Blood spurted from her nose.

He didn't hesitate to come at her again.

She raised her hand, pressed the button, and sprayed him with Mace.

He grunted and cursed, wiping his face with his sleeve, but his damn sunglasses had stopped the Mace from doing much damage.

As she scrambled to her feet, he came at her again with incredible speed. She ducked. He missed, but then he slammed his knuckles across her jaw and she hit the ground hard.

He hovered over her.

Afraid she might lose consciousness, she tried to get a good look at his face, but it was no use. Between a hood and aviators, she couldn't see a thing. He grabbed hold of her feet and began dragging her to the area in the middle of the park that was thick with trees and brush.

No fucking way was she going to let him drag her into the woods. She kicked and shouted. Every pebble and divot in the pathway cut into her backside. She lifted her neck to keep her head from hitting concrete. Over a decade of teaching self-defense and yet she felt helpless. *Fuck him.* She tried to wriggle free of his grasp. It was no use. She kept screaming. Her attacker was determined.

Twigs and pine needles bit into her skin as he dragged her along.

She grabbed hold of a good-sized branch on the ground and held it close to her side. When he finally stopped, he put a foot on top of her chest, pushing hard, crushing her ribs. "You should have learned by now to mind your own business."

"Who are you?"

"I'm the darkness when you're afraid. I'm the screams you hear in your sleep. I'm the creak in the other room when you're all alone."

"Don't flatter yourself," she said through gritted teeth. "You're the fucking pimple on prom night and the asshole every girl avoids at Uncle Bob's Christmas—"

His foot crushed down on her chest, stopping her from finishing.

Every lesson she'd ever taught came roaring to life, exploding within her head like fireworks. Fight. Bite. Kick. She swung the branch, hard and fast, hitting the side of his face.

Caught off guard, he fell to the ground.

Crawling on all fours, Lizzy grabbed his leg and bit through fabric and into his flesh, drawing blood and making him squeal like the pig he was.

The fucker was not going to get away with this.

His kicking motions became frantic—like a kid trying to keep his head above water as she climbed on top of him, straddling him and then slamming her open palm into the bridge of his nose, hitting gold. Blood sprayed across his face.

She reached for his aviators, intent on seeing his face, but he bucked her off, jumped to his feet, and grabbed the branch she'd used on him. He raised the branch above his head, ready to strike.

"Hey you! Get away from her!"

Her attacker looked up, tossed the branch, and took off through the brush.

Lizzy pushed herself to her feet and headed back for the trail.

It was William, the same man Erica had waved to earlier. "I called 911," he told her.

"Thanks."

He reached out to help her. "Maybe you should sit down."

Panicking, she pushed his hand away and then jogged toward the open path. She couldn't breathe. She tasted blood. She needed air.

"I've never seen anything like that," William said as he followed her out of the brush and onto the pathway. "My name's William."

"I know." She kept moving, walking faster, trusting no one. She staggered more than walked, but she couldn't stop.

"You know my name?"

"Erica told me."

"Ahh. She's a nice gal."

Lizzy wanted to ask William to please shut the fuck up for a minute so she could think. Instead, she pulled out her cell and was about to call Jared when she remembered that he was on a plane headed for Los Angeles. He hadn't wanted to go and he was adamant about her skipping her morning run. *Shit.*

She tucked her phone into her pocket and tried to ignore the guy as he rambled on about how lucky she was that he'd heard her screams, wondering what she would have done if he hadn't come.

The pain was excruciating; her skull throbbed as if somebody were stomping on her face. She could hear sirens in the distance, but she had no intention of sticking around. Too bad her body and her mind were not on the same page. Her legs wobbled. Her knees quivered. She was going down, right into William's arms.

Sacramento
Monday, May 28, 2012

Hayley walked with her arm extended and her thumb pointed at the sky. Ever since Tommy had replaced her ankle bracelet, she'd been free to roam, but a lot of good that had done her. Every time Jared left for work, Lizzy seemed to find a reason to stay at the house. Then Lizzy would leave and Jessica would stop by to check up on her. Between the break-in, the weird car accident, and her mom's visit, nothing had been going as planned. But today, Hayley didn't care. She'd left a note on the bedroom door that said she was sleeping. If she was found out, so be it.

The first place on her list of places to go was My House, the shelter for battered women Lizzy had lined up for her mom. Hayley wanted to see how she was doing. She'd thought about stopping by her mom's house first—to see if Brian was there—but after mulling over the idea, she'd decided she didn't care if Brian lived the rest of his worthless life in that house. Not too many good memories had come from inside those walls.

Keeping her arm stretched outward, she breathed in a lungful of unsullied air after a night of rain. Up ahead, gravel spewed every which way as a faded red Volvo pulled to the side of the road.

As cars passed by in a blur, she noticed that the driver looked familiar.

Shit.

Here she'd been worried about a cop pulling over, but not once had she considered that Jessica might be the one to catch her out of the house. As cars sped by on the opposite side of where she stood, Hayley stooped over and looked into the open window on the passenger side of the vehicle.

"What are you doing?" Jessica asked.

"I'm hitching a ride."

"I can see that. Are you crazy?"

Hayley straightened and was about to continue on, when Jessica said, "Would you please get into this car before a police officer pulls over to see what's going on and realizes I'm aiding and abetting a fugitive?"

Hayley opened the door and climbed in. She couldn't help but smile at the fugitive remark. Jessica was still staring at her. "Jesus," Hayley said. "What now?"

"Could you buckle up? It's a law, you know?"

She located the end of the seatbelt tucked between the door and the seat and snapped the belt in place. "Happy?"

While Jessica merged onto the highway, Hayley took a good look at the inside of Jessica's car. There was wall-to-wall shag carpet and it smelled like moldy cheese. "Nice car," she lied. "Where did you get it?"

"Craigslist."

"What happened to the Mustang?"

"I returned it to the original owner."

"Did he give you your money back?"

"Not yet, but he promised me he would before the end of the month."

It was quiet for a moment before Jessica glanced toward Hayley's feet. "Where's your ankle bracelet?"

"It's there," Hayley said.

"It's a fake, isn't it?"

"Yep."

"How could you risk so much after everything Jared and Lizzy did to get you out of that place?"

"You wouldn't understand."

"Try me."

"I don't like being confined. If I could have found a way out of the detention center, I would have left that place, too."

"And if you were caught, you would spend the rest of your life behind bars."

Hayley shrugged.

"Don't you have dreams and goals?"

Silence.

"I realize we've never seen eye to eye, but for some weird reason I sort of like you. There are a lot of people in this world who care about you."

"So, you think I should let the past go and become a model citizen?"

"That would be great, but that's not what I'm saying."

Having no interest in what Jessica had to say, Hayley bit her tongue and tried her damnedest to tune her out.

"What I'm saying is that life is short."

"Got it."

"I'm not done."

Hayley clenched her jaw. *Fuck.*

"You are intelligent. Your mom must be an incredible human being to have managed to raise such a smart daughter—against all odds. Surrounded by druggies and rapists, the worst kind of scum, and yet she is still trying to overcome ridiculous obstacles in her life."

Hayley had nothing to say to that, but she didn't like the tightness she felt in her chest.

"Your mom," Jessica continued, "after years of neglect and mistreatment, has not given up. She's trying to make a better life for herself. She's an inspiration, and maybe just for her, you should try to change things around, too."

Hayley watched the scenery outside—gray and dreary.

"Are you running away? Is that what you're doing?"

"Just getting some things done."

"So, your plan is to run around for a few hours and then return before Lizzy gets home?"

"That's the plan."

"I was just at the house to pick up some files. I saw the note on your bedroom door and figured you were sleeping."

Hayley wasn't listening. She pulled out a piece of paper. "I'm going to My House, a shelter for battered women, located at Center Street in Sacramento. If you're going to the office, you can drop me off at the exit."

"This is crazy."

"You're repeating yourself."

"No, I'm not. First, I said that *you* were crazy. Now I'm saying that *what you are doing* is crazy."

"Thanks for the clarification."

Jessica gritted her teeth. "I'll take you to the shelter and I'll wait for you outside."

"After the shelter, I'm going to Rancho Cordova."

The sound that emerged from Jessica's throat sounded a lot like a growl.

Hayley tried not to laugh.

"What's going on in Rancho Cordova?"

"I've been doing some research on Adele Hampton, the girl who was given up for adoption eighteen years ago."

"Did you find her?"

"Not yet. According to the receipts in the file, she visited quite a few shops, all within a few blocks of one another. I want to show her picture around and find out if anyone recognizes her."

Hayley expected flack, was surprised when she got a regular question instead.

"Do you think she might still live in the area?"

"I do."

"That wouldn't make sense, would it?" Jessica asked. "I mean, why would the girl stay in that city unless she wanted to be found?"

"Maybe she never thought anybody would ever bother to look for her."

For five blessed minutes, it was quiet, until Jessica thought of something else she wanted to chat about.

"I have another problem I was hoping you could help me with."

Hayley looked at Jessica's profile and waited.

"I'm supposed to meet Magnus, the guy I told you about, for coffee tomorrow. I have no idea if can trust him, but I need to at least try to find out what he's up to."

"What do you have in mind?"

"After I meet with him, I'd like to find out where he goes next, but I can't follow him myself because he knows what car I drive and this car of mine is hard to miss."

"I'll talk to Tommy—see if he can follow him."

"You would do that?"

"I just said I would, didn't I?"

CHAPTER 19

If I could dig up my mother's grave,
I'd take out her bones and kill her again.
—Joseph Fischer

Sacramento
Monday, May 28, 2012

Eli Simpson sat in his dad's old Buick and stared at the house where he was sure his sister had died. His heart no longer raced out of control when he visited. He was empty. Well, not entirely empty. His insides felt bleak, maybe even ominous.

It was dark out tonight, but it didn't matter because he'd been here often enough to know what the house looked like, even in the dark. The house was 1,400 square feet, give or take. It was old and neglected. The cracked path leading to the door, the dead lawn, and the oak with arthritic branches emphasized its decay.

He rolled his head from the right to the left, hoping to get the kinks out. He'd been sitting in the same position for over an hour. Although he had yet to see any movement inside the house, the kitchen light was on.

He couldn't recall a time in the past five years when John Robinson might have had a visitor, which made sense since killers were not human beings. They were monsters.

Exhausted from a long day at work, he leaned his head on the headrest and shut his eyes. Visions of his sister popped into his mind—smiling, of course. Rochelle didn't know how not to smile. He was her older brother, but only by ten months. He and Rochelle had always had a special connection, the same sort of connection people often talked about twins having.

Five years ago, when Rochelle first brought John Robinson home to his parents' house for Sunday dinner, he'd known straight off that she was just being nice. Bringing the guy home was like bringing home a stray cat. Rochelle felt sorry for him. She probably thought she could feed him and give him some attention and he'd be a better person for it.

Compassionate—that was his sister in a nutshell, compassionate and caring. She was a true angel, one of those unique individuals who made a difference simply by existing. People wanted to be near her. Not only was she a great listener, she made everybody feel important.

The darkened street was suddenly lit up by twin headlights.

Sinking lower into the seat, he saw the garage next door to the house he was watching creak open, crying out in a slow eerie wail as if it were dying like the rest of the shit neighborhood. A woman with dirty-blonde, shoulder-length hair sat behind the wheel. The garage was tidy and neat. He couldn't help but wonder if the woman had ever met the killer next door. He'd knocked on her door once or twice, hoping to ask a few questions, but she never answered.

The neighborhood was like a ghost town. Maybe most of Robinson's neighbors were dead, stuffed in the attic or in an old freezer. As the garage door closed, he looked around again, his gaze stopping to focus on the house belonging to Claire Schultz, the only person who had ever allowed him inside their house. He had talked to her five years ago, in those dark months after Rochelle disappeared.

He'd shown the elderly woman a picture of his sister, and the look of surprise on Claire's face had told him she knew something. She'd even proceeded to tell him what she'd seen the night John Robinson brought home a girl—the same girl in the picture.

Eli had asked her if she would talk to the police, tell them what she'd seen. She had agreed. And he'd been sure he would be able to prove that John Robinson had something to do with his sister's disappearance. He thought he had a witness.

Eli shook his head at the remembrance. By the time the police finally talked to her, Claire changed her story and said she didn't recognize the girl in the picture. Claire Schultz was suddenly adamant about the fact that she didn't know anything at all about the missing girl. She told the police she didn't recall one damn thing about the night John Robinson brought a girl home—the night she'd told Eli that she'd watched as John slammed a hand through a window and choked a woman. She claimed her memories had been foggy since her fall. She told the police all about her broken hip and how she'd spent longer than most recovering from surgery.

Somewhere between his talk with Claire and the police finally getting off their asses, she'd changed her story.

Why? What had John Robinson said or done to her to make her clam up like that?

Sacramento
Tuesday, May 29, 2012

Yesterday, after the EMT had finished looking at Lizzy, she had followed the ambulance to the hospital, where an elderly doctor had checked her out: no X-ray or CT scan was needed. Her nose had stopped bleeding and it wasn't broken. The doctor recommended ibuprofen, ice, and a nasal decongestant. Bruised and battered, she had been sent on her way. Lizzy had decided not to tell Jared about the incident in the park. She would tell him when he returned home at the end of the week. Overwhelmed and too exhausted to make a police report, she'd turned off her cell and gone straight to bed.

It was now Tuesday morning and Hayley was still sleeping, so Lizzy left her alone.

She climbed into her car. A peek into the rearview mirror confirmed that most of her face was black and blue. She looked like roadkill, but the bruises looked worse than they felt as she drove to the Sacramento police department. She wished she could say the same for her body. Every bone ached, every muscle was sore.

Lieutenant Greer was out for the day, which meant she would receive no preferential treatment today. Upon arriving at the station, she filled out a report about the incident in the park, and then she was led through a sea of desks to an empty chair in front of Detective Mark Goldberg's desk. Her head was throbbing again, but since she was here, she wanted to see if they had learned anything about the driver of the truck who had hit her car.

As she waited for Detective Goldberg to finish with a call, she overheard a disgruntled man talking about his dead sister. The voice was familiar. The man was angry and he was talking loudly enough to be heard by anyone who was inclined to listen.

Taking a peek over her shoulder, her breath hitched when she saw that it was Eli Simpson, the same man who had caught her peeking in the front window of his house.

None of the other detectives or officers sitting at their desks appeared to pay him any mind, as if they'd heard it a million times before. The officer assigned to listen to Mr. Simpson seemed to be merely going through the motions, nodding his head as he shuffled papers on his desk.

She turned away, hoping Mr. Simpson wouldn't notice her, suppressing a cringe when she heard him relay the story about catching a woman looking through his window at his home. According to his neighbors, he said, the Peeping Tom had been trolling his house for days. He was certain that his sister's murderer had put the woman up to it. Mr. Simpson wanted the police to set up camp in front of his house; he wanted protection for him and his dad.

Before she could decide whether or not she should go over there and set Eli Simpson straight, Detective Goldberg hung up the phone.

"Sorry about that," he said. "Looks like you've had a rough week," he added, gesturing toward her face.

"I was attacked in the park yesterday morning. It's all in the file," she said, "but I thought since I was here I would check on another incident. About two weeks ago, a truck deliberately hit my car—more than once. I filled out a report, and there were half a dozen witnesses who did the same. I was hoping you could give me an update as to whether or not the truck has been located."

He examined her closely, probably wondering how one woman could get into that much trouble. "Do you have the case number?"

She gave him the number as he typed the info into the computer. "The system is a little slow today, but if we're patient, this shouldn't take long."

"That man over there," Lizzy said, gesturing toward Eli Simpson, "I couldn't help but overhear him talking about his sister. Is it true? Was she murdered?"

"As of today, she's listed as a missing person. Been missing for five years now." He straightened his spine and rolled his neck to get the kinks out. "Eli Simpson comes in here every month, rain or shine, to get an update."

"Why does he think she was murdered?"

"His sister used to date a man he wasn't fond of. She disappeared and Simpson is convinced his sister's boyfriend had something to do with her disappearance."

"Coming here month after month for five years…that's a long time…could he be telling the truth?"

Goldberg shook his head as he reorganized files and papers on top of his cluttered desk. "We've been inside the accused man's house on more than one occasion. The house is clean. That guy over there has also been inside the man's house, which is why there's a restraining order against him."

"What's the boyfriend's name?"

"I can't tell you that, ma'am. In fact, I've said too much as it is. And look here," he said, squinting his eyes at the computer screen. "The truck that hit you was reported missing on the same day as the incident."

"And it's still missing?"

He nodded, still looking at the screen, his fingers clacking away at the keyboard. "Afraid so." He turned the screen in her direction. "Is all of your personal information up to date?"

Nothing had changed since she made the report, so she nodded her head.

"Well, then, is there anything else I can do for you? I made a note that you were here to inquire as to the status of your case. If we hear anything, we'll give you a call."

"Thank you," she said.

Eli Simpson's tone increased another octave as he ranted about the entire police department being incompetent. Hoping to escape before he noticed her, Lizzy stood, thanked Detective Goldberg for his help, and headed for the door.

By the time Lizzy returned to her car, she'd changed her mind about avoiding Simpson and even decided to wait for him. She didn't have to wait long.

"It's you," he said as he made his way through the parking lot and spotted her leaning against her car. "What happened to your face? No, never mind, don't tell me. You were snooping around somebody's backyard and you went and pulled out your gun."

"No, actually, I was attacked in the park yesterday."

"Maybe you should go home and put some ice on that face of yours."

Before she could say another word, he narrowed his eyes and said, "What are you doing here, anyway? Are you still following me?"

"I realize it must look bad, but actually I was checking up on a personal matter."

"You won't get any help in there. Too many tax dollars being wasted inside that building."

"I was talking with Detective Goldberg when I heard you talking about your sister."

He didn't respond. He just kept walking.

Lizzy followed him across the parking lot, trying her damnedest not to limp since one side of her body felt like Bruce Lee had used it as a punching bag. Before opening the door to his truck, he turned and pointed his keys at her. "What do you want, lady?"

"Like I said, I heard you talking to the officer in there. You don't believe I was hired by Michael and Jennifer Dalton?"

He snorted.

"After I left your house," Lizzy continued, "I thought about who might have used your name to apply for workers' compensation. Whoever it is might be using your name for all sorts of illegal dealings."

"And?"

"And you don't care?"

"Listen," he said, clearly frustrated, the veins in his forehead suddenly accentuated as he spoke, "I know exactly who's using my name—the same guy who has been fucking with me for years. The same guy who I bet hired a private eye who's this close"—he squeezed his fingers together for emphasis—"to prematurely firing her gun and losing her license for good."

Lizzy sighed.

"I guess what I'm really wondering, Lizzy Gardner, is why you would care at all."

"Like I've been telling you from the start, I'm just doing my job. I was hired and paid to find out if Eli Simpson was injured on the job. If not, I need proof, and then I need to let the insurance company know they don't have to pay. That makes them happy and it makes me happy, especially when I stamp the file CLOSED and move on to the next asshole who's trying to work the system. I already told you who hired me to watch you, and I really don't understand what the big deal is. If you give me the name of the man who you believe is impersonating you, then I can watch him instead of you. It's a win-win for you and me, Mr. Simpson."

Eli Simpson relaxed a little, but he seemed to be doing a lot of thinking, which didn't make any sense to Lizzy.

She tried once more. "Can you just give me his name?"

"Whose name?"

"The name of the man you think had something to do with your sister's disappearance."

"How much did Goldberg tell you?"

"Not much."

"Well, the man in question didn't take her, he killed her."

"Do you have any proof?"

"Nope."

"OK, but you think he was the one who used your name on the workers' comp claim?"

"No doubt in my mind."

"If you give me his name, maybe I can help you, too."

"And how would you propose to do that?"

"You're not allowed to go near the man, right?"

"Is that what Goldberg told you?"

Damn. Eli Simpson was as stubborn as an ox. "Is there a restraining order against you, or not?"

He crossed his arms, but didn't answer the question. "So what is it you think you can do for me?" he asked.

"I could watch the man's house."

"I'm already doing that."

"What about the restraining order?"

"What about it? I'll do whatever it takes to find my sister."

She sighed. "If he is the same man who is using your name, he could be arrested for fraud."

Eli said nothing.

"I just need the man's name and address so I can do my own investigation. Workers' comp fraud is a huge crime in America. Billions of dollars are paid out in false claims every year. Scams like this are draining business profits and costing honest workers their jobs. I take my job seriously, Mr. Simpson, and I like to think that taking one bastard down at a time actually makes a difference."

His eyes were intense as he stared down at her, making her uncomfortable. "If I give you his name, what's in it for me?"

"I'm an investigator, remember? If you give me the man's name and provide me with information about your sister—date of birth and Social Security number—I could do an investigation on the man you believe is screwing with you and see what comes up. No charge."

"Oh, yeah?"

She nodded. "Have you hired an investigator in the past?"

"Nope, can't say that I have."

"Why not?"

"Because I already know who took her."

Lizzy tried not to grit her teeth. No wonder the police all but ignored him. "You give me the name and I'll help you search for your sister. I would need to ask you some questions, find out if she has any identifying marks, like tattoos or piercings, who were her closest friends, did she have a cell phone or a pager before she—"

"She's dead."

Lizzy inhaled. "How do you know?"

"She would have called or come home if she wasn't."

"Well, then, in that case, if you can tell me everything you know about this man who you believe might have stolen your identity, I can get my people on it and we can put that fucking killer behind bars once and for all."

"Now you're talking, honey. Now you're talking."

Shady Coffee & Tea
Roseville
Tuesday, May 29, 2012

"I like you," Magnus told Jessica within ten minutes of arriving at the coffee shop. He sat across from her, one hand on top of the other. "I'd love to take you out on a date."

She glanced over her shoulder to make sure a tall blonde wasn't standing behind her. *Nope.* All clear. She turned back to him, eyed him warily, and said, "It's way too early for a date. I hardly know you."

"OK, then what would you like to know? Ask me anything."

She fidgeted in her seat. She'd come here today to find out more about his boss, Dominic Povo, but at the moment, she couldn't care less about any of that. Magnus looked like a whole different guy in his slacks and newly pressed button-up shirt. He smelled good, too. "How old are you? Have you ever been married? How long did your last serious relationship last? What's your idea of a romantic night out? And is working construction your passion?"

"Twenty-nine. No. Two years. Walking hand in hand on the beach. And no."

She sort of wished he wouldn't keep looking at her the way he was, like she was beautiful and interesting. Not just because he made her nervous, but because she didn't know if she could trust him. Nobody had ever looked at her like that before.

He smiled and crossed his arms, well-muscled arms that bulged beneath his light blue, fitted shirt. "Where do you see yourself?"

"Excuse me?"

"Down the road…the future…where do you see yourself?"

"I haven't put a lot of thought into it." That was a big lie. The future was pretty much *all* she thought about. She knew exactly what she wanted to be when she grew up. She wanted to be an FBI profiler. She wanted to spend her days doing criminal investigative analysis. Exploring the human mind intrigued her, but this wasn't supposed to be about the two of them, she reminded herself. This was coffee with a guy way out of her league. A guy she wanted to trust, but didn't. "What about you?" she asked, hoping to put the focus on him, where it belonged, figuring they could talk about Povo in a minute. "Tell me more about yourself."

"I'm a rare breed—a mix of overconfidence, competitiveness, and salesmanship, with only a touch of compassion."

"Oh, really," she said, thoroughly amused and intrigued, especially by his mouth and his dark, smoldering eyes.

He laughed. "I'm kidding. I have a degree in finance, but at the moment, I'm working construction to pay off my student loans. Since working this job, I've been burning the candle at both ends. I like to rock climb, play a little golf, read financial books, and visit family when they come to town." He put both hands on the table between them and leaned forward. "Secretly, I'm looking forward to the day I can settle down with the right woman. How about you?"

Jessica sighed. Guys like Magnus didn't usually pay her much attention, and that was her first clue that something wasn't right. Not that she wasn't worthy of a date with a hot guy; she was an eight out of ten in the looks department—not too thin or overweight. She had curves. She wasn't a genius like Hayley, but she was no dummy, either. And she liked to think she had a sense of humor. "My life isn't too exciting. As you know, I work for a private investigator, and I'm going to be straight with you. I need you to tell me what's going on with Dominic Povo."

"Who wants to know?"

"His fiancée."

He exhaled and then seemed to relax a little before he said, "Tell her to run as fast as she can."

"I suppose you're not going to tell me why?"

He shook his head.

"Is he dangerous?"

"Extremely."

"Can you tell me anything about the garbage bags delivered to the site a few weeks ago?"

He looked taken aback. "I'm not sure what you're talking about."

She wasn't sure whether or not she believed him, but the truth was she hadn't seen Magnus in the area when the delivery was made. "There were a couple of bulky plastic bags delivered to the site," she told him, "and the shape and size of the bags, together with the lumpiness of the delivery, made me think there could be a dead body inside. But I have an overly active imagination and I've been known to jump to conclusions, which is why I haven't yet called the police."

"Leave the police out of this."

"Why should I listen to you?"

"Because I like you and I'm trying to help you."

"But you can't tell me what Povo's up to?"

He shook his head.

"If you're in some sort of trouble, Magnus, you need to get away from Povo, because in two weeks, when his fiancée returns from Europe, I'm going to set up a meeting with her and my boss and tell them everything. At that point, since I have no proof, I'll let them decide what needs to be done."

He scribbled his number on a napkin and handed it to her. "Here's my number in case you ever need to talk." He looked at his watch and then gazed into her eyes as if he were trying to decide how much he could tell her. "Stay safe, Jessica."

And that was it. She watched him walk away, wishing they had met under different circumstances. She didn't bother following him outside to see what kind of car he drove. She needed to think about things. Coffee with Magnus had been bittersweet.

She liked him. But he was hiding something, which meant he was too good to be true. Hayley was right. She needed to be careful. She needed to use her instincts, too. Magnus was twenty-nine. If he wasn't exaggerating about his degree or his fondness for rock climbing, he was smart and adventurous, and he was also a bad boy.

What's not to like?

Butterflies had flittered inside her belly the entire time he sat across from her. *Pathetic.* High school all over again.

For the next ten minutes, she sipped her coffee and read one of the magazines the coffee shop made available to customers. Her phone vibrated. She glanced at the caller ID and hit Talk. "He couldn't have possibly gotten to work already."

"He didn't go back to work," Hayley said.

Jessica's heart skipped a beat. "Where did he go after he left the coffee shop?"

"You're not going to like it."

"He met with Dominic Povo, didn't he?"

"Yes. Tommy's still watching him, but he called to let me know."

"Damn."

Silence.

Jessica let out a breath. "I need to check out the construction site when nobody else is there, maybe this Friday after the crew is gone. Do you think you could go with me?"

"I would love to."

"Thanks. I'll talk to you later." Jessica disconnected the call and stared straight ahead. The woman working the main counter came over and asked her if she needed anything.

"Men, boys, whatever," Jessica said, "they all suck."

"Yeah, they do. More coffee?"

"Sure."

CHAPTER 20

You feel the last bit of breath leaving their body. You're looking
into their eyes. A person in that situation is God!
—Ted Bundy

Sacramento
Thursday, May 31, 2012

As he lay in bed, staring at the ceiling but seeing only shadows of
darkness, his mind worked overtime.

Three days had passed since the bitch had bashed his nose
in. He didn't have the luxury of going to the hospital, but he was
certain it wasn't broken—maybe just fractured. But that didn't
mean he wasn't in pain. His face felt as if he'd been hit by a car.
It was a mess, a kaleidoscope of colors, and there was no way he
could stay on schedule now. His plan had been to be inside Kassie
Scott's house tomorrow afternoon. Now, with the way he was feeling, he was going to have to put things off for a week.

Lizzy Gardner was going to suffer for her bad behavior. No
more silly cat-and-mouse games. She would die, but not before
he strategized long and hard over her demise. There would
be torture involved, of course, and darkness and endless days
and nights of not knowing what would happen next. He knew

that going after her these past weeks had been a gamble. Just as screwing with Eli over the years was an added risk he didn't need to take. But fucking with other people's heads was just plain fun. When people like Eli tried to get into his business and mess with his everyday life, he liked to turn their nosy ways on them and show them who was boss—show them how powerless they really were.

He would lie low at his parents' house for a few more days.

He thought about better days when Mrs. Beck cooked for him, always aiming to please. The Becks had coddled him and treated him like he was still thirteen years old. It used to drive him absolutely insane; all that petting of his head and oohing and ahhing over his bullshit accomplishments.

But after the embalming incident, it seemed they spent their days and nights watching TV.

Their sudden coldness and lack of interest in him had been the turning point.

Everything had changed after that. Inevitable? Perhaps.

It was almost midnight, but he couldn't sleep. Pushing himself off of the bed, he caught his balance before he made his way to the window. It was an old window with a crank handle, and he had to put his muscle into it to get the window to open a few inches. No longer a young boy, he felt at ease amid the eerie high-pitched sound of the pine sawyer beetles.

Look. There was one now.

It took some doing, but he managed to get ahold of the beetle before it could disappear in the crevice of the window frame. He picked up the beetle and brought it within millimeters of his eyeball so he could examine it more closely, wondering why the beetle had ever spooked him to begin with. Then he popped the bug into his mouth and enjoyed the feeling of its legs on his tongue as it moved around, trying to find a way out. When he grew bored, he crunched down on its hard brittle body, enjoying its squeals right before he felt a squirt of bug juice drip down his throat. As he chewed and then finally swallowed, he tried to imagine what it would be like to be an insect with no brain, no thoughts, just a big dark canvas of nothingness.

Antelope
Friday, June 1, 2012

It was five minutes past eight and the sun was setting as Jessica parked her car. Hayley was sitting on the curb waiting for her just as she had said she would be. They were headed for the construction site to look for anything that might be suspect, like dead bodies. Povo and his crew should be long gone.

Hayley opened the passenger door and climbed in.

"What's going to happen if Lizzy beats you home and you're gone?" Jessica asked.

"I locked my door and went through the window. She'll think I'm sleeping."

It took them only a few minutes to get to where they needed to be. Jessica drove up to a curb and shut off the engine. They would walk over an empty field of dirt to get to the house.

Hayley pulled a tight cap over her head and then fastened an elastic band with a tiny flashlight around her forehead. Jessica had worn her hair in one long braid. No head covering needed.

Locate the garbage bags. In and out, that was their goal.

Neither of them said a word as they made their way across the field. The construction site was in a cul-de-sac. If they had parked next to the model homes or anywhere on the same street and somebody showed up, they would be trapped.

As they approached the site, Jessica scanned the area for vehicles. There were no cars or trucks parked near the unfinished home. No lights on in the trailer where Dominic Povo and his men worked during the day. Jessica had to jog to keep up with Hayley, who always walked with focus and determination. Tonight was no different.

The construction workers had done a good job of keeping debris in piles, no loose nails or random pieces of wood scattered. Jessica followed Hayley through the garage. All of the walls had been framed, as had the stairs. There were shingles on the roof, but doors and windows were still missing.

Hayley stopped and pointed to a dark plastic bag close to the door leading into the house. After turning on the minilight on her forehead, she undid the knot on the top of the bag and looked inside.

Jessica held her breath.

"Trash."

Thank God. "OK, let's check the house."

"Wait a minute," Hayley said. "Look at the ground."

Jessica came closer and peered at the area where Hayley pointed. Smooth gray concrete. "What is it?"

"The foundation is usually the first thing they pour before the framing begins. But this flooring was poured in the past forty-eight hours. It was just cured. I can smell it."

Shivers coursed up Jessica's spine. "This was a really dumb idea. I think we should go to the police."

"What are you going to tell them? That you saw a couple of large plastic bags being delivered to the site and you think there might be dead bodies buried beneath the garage floor?"

"OK, fine. Let's do a quick search and get this over with. In and out. We've already been here too long." Jessica decided this was by far the dumbest idea she'd ever had. She should have listened to Magnus and stayed away.

They headed inside. Jessica went upstairs while Hayley moved straight through the lower part of the house.

Upstairs, there were three bedrooms, all with good-sized closets. Jessica stepped into the master bedroom. Moonlight filtered in through the window opening. All of the rooms had been swept clean. An empty package of Camels sat on one of the windowsills, but that was it. No plastic bags stashed away in the unfinished closets.

Jessica froze at the sound of a car pulling into the driveway.

"Shit."

There were two windows in the room. She peeked out the window overlooking the driveway. Two vehicles pulled in and parked in front of the garage. Jessica ran to the top of the stairs. She took two steps down before she could hear male voices in the garage. If she took another step, they would see her for sure. She ran back to the room she'd just left and hid in the closet. She sank quietly down to the floor. Her heart thumped against her chest.

What was she thinking, coming here? She wanted to be a criminologist, not a policewoman or an investigator. Hoping Hayley had heard the cars and escaped through a window opening, she stuck her head out of the closet space and listened. The voices had moved to the backyard. She crawled across the floor and stopped beneath the window overlooking the yard. A patio area had also been newly poured with concrete, and there was a Dumpster half-filled with garbage.

Three male voices—they were arguing about something.

"Where's Povo?"

"He should be here any minute."

"We don't have time for your bullshit. Did you bring the money, or not?"

"He said he'd put it in that storage bin over there."

The last voice sounded familiar. Pressed to the wall, Jessica slid upward until she could see shadows outside. Based on his build alone, she knew one of the men. It was Magnus. As Magnus led the way to the storage bin and began to work on unlatching the bolt, she saw one of the guys following him pull out a knife.

She sprang to her feet, gasping and knocking the cigarette package out the window in the process.

All three men turned toward the sound.

Magnus must have seen the knife, because a struggle broke out. As they wrestled on the ground, she couldn't tell who was who.

"What are you doing?"

Jessica looked to where a door should be. Hayley stood under the frame, scowling. She ran inside, grabbed Jessica's arm, and ushered her down the stairs and out the way they had come, through the garage.

Pop. Pop.

Gunshots? Were they being shot at?

Hayley grabbed her arm, pushing her to run faster. The only sounds were their heavy breathing and the slap of their shoes against pavement as they sprinted down the street, across the road, away from the dirt field they had crossed to get to the house.

Hayley half climbed, half jumped over a four-foot chain-link fence that surrounded the model homes. "Hurry up," she said, pulling Jessica to the other side before she could jump.

Jessica's shirt snagged on something and ripped. Her left knee hit the sidewalk on the other side, but Hayley hardly gave her time to find her balance before she grabbed her arm again.

They were in the backyard that all three of the model homes shared. Hayley went to the house in the middle. She pulled out her keys and used them to fiddle with the screen on the window.

"What about the alarms?" Jessica asked. "There are signs all over the place."

"Those are fake. Besides, I already called the police."

"You could go to jail."

Hayley ignored her as she slid the window open and climbed inside. No alarms went off.

Once Jessica was inside, Hayley fixed the screen, closed the window, and then made sure the latch was secure before she went around making sure all of the doors and windows were locked.

"How did you know that window was unlocked?"

"I did a little research online."

"Oh."

"I figured the security signs they posted were bogus. The company is hanging on by its fingertips. They need to cut costs wherever they can."

"Those were gunshots, weren't they?"

"I think that's a safe bet."

"I never should have asked you to come here with me," Jessica said. "I'm sorry."

"You worry too much."

Jessica's hands shook. "Magnus could be dead or bleeding to death. I can't sit here and do nothing to help him."

"You have no idea if he's the good guy or the bad guy. Are you ready to die for him?"

Jessica knew she was right. She listened for the police sirens. Nothing yet.

Hayley disappeared upstairs while Jessica walked back and forth, worried about Magnus, wondering what the hell had just happened. She ran to the kitchen and peeked out through the wood blinds. Both trucks were still parked outside. She saw a shadowy figure step out of the garage.

She ducked, got down on all fours, and scrambled out of the kitchen. When she reached the stairs, she ran to the top of the landing, frantically searching room after room. "Hayley, where are you?"

"Over here. Keep your voice down and stay away from the windows. He's heading this way."

Jessica remained on the floor, her heart hammering against her chest. Not until she heard the sounds of the sirens did she dare to take a breath.

Sacramento
Friday, June 1, 2012

Lizzy's eyes darted from one side of the street to the other as she drove. Her car window was half open. Ten seconds ago, she had seen Eli Simpson make a right on this very street.

Where did he go?

Watchful and alert, she drove down the quiet street with her window rolled down. It was late and it was dark. The air outside was brisk. The only sound was the slow grinding of tires against asphalt. Thunder rumbled in the distance.

Unlike the street where she lived now, there were no street lamps on Bunker Street—no signs of life, for that matter. Most of the houses were dark, inside and out. There were a few cars parked in driveways, but that was it.

Her hands held tight to the steering wheel.

She finally spotted Eli's truck, parked to the left, empty. He had to be around here somewhere. Yep, there he was. Two blocks down, a shadow of a man. So this was where he spent his nights. Although Eli Simpson had given her his cell phone number, he hadn't answered any of her calls since she'd talked to him in the parking lot at the police station. She'd finally given up and driven to his house instead. No sooner had she turned onto his street than she had seen his truck pull out of the driveway. So she had done what any curious private eye would have. She had followed him.

She didn't know Eli, nor did she trust him, but there was something about him that made her believe his story. She had also run a quick search on Eli Simpson. His parents used to live in Lincoln, California. His mother had passed away recently from cancer. His parents' house was sold, and Lizzy assumed Eli's father had moved in with him at that time. Eli had two sisters. One was married with two kids and lived in Citrus Heights. The other sister had gone missing five years ago. There was no mention of her being murdered. No names had been cited in connection with her disappearance. In an article run in a local paper at the time of her disappearance, friends of Eli's sister told reporters that Rochelle was friendly and outgoing, the type of person who would never hesitate to help someone out if she could. For that reason, they suspected she might have been abducted.

Nice girls finished last.

A few feet away, Lizzy saw Eli's dark shadow. She pulled up to the curb next to him and shut off her lights. Eli Simpson was not a small man. He worked construction and it showed even beneath a dark hooded sweatshirt and denim.

She hit a button and rolled down the window on the passenger side.

He hesitated, but did finally come to the passenger side of her car and bend down so that he could pin her with a steely-eyed gaze.

"What are you doing here?" he asked.

"You wouldn't answer my calls. What was I supposed to do?"

"You were supposed to take a hint and leave me the hell alone."

"Yeah, well, there is that, but I don't give up easily. Last time we talked, you seemed interested in having me help you."

"Changed my mind." After a short pause he added, "I don't think you should be here."

"I know *you* shouldn't be here," Lizzy said. "Get in the car. Please. We need to talk."

He shook his head. "I don't think you should be here. The man is dangerous."

"Are you worried about me, Simpson?"

He said nothing.

"Tell me something: Let's pretend this man really did take your sister. If that were true, why would he take the risk of using your name on a workers' compensation claim? Why take the added risk of being found out?"

Both of Eli's hands were on the frame of her car door, his forehead pressed against the top part of the window frame. "I told you the guy was fucked up. Fucked-up people don't think logically. They just do."

"They just *do* what?"

"They screw with people's minds. Screw with people any way they can. A dozen people were shot and killed last month at a popular fast-food restaurant in Idaho."

"I heard."

"People sitting there having a bite to eat, everyone minding their own business, taking a break after a long day at work and school—families bringing their kids for a bit of fun. So some asshole comes in the place and blows their heads off. They didn't have a chance. Evil never dies."

Chills raced up her spine. She pointed to the house she assumed he'd been watching when she drove up. "So, who is that guy? What's his name?"

A light went on in the house.

They both watched as somebody moved around the front room. Eli's gaze was intense as he observed every movement the shadow made.

"Is that him? Is that your guy?"

Without answering her question, he looked back at Lizzy. His eyes were filled with distrust. "How did you find me?"

"I've been digging since I saw you last, looking up anything I could find regarding your missing sister—"

"You followed me here."

She nodded.

He arched a brow. "So you consider yourself to be the real deal?"

She figured he was asking whether or not she was a real investigator, so she answered in the affirmative.

"I already know you carry a gun."

"I do."

"Do you understand privacy rights—the difference between videotaping from the building across the street versus looking into someone's front window?"

She sighed. "I crossed the line. I'm sorry about that."

"I bet you're only sorry you were caught."

"Not in this case," she said. "If you hadn't caught me, I would still be watching your father collect the mail every day—boring and a huge waste of time."

"Are you calling my father boring?"

Before she could attempt to pull her foot out of her mouth, he said, "I bet you cross the line more often than you would care to admit."

"Truthfully," she said, "I don't think I cross it nearly often enough."

He smiled, realized he was doing so, and quickly put a stop to it.

Lizzy was beginning to see that Eli Simpson was a lot of bark and not too much bite. She relaxed, but only a little. "So, how many of these people in the neighborhood have you talked to?"

"I've knocked on every door dozens of times over the years. Only one person agreed to talk to me in all the years I've been coming here. By the time I convinced a detective to follow up, she recanted her story."

"Why?"

"I'm guessing my guy, as you're fond of calling him, had a chat with her, threatened to put an end to her Tuesday-night bingo or maybe kill her pet canary. Whatever it was, it worked."

"Not too much action around here, then?"

"I don't come here every night. I do have a business to run."

"Can I ask you for a favor?"

"You can ask."

She reached into her glove compartment and pulled out a sleek little camera. "This beauty takes pictures, close up and far away, night and day. Since you're here anyhow, could you try to get a picture of him?"

"Of John Robinson?"

"Is that his name?" Lizzy asked.

"I thought you said you've been digging."

"Let's just say I've been preoccupied. That's why I followed you. I needed a name."

"Well, now you have one."

"So, you'll take a picture if you get the chance?"

He took the camera. "Digital?"

She nodded.

"I hope the pay is good."

"It depends on the quality of the picture."

"I was joking."

"I know."

"So, I guess this means we're working together."

"I guess it does."

"What's next?" he asked.

"Do you know what John Robinson does for a living?"

"He works for a small business downtown. He also buys nice clothes and drives a Camry. Every once in a while he has some work done in the house or in the backyard, which tells me he must be independently wealthy."

She gave the house and the neighborhood another fleeting look. "If that were true, why would he live here?"

"Because monsters don't just live in closets and caves; they live in dark scary houses on neglected streets like this one."

She looked more closely at Eli and asked, "Why is there a restraining order against you?"

"Are you being nosy?"

"We're working together," she said with a shrug. "I need to know who and what I'm dealing with."

He leaned his body closer, his face jutting in through her window.

She stiffened as she watched him transform back to his intimidating self.

"What you need to know," he said, "is that you're now working with one pissed-off motherfucker. I've done nothing wrong and yet the monster living in that house over there has managed to turn my entire family against me. *Me*," he said with annoyed emphasis, his face a maze of angry lines. "The only guy in the world who seems to care enough to want to know what happened to Rochelle Simpson, my sister."

Silence hovered over them, thick and palpable. Lizzy remained silent.

"Rochelle didn't deserve to die."

It made Lizzy nervous, the way he kept talking about his sister being dead as if he truly knew that for a fact. Nobody could know whether or not a person was dead until a body was found.

He pulled away, giving her some distance, and rested his arms against the window frame.

She took a breath.

"John Robinson wasn't the first loser Rochelle brought home to meet the family," Eli said. "She liked to make everybody's day a little brighter. I wasn't the only one who told her that one of these days her kindness was going to get the best of her, but I was definitely the last person to tell her so."

"Was she dating him?"

His shoulders sank, not in defeat but in maddening resentment. It was obvious he was fighting to control his own monstrous demons, fighting to keep them tucked away somewhere inside him where they belonged. Finally he lifted his head, his jaw clenched as he said, "Nope. Never. Read my lips: she was just being nice."

"Did John Robinson think they were dating?"

"Absolutely."

CHAPTER 21

There is no happiness without tears, no life without death.
Beware! I am going to make you cry!
—Lucian Staniak

Carmichael
Saturday, June 2, 2012

Lizzy hadn't comprehended how much she missed Jared. And the funny thing was that at that very moment, she was sitting in the passenger seat of his car, admiring his hard jaw, handsome lips, regular chin, and nose. He was right there. If she reached out, she could touch him, yet she still missed him.

"Thanks for coming with me," she said. Lately he'd been away more than he'd been home. Long conversations were no longer the norm. They rarely had time to talk, which had led to a downward spiral in the intimacy department. She hadn't helped matters by keeping the attack in the park from him. He felt betrayed, as if she didn't trust him enough to tell him what had happened. Clearly, he was disappointed.

Thirty-two years old and she'd never been in a long-term relationship before now. Maybe this was how the whole thing worked:

incredible highs and depressing lows, inner turmoil, loud silence, hot sex, no sex, start over again.

Although Jared had his own caseload to deal with, they were on their way to Michael and Jennifer Dalton's house. Soon after Michael was arrested, his parents had moved into his house so they could take care of things like collecting mail and feeding the cat. They knew that Lizzy believed Michael was innocent, and since they wanted to help him, they agreed to let her look around. Mostly, Michael Dalton's parents wanted their only son back home, where he belonged.

"Anything new on the case you're working on?" Lizzy asked.

"The Lovebird Killer is doing a decent job of staying one step ahead of us, which tells me he's a quiet man, living what appears to most to be a normal life."

"Haven't most of the killings occurred in Sacramento?"

Jared nodded. "I suspect the unsub is living in the area."

"What's his MO?"

"In three of the cases, including the most recent one, the female is taken first. Husband, boyfriend, or partner reports female missing, and within forty-eight hours husband disappears, too. Every police department within Sacramento County has been instructed to inform the FBI immediately of any missing person reported."

"Do you think he targets couples because of a relationship gone bad?"

"I would guess that the unsub is lonely and has had continuous problems with lasting love. Maybe he doesn't want others to have what he feels he's been denied."

"Any suspects?"

"Nobody specific. Caucasian. Single male. An introvert. A man in his thirties who likes to inflict pain because it makes him feel powerful and in control."

She reached a hand to Jared's shoulder and squeezed. His muscles were tight. "I'm sorry I didn't tell you right away."

"Are you going to fight me on hiring security?"

"No."

Following the navigator's instructions, he took the next exit. A few minutes later, they arrived at their destination. Jared shut off the engine and then looked at Lizzy and said, "It's going to be OK. Me, you, Hayley, life…everything is going to be OK."

Davis
Saturday, June 2, 2012

Before Jessica reached the entrance to Lizzy's house, Hayley opened the door and said, "Lizzy and Jared left, let's go."

Jessica made an about-face and limped back toward her car while Hayley locked up the house.

"Something wrong?" Hayley asked as she caught up to her.

"No."

"You're usually all saccharine and gushy smiles."

"I'm fine."

"You're limping."

"I'm not as good at jumping fences as you are," Jessica said. "Did you tell Lizzy what we did last night?"

"No, she has enough problems right now."

"What did Jared say when he saw Lizzy's face?"

"He was upset with her. I have a feeling he's going to be her shadow for a few days."

"What do you think is going on? Break-ins, car crashes, weird bugs left in her office, and then she's attacked in the park. It's like Spiderman all over again."

"She definitely attracts the weirdos," Hayley said.

Jessica looked from her left to her right and then over her shoulder.

"What are you looking for, a hit man?"

That was exactly what Jessica was afraid she might see: a giant of a man with bulky arms, hands the size of melons, and shiny metal teeth like the guy in the Bond movies.

The man coming toward the model home last night had been scared off by the blaring sounds of the police sirens. When Jessica peered out the window again, both cars in the driveway across the street were gone. A few minutes after that, two patrol cars showed up. It took three uniformed officers only ten minutes to check out the house before they returned to their vehicles and drove away.

"You need to settle down," Hayley said. "Everything's going to be fine."

Easy for her to say. Was Magnus OK? Jessica wondered. Had he driven away in one of the cars? She wished she had given Magnus her number, because then he might call. If she could at least hear his voice, she would know he was alive.

Jessica climbed behind the wheel and started the engine. It was Saturday. She should be sitting on a park bench reading a good book, or reorganizing her closet. Instead, she was headed for a strip joint with one of the surliest, most hardheaded people she'd ever met.

Hayley was grateful for the quiet while they drove on Highway 50 toward Rancho Cordova. During her last visit to the same city, Hayley had shown Adele's picture around, and it wasn't long before she was told by a man working at a doughnut shop that Adele Hampton worked at Centerfold. He'd recognized Adele right away—not that the doughnut man ever went to Centerfold, of course, but because, apparently, as the man stated, "Adele was pregnant at the time and she really liked doughnuts."

When Hayley did a search on the Internet, sure enough, Adele's photo had been listed on the Centerfold website, and she was scheduled to dance this afternoon.

"Are you sure you only have to be eighteen to get into this place?"

"Positive," Hayley said. "They don't serve alcohol. It's just a bunch of half-naked women walking around selling lemonade and sandwiches."

"Wonderful."

"You don't have to go inside if you don't want to."

"I can handle it."

Hayley rolled the window down so she could get some air.

"Can I ask you something?" Jessica asked.

Hayley breathed in, filling her lungs with fresh air, before she said, "Sure."

"Have you ever really felt strongly about a guy, someone you just met? Someone you hardly even knew?"

"You're talking about Magnus, aren't you?"

Jessica kept her eyes on the road as she nodded.

"You hardly know him and he's obviously not the kind of character you want to get to know better."

Jessica sighed. "I keep telling myself it's crazy, but I'm worried about him. What if they hurt him last night?"

More silence.

"What if there are bodies buried in that garage?"

"Right now we need to stay away from that place and lie low. You could call the police again, but they've already been there once and I don't think they're going to start jackhammering the garage floor based on what little you saw. You never gave Magnus your number, right?"

"No, but he did give me his number when we met in the coffee shop."

"The business card he gave you was a fake, by the way."

"Why didn't you tell me?"

"I'm telling you now. I called the number and it was disconnected. Then I did a quick search on the handyman business, and his name doesn't exist. What did he tell you in the coffee shop? Was he expecting you to call him?"

"I'm not sure, I guess so," Jessica said. "I don't know if I can handle this—"

"Handle what?"

"Working for Lizzy. It's dangerous and I don't think I'm cut out for this type of work."

"You can't quit, Jessica. Not right now, not yet. Lizzy needs you. Tell me about the woman who hired Lizzy to watch Dominic Povo. Have you talked to her about everything that's going on?"

"She's in Europe for a few weeks."

"Then let's hold off on the Povo case until she returns. Until then, don't go near the construction site and, whatever you do, don't call the other number Magnus gave you. He could be dangerous."

Carmichael
Saturday, June 2, 2012

The Dalton house was a two-story set in Carmichael off Clover Street. Michael's mother, Mrs. Dalton, was in her seventies. Her eyes were kind, but the pain there was unmistakable. After introducing her husband, Harold, she busied herself in the kitchen. Harold Dalton was short and stocky. His hair was more white than gray. His khaki pants were pulled high on his waist and his brown belt was cinched tight. Harold followed close at Jared's heels as Jared made his way upstairs, giving Lizzy the perfect opportunity to cut to the right.

She opened the first door she came to and found herself inside the garage—an oversized room with plenty of workspace.

One corner of the garage was reserved for tools: a gray steel toolbox filled to the brim with nails, screwdrivers, and wrenches. A half wall above the workbench was covered with hammers and saws, all neatly hung. Most of the back wall was made up of open-wire shelving. She headed that way and began to search through the mishmash of items: endless piles of books, picture frames, paint supplies, holiday decorations. There were golf clubs to her left and bikes hanging from the ceiling to her right.

Lizzy looked at the only car parked inside the garage. It was the same one she'd seen parked in front of Jennifer's office downtown. She opened the door, climbed in behind the wheel, and simply sat there for a moment. Then she opened the center console: gum, tissues, loose coins. She checked the glove compartment next. Neatly folded papers, owner's manual, proof of insurance. Nothing unusual. Nothing out of place.

She climbed out of the car, shut the door, then moved to the rear and popped the trunk.

Empty and clean.

With a sigh, she moved to the door leading into the house and gave the garage one last look, her gaze slowly scanning the entire room. There was an attic marked by a wooden door with a pull-down chain. She would find out if they could move the car so she could climb up for a quick look. Next, her gaze fell on the shoe rack by the door. Two rows of neatly placed shoes beneath a row of winter coats. There were hiking boots for him and her. Two pairs of women's running shoes. One pair looked brand new. She leaned forward to get a closer look at the pink mesh and flex grooves along the length of the midsole. Something was stuffed inside.

She picked up the shoe. Those were not socks inside. Kneeling down, she turned the shoe over and gasped as dead pine sawyer beetles fell to the ground.

Rancho Cordova
Saturday, June 2, 2012

The Centerfold parking lot in Rancho Cordova was filled with eighteen-year-old boys loitering around. Nobody paid any attention to Jessica and Hayley as they made their way inside.

The cover charge was steep at twenty dollars each. No alcohol allowed, but there was unlimited lemonade and raspberry punch. In one of the booths, a guy was getting a private lap dance that really wasn't very private. Jessica cringed.

There were two stages. The place was dank and dark and not overly crowded. She walked stiffly behind Hayley, who seemed perfectly at ease as they took a seat near the front of the first stage.

After the waitress took their order, Jessica did her best to keep her gaze straight ahead and away from the lap dance going on nearby. It wasn't easy to ignore. "Why do guys come to these places?"

Hayley shrugged. "To hang with their buddies. To socialize. They can't touch the girls, so the lap dances are a big tease."

The waitress set two lemonades on the table and said she'd be back with the food in a minute.

"I'd rather live on the streets than work in a place like this."

"These women are trying to earn a living like everyone else in the world," Hayley said. "And they understand what men like and need. What's the big deal?"

"I guess you're right." Jessica drank the lemonade they served, but ignored the food when it was brought to the table. She'd lost her appetite the moment she'd walked inside the place. Two different girls were dancing on stage, making Jessica blush. She wanted to find Adele Hampton and get out of here. The walls were covered with eleven-by-fourteen pictures of the strippers who danced at the club. The music was loud techno remixes of popular songs of the day.

"That's her," Hayley said.

Jessica looked up and saw a new girl on the stage in front of them. Hayley waved a twenty-dollar bill at the girl, making Jessica even more uncomfortable.

The girl climbed down the stairs and approached Hayley.

"Is your name Adele?" Hayley asked.

"Who wants to know?"

"We do. This is Jessica and I'm Hayley."

Adele took the twenty and slipped it between her breasts, where it disappeared completely. "I'm Adele. Enjoy the show."

Hayley pulled out another twenty. "Your mom is looking for you."

Adele rolled her eyes and started to turn away again without bothering to touch the second bill that Hayley held outward.

"Your biological mom," Hayley added, "not the one who raised you."

Adele turned to face Hayley again. "Does she know I work here?"

It was hard for Jessica to tell if the girl was worried or excited.

"No," Hayley said. "Nobody knows but the two of us."

"Did she hire you?"

"Yes. We work for a private investigator in Sacramento."

"Does she live in the area?"

"Your biological mom lives in New York, but she located your adoptive parents. When you used their credit card, you left an easy enough trail to follow."

"It couldn't have been that easy, since my parents didn't find me."

"They never looked," Hayley said.

Jessica felt sick at how callous Hayley's words sounded. The girl's adoptive parents had never bothered to look for her. Adele tried to hide the hurt beneath a grunt and a smirk, but the pain and the sadness of it all was right there in her eyes, plain as day.

Adele spared Jessica a quick glance before she looked back at Hayley. "Do you know why I left?"

Hayley shook her head.

"I was pregnant. I didn't know what to do. I was scared, and for the first time in my life, I think I understood why my mother gave me up."

Hayley didn't ask Adele to explain, Jessica noticed, she just waited patiently.

"I was told that my biological mother got pregnant at a young age. I never understood why she would give her baby up. I never wanted to understand it—not until it happened to me." Adele tapped the table with her long, manicured nail. "My adoptive parents had big plans for me, high hopes. Harvard, Stanford, only the best for their little girl. God, I was such a bitter and angry little girl. They gave me everything. I gave them nothing in return. No, that's not true. I gave them grief, plenty of grief. I don't blame them for not looking for me. I wouldn't have looked for me either. So," Adele added after a short pause, "what's next?"

"Did you have the child?" Jessica asked.

Adele smiled. "Yes, I did. She's the sweetest little girl in Placer County."

"I don't get it," Jessica said. "Your adoptive parents went to all the trouble of adopting you and raising you as their own, but they let you walk out of their life because you were pregnant?"

"They knew they had raised me better than that. I knew better, I just didn't do better. I don't blame them."

"Do you want to meet your mother?" Hayley asked.

"I'm not sure."

Hayley grabbed a napkin from the canister and scribbled her name and number on it. "If you decide you want to meet her, give me a call."

Jessica wondered what Hayley was up to. That wasn't part of the deal. If a client hired them to find somebody, that was that.

"Keep this, too," Hayley said, handing her the other twenty.

Adele took the napkin and the money and walked off.

"You can't keep this from Lizzy," Jessica told her. "You have to tell her that you found Adele."

"I can and I will keep it from Lizzy, and so will you, because it's the right thing to do."

"It's unethical."

"Are you fucking kidding me? Who are you? When are you going to wake up and get it?"

"Get what?"

"That the world is not black and white. It's fucking yellow and purple and gray and blue."

"What does that even mean?"

"It means that the world is a kaleidoscope of colors, people, places, situations. People think they have to follow the stupid-ass recipe because it's in writing. If you don't like salt, leave out the salt, for God's sake!"

Jessica stiffened, praying that nobody else was listening to the crazy girl sitting across from her.

"Right and wrong—that's what it all comes down to," Hayley went on. "Plain and simple. Nothing else matters. If it feels wrong, it is wrong. If something you do," Hayley said, pointing at Jessica, "hurts another person, causes them pain in one form or another, then it's wrong. If something you do hurts no one but yourself, then you have a choice to make. Your choice. Not mine, not the guy over there jacking off in the corner, not Lizzy's."

"But what if it's your job to find out information and you're getting paid to do it?"

"Let them fire you. If something is wrong, then it's wrong. Getting paid to hurt someone is double wrong. If Adele doesn't want to be found, I'm not going to be the one to tell everyone where she is. Lizzy can hire someone else to find her if she doesn't like it."

Jessica sighed. Then she stood and said, "I get it. Can we go now?"

Carmichael
Saturday, June 2, 2012

By three o'clock, the Dalton garage was roped off as an official crime scene.

Lizzy and Jared stood outside the garage, looking in. It was raining again. An hour ago, the sun had looked as if it might make an appearance, but the dark clouds had won out and now the rain was coming down hard.

Lizzy had borrowed an umbrella from the garage. She'd been afraid to open it, afraid a zillion beetles would fall out onto the street, but this was her lucky day, she supposed, since the umbrella turned out to be bug-free.

Although she tried to share the umbrella with Jared, he kept coming and going, talking on his phone one minute, and then instructing the technicians the next. At the moment, he stood at her side as water dripped down his face and off his nose and chin.

"So, what do you think?" Lizzy asked him.

"Definitely a connection between the Lovebird Killer and the Daltons," he said. "Might be a bigger connection than even you imagined."

"What do you mean? They're not pointing their finger at Michael, are they?"

"Lizzy," Jared said in a tone he usually used on Hayley, "what is it with you and this Michael guy?"

"What do you mean?"

"You're very protective of him and you supposedly met him… what…a total of three times?"

"What do you mean *supposedly*? I met him three times."

"I talked to Greer. He said that you met with Stacey Whitmore, the reporter, at her home in Granite Bay."

"I did. What about it?"

"What did she say about Michael Dalton?"

"Stacey says he's about as good as any man can be."

"She's married to Dan Whitmore, the divorce lawyer who is in the news more often than not."

"That's right. I believe he's also serving as a consultant for the popular nighttime drama *Cheaters*. I haven't met Dan, but Stacey did share one of their family albums with me. Stacey Whitmore and Michael Dalton dated in college, but that relationship ended when Michael met Jennifer. The two remained friends, and both couples have been enjoying family vacations together for years."

"They were having an affair," Jared blurted.

"What?" Lizzy was completely thrown off guard. "Who?"

"Jennifer Dalton and Dan Whitmore."

Lizzy couldn't believe what she was hearing.

Jared didn't say anything more, he merely stood in the rain and let the information settle in until Lizzy probed further.

"I'm assuming Greer just gave you the news?"

He nodded.

"That bitch."

"Who?"

"Jennifer Dalton, who else?"

"What about Dan Whitmore?"

"He's an asshole, but that goes without saying. What about Stacey?" she asked.

"What about her?"

"Did she have any idea?"

"She's known about the affair for years."

Lizzy stood there and let it all sink in. "Jesus Christ."

"I don't think this information is going to help Michael's case much."

"I think not."

Lizzy gestured toward the garage. "I guess this makes Michael Dalton look like a jealous and angry man and now, with the bugs, also your prime suspect?"

"Possibly."

"I've been working my ass off trying to free a serial killer?"

"It's too early in the game to go down that road, Lizzy. If not for you, we wouldn't be standing here now in front of the Daltons' garage. Give yourself a pat on the back instead. Will you do that?"

She snorted.

"Just this once?"

"Don't worry," she finally said. "I'm not going to blame myself for every crazed lunatic out there." As Lizzy stood there watching the technicians gather evidence, she realized the idea of Michael Dalton being the Lovebird Killer did not compute. She had looked into the eyes of a serial killer for months on end—flat, empty, lifeless eyes. Michael Dalton was not a killer, and nobody, not even the man she loved, could convince her otherwise.

"I'm not perfect," Jared said, "but I'll promise you one thing."

She lifted the umbrella higher so she could get a good look at him as he spoke.

"I'll never lie to you. And I would never cheat."

"I know," she said. And it was true. If there was one thing in this godforsaken world that she could count on, it was Jared Shayne. She never had to question his love for her. Before she could offer him any promises of her own, his cell rang and he put the phone to his ear and walked away.

CHAPTER 22

I took her bra and panties off and had sex with her. That's one of those things I guess that got to be a part of my life—having sexual intercourse with the dead.
—Henry Lee Lucas

Davis
Tuesday, June 5, 2012

After disconnecting the motion sensor Jared had installed, Hayley opened the window and crawled out. As she shut the window, she felt a twinge of guilt at the thought of leaving the house unsecured. Not wanting to disturb any dogs in the neighborhood, she walked as fast as she could without letting her heels clap too hard against the pavement. She'd asked Tommy to meet her at the corner of Meadow and Leighton. At first she thought he might have chickened out, but then she saw him sitting on the curb near his bike. He wore all black and blended into the night. Until this moment, she'd never seen him wearing anything other than bright colors.

An unfamiliar fluttering of excitement raced up her spine.

"Hi," she said as she approached, feeling twitches of happiness, something she hadn't felt in a very long time.

"Hi," he said, pushing himself to his feet.

She let her gaze roam down to his boots. "The whole black thing looks good on you."

"Thanks."

He unhooked an extra helmet from his bike and handed it to her. "We should get going before the neighborhood wakes up and comes out here to see what's going on."

He climbed on the bike first.

She put on her helmet, fastened the chin strap, and hooked a leg over the seat. She barely had time to latch onto him before he turned on the ignition and took off. She held tighter. Maybe that was his plan. Either way, she didn't care.

She was enjoying herself.

The air smelled crisp and fresh. She was free.

For thirty minutes, she held her arms snug around his waist as he headed down a maze of dark and narrow streets. When they finally slowed, he turned onto a dirt road. It was long, windy, and steep, and she had to use muscles she didn't know she had to keep from falling off the back of the bike. Once they reached the top of the hill, he turned off the ignition.

She climbed off and so did Tommy. No words were spoken between them as he opened a bag hooked to the tank, pulled out a blanket, and laid it out on the ground. They both lay flat on their backs and stargazed. The night was cool. The rain had stopped hours ago.

"I'm glad you called me," he said, gazing upward.

Hayley didn't know what to say to that. She wanted to thank him, but that sort of thing did not come easily to her, if at all. Every emotion inside her felt raw and new. Anger she could handle. Disappointment, fear, sadness, she knew them well, but surprise and joy—not so much. One thing for sure, it felt good to be free.

They both lay straight and stiff, arms at their sides.

"Are you OK?" he asked.

Frogs croaked in the distance.

"I am," she said. "I'm OK."

"Life is strange," he said next.

"How so?"

"The two of us here right now, stargazing. Didn't see that coming."

She smiled. "Do you come here often?"

"I've been coming here for years."

Silence.

"You're the only one I've ever brought here with me," he said.

"I'm flattered."

He laughed.

"You're a contradiction," she told him. "Color coordinated one day and all black and mysterious the next."

"I don't try to be anything I'm not. I just go with the mood. I'm far from mysterious."

She tried to find a constellation and finally gave up. "What made you become a karate expert?" she asked.

"I grew up being bullied—verbally and physically. Those kids you hear about who had their lunch taken from them? That was me. Every single day the bullies came after me."

"What about your family?"

"They're great—Mom, Dad, two sisters—but they couldn't help me."

"Why not?"

"For years I didn't tell anyone. I didn't want to upset my parents. My sisters figured it out when they saw firsthand what was going on at school. They tried to help when they could, but at my particular school there were more bullies than not. One of my sisters finally told Mom and Dad, but my parents had no idea how bad it had gotten, not until I ended up in the hospital in my junior year of high school."

"What happened?"

"A few broken bones, a cracked rib. My straight aristocratic nose has not been the same since."

His attempt at humor didn't work. "So, you started taking karate lessons?"

"My dad brought a friend to the house—a karate expert named Kyro. He gave me private lessons, taught me everything I know. After I returned to school, it wasn't long before I had the chance to show a few kids what I'd learned over the summer. Things improved after that, but I refused to change. I didn't want to dress differently just to fit in. By then, I didn't want to fit in, period. I didn't mind being different. In fact, I always found myself drawn to the kids who danced to their own music."

"And that's what you do, isn't it? Befriend misfits, people like me?"

"Is that what you are, a misfit?"

"I don't like to put labels on people, especially on myself," Hayley answered. "I'm sure I have misfit qualities, though. I'm an introvert and I tend to follow my own beliefs. If people don't like me, that's their problem. I don't intentionally go out of my way to hurt people. Although I'm sure you heard that I cut off a man's penis, I'm not insane. He deserved everything he got."

"Did you feel better afterward?"

"No."

"Would you do it again if you had the chance to go back in time?"

"I wouldn't want to find out."

The stars were incredibly bright, Hayley thought. She was actually living in the moment and she liked it. Her breathing was slow and even as awareness settled over her: the croaking of frogs, the woodsy smell after a good long rain, and the feel of his warm hand settling upon her left hand.

She wasn't sure how she felt about his hand being on hers. She didn't like people touching her, but his fingers felt warm, so she let it be.

Sacramento
Wednesday, June 6, 2012

Early Wednesday morning, Stacey Whitmore marched into Lizzy's office on J Street in Sacramento. She was dressed in a tweed suit jacked trimmed with fringe and a matching skirt. Her expression was grim, her face pale. "You have to help him," Stacey said as the door closed behind her. "You can't abandon Michael now, when he needs you most."

Lizzy angled her head. "Are you kidding me?" She stabbed a finger toward Stacey and added, "You're the one who deserted him. The moment you lied to me, you muddled the facts and lost all credibility. Get out of my office."

Stacey didn't seem to be afraid or intimidated by anyone. A grizzly bear could appear out of thin air and the woman wouldn't flinch. She stepped closer to Lizzy's desk, her expression unwavering. "Michael is innocent," she said. "Nothing else matters."

"Are you in love with Michael Dalton?"

"Yes."

"Is he in love with you?"

"No."

"His wife was sleeping with your husband," Lizzy said. "More than likely, she would still be sleeping with him if she wasn't dead. But you are determined to help Jennifer's husband?"

"Because he's innocent."

"Justice for all. That's all that matters?"

"That's right."

"Why would you go to all the bother of getting me involved and yet not arm me with all the information you had?"

"Because I knew if I told you about the affair, Michael's innocence would get lost in the middle of all the dirty laundry."

Lizzy narrowed her eyes as she thought about Stacey's answer. "How is your husband handling Jennifer's death?"

"I wouldn't know. I hardly ever see him. I'm sure he's dealing with it the same way he's always handled disappointment: drowning his sorrows in his work."

"Does he believe Michael's story?"

"Absolutely."

"So, I take it you and Michael both knew that your significant others were messing around?"

She nodded.

Lizzy wasn't sure what to think about that, so she let it go for now. "Please explain to me why you are so intent on me being the one to help Michael."

"Forget about who's sleeping with whom," Stacey said. "You know Michael is innocent. And the media is still fascinated by you. If you believe he's innocent, others will, too. It's the way the world works. That's why celebrities can sell ice water in Alaska."

Lizzy sighed. "And here I was hoping it had something to do with my reputation as a decent investigator."

"That, too, of course."

"I need some time to think."

Stacey's smile looked strained, but she nodded and then turned to leave.

Lizzy wanted to tell her about the beetles found at Michael's house. She wanted to let her know that the man she was in love with could very well be a serial killer. But she wasn't about to jeopardize the case. Stacey would find out soon enough.

As she watched Stacey cross the street to her car, she couldn't shake the feeling that Stacey was right—Michael was innocent. And the answer was right there under her nose: the pine sawyer beetle.

The beetles had been left in her office for a reason. If Michael was truly innocent, then whoever had left beetles in Jennifer's shoe was the same man who had left beetles in Lizzy's office. And whoever it was, he didn't like Lizzy getting involved.

Sacramento
Friday, June 8, 2012

As he walked through the Scotts' house, he decided that being forced to wait an extra week had heightened his enjoyment now that he was here. His nose was still sore, but doing much better. He had big plans for Lizzy Gardner, and he looked forward to strategizing further, even planned to call her later and get the dialogue going. But for now, his plan was to focus solely on Kassie and Drew Scott.

He thought about how he would tell Kassie exactly what he planned to do with her. That was his favorite part. He would explain in detail how he was going to kill her first, dismember her, and then have sex with her corpse while her husband watched. When he was done with her, he would kill her husband and dismember him, too. And then, purely for shits and giggles, switch arms and legs and sew them back together again.

A smile curved his lips as he thought about reconstructing her best features with her husband's. It was something he'd fantasized about doing when his foster parents embalmed more than one person at a time. The Becks, his adoptive parents, had had a wicked sense of humor, but they'd had no clue that their "son" had an even more bizarre side to him—not until investigators showed up at their door to discuss two bodies embalmed by their company. Both corpses, it was discovered, had been stuffed with live pine sawyer beetles.

He was only seventeen at the time. His parents hadn't even questioned him. They knew. To keep the media at bay, though, they quickly pleaded guilty, paid a fine of $1,200, and got a reverse mortgage on their rental across town to pay off the parents of the victims. It was all dealt with in a matter of weeks, then quickly swept under the rug and left there for good.

The people were already dead. What was the big deal?

After that incident, it was never the same between him and the Becks. They stopped calling him "son," and he stopped calling them Mom and Dad.

Love was fleeting.

Now you see it, now you don't.

As he admired dozens of framed pictures of Kassie and Drew hanging on the wall, the memories of his past quickly faded. He looked closely at the picture of the Scotts hiking the Appalachians, Kassie and Drew on a raft in the river, Kassie and Drew on their wedding day, both smiling and happy.

He moved onward. His shoes sank into the plush cream-colored carpet. His heart beat faster and excitement built with each step. He'd been watching Kassie and Drew Scott for months now. Stalking his prey was pleasurable, but nothing compared with the gratification he got when it came to torturing them—the fear in their eyes and the diminishing hope. His favorite act was to perform spur-of-the-moment surgeries. No anesthesia needed, just a strip of duct tape over the mouth.

It was almost 2:00 p.m. on Friday. Every Friday night, Kassie's husband, Drew, shot hoops with the guys after work. Shooting hoops was sometimes followed by a trip to a local watering hole where they drank a few beers. Drew wouldn't be home until later; seven would be his earliest time of arrival if he skipped the beers. Kassie, too, often took off from work early on Fridays. She was a highly regarded psychologist who worked with emotionally disturbed children. That was one of the things about her that had put her and her husband at the top of his list.

Kassie Scott intrigued him. He looked forward to dissecting her brain—literally and figuratively.

The excitement and power he felt as he strolled through the Scotts' house made him dizzy with excitement. A curio cabinet with two-way glass sliding doors showed off a display of wedding pictures, crystal flute glasses delicately engraved with messages of love, and handwritten vows. All the memorabilia sent him over the top. He slid open a door, reached inside, and removed the lid from a heart-shaped crystal dish. He then dug into his pant pocket and withdrew two live beetles. The insects appeared dazed by the journey. He used the tip of his finger to play with them, petting each one equally before placing them inside the dish and replacing the lid.

As he wove a path through a maze of ultramodern furniture, his musings focused on what he was going to do with Kassie when he was alone with her, just the two of them. He hadn't brought anyone to his special hideout in quite a while. It took a lot of planning to get someone to his hideout unseen, which is why he didn't do it as often as he'd like.

One of the reasons he'd waited so long was that the people of Sacramento were beginning to get a little too vocal with talk of forming vigilante groups. Their fear was driving the FBI to work longer and harder on his case. But he knew better than most that the good guys were understaffed. By the time they responded to leads on one homicide, he'd already disposed of his next victims. As long as he mixed things up and dished out unreliable leads like Michael Dalton, he wasn't worried.

The show must go on, he thought, then chuckled to himself.

The dining room table was one of those modern tables with a marble top. It was surrounded by four chairs with black leather upholstery and accented with a crystal bowl of fruit. He reached for the grapes and didn't realize they were plastic until they were inches from his mouth. Using the tip of his long tongue, he licked one grape and then another.

The sharp ring of the doorbell caused his heart rate to soar. He could literally feel the rich fluid pumping through his arteries, spreading nutrients and oxygen to his cells. Tossing the grapes back into the bowl with a *clink* and a *clank*, he moved quickly to the bedroom in the front of the house so he could peek out the window and see who was at the door.

False alarm.

A delivery truck was parked at the curb. The driver, a young man in a brown suit, had left a package at the door and was already in the process of climbing behind the wheel of his truck.

The unexpected ring of the doorbell had given him a wonderful jolt of pleasure. He liked a good challenge, and couldn't help but imagine all the ways he could have entertained the driver until Kassie arrived home. That guy would never have known what hit him. And yet, of course, he never would have tried such a stunt. He wasn't stupid.

A killer could fantasize, right?

He inspected the guestroom: green walls, a four-poster iron bed, and a huge picture of a naked woman wrapped in a towel, her back to the artist. Boring. Nothing to write home about. He exited the room and headed upstairs. He stepped inside the master bedroom and smiled. The room was open, spacious, and tastefully decorated. He relished going through other people's things. The master bedroom often held the most intimate items, even secrets if you searched long enough.

Every part of him tingled as he looked around, trying to decide where to start. In the dresser drawers? The closet? Under the bed?

An open book lay facedown on the bedside table on the right side of the bed. The title caught his attention: *Love Is Not Enough: The Treatment of Emotionally Disturbed Children* by Bruno Bettelheim. He sat down on the bed and then stretched himself out, facing the ceiling. He wiggled his legs and arms to test the firmness of the mattress.

Not too bad.

Rolling to his side, he removed a pillow from beneath the top cover, gently stuffed his nose into it, and took a long whiff, breathing in and out until he began to feel dizzy. Then he grabbed the book from the table and began to read where he assumed Kassie, not Drew, had left off.

Davis
Friday, June 8, 2012

After calling Hayley and Jessica to tell them she wanted to regroup and talk about what everyone was working on, Lizzy left the office and returned home.

At 2:00 p.m., all three of them were sitting in the living room. Files and papers were spread across the floor and the coffee table. Every available space was taken. Nobody could move without disturbing a file or two.

Lizzy wore her hair in a ponytail and had changed into jeans and a T-shirt. Hayley wore her standard attire: black pants and a black T-shirt with a skull design. Jessica wore jeans and a bright green shirt beneath an off-white cardigan with tiny buttons. She was the fresh-looking one in the group, the only one who looked put together.

Lizzy took a sip of her coffee and noticed Jessica staring at her. "What is it, Jessica?"

"Does your face hurt?" Jessica scrunched her face. "It's turning yellow. It looks like it hurts."

"It's not as bad as it looks," she said as she held up a piece of paper. "OK, here's something I need to find out pronto. I need to know who owns the house on 1032 Bunker Street in West Sacramento."

She looked at both of them, making sure they were taking notes. Hayley was typing on her keyboard while Jessica scribbled in her notebook.

"I also need a thorough search done on the man who lives there. His name is John Robinson."

"That name sounds familiar," Jessica said. "Did we used to have a client who went by that name?"

"Not that I know of," Lizzy said. "Any more questions before I continue?"

"Are we working this weekend?" Jessica asked.

"Absolutely," Lizzy said. "I'm up to my eyeballs with assholes trying to mess with me, and beginning Monday morning, I'll have security on my ass twenty-four-seven. Excuse the bad language," she added. "It's just that I've had enough."

"So you think one of the cases we're working on is somehow related to all of the recent incidents?" Jessica asked.

"Yes," Lizzy said. "I do." She exhaled. "So, what have you two found out about Adele Hampton?"

"Hayley is working on that one," Jessica said a little too quickly.

"Hayley?"

Hayley stopped typing and looked up. "The guy's name is Dennis Nilsen. He's thirty-four years old. He's a photographer."

Jessica was being evasive, and now Hayley was talking in riddles. "What guy?" Lizzy asked.

"The owner of the house on Bunker Street in West Sacramento. The address you just gave us. Dennis Nilsen is listed as the owner of the house."

"Good job," Lizzy said. "I wonder if Dennis Nilsen lives there with John Robinson. Does it say anything there about whether or not he lives in West Sacramento?"

"According to the records I found, Dennis Nilsen lives on fifty acres in Lincoln, California. I have an address if you need it, but no phone number is listed."

Jessica was staring at Hayley as if she had two heads.

"What's your problem?" Hayley asked her.

"How could you possibly find out who owned that house that quickly?"

"It wasn't that quick. It took ten minutes."

"Nope," Jessica said, shaking her head. "More like two minutes. You have outside help, don't you?"

Hayley shook her head at Jessica as if she were a lost cause and went back to what she was doing.

Lizzy stood and gathered her purse.

Jessica frowned. "Where are you going?"

"Do you want me to call your cell if I find anything on John Robinson?" Hayley asked.

"Absolutely," Lizzy said.

"You just got here," Jessica said. "You can't leave without telling us who John Robinson is."

Jessica was right. It wasn't fair to leave them hanging. Lizzy sat down and explained, "Michael and Jennifer Dalton hired me to look into an employee of theirs who filed a workers' compensation claim. As you know, Jennifer was murdered and her husband is in custody."

"But you're not convinced he killed her," Jessica stated.

"That's right," Lizzy said, deciding to leave out the part about Michael being the FBI's number one suspect—at least for now. "Since I had already signed a contract and I was paid a deposit, I didn't feel right letting their employee get away with fraud, so I decided to finish what I had started."

Hayley held up a file. "You're talking about the Eli Simpson case."

Lizzy nodded. "It's complicated, but in the midst of my investigation on Eli Simpson, he and I had a chat, and it turns out he never met or worked for Michael and Jennifer Dalton."

"What if he's lying?" Jessica asked. "What if he *was* the guy who worked for the Daltons but only wants to get you out of his way?"

"I wondered the same thing, but then I talked to a woman at Sunset Realty, a company that the fake Eli Simpson had listed on his application as past employment. It turned out he never worked at Sunset Realty, but he did interview for a job there. The Eli Simpson they interviewed was five foot ten, thin, and bald. The Eli Simpson I met is well over six feet. He's also big, as in well muscled, and he has a thick head of dark hair, a crooked nose, and brown eyes."

"Not even close."

Lizzy nodded. "Eli Simpson believes that John Robinson is using his name for the sole purpose of screwing with him. It seems they have a history. A few years ago, John Robinson even went so far as to file a restraining order after Eli broke into his house."

"Why would he do that?"

"Eli believes that John Robinson had something to do with his sister's disappearance five years ago."

"What do the police say?"

"They have no proof of any wrongdoing."

Jessica scratched her chin. "What are you going to do?"

"If Eli Simpson is correct and John Robinson is the man who worked for the Daltons, then I need the usual pictures to prove that he's able-bodied so I can close this case. It should have been an open-and-shut case."

"If John Robinson lied about who he is on the workers' comp form," Jessica asked, "couldn't he be arrested for fraud?"

"That's a possibility."

"If he's lying about who he is, he could be dangerous," Jessica said. "Have you talked to Jared about this?"

"He's busy," Lizzy said. "Besides, I only discovered John Robinson's name the other night after talking with Eli Simpson again."

"You went alone?"

"She's a private investigator," Hayley reminded her. "They talk to people they've never met—complete strangers. That's what they do."

"You're such a bitch," Jessica said.

Hayley shrugged. "Just stating the facts."

Lizzy ignored their bickering. "Any more questions before I take off?"

"I still don't get the Dennis Nilsen connection," Jessica said, "and why you would want to talk to him."

"I promised Eli that if he gave me the name of the man who he believed used his name on the workers' compensation claim, I would do some investigating of my own into the case of his missing sister." Lizzy fished for her keys at the bottom of her purse and looked at Jessica. "I'm hoping Dennis Nilsen can tell me something about his tenant, John Robinson. Want to go?"

"No thanks," Jessica said. "I'll pass, but I still need to talk to you about the Dominic Povo case."

"Can it wait a few more hours?"

"Sure, I guess."

As soon as Lizzy reached the door, she snapped her fingers and turned to face the girls. "Two more things: Best Limousines and pine sawyer beetles. I've done a search, but I can't find anything on Best Limousines. I also need everything and anything you can find out about the pine sawyer beetles: what they eat, how long they survive, where they hang out, any hidden meanings, et cetera."

CHAPTER 23

I love to kill people. I love watching them die. I would shoot
them in the head and they would wiggle and squirm all over the
place, and then just stop. Or I would cut them with a knife and
watch their faces turn real white. I love all that blood.
I told one lady to give me all her money. She said no.
So I cut her and pulled her eyes out.
—Richard Ramirez

Sacramento
Friday, June 8, 2012

The sound of the door alerted him to Kassie's arrival. He glanced
at his watch. She was thirty minutes earlier than expected, which
meant he would have to work a bit faster than planned.

He set the book on the bedside table, stood, straightened the bed-
covers, and went to the bedroom door so he could listen. The heels
of her shoes clicked against the tiles in the front entrance leading to
the kitchen. Cupboards opened and closed. He heard running water.

Although he wouldn't mind hiding in the bathroom, hoping
to catch a glimpse of her undressing, he preferred to take her to
his place fully clothed. She habitually parked in the garage, which
would make it easy for him to drag her into the trunk of her car

unseen and head back to his place from there. He'd brought his standard kidnapping attire: a wig, sunglasses, and lipstick, in case a nosy neighbor caught a glimpse of Kassie leaving so soon after arriving home from work.

Now he could hear her talking on the phone, probably chatting with her mother or her husband. He liked the sound of her voice, smooth and velvety, with a calming lilt. Since she was a child psychologist, he imagined he would have benefited from long talks with her when he was young.

Strange, he mused, *that she became a child psychologist but bore no children. Hmmm.* He'd have to remember to ask her about that. Her voice was getting louder. She was coming this way. He looked around, smiling, alert, excited.

His mom used to play hide-and-seek with him. It was his favorite game. The Scotts' shower was one of those glass-enclosed types, no curtain to hide behind, so he opted for the closet. Tiresome and uninspiring, but it would have to do. If he ran for another room, she might see him as she came up the stairs.

The walk-in closet was one of the largest he'd ever had the pleasure of hiding within. There was an island in the center, made of rich mahogany. He went to the far side, where she wouldn't be able to see him right away. Then he plunked down and made himself comfortable.

A minute later, he heard random little noises within the main part of the bedroom.

"No, I haven't had a chance to tell him yet," she said. "I tried calling him, but it's his night out with the boys. I'll have to tell him later. Please don't tell anyone else until I've had a chance to tell Drew."

Apparently she had news to share. The notion made him giddy. He could barely contain his excitement. As he sat alone in the dark, the anticipation of taking her was almost too much.

Restless, he rubbed his arms as if he were cold, though he was anything but. He was hot—eager and hopeful with high expectations, maybe too high.

In an attempt to calm himself, he closed his eyes and thought of his mother instead. Thoughts of Mom calmed him, reminded him of why he was here and what he had to do. He heard a noise and when he looked up she was standing there, not even a foot away, staring at him as if he were a ghost.

He was no ghost.

He was the real deal.

When she finally grasped the idea that he was not an apparition, it was too late. She was fast, but he was faster. He was the pursuer, the one with the plan. He lunged for her and grabbed her ankles before she could escape from the closet. He dragged her back toward him. Her screams were piercing, slicing through the quiet. His plan was to choke her until she passed out, but the bitch was stronger than she looked. He considered her to be tall, at five foot seven, but she was small boned and had little meat on her body. No padding at all, all sinewy muscle and well-worked tendons.

She was on her back and he straddled her waist while she kicked and clawed. Reaching out with his right hand, he yanked loose the first thing he could grab hold of, which turned out to be one of her husband's long-sleeved shirts. While she took his skin under her nails and left her mark on his arms and neck, he stayed focused, oblivious to any pain she caused him, even enjoying it as he shoved the overly starched cotton into her mouth.

Her eyes bulged with fear.

That look, that moment when she realized he might get the best of her, was the moment he got a hard-on. She had no choice but to concentrate on keeping an open airway. Using both hands to grab for the shirt, she gave him the chance to bind her wrists together, using the same shirt that had been clogging her airway only moments before.

He ripped another shirt from a hanger and used it to tie her ankles. Breathless, he worked fast, choking her until she passed out. He then pulled out his handkerchief and enjoyed one of the finest orgasmic thrills of his life.

Getting Kassie Scott from her walk-in closet upstairs to the trunk of her car parked in the garage did not go as planned. With his hands grasping her ankles, he pulled her from the closet. He dragged her body down the stairs and through the living room. But along the way, she woke up and managed to untie her hands.

Kassie Scott was doing everything she could think of to stop him from taking her any farther. Chairs were knocked over and decorative items were broken. A hard object struck the side of his head, pissing him off. Another knot on his head.

The bitch was going to wish she had cooperated.

As he pulled her through the kitchen, she screamed and kicked, so he decided to take a moment to teach her a lesson. He grabbed the biggest knife he could find, held it to her throat, and threatened her into submission. His hands shook. He wanted nothing more than to stab her, slice her open, and play with her innards. She must have seen the resolve in his expression because when their eyes met, she stopped fighting him.

By the time he secured her arms and legs, shoved her inside the trunk, and slammed it shut, he'd come down a long way from his incredible high.

He returned to the house and righted fallen chairs, cleaning up the path of destruction as best he could. After returning to the garage and climbing behind the wheel of Kassie's car, he shuffled through his bag for the blonde wig and slid it over his smooth bald head. Using the rearview mirror, he made a few necessary adjustments, and then slipped on a pair of sunglasses. Lipstick came next. "Impassioned" was the shade of the day. He rubbed his lips together and admired his new look.

Beautiful.

Next, he pulled out the disposable cell phone he'd bought to make contact with his favorite private investigator.

It was time.

He couldn't help but wonder what Lizzy was up to. Had she gone for a run this morning? He laughed at the notion. Had she found the gift he left in her office? *Did she have any fucking clue who she was dealing with?*

He already knew her number by heart, but he'd never called her before. He pushed Favorites, and one more push of a button was all it took before he felt a rush of adrenaline stream through his veins as he listened to the ringtone. "Come on, Lizzy, answer your phone. Let's play."

Davis
Friday, June 8, 2012

The moment Lizzy drove off, heading for Lincoln, Hayley went to her room to grab her backpack. She made a mad dash back into the living room and said, "Come on."

Jessica looked frantic, her eyes wide, her face pale. "What are you talking about? We have to stay here. There's work to do."

"That's what we'll be doing," Hayley said. "Working. Come on."

"What's in that backpack?"

"Nothing that would interest you. I would borrow your car and go alone," Hayley added, "but I need a lookout."

"A lookout?"

"Yeah, you know, the person who calls you on your phone to tell you somebody is coming and that you have two minutes to get out of the house if you want to get out alive."

Jessica crossed her arms over her chest, something she often did. Her lame way of saying she wasn't going to budge.

"If you don't take me," Hayley told her, "I'm going to call Lizzy right now and tell her all about you aiding and abetting a fugitive the other day."

"That's blackmail. You wouldn't dare."

"Do I look like I wouldn't dare?"

"You can stop with the threats. You wouldn't do it because you would be giving up your own freedom."

"Good point."

"If you do this," Jessica said, "Lizzy is going to return home and see that you are gone. You'll get caught for sure."

"She's going to Lincoln. That's almost an hour away. We have plenty of time. Besides, if you don't take me, I'm calling Tommy. I'm sure he'll be a perfect lookout."

Jessica practically growled as she came to her feet and tugged the strap of her purse over her shoulder.

Hayley held open the door for her.

"I'm going to remember this," Jessica said.

"I'm sure you will."

Lincoln
Friday, June 8, 2012

Lizzy made a left off Forbes Road onto a narrow street. There were tall pines on both sides of the road, which made it feel less like day and more like night.

She followed the road for about a mile until she came to a road block. A chain was hooked from a tall pine on the left to a wood post on the right. Pulling to the side of the road, she parked the car and decided to go the rest of the way by foot.

The majority of the property was made up of a forest of trees. The ground was covered with dirt and leaves still damp from recent rains. Towering redwoods, oaks, and pines filled the air with a woodsy smell. As she walked along, she heard a strange sound. She stopped and listened. It wasn't the high-pitched sound of cicadas—it was a low, eerie hum, a quiet munching, distinct and rhythmic.

Not far ahead, she spotted the roof of a single-story house. A closer look showed that the house was bigger than she'd first thought. It was L-shaped, with a surrounding porch. There was an unattached barnlike building in the foreground. The wood paneling on the house was faded and weathered. More than half of the foundation appeared to be gone, giving it a slant that made it look as if part of the house might topple over at any moment. The bottom edge of the siding appeared to have extensive termite and weather damage.

She might have thought the house was abandoned, except once she made her way up the three wooden steps leading to a new cedar porch, the place showed signs of life. An umbrella leaned against the wall near the door, nearby work boots were covered with dried mud, and a stack of wood was shoved against the siding. She opened the screen door and knocked. After a minute, she knocked again. Backing away, she let the screen door shut on its own.

As she followed the length of the porch, every step echoed off the wood planks.

"Anybody home?" she called as she worked her way westward until the porch ended. From where she stood looking over the

lly get a
chance to talk to you."

It was a man. She stopped at the top of the porch stairs. "Who
is this?"

"I am a big fan. I've been reading up on your story of perse-
verance: overcoming your fears and phobias in hopes of leading

a normal life. Your story warms my heart. I was hoping we could meet face-to-face."

As she waited for the caller to elaborate, out in the distance, where large boulders and tall trees dominated, she heard the same rhythmic munching noise she'd heard earlier. "Who is this?" she asked again.

He laughed. "Truthfully, I'm your worst nightmare," he said, his voice suddenly low and gravelly.

Her spine stiffened. "My worst nightmare is dead."

"Don't you wish," he said with a chuckle. "Don't you wish."

Sacramento
Friday, June 8, 2012

The wind had kicked up a notch as Jessica drove at a steady sixty-seven miles per hour, two miles over the speed limit. She kept a good grip on the steering wheel and her eyes on the road in front of her. "Where are we going?" she asked again.

"We're going to John Robinson's house."

"Didn't you hear anything Lizzy said? He could be danger-ous."

"I live for danger, remember?"

Jessica's eyes narrowed. "You're insane."

"And don't forget crazy."

"You just like to piss me off."

"Because it's so easy to do," Hayley agreed.

For the rest of the ride, silence devoured the air between them until Jessica couldn't take it anymore and turned up the radio.

"Take the next exit," Hayley said a few minutes later.

Jessica was not happy as she exited the freeway as instructed. She did not like taking orders, and she certainly didn't appreciate being blackmailed. Mostly, she didn't like the idea of Hayley getting hurt or being thrown in jail again if she were caught. She took the next exit, and after a few more turns, she pulled her car to a stop at the curb and looked at Hayley. "You need to tell me the plan."

"We're not there yet."

"I'm not going any farther until you tell me the plan."

"Fine," Hayley said. "Once we get to the house, you're going to park about a half a block away from Robinson's house, facing east. I'm going to knock on the door. If anyone answers, I'm going to use my phone to take a picture."

"That's illegal. You can't simply take pictures of anyone you want."

"I'll be discreet. He'll think I'm making a call."

"And what if nobody answers the door?"

"I'll take a quick look around and see what's going on."

"Promise me you won't break into the house."

"I won't break into the house."

Jessica stared at Hayley, wondering if she was lying. "I thought you didn't make promises."

"I don't."

Jessica huffed. "And this impromptu reconnaissance of yours will take how long?"

"Ten minutes at the most."

Jessica thought about it for a second as she watched the wind swoosh through the branches of the trees lining the street, making them dance. "OK. Ten minutes. Otherwise, I'm calling the police."

"Do not call the police."

"I was kidding."

"Don't call them until the twenty-minute mark," Hayley added.

Jessica didn't like the sudden gravity of Hayley's voice, let alone the idea of having to call the police at all. She hadn't been serious about calling the police, but obviously Hayley was.

"And this is the most important part," Hayley continued. "If a car pulls into the driveway or you see anyone at all approaching the house, you need to give me a call. My phone is set to vibrate, so nobody will hear a ringtone."

Jessica felt sick to her stomach.

"Are we good?"

"Yeah, we're good," Jessica said as she pulled back into the street. "Let's get this over with. It looks like it's going to rain soon. Which way?"

"Make a left at the next stop sign."

CHAPTER 24

I hate a bitchy chick.
—Gerald Stano

Lincoln
Friday, June 8, 2012

"Why don't you tell me who's calling?" Lizzy asked.

"And ruin all my fun?"

"Are you the same man who attacked me in the park?"

"I need to go, Lizzy. I have important business to attend to, but I really wanted to hear your voice."

"Before you go," she said, "I have something very important to tell you."

"I'm still here."

"Good, because I want you to listen carefully. I'm *your* worst nightmare, asshole. I'm the shadow lurking in every dark corner from here on out. Maybe you've read a few articles about me. Maybe you believe everything you read and you think I'm teetering on the edge of a dark abyss. Well, guess what? You're right. I'm teetering, all right, but I'm teetering on the edge of enlightenment. I get it. I'm all fucked up and because of my past history I tend to attract lunatics like you. But your plan to push me a little too far has backfired, because I'm the bitch who is going to find you and haul your sorry ass to prison, and the only thing you'll be wishing is—"

She heard a dial tone and realized her worst nightmare had just hung up on her.

The nerve.

For the first time in months, Lizzy felt something much stronger than fear. It was anger, raw, dirty anger. And in the blink of an eye, it smothered all her apprehensions and terror within. What she felt was not the fleeting kind of annoyance most people encountered throughout their day; this was full-fledged rage. And it felt good.

A smirk formed as she walked along the dirt path back to her car.

Sacramento
Friday, June 8, 2012

Hayley counted to ten. Clearly, nobody was home. The entry door to John Robinson's house was solid wood—no way to peek through. The large-paned window was covered with dark curtains—nothing to see there, either.

On to Plan B.

It was easy enough to find the side gate, but not nearly as easy to open it. She reached over the gate, stretching her arm as far as she could, catching splinters along the way. Finally, she felt the metal latch, but it wouldn't budge. Her fingers brushed over a heavy-duty lock—the kind of lock that needed a key.

The old, weathered fence was warped, making it easier for Hayley to see through the cracks. The backyard was an exact replica of the front yard: dead lawn, no greenery other than weeds. There was a dented aluminum garbage can overloaded with trash.

She glanced over her shoulder and saw Jessica peering out the window, looking worried.

Their eyes met.

Jessica shook her head and used both hands to gesture for Hayley to return to the car.

Hayley shook her head right back at her and pointed to the backyard, letting her know she was going to climb the fence. Then she jumped. Gritting her teeth, she used all her strength to pull her body up and over. She landed on her feet, but then lost her balance and fell on her ass. Pushing herself up, she wiped herself off. The stench caused her nose to wrinkle. The air smelled like raw sewage and skunk, making her feel right at home.

Her phone vibrated. She ignored it, knowing that Jessica was just being a worrywart.

Hayley could see the driveway through the wood slats. Nobody had driven by and there were no new cars parked in front.

As soon as Hayley left the car, Jessica began her countdown. It was past five. She turned off the music. She needed to concentrate. She didn't like this street. The neighborhood looked abandoned: houses with broken windows, and an old mattress on the curb farther down the street. Nearly every mailbox lining both sides of the street had been destroyed, flattened with a hammer or a baseball bat. She couldn't help but wonder how many of these homes, if any, were actually occupied.

She'd read about streets like this. Houses were foreclosed and then deserted, leaving the empty homes for drug users and criminals. The entire street smelled foul.

From where she sat, she could see Hayley at the front door to John Robinson's house.

Come on, Hayley. Nobody's home. Let's get out of here.

Highly annoyed, she watched Hayley walk to the side of the house, stand on her tiptoes, and reach an arm over the top of the gate. The gate was obviously locked; otherwise she would have opened it and gone inside. When Hayley looked her way, she was relieved to finally make eye contact. Jessica gestured for her to return to the car, letting Hayley know her time was up. Instead, she watched Hayley jump and pull herself up and over to the other side.

Shit. She should have known that Hayley wouldn't give up so easily.

Whatever.

If Hayley wanted to risk her life, that was her prerogative… but for what? That girl was foolish. She had just climbed over the fence of a potentially dangerous man. Only Hayley would be so careless.

Jessica refused to sit here and worry. She was going to get an ulcer if she kept it up. Hoping to distract herself, she looked at her phone. No missed calls. No new texts. Still no word from Magnus. It was killing her not to give him a call. She reached into her purse and pulled out the piece of paper with his number scribbled on it—the paper he had given her at the coffee shop.

If she could hear his voice, she would feel so much better. She dialed his number, her heart racing a little faster with each ring.

He didn't answer.

Out of the corner of her eye, she saw movement. She shut her phone and put it away. Outside, she saw a dog—a small scruffy dog with no collar. The dog looked like a mutt—a cross between a Maltese and an unidentified ancestor. Its ribs were showing.

Aw, the poor thing looked hungry.

She looked up and down the road—nobody outside looking for a lost dog. She scrounged around inside her purse until she found the snack bar she kept stashed away for emergencies. She grabbed her bottled water, too, and climbed out of the car. "Hey, pooch," she called.

The dog turned and looked at her.

"Are you hungry?"

The dog's tail wagged a little, but he wasn't ready to come toward her.

Jessica opened the bar, broke off a tiny piece, and held it out for him. "Here you go, pooch. Come on, you can do it."

He took a step forward, but then a truck came into view and ruined everything. The dog ran off and the car pulled into the driveway next door to John Robinson's house.

Jessica hurried back to her Volvo and slid behind the wheel. She pulled out her phone and dialed Hayley's number. One ring, and then two…three…four.

"Answer your phone, Hayley."

What's the point of having a lookout if you aren't going to answer the phone?

Jessica scooted lower in her seat and watched the man exit his vehicle. He was a large man. Instead of heading for the front door, he headed for John Robinson's house. He didn't bother going to the front door. He went straight for the same side gate Hayley had jumped over and shoved a booted foot right through the wood, sending pieces of broken planks flying.

Jessica gasped. What was the man doing? What was going on?

He didn't even look up to see if anyone was watching. He appeared to be completely at ease, as if kicking down doors and gates was something he did every day, before he ducked low and disappeared through the opening. The entire neighborhood appeared to be alive with crazy people. Jessica grabbed her phone.

Hayley reached into her backpack and pulled out a tension wrench. It took less than thirty seconds to get the side door into the garage open. Once inside, she took a good look at the blue Toyota Camry, all shiny and clean. Even the rims sparkled like new. The entire garage was neat and organized. One entire wall was devoted to tools: saws, an axe, shovels, and an assortment of gardening tools.

The fact that there was a car parked in the garage at all bothered her, since there had been nothing in John Robinson's records about his being married. If he wasn't married, the probability of his having more than one car was slim to none. And if he had only one car, then he was probably home. *So why didn't he answer the door when I knocked?*

She planned to find out. But first, she lifted her jeans to make sure her knife was safely tucked within the sheath strapped to her calf. She reached for the knife, grabbed the handle, and whipped it out, the blade pointing outward in front of her. Glad she hadn't lost her touch, she put the knife away. Using the same twisted tension wrench, she then made her way into the house. She stood in the kitchen for a long moment and listened. All was quiet. No television on in the background. No radio. No washer or dryer or any sounds of any kind.

The kitchen counters were yellow Formica. The table where John Robinson ate his meals was a midcentury vintage chrome-and-avocado piece surrounded by four aluminum chairs. The shag carpet was multiple colors. Like the garage, everything was orderly and clean. Even the walls looked newly painted.

Her phone vibrated again, prompting Hayley to walk to the living room window and peek through the heavy curtain.

Jessica was looking her way and making stabbing motions with her finger at the neighbor's house. Hayley couldn't see a thing and she didn't care about the neighbor, so she gave her a thumbs-up and shut the curtain.

It took about five minutes to do a quick run-through of the house. There were only two bedrooms. Nobody sleeping in the beds. In fact, the entire house hardly looked lived in. No pictures on the wall, nothing to tell her who lived here.

She was in the bathroom, searching inside the medicine cabinet, when she heard loud noises coming from the house next door. She exited the bathroom, ran to the bedroom on the far side of the house, and looked out the window. The house next door was a clone of the house she was in right now. She could see the side yard and the door leading to the garage.

Thump. Thump.

What was going on over there?

The neighbor was probably working inside the garage. *No big deal. Focus.* She needed to finish looking around and get out before Jessica called the police. Upon returning to the bedroom, Hayley noticed that the rectangular table at the end of the bed was actually a wooden chest. She lifted the lid. The chest was filled with women's clothes, everything neatly folded. There was a pair of black pumps and a pair of size 8 leather boots. She reached for a cloth bag, tied with a silk rope. Inside were two blonde wigs. She pulled one out. It was shoulder length, with a wispy modern side-sweep of bang. It felt like real human hair.

At the sound of a scraping noise in the other room, Hayley shoved everything into the chest, closed the lid, and hurried back to the main room. She stood there for a moment, listening, waiting to see if she would hear the noise again. That's when she saw movement beneath a table between two chairs. A large section of the shag carpet was coming loose.

A trapdoor?

Shit!

She made a run for it. Before she could escape, a hand shot out and large fingers grasped her ankle. She fell and hit her head on the corner of a chair. Rolling to her side, she used her free leg to kick him in the face.

He grunted, but held tight. "Who the hell are you?"

"Who the hell are you?" she shouted.

"I'm just making my weekly rounds," he gritted out, "looking for my sister."

Hayley's eyes narrowed. "Eli Simpson?"

"Now how in the world would you know that?"

"I work for Lizzy Gardner."

He released a frustrated breath and let go of her ankle. "Is that an ankle monitor?"

"What's it to you?"

"Nothing, I guess." He climbed out of the hole and replaced the lid to the trapdoor. "This creep has more traps and rickety stairs than the Mousetrap game."

Hayley came to her feet and brushed herself off. "Anything down there?"

"Nothing but an empty, windowless room with a workbench and some tools. I've been wondering how the guy has been getting in and out without being seen. He had some work done on his backyard a while ago. Sure enough, I found a tunnel leading from the greenbelt behind his house to the room below."

"Did you find anything in the tunnel?"

He shook his head. "Did Lizzy send you here?"

"No." Hayley pointed toward the front door. "I've gotta go or the crazy girl who drove me here is going to call the cops."

He pointed at her face. "You're bleeding."

She touched her face, felt the blood with her finger, surprised at how fast her heart was beating as she headed for the door.

"What about you?" he asked before she left. "Did you find anything?"

"A chest full of women's clothes and some wigs."

"Yeah, he likes to play dress-up," he said, waving her out. "I'll take it from here."

She looked over her shoulder at Eli, even felt sorry for him as she shut the door behind her. She jogged across the street. Jessica had the passenger door open and ready.

Hayley climbed in and Jessica took off the minute she shut the car door.

Hayley's heart thumped hard against her chest. She kept waiting for Jessica to ask her what had happened or at least yell at her and tell her she was a crazy bitch, but she was driving at the perfect speed limit and stopping at the end of every street, checking both ways before hitting the gas. If it weren't for the big droplets of tears running down the side of her pale face, Hayley never would have guessed that Jessica was feeling any emotion at all.

CHAPTER 25

One side of me says, I'd like to talk to her, date her.
The other side of me says, I wonder what her head would
look like on a stick?
—Edmund Kemper

Sacramento
Friday, June 8, 2012

The metal garage door made a loud whirring noise as it closed. Once it shut, he pulled off his wig, tossed it on the passenger seat, laid his head on the headrest, and took a breath.

He was still feeling the lingering effects of his talk with Lizzy Gardner. She was a sassy bitch. Just the way he liked them. She was cocky and overly confident and she wanted him to think she had him right where she wanted him. The notion made him smile.

She had no idea what was coming, no idea what he had planned for her. If only he had a way to videotape her reaction when her life came tumbling down around her.

A loud thumping noise caught his attention. No doubt about it, he thought as he climbed out of the car and shut the door,

Kassie Scott was a stubborn one. And she would regret causing him so much grief.

He used the key to unlock the trunk, and when he lifted it open, he saw a flash of movement and felt a sharp ache in his side. He staggered backward and looked down at the knife protruding from his body.

Clever girl.

Dazed, he watched her climb from the trunk.

As the scene unfolded before him, he realized watching Kassie's escape would be funny if it weren't so ludicrous. Feisty little lady obviously thought one little steak knife would be the end of him. She had no idea who she was dealing with. All he could see in his mind were all the ways in which he wanted to and, more importantly, *would* cause her pain. A lot of pain.

Taking unhurried steps, he followed after her, determined to show her who was boss.

As she tried to slide open the bolt that would allow her to escape, he pulled the knife from his side and plunged it into her thigh. Her high-pitched scream forced him to slam her head into the wall and knock her out. He grabbed some rope and tape from his work area, tied her hands and feet, and then placed duct tape over her mouth.

Standing straight and tall, he looked down at her for a moment before bending down so that his face was level with hers. After a while, her eyes fluttered open as she slowly became aware.

"This is only the beginning," he warned her. "In the end, when you come to terms with death and believe dying will bring you peace, you'll be wrong. I will be sleeping with your corpse. These hands," he said, showing her both hands, palms flat, fingers pointed upward, "will be playing with every part of you. These fingers, each and every one, will be intimately devoted to your body for hours on end."

She was trembling now, and he was glad. He closed his eyes and felt a shiver course through his body.

Friday, June 8, 2012

As her anger dissipated on the drive home, Lizzy stared at the road ahead and couldn't help but wonder where she'd gone wrong. All the bravado she'd felt earlier on the phone had vanished. Just when she was beginning to think her future looked promising, everything began to disintegrate. She hadn't talked to her sister or her niece in weeks. She missed them both. She couldn't remember the last time she'd thought about her mother, but she thought about her now. Mom lived in Hawaii. Cathy and Brittany had visited her in Maui a few months ago. They said she looked healthy and happy. Cathy never mentioned whether or not Mom had asked about Lizzy, but she didn't have to say anything; Lizzy knew. Even now, after all these years, her mother and father blamed her for everything that had gone wrong in their lives. Lizzy's therapist often reminded her that her parents were deflecting the responsibility away from themselves. Blaming someone else helped relieve them of some of the guilt they felt.

And then there was Jessica. She was young and bright, and it seemed every time Lizzy looked at her lately, she could see that Jessica was scared. Lizzy knew what needed to be done. She needed to fire Jessica, force her to move on before she got in too deep and allowed the darkness to swallow her whole.

Her phone rang and the screen displayed the caller ID. It was Jared. *Thank God.* She had left him a message asking him to call. She hit the Talk button on the console and said, "Are you OK?"

"I'm fine," he said, his voice hurried. "I wanted to let you know that I won't be coming home for a few days."

"Are you going back to Quantico?"

"No. I'll be here in Sacramento."

"What's going on?"

"A woman went missing today—Kassie Scott. Married for fourteen years. No kids."

"Has it been on the news?"

"No. Her husband reported his wife missing a few hours ago. The FBI will be keeping this one under the radar. Every police department in Sacramento County was instructed to keep us informed in the event any females fitting the Lovebird Killer's signature went missing."

"I thought he didn't have a signature."

"He doesn't, not really, since he tends to kill, kidnap, and dispose of the bodies in any number of ways. In the case of the most recent victims, though, the male was abducted twenty-four hours after he reported his partner missing. New evidence revealed the same thing happened with Rene and Harold Lofland. Apparently, one of Rene's cleaning ladies had stayed behind to pocket a diamond bracelet, along with other expensive jewelry, when Mrs. Lofland arrived home. The cleaning lady was hiding out when she overheard Rene's abductor tell her he would be returning for her husband."

"And she didn't report this until now?"

"She was caught trying to pawn the diamonds and was eager to escape jail time in exchange for information concerning Rene Lofland's murder."

"So, what's the plan?"

"We need to act fast. This could be our chance to catch the Lovebird Killer in action. I'll be staying with Drew Scott until the unsub makes contact."

"What if the killer is expecting you?"

"There will be unmarked cars in the vicinity of where I'll be staying. How's your face?" Jared asked. "Are you still in pain?"

He was redirecting the conversation again, an art he had perfected. "I'm fine," she said. "Don't worry about me."

"I love you," he said. "I have to go. I'll talk to you in a few days."

"Jared," she said, but the call was disconnected before she could tell him about the threatening phone call she'd received. She pulled into the driveway and sat in the car for a moment. She dialed his number. No answer.

She closed her eyes and tried to imagine a life without Jared in it. For the first time since she'd moved in with him, she knew that she was right where she needed to be. This was their home. This was where she belonged.

Jessica and Hayley had returned moments before they heard Lizzy's car pull into the driveway. Files and papers were spread across the coffee table. They quickly moved things around, trying to make it look like they had been at the house all along.

Lizzy walked through the door at the same moment they both took a seat on the couch.

Although Lizzy's face was still bruised from the attack in the park, Jessica saw dark shadows of exhaustion making half-circles under her eyes. Lizzy said a quick hello and then told them she was going to change her clothes and be right down.

While Lizzy was upstairs, Jessica whispered to Hayley, "That was too close."

"Stop worrying. We made it back in time."

"I'm going to tell Lizzy about Magnus and what's going on with the Povo case."

"Do what you have to," Hayley said, "but leave out anything to do with my involvement. If Lizzy found out about my copycat ankle bracelet, she would be obligated to tell Jared since they're both under court order to see that I follow the rules. They are officially, albeit temporarily, my legal guardians."

"Got it," Jessica said.

"I would leave out the part about the men wrestling with the knife, too."

"Why?"

"What if she feels the need to call the police? What if they figure out where he lives? What would happen to your friend?"

Jessica didn't like keeping anything from Lizzy, but Hayley was right. She didn't know what Magnus was up to, and therefore she didn't like the idea of getting him into trouble. Not yet. Not until she had a chance to talk to him. She needed to calm down and stop being so paranoid. Before she could say anything more to Hayley, she turned toward Lizzy, who was already making her way down the stairs.

Lizzy looked from Hayley to Jessica. "What's going on?"

Without taking an extra breath, Jessica told Lizzy all about the Dominic Povo case: the bulky garbage bags and the impromptu meetings held in Povo's trailer and the possible blood splatter. She also mentioned that she'd met with Magnus at a coffee shop and later went to the construction site again and saw Magnus threatened by two men. She left out anything to do with Hayley's involvement.

"I don't want you going anywhere near that construction site again, do you understand?"

The panic in Lizzy's voice was unmistakable. "You don't have to tell me twice," Jessica said, "but what about Magnus?"

"Magnus is the man you met in the coffee shop?" Lizzy asked.

Jessica nodded. "He works for Dominic and I'm worried about him."

"He's bad news," Hayley told Lizzy. "Magnus knows that Jessica works for you. How would he know that unless he did some investigating of his own? And why would he investigate some girl sitting in a car watching them unless he was up to no good?"

Jessica gave Hayley dagger eyes. "But—"

"No buts," Lizzy said, stopping Jessica from saying anything more. "We're going to drop the Povo case until Danielle Cartwright returns from Europe. She's our client. We'll hear what Danielle has to say and then take it from there."

"OK, fine," Jessica said, sinking back into the couch.

Lizzy took a seat and looked directly at Hayley. "Why don't you get me up to date on the Adele Hampton adoption case?"

"I made some calls, but long story short, the few leads I had turned cold," she lied. "I've talked to Adele's mom and I have to say…I believe she wants to find Adele so she can use her daughter as a publicity stunt for her husband's campaign."

"What did she say to make you think that?" Lizzy asked.

"It's what she didn't say." Hayley exhaled. "Either way, I'm working a few different angles, and I should have more information in a few days."

Jessica pretended to take notes, but she felt a tremendous urge to quit right then and there. She was tired of all the lying, the danger, and the stress that came with the job. Unfortunately, she needed the money and she happened to adore Lizzy Gardner. The last thing she would do was leave Lizzy when she needed her most. Hayley was another story. Jessica was tired of being manipulated by her, tired of her constant lying and playing games—tired of breaking the law. They had barely escaped John Robinson's neighborhood unnoticed, and she was still feeling the effects. If Lizzy knew they had gone anywhere near John Robinson's house today, what would she do?

"Is there a problem?" Lizzy asked Jessica, obviously sensing her anxiety.

"Nope."

"Jessica has been busy," Hayley said. "Not only did she check on my mom, she's going to school, studying, and working too many hours on the Dominic Povo case. She also managed to get pictures proving that two of the six workers' compensation claims were fraudulent. Both cases were closed in record time. The insurance company is impressed."

Lizzy nodded. "Perfect. Thank you, Jessica."

"Sure, it's what I do," Jessica said without looking up. Yes, it was true, two cases were closed, but Hayley was the one who had done all of the work, pictures included. But, of course, Hayley had no choice but to give Jessica the credit, since nobody could know that Hayley was out gallivanting around town.

"Somebody's at the door," Hayley said.

Lizzy walked across the room, looked out the peephole, and then opened the door.

It was Stacey Whitmore from Channel 10 News.

"I need to talk to you," Stacey said.

"Come on in."

As Lizzy locked the door behind her, Stacey stepped farther inside. Instead of her usual two-piece suit, she wore dark designer jeans and black ballet flats with gold chain accents. A white silk blouse peeked out from beneath a fitted red jacket. Every hair was in place. Although the woman was well dressed and looked put together, it was easy to see that she was on the verge of having a mental breakdown. Jessica knew the feeling, and her heart went out to the lady.

"These are my assistants," Lizzy said, gesturing toward the girls. "This is Jessica and Hayley."

Stacey nodded. With introductions out of the way, Lizzy and Stacey moved to the kitchen. "Can I get you anything?" Lizzy asked.

"No, thank you. I came because I need to get something off my chest."

"Should we move to the backyard for privacy?"

The woman looked at Jessica and Hayley and then shook her head. "No need. Here's fine."

"OK, what's going on?"

"It's about Michael." Stacey gestured toward the television set. "It's all over the news. They think he's the Lovebird Killer. He's the FBI's number one suspect."

Michael wasn't the only suspect, but Lizzy didn't say anything about that.

"You knew about this." Stacey rubbed the bridge of her nose. "Why didn't you tell me?"

"I couldn't."

"What does the FBI have on Michael? You told me yourself you were at his house. What did they find?"

Hayley looked at Jessica and mouthed the words "What's going on?"

Jessica shook her head, letting Hayley know she had no idea.

"Off the record?" Lizzy asked.

"Off the record," Stacey answered.

"The connection between Michael and the Lovebird Killer has to do with the pine sawyer beetle."

Stacey narrowed her eyes, her surprise apparent. "Pine sawyer beetles," she said under her breath.

Lizzy nodded. "Right now, it's my understanding that the beetle is their only connection."

Stacey pulled out a stool and took a seat. She looked dazed.

"Evidently, the Lovebird Killer is fascinated with the beetle. Over the past five years, he's left the beetles somewhere in the vicinity of the bodies, on or near his victims."

"So what you're telling me is they found this beetle at Michael's house. The real killer could've planted the insect there. It's just as he said—he's been set up. That makes sense, don't you think?"

Lizzy said nothing. Kassie's abduction changed everything, and yet she didn't want to say too much and risk putting Jared in further danger.

"If I remember correctly, Channel 10 News ran a story about the pine sawyer beetle once," Stacey said, her eyes suddenly alert. "God, it had to be at least ten years ago. The story involved an elderly couple. If I remember correctly, they were embalmers and it was discovered that they had stuffed two dead bodies with those same beetles."

"You weren't working for Channel 10 News at the time."

"I've been watching every show since I knew I wanted to be in broadcasting. I would memorize every movement the reporters made: how they talked, their expressions, what they did with their hands. I was in my last year of college and the media had Lewinsky and Clinton, Mark McGwire and Sammy Sosa. We had economic turmoil and hurricanes over the Caribbean to worry about. Nobody cared about a few bodies stuffed with beetles."

Jessica felt sick to her stomach. Gross. A few minutes ago, when she and Hayley had been scrambling around, Jessica had grabbed a file from the coffee table, hoping to look busy. A business card had slid out of the file and onto her lap. Jessica fiddled with the card while she listened to Lizzy and Stacey talk. When she finally examined the card closer, she saw the name "Belle Gunness" scribbled on one side. Something wasn't right. The name was familiar, but she couldn't put her finger on where she might have met the woman or why the name was so familiar.

Hayley was clacking away on her keyboard, as usual. "Yep, she's right," Hayley said. "The couple's names were Karen and Todd Beck. They were embalmers and they lived in Lincoln, California." Hayley looked at Lizzy. "Didn't you go to Lincoln today?"

Lizzy nodded.

"It looks like the Becks pleaded guilty and were let off with a slap on the wrist," Hayley added.

"I'll call my assistant," Stacey said, "and see if she can locate the transcript."

Jessica looked at Lizzy and held up the card for Lily's Flower Shop. "This business card for Lily's Flower Shop was one of the vendors Jennifer Dalton was using for her anniversary party, is that right?"

Lizzy nodded.

"Did you see the name scribbled on the back of the card?"

"I did," Lizzy said. "I went to the shop and talked to the owner."

"Did you talk to Belle Gunness?"

"I asked about her, but the owner said she would be gone until Thanksgiving. What's going on?"

"I'm not sure," Jessica said. "Her name sounds familiar, that's all."

CHAPTER 26

I hated all my life. I hated everybody. When I first grew up
and can remember, I was dressed as a girl by my mother. And
I stayed that way for two or three years. And after that I was
treated like what I call the dog of the family. I was beaten. I was
made to do things that no human bein' would want to do.
—Henry Lee Lucas

Sacramento
Friday, June 8, 2012

The call that Kassie Scott was missing came in at exactly 7:43 p.m.
on Friday. By 9:22 p.m., the FBI had a plan.

Drew Scott, the man who had called in saying his wife was
missing, was instructed to go immediately to the market on 10th
and Oak. He was to go into the store, buy milk, and return home.
He was told where to park and to leave his car unlocked. He was
to be quick, get in and get out.

Furthermore, the agency told Drew not to be alarmed when he
returned to his car and found a man hunkered down in the backseat. That man would be FBI agent Jared Shayne. If Drew's wife,
Kassie, had been taken by the Lovebird Killer, then that meant,
more than likely, the killer would be watching Drew's every move.

Two minutes after Drew parked his car at the market, exactly as instructed, a large delivery truck obstructed all views of the vehicle, allowing Jared less than thirty seconds to climb into the vehicle unseen. The plan had been put into place after it was determined that the chance of being seen sneaking an agent into Drew's car was far less risky than sneaking an agent into Drew Scott's house.

It all happened fast, so fast that not even fifteen minutes passed between Drew's leaving his house and returning home with milk and an FBI agent's being stashed in the backseat.

Drew pulled into his two-car garage and hit the remote clipped to his visor. Once the garage door came to a close, he said, "You can come up for air now. It's all clear."

Jared put a finger over his mouth, letting Drew know that it would be in his best interest if he didn't talk aloud. Jared quietly opened the car door and climbed out of the vehicle, bringing with him a bag filled with tools to collect evidence. Since the crime technicians would not be allowed inside until this was all over, which could be days, he had been instructed to collect all the evidence he could on his own.

He would start with evidence that was considered fragile, anything that could be contaminated, like blood, hair, fingerprints, and fibers. First on the list: photograph any and all areas that looked as if they had been disturbed. He had a bright light and a magnifying glass, but if he got really lucky and the perpetrator washed his hands with, say, a bar of soap, a photograph could possibly do the trick. Otherwise, Jared would use his flashlight and black powder.

He would be looking closely at entries, exits, and all hard surfaces. If furniture had been moved or objects had been disturbed, that would be his starting point for gathering evidence.

Before he did any of that, though, he would make sure the place was empty and secure, and that nobody was hiding out.

Although agents had been planted on the street within minutes of being made aware of Kassie Scott's disappearance, they had been instructed to stay well hidden.

With the bag strapped over his shoulder, Jared slipped on a pair of latex gloves, pulled out his Sig P226, and motioned for Drew to remain quiet and stay where he was until Jared was finished checking out the house.

Jared stepped into the kitchen. The only light in the house came from a couple of wall sconces in the next room. He flipped the switch on the wall to his right. At first glance, everything looked sterile and untouched. At second glance, he bent down and saw a small knife protruding from under the cabinet where often molding called toe kick was installed in newer homes. He returned his gaze to the garage, where he could see Drew frozen in place, nervously watching Jared's every move.

It was difficult to tell what Drew might be thinking. He was pale, his eyes unblinking. The man probably had a million questions. More than likely, he was worried about his wife. And yet he seemed calm—too calm.

Jared didn't want to put himself in Drew Scott's shoes, not even for a minute.

Leaving the knife for now, Jared continued on to the main living area at the front of the house. He flipped another switch, lighting up the room. The front door was locked. No sign of a break-in. Four high-back chairs surrounded the dining room table. One of the chairs was knocked over. The table's centerpiece, a bowl of plastic fruit, had also been moved. He added those two things to his mental what's-wrong-with-this-room list and continued on, gun loaded and ready.

Next stop was a cherrywood curio cabinet in the dining room. The glass door was partially open. Empty spaces were obvious because of the markings left in the thin layer of dust, though the open door and the missing items were not what had immediately caught his attention. It was two live pine sawyer beetles crawling inside a lidded crystal heart dish.

They had their man.

Lizzy's face flashed within Jared's mind. He gave his head a quick shake to clear his vision. *She's fine*, he told himself. He had seen her this morning and talked to her less than an hour ago. Something kept niggling in the back of his mind, though, making it difficult to concentrate.

He looked at the beetles. The Lovebird Killer had been here—might still be here. Focused, he continued onward. He checked the guestroom: nobody under the bed, nothing but winter coats and a collection of ski boots in the closet—nothing out of place. Moving on, he exited the bedroom and headed upstairs. At the top of the landing, he stood still. There was a noise—a dripping faucet to his right.

With slow, methodical steps, he entered the master bedroom. The right side of the bed had been disturbed. Another mental note: ask Drew if he had sat on the bed or taken a nap before reporting his wife missing. Jared glanced at the open book, but didn't touch it.

Drip. Drip. Drip.

An insomniac's nightmare.

The bathroom was all glass, marble, and titanium fixtures. It was an open layout with nowhere to hide. He shut off the valve that was making the racket. And that's when he heard a scratching sound coming from the bedroom. Could be a rat in the attic—could be a killer.

On full alert, he stepped out of the bathroom and listened. The door to the closet was shut. As he walked that way, his feet sank into plush carpet. Pushing down on the chrome handle, he opened the door to the closet.

The inside of the closet was dark, nothing but shadows. He reached his left hand inside, brushed his fingertips against the wall until he found the light switch and flipped it on.

The inside of the closet was shaped like a horseshoe and nearly as big as the guestroom downstairs. His gaze went from the disheveled shirts hanging precariously from wood hangers to the carpeted floor beneath. A section of the carpet was tousled and stained. There had been a scuffle, and this, Jared quickly concluded, was where it had all started.

Gun drawn, he took slow steps toward the island in the middle of the walk-in closet where both sides met. A walk around the island gave him a full view of the entire closet. The shelves above his head were covered with shoeboxes and an assortment of accessories like purses and hats.

He stopped to listen again. The scratching noise had stopped.

He would open drawers later. For now he focused on the shirts near the light switch. Heading that way, he bent down and noticed a lone button and what looked like blood smears on the carpet.

John and Rochelle
Sacramento
June 2007

"Oh, God, what have I done?" Rochelle cried out, her hair dirty and stringy around her face.

Both of his hands were unrestricted now, and John worked frantically at the ropes around his ankles. The right leg came loose. One more ankle to go and he'd be free. "Rochelle," he said. "It's OK. We're going to get out of here."

She appeared to be delirious, her eyes wild as she rambled incoherently, her chains clinking as she paced a small area of the room. She was confused. In all the frenzy she had accidentally stabbed him more than once with the screwdriver, and she couldn't handle the possibility that she might have hurt him. The pain was intense, but he tried not to alarm her. He used his shirt to stanch the flow of blood.

"You're going to let me go?"

"I'm going to free us both, if that's what you mean."

He had no choice but to ignore her ramblings as he worked at getting loose. If he wanted to get them out of here, he needed to stay focused. He was almost there. Another minute, and he'd be able to work on the chains around Rochelle's leg.

A siren sounded in the distance.

Rochelle's head snapped up, her eyes wide, alert, hopeful.

John didn't have the heart to tell her that nobody could possibly hear them down here. There were no windows, no way for anybody to hear their cries for help.

Rochelle must have sensed this, especially since the sound of the siren was growing fainter instead of louder.

She sank down to her knees, crawled away from him, and huddled in a corner, shivering.

John wanted nothing more than to get upstairs and beat the shit out of the guys who had done this to them, but his left leg was still tied to the chair. Until he could break free, he was defenseless. He grabbed the screwdriver and worked furiously at the rope on his left leg. Gritting his teeth, veins popping, he pulled his foot free.

I did it! For the first time in days, maybe weeks, he was able to push himself to his feet. Unsteadily, he stood there for a moment, his legs bent at the knees while he found balance. He took a step and then another. He wobbled, slipped on blood, and fell to the mattress where Rochelle had been sleeping every night for weeks. The smell of her brought tears to his eyes.

She didn't move as he tried to remove her chains. Her despondency worried him. She'd been pushed over the edge and seemed to have given up. Each metal link was two inches in diameter. There was no way he could free her without the right tool to cut the metal clamp from her ankle.

He'd heard the men talking earlier, and he knew they could return at any moment.

They were running out of time.

He pushed himself to his feet again, staggered to the area where the tools were kept. There was nothing that could cut through metal. He made his way to the bottom of the steps and crawled his way to the top. His arms and legs felt like noodles. His breathing was shallow, his strength nearly gone. Dread prickled his skin. How was he going to save Rochelle?

The door opened easily. *Thank God.*

He hung tightly onto the wall and pulled himself to his feet. He looked from left to right. If one of the men returned and saw him, he was a dead man.

He hated leaving Rochelle, but it was the only way he could possibly save them both. Rochelle called out for help. Her cries squeezed at his heart as he staggered through the main room to the front door.

Slowly, quietly, in case someone was sleeping in one of the rooms, he turned the knob and opened the door. Fresh air touched his face. He breathed in.

The neighborhood was quiet; the streets were clear. Everything looked the same except that his car was gone.

Rochelle cried out for help.

He turned toward the main room, thought about trying to find another way to free her, but it was too risky. They would die—that much he knew. Every single one of the men who had done this to them would die by his own two hands—and soon.

But for now, he needed to get help. There was no other way. Stepping outside, he stumbled over leaves and dead branches scattered around the yellowing lawn. The sun was half hidden behind a layer of thick clouds. The neighborhood appeared sad and lifeless. Moving as fast as he could, which didn't feel all that fast, he limped his way over a cracked, uneven sidewalk. He had no idea what day it was; he didn't care. He knew only that he needed to find help for Rochelle before darkness descended.

CHAPTER 27

All of the sudden I realized that I had just done something that
separated me from the human race and it was something that
could never be undone. I realized that from that point on I could
never be like normal people. I must have stood there in that state
for twenty minutes. I have never felt an emptiness of self like I
did right then and I never will forget that feeling. It was like I
crossed over into a realm I could never come back from.
—David Gore

Sacramento
Saturday, June 9, 2012

Jared spent most of the night trying to calm Drew down, reminding him that he wouldn't be able to help his wife if he didn't find
a way to keep his composure. Since much of the evidence that
needed to be collected was in Kassie's and Drew's bedroom, the
upstairs was off-limits and Drew was forced to sleep in the guestroom while Jared took the couch.

Jared hadn't slept much, but he must have dozed off for an
hour because it was 4:00 a.m. when he awoke to the sound of a
car door being shut. Jared headed through the kitchen to get to
the garage. He found Drew Scott sitting behind the wheel of his

car while holding a cell phone to his ear. He clicked his cell shut as soon as he saw Jared.

Jared noticed perspiration on Drew's forehead.

"He made contact," Drew said.

"Who made contact?"

"The guy who took my wife."

Drew's hands were shaking. His eyes darted from one side of the garage to the other. Something wasn't right. Jared walked over to the car and peered inside. The backseat was empty. "Open the trunk," he said.

Drew popped the trunk. It was empty.

"What are you doing?" Drew asked. "The man you're looking for made contact. Aren't you going to do something?"

"I'm doing it," Jared said as he returned to the front of the car. "You need to stay calm."

Drew snorted and turned on the ignition.

"Turn off the engine and hand me the keys," Jared told him, his voice firm.

"I'm going to save my wife."

"Turn off the engine. Now."

"Not until you tell me what's going on. What did you find upstairs, and how long are we going to sit here doing nothing?"

Jared needed to calm the man down. To do that, he would need to be honest with him. "There was a struggle upstairs in your bedroom closet."

Drew's head fell forward, his chin hitting his chest, his shoulders moving. He was crying.

Jared reached into the car, shut off the engine, and took the keys. "Where did he tell you to meet him?"

"I'm not supposed to tell you."

"He knows you're cooperating with the FBI?"

"I didn't say anything about that," Drew said, his voice flat, his eyes bloodshot. "He told me that if I made contact with the police or the FBI, the deal was off and Kassie would die."

"Tell me where you're supposed to meet him."

"I can't. He'll kill her."

Jared exhaled. "We're here to help you and your wife, Drew. Tell me where you're supposed to meet the man who called."

"You don't understand. I can't live without her."

"I do understand, Drew. I would never do anything to jeopardize Kassie's life. You've got to let us help you."

"The Shell station on Madison Avenue," Drew said in a low voice. He closed his eyes. "He's going to call again."

"Did he say when?"

"No."

"Tell me exactly what the caller said, Drew, so we can help Kassie."

"There's a pay phone at the Shell station on Madison," Drew said, looking at his lap as he spoke, his voice shaky. "I was instructed to wait until the phone at the station rings. I am to go to the gas station alone. If I'm not the one who answers the phone, the deal's off."

Jared pulled out his cell phone and called Jimmy Martin. "It appears the unsub made contact with Drew during the night. He's been instructed to drive to the Shell station on Madison Avenue."

After relaying the rest of the information, Jared was given the go-ahead: Drew would be allowed to drive to the pay phone and wait for instructions. Jared disconnected his call with Jimmy and returned the car keys to Drew.

It wasn't until Drew had a hold on the keys that he managed to look Jared square in the eyes. "I'm sorry," he said, his eyes tearing, his voice sincere. "I didn't have a choice."

"Didn't have a choice?" Jared asked. But there was no need for Drew to explain, because even before Jared heard the loud static popping or felt the jolt of shocking pain in his neck, he saw movement to his right and realized he'd been duped.

Drew stepped out of the car and hovered over Jared, his face grim. "I had no choice," he said again. "He's going to let Kassie go now. It was the only way I could save her."

The pain was intense. Jared's body cramped, every muscle contracting. He had zero control over his body.

"Get in the car," a man ordered, the same man who had hit Jared in the neck with a high-voltage stun gun.

Drew climbed in behind the wheel while the man hovering over Jared readied a needle.

"The effects of the stun gun won't last long. That's why I'll need to inject you with a tranquilizer. It's the only way I'll be able to get you from Point A to Point B without being seen."

Jared focused on the Lovebird Killer.

He'd spent the past nine months profiling the man, trying to get into his head using an in-depth analysis of each crime scene to gain insight into the motives of the man standing before him now. The Lovebird Killer was Caucasian, five foot ten, and bald. Everything about him appeared stretched out: a giraffe neck, long legs, and abnormally long fingers. His eyes were large, hollow, and blue, and appeared much too big for such a narrow face.

The spasms of pain from the Taser were beginning to subside when Jared felt the prick of a needle in his arm. His vision blurred.

"Where's Kassie?" Drew asked the killer, his voice pleading. "Where can I find her?"

Jared looked at Drew. The man was a fool. He had no idea what he'd done. It was an unwise choice to think he could make a deal with a madman. Sadly, he'd find out soon enough that he might as well have just killed his wife with his own two hands.

"Look at your watch," Jared heard the killer instruct Drew. "In ten minutes, not a second before, you're going to open the garage door and drive to the gas station on Madison, exactly as we discussed. Once you arrive, you'll get a phone call from me telling you where you can find your wife. Now shut the door."

Jared heard the car door shut.

Right before he lost consciousness, he felt his body being dragged out of the garage, through the kitchen, and out the sliding door leading to the backyard.

Sacramento
Saturday, June 9, 2012

Jimmy Martin was already parked across the street when Drew Scott pulled into the gas station on Madison. Another undercover agent had followed Drew to the premises and was now parked kitty-corner to the station. They used their car radios to acknowledge each other's presence.

Drew parked to the left of the pay phone and jumped out of his car. Standing by the phone, he continuously raked his fingers through his hair, clearly agitated. After a few minutes, he began to pace.

While Jimmy and his men waited for the killer to make contact, Jimmy called Jared again. Still no answer. He didn't like the unwelcome thoughts running through his head. Something had gone wrong. He called one of his agents still positioned outside the Scotts' house. "What's going on?"

"Nothing. No movement. No calls."

"When did you talk to Jared last?"

"I've had zero contact."

"I want you to move in, see what's going on. Call me once you're in." Jimmy clicked his phone shut, exited his vehicle, and headed across the street. He showed Drew his badge. "Jimmy Martin, FBI."

Drew's face grew pale.

"What's going on, Drew?"

"What do you mean?"

Jimmy didn't like the guilty look he saw in Drew's eyes. "Tell me what's going on or I won't have any choice but to cuff you and take you in."

"You shouldn't be here," Drew said. "He's going to call."

"What else did the man who took your wife tell you, Drew? Did he make you promises? Did he guarantee you that he would return your wife unharmed if you did exactly as he said?"

"How could you know that?"

Jimmy raked his fingers through his hair again. His phone rang and he picked up his cell.

"I'm inside," the agent told Jimmy.

"What do you see?"

"It's apparent that a heavy object, more than likely a body, was dragged through the house, dumped into a wheelbarrow, judging by the tracks in the lawn, and then pushed through a private gate that leads to a greenbelt—twenty acres of trees and tall weeds."

"No sign of Shayne?"

"Afraid not."

"Get forensics in there, pronto."

"Already on it. They're scouring the grounds, inside and out."

As soon as Jimmy hung up, his phone rang again. "What's up?"

"The pay phone is out of order. If Drew Scott has a telephone conversation, it's not going to take place on the phone next to you."

Jimmy clicked his phone shut, looked at Drew, and said, "Come on. You're coming with me."

"You don't understand. I can't leave. When that phone rings, I have to be the one to answer the call or he'll kill her."

"Nobody's going to call."

"That's not true."

Jimmy reached over and picked up the phone, listened for a second, and then handed the receiver to Drew. Panicking, Drew dug into his pocket, deposited a few coins, and then frantically pushed the lever up and down.

The phone was dead.

Davis
Saturday, June 9, 2012

"We've been at this all night," Lizzy said when she saw Jessica asleep on the couch. "Stacey probably needs to get home to her family. Let's go over what we have so far and then reconvene—" Her phone rang, interrupting her announcement. She checked the ID and saw that it was Jimmy Martin. She hit Talk. "Hi, Jimmy. What's going on?"

"It's not good, Lizzy. You might want to sit down."

She didn't bother looking for a chair. "Out with it, Jimmy."

The tone of her voice was gruff enough to cause everybody in the room to look her way.

"He's got Jared."

"Who?"

"The Lovebird Killer."

That didn't make any sense. Jared was competent and smart. He carried a gun, for God's sake. There was no way he would have walked off with a killer, but Jimmy wouldn't screw around with her, wouldn't call at all unless what he was telling her was the truth. "How?" she asked. "How could that happen?"

"He was betrayed by Drew Scott. We have the man in custody. He helped the killer overpower Jared after being assured his wife would be spared if he did as the killer asked."

Lizzy did find a seat on the couch; she sank into the cushions and tried to wrap her mind around everything Jimmy was telling her. "Do we have any idea where he might be, any idea at all?"

"No."

"Nobody saw a car leave?"

"Drew was instructed to drive to a pay phone on Madison. Two of my men followed him. Jared had made contact minutes before. There was no reason to believe there was a problem. He did not sound as if he was under duress. He must have been overpowered soon after making contact."

"But how could the killer have gotten Jared out of the house without being seen by you and your men?"

"There's a greenbelt running through the backyard, behind the house. Jared was moved across more than ten acres of weeds in a wheelbarrow, probably to a car that was waiting. After the tracks in the field end, there are no trails. It was still dark and there are no witnesses so far."

Lizzy rubbed her temple and tried to remain calm. "I have my task force here, Jimmy. There's been a lot going on these past few days. I've received strange calls. I wonder if there might possibly be a connection to the case you're working on. I think you might want to come by the house so we can talk."

After Jimmy agreed to meet with her, Lizzy hung up the phone and looked toward the dining area, where Hayley and Stacey had been working all night long: making calls, taking notes, and searching for information on the Internet. Five minutes ago, Stacey had been getting ready to head home. Now her jacket was off and her sleeves were rolled up to her elbows. She looked at Lizzy. "We're going to find him."

Saturday, June 9, 2012

Jared awoke with a pounding headache. Dazed and groggy from whatever had been shot into his bloodstream, he tried, unsuccessfully, to lift his head. He put a hand to his forehead, feeling strangely disconnected, as if he were floating. For the next ten minutes, he concentrated on his breathing until his surroundings became less hazy.

He was inside a cage: a ten-by-ten cage with the same diamond mesh used as fencing around most sports fields. All four sides and the roof were made from the same material. Jared wasn't sure how much time passed as he drifted in and out of consciousness.

When he opened his eyes again, Jared heard someone moan. He was lying on a thin mattress with no blankets. He crawled off the mattress and used the diamond mesh to pull himself to his feet. As his eyes adjusted to the dark, he saw that there were two cages in the room, only inches separating them. It took a moment to figure out what he was looking at. There was a woman in the cage next to him. She was lying faceup. She wore no clothing. Her long hair drifted over the edge of the mattress behind her head.

"Kassie?" he called out, his voice raspy.

Another moan.

Jared looked around, his eyes settling on another woman, sitting in a chair in the corner of the room. She had on a colorful dress, tights, and black heels. Her head rested to one side. A large hat made it impossible for him to see her face, but she had long auburn hair that fell across thin shoulders. "Hey!" Jared called out. "Wake up."

The woman in the chair didn't move.

The woman in the cage next to him moaned again, but his gaze was now focused on the wall of souvenirs: teeth, bones, fingers, and toes. Driver's licenses and scalps with hair. Pushpins and nails had been used to hang jewelry, pictures, newspaper clippings, dried organs, and skin. If these were the doings of the Lovebird Killer, it appeared he'd killed many more people than they'd given him credit for.

Jared felt for his gun. Of course it was gone. He shoved his hands deep into his pockets. No cell phone or wallet. His gaze returned to the room he was being kept in. There was a desk pushed up against the souvenir wall. To his right was an old model television set atop a small table. Above the table was a shelf covered with jars of all sizes filled with what he assumed was formaldehyde, since the organs inside looked to be well preserved.

"Leave me alone," the woman in the cage cried. "Don't touch me."

Jared returned his gaze to the woman in the other cage. "My name is Jared Shayne," he told her, his voice calm. "I'm with the FBI. I'm not going to harm you."

The woman turned her head so that she could see him. Her eyes were wide and fearful. "Are you here to help me?"

"If I can get out of this cage, I'm not going anywhere without you."

"I'm cold," she said.

"Can you move?"

She nodded, and then winced in pain as she tried to climb off the mattress.

Jared took off his jacket and then peeled off his shirt since his jacket was too thick to fit through the wire mesh. He rolled his long-sleeved button-down shirt into one long piece of fabric and began to snake the fabric through the wire mesh until the cotton fabric touched her cage.

She saw what he was doing. It took her a while, but she managed to crawl across the cage floor, reach for the end of his shirt, and pull the fabric through. Upon closer view, Jared could see she'd been cut in more than one place. The incisions were neatly sewn, each stitch short and precise. One of the longer wounds across her collarbone looked red and swollen. He leaned close to the cage for a better look, and that's when he saw movement beneath her flesh. "What the hell did he do to you?"

Tears slid down both sides of her face as she struggled to slide her right arm into the sleeve of his shirt. There was nothing he could do to help her and it frustrated him. They needed to open the wound and get whatever the hell was crawling inside out of her.

She looked at him and easily read his thoughts. "The stitching is small and precise and the wound hurts too much to touch. I can't do anything about it."

Jared gritted his teeth. *Stay calm. Find a way out.* "Your husband reported you missing," he said as he walked from one side of the cage to the other, pushing here, pulling there, checking for weak links.

"Is he all right?"

Jared climbed the cage to see if he could find a way to push through the top. The cage was made of galvanized steel and was wired together. He would need wire clippers. "Your husband is worried about you, but he's fine. He won't be harmed."

"How can you be sure? He got you, didn't he?"

"Apparently, the abductor wanted me instead of your husband."

"Why?"

"I'm not sure."

She crawled to her mattress and then propped herself up against the wire mesh, legs straight out as she buttoned the shirt. "Does the FBI know where we are?"

"No." If they did, Jared thought, they would have knocked down a few doors already.

Jared gestured toward the woman in the corner. "Is she sleeping?"

Kassie shrugged. "She hasn't moved since I've been here. Wherever here is."

"Are we inside a house?"

"I was locked inside a trunk on my ride here. I have no idea."

"We're going to get out of here," Jared assured her.

Their gazes locked and she forced a tight smile. "I'm a big girl," she said. "You can save the glass-is-half-full bullshit for somebody else."

"Sorry. You're right." Jared slid on his jacket. "Habit. I'm usually sitting on the other side of the table from the bad guy after he's been caught, not before."

"No," she whispered. "I'm sorry. You're not the one to blame." Her eyes probed his for answers. "Were you looking for this guy before I was kidnapped?"

Jared nodded.

"Who is he?"

"He's known as the Lovebird Killer. He seems to focus on couples, taking the female first, and within twenty-four hours, the husband or partner goes missing, too. As soon as your husband reported you missing, we went with a hunch. We talked to Drew, asked him to play it cool and take a trip to the market so I could climb in his car and get inside your garage unseen. The killer found a way to make contact with your husband and make a deal—me in exchange for your release."

"Oh, Drew," she said.

"He was desperate," Jared said in her husband's defense.

"While I was in the trunk," she said, "I kept track of how long it took to get here. It was no more than twenty minutes from my house to wherever we are."

Jared continued to examine the cage. He tried to lift one of the corners, but it wouldn't budge. Metal clamps and concrete screws had been used to keep the cage in place.

He opened and shut the porta potty, picked up the mattress, examining it closely, looking for something he might be able to use as a weapon. There were two water bottles and a granola bar next to his mattress. He looked inside Kassie's cage, wondering whether she had water and food. He followed her gaze across the room, where he could see two full bottles on the ground and out of reach.

"I lost my cool," she told him. "I threw the water bottles at him; didn't even take a good shot. At least I was able to stab him with a steak knife when he opened the trunk to get me out. I didn't hit any major organs, but I tried."

Jared remembered seeing a steak knife on the floor of her kitchen. She must have dropped one and hidden the other as he dragged her out of the house. He squeezed one of his water bottles out of his cage and pushed it close enough to her cage that she could get to it.

"Thanks."

Jared nodded.

"I'm a child psychologist," she said when Jared took a seat on the mattress. "Every day I talk to emotionally disturbed children, kids who have been verbally and physically abused. I try to convince them that everything will be OK. I tell them how brave they are and how sorry I am that these horrible things happened to them. I tell them they're not alone and that I'll do everything to help. But you know what? In the end, they really are alone. I'm not there in the middle of the night when they wake up in a cold sweat. Until now, I never really understood the true horrors of what some of those kids have been through." She shook her head. "At the time, though, as I listened to their stories of horrific abuse, I really thought I understood. Nobody understands what another person has been through until they have walked in their shoes." She sighed. "I've always been passionate about my work." She winced in pain and clutched her stomach as if she were cramping. When she recovered, she said, "I realize now that I'm a fraud—nothing but an impostor."

Jared was about to try to comfort her when he heard a sound and saw the man's giant booted feet descending a steep set of narrow wooden stairs.

"Ah," the man said as he finally stepped onto solid ground. "I see you two have become fast friends. Charming."

He focused on Kassie and shook his head. "Poor, stupid Drew. Do you think he's still waiting for my call?"

Jared didn't take the bait. Neither did Kassie.

"You gave her the clothes off your back, I see," he said to Jared, then chuckled. "So gentlemanly of you." As he continued to stare at Jared, his head cocked in a bizarre manner, his eyes widened. "You don't appreciate a woman's body?"

"She was cold," Jared said flatly.

"Ah, silly me. Why didn't I think of that?" The man rubbed his bald head as he looked around. "What do you think of my special place?"

Silence.

"Is that woman in the chair OK?" Jared asked.

The man turned toward the woman in the corner of the room. "The nice FBI man wants to know if you're OK." He walked toward the woman, leaned over, and whispered into her ear. Then he put his ear to her mouth and nodded like she was whispering into his ear.

He straightened and said, "She appreciates your concern, but she had a long day and she's tired."

"Who is she?" Jared asked.

"She's the love of my life—my everything. She's *my* Lizzy."

Jared tried to appear undisturbed by his answer, although he was anything but. By mentioning Lizzy's name, this man was letting Jared know he knew intimate details of his life. Most killers liked to get a reaction, which was why Jared refused to give him one. "What's her name?" Jared pressed on, wanting to know more about the woman in the chair. He couldn't tell if she'd been drugged or if she was dead. Hell, he wasn't even sure if she was real. She was sitting in the darkest corner of the room. She wore tights and gloves. A scarf covered her neck and a hat covered her face. Her head appeared to be resting on her shoulder as if she were sleeping.

"She'll tell you her name when she's ready." He rubbed his hands together. "I have a big day planned—there's a lot to do."

Jared noticed that Kassie was now lying on the mattress, her body shaking. "Let Kassie go," he said.

The killer looked at Jared. "Your chivalry has no end. No wonder Lizzy is so drawn to you." He crossed his arms. "Sorry, no can do. The woman stays. I have big plans for Kassie. Plans I have no intention of telling you. Show, don't tell. That's my new motto; do you like it?" He didn't wait for an answer before he said, "Kassie is fully aware of what her fate will be." He cupped a hand around his mouth as if he didn't want the woman sitting in the chair to hear what he was about to say. "To be honest, I would tell you, but I can't...not in front of my fiancée. She doesn't like it when I bring other ladies home. She's a jealous female," he said with a wink.

CHAPTER 28

I was born with the devil in me. I could not help the fact that I
was a murderer, no more than the poet can help the inspiration
to sing…I was born with the evil one standing as my sponsor
beside the bed where I was ushered into the world,
and he has been with me since.
—H.H. Holmes

Davis
Saturday, June 9, 2012

It was seven o'clock on Saturday morning. They had been up all
night. Jessica had dozed off for a few hours, but she was awake
now and making a fresh pot of coffee in the kitchen.

Stacey had been making calls for hours. At 5:30 a.m., her
assistant had personally delivered the transcript Stacey had been
looking for, the story she'd been talking about. The embalmer
couple who stuffed dead bodies with pine sawyer beetles. Sure
enough, Karen and Todd Beck used to live at the same address in
Lincoln where Lizzy had gone yesterday.

Lizzy clicked shut her cell phone. "That was Jimmy," she said.
"The FBI talked to the Becks about a year ago. They searched the
property and found nothing to tie them to the Lovebird Killer, but

he's agreed to take another look. They're scouring the grounds in Lincoln now. The trees are infested with the beetles, but nobody appears to be home and they won't be able to get inside the house until they have a warrant."

"You have to look at this," Hayley said. "I found a listing for Beck's Limousine Service. Could Jennifer have written Beck's Limousine instead of Best?"

"I'll talk to Jimmy about that," Lizzy said. "Have you learned anything about the Becks' adopted son? Do we know where he is or what he's doing?"

"Robert Beck, who lived with quite a few families before he was adopted by the Becks, was eleven or twelve when he was taken in by the Hargroves. The Hargroves were the last foster family to take Robert in before he went to live with the Becks. I can't find much information on Robert Beck, but when I searched the name "Hargrove" I learned that the Hargroves had taken in three boys and they all attended the same school. A boy named Robert was listed as a student of Maria Trumble. His age is consistent with Robert Beck's age at the time. In a blog written by a teacher of that same name, she wrote a post about a boy in her class who once had extreme discipline problems. He'd been passed from foster home to foster home, but she believes he was finally adopted. She doesn't mention a name, although he was only in her class for one year, which is consistent with my records of Robert Hargrove being at Twin Rivers Unified School District, where she still teaches. I have her home address if you need it."

Fifteen minutes later, Lizzy was in her car, headed for Maria Trumble's house on Cottage Way in Sacramento. The traffic was heavy for a Saturday morning. Lizzy counted to ten, trying to keep her mind off Jared and what he must be going through.

What if something happened to him?

She couldn't think that way. She couldn't live without him.

*One. Two. Three...*She counted all the way to Maria Trumble's house.

Cottage Way was a quiet street in Sacramento. The house was surrounded by colorful flower beds and a nicely manicured lawn. Lizzy parked at the curb and headed for the front door. There was a gray Prius in the driveway. It was early, but the only thing on Lizzy's mind as she pushed the doorbell was finding Jared.

Before she could hit the doorbell again, a gray-haired woman peeked through the living room curtain, then opened the front door a few inches, leaving the chain in place. "It's Saturday and it's early. Do I know you?"

"I'm Lizzy Gardner. I'm a private investigator and I need to talk to you. It's an emergency; otherwise I would never have bothered you like this."

"I don't see how—"

"I read something you wrote on the Internet," Lizzy blurted. "It was about a child you once had in your class...I believe his name was Robert."

The woman stiffened. "I taught Robert twenty years ago," she said. "I don't see how anything I could possibly tell you about that boy could help you."

"Please. I'm begging you to let me in so we can talk. I have a friend who is in immediate danger, and you might be the only person who can help me find him."

The woman sighed. She shut the door, and Lizzy could hear her unfastening the latch before she opened the door again and gestured for Lizzy to come inside.

Sacramento
Saturday, June 9, 2012

After Lizzy had left the house, Stacey headed off, too.

Hayley couldn't stop thinking about John Robinson. She was convinced they needed to learn more about him: first, John Robinson's landlord happened to live in the same house where bodies were once stuffed with pine sawyer beetles. *Coincidence?*

Second, somebody was determined to mess with Lizzy, and the only person who made sense was John Robinson. Maybe he *was* the man pretending to be Eli Simpson and he'd found out that Lizzy was helping the real Eli Simpson investigate the disappearance of his sister.

Third, if John Robinson was capable of impersonating other people and making Eli's sister disappear, then maybe, just maybe, he was fucked up enough to go after Lizzy, too.

Hayley finished reading the police reports in the Eli Simpson/John Robinson file and handed it to Jessica to read. According to Eli Simpson, John Robinson's neighbor Claire Schultz had seen everything, and she knew exactly what had happened to his sister five years ago.

It took some doing, but Hayley convinced Jessica to drive her to Claire's house. She refused to sit there and twiddle her thumbs.

Hayley knocked on Claire Schultz's door while Jessica looked down the street toward John Robinson's house. Lizzy had told them about the beetles' connection to the Lovebird Killer, which made Hayley wonder if John Robinson's ties to the Becks could mean he was doing more than just screwing with people's minds. Before she could say as much to Jessica, an elderly woman opened the door. She reminded Jessica of an apple doll: deep-set eyes, a sizable nose, and a slit for a mouth set within a maze of deep facial creases and wrinkles. The woman was short. A thick colorful scarf around her neck emphasized a hunched back. "I don't need any more Girl Scout cookies. Go away."

"We're not selling cookies," Hayley told her. "We need to talk to you about your neighbor down the street, John Robinson."

The woman's face turned ashen. She tried to shut the door, but Hayley jammed her foot inside to stop the woman from closing the door all the way. "There are two people in grave danger. You might be able to help."

"Please," Jessica added.

"If you don't leave this minute, I'm calling the police."

"You know something," Hayley said. "Why won't you help?"

"Sometimes it is best if we mind our own business," the woman said. "Now leave me alone."

Jessica touched Hayley's arm. "Come on, Hayley. She doesn't want to talk about it."

"God, that's what I hate about you," Hayley said, her face red and angrier than Jessica had ever seen her look.

"Jared might die," Hayley went on. "He could be dead already for all we know, but you don't even care. If you did care, you wouldn't take no for an answer. This woman knows something and yet she's going to die knowing because she's afraid of some maniac down the road. The real killers are the people who say nothing."

"That's enough, Hayley. She doesn't have to talk to you or anybody else. It's her right as a citizen of the United States. Leave her alone." Jessica turned to leave. She'd had enough.

"I'll talk to *her*," the woman said, pointing to Jessica.

Jessica turned to face the elderly woman. Sure enough, she opened the door wider, allowing Hayley to step inside. Then she waited for Jessica to enter, too.

Sacramento
Saturday, June 9, 2012

Maria Trumble pulled her robe tight around her waist before she took a seat on the couch facing the chair where Lizzy sat, and said, "In all my years of teaching, I've never met a more disturbed child."

"How so? Loud and obnoxious?"

"Quite the opposite. Robert was quiet—too quiet. In the beginning I thought he was shy, but it didn't take long to recognize that not only was he smart, he could also be very social. As soon as it was time for recess, his dull murky eyes would come alive, except on the days I was scheduled for yard duty. That's when Robert would sit quietly on a bench and read."

"That doesn't sound social to me."

"No, it doesn't, does it?"

Lizzy had no idea where the woman was headed with this story, but she knew she had to be patient if she wanted to keep her talking. What if the Becks' adopted son was somehow connected to the Lovebird Killer? What if he *was* the Lovebird Killer? It was a long shot, but it was the only lead they had. The problem was nobody knew what had become of Robert Beck. Where was he now? Jimmy and his men were in Lincoln, waiting for a warrant so they could get inside the Becks' house. She kept glancing at her cell phone, praying he would call and tell her he'd found Jared.

"Whenever I was on playground duty," Mrs. Trumble said, "Robert was on his best behavior because he knew that I was watching him."

"But on the other days? The days you weren't on duty?"

"On those days, all bets were off. On those days something always happened. A child would 'fall' off the bars and break an arm or a leg. Fire alarms would go off or a dead animal would be found in one of the bathrooms." She shook her head. "Never failed."

"And you think Robert was responsible?"

"I *know* Robert was responsible."

"How could you know for sure?"

"Because he told me."

"He would push a child off the bars or start the fire alarm and then tell you what he did?"

She nodded. "And then, as I'm sure was all part of his devilish plan, I would report him to the school principal. He would be called in to the office, too, and that's when Robert put on the charm. All it took were clever words and an innocent look to convince the principal that I had it out for him. Sometimes he would blame another innocent child, but either way, the end result was the same: he would walk out of the principal's office with a smirk."

"On a few occasions you walked Robert home from school, is that right?"

She nodded. "I knew Mrs. Hargrove personally. She had fostered two other boys, and she was a lovely person and a wonderful mother."

"And so you wanted to tell her what was going on?"

"Absolutely. I wanted to warn her. She needed to know. I was afraid for her."

"Afraid that Robert would hurt her?"

"Afraid he would kill her."

"He was only eleven years old at the time," Lizzy said, surprised by the woman's serious tone.

"Yes, he was only a boy, but he had a dark mind. The boy was delusional. On a few occasions I walked Robert home and had a talk with Mrs. Hargrove. She told me that all three of her boys had spent time with a therapist. She said Robert was diagnosed as having an uncommon psychiatric condition known as delusional disorder. He would make up stories in his head. For example, he was convinced that he was popular and well liked, while the truth was most children his age were afraid of him."

"What causes delusional disorder?"

"Many things, including a traumatic childhood, but they believe Robert's disorder occurred after his mother disappeared and he was sent to one foster home after another."

"Was he given medication?"

She shrugged. "I believe so, but I never saw an improvement."

"Did you go to the police?"

She shook her head. "I certainly thought about it. He wrote a paper once, describing in detail how he planned to kill Mrs. Hargrove. After he killed her, he planned to kill his teacher, too."

"A past teacher from another school?" Lizzy asked.

"No, he included little drawings in the margins. He wanted to kill me. I saw it in his eyes. I saw it every day."

"But nobody would listen to you even though you had proof?"

"I don't know how he did it, but somehow Robert got ahold of the paper he'd given me. It disappeared from my desk drawer that I kept locked at all times. It wasn't until a concerned friend came in one weekend and set up cameras that I was able to catch Robert defecating on the top of my desk."

"That's horrible."

"That was nothing. I wasn't sure if that would be enough proof, so I kept the camera rolling for two weeks. That was no child; he was a demon. He poked other kids with sharpened pencils. He left dead lizards and frogs inside the other children's desks. He convinced little girls to touch him improperly and they would allow him to touch them, too. To this day, I don't have a clue as to what he said to get them to follow his orders, since there was no audio on the tapes, but that was the last straw."

"But his classmates never told on him?"

She shook her head. "Never. Not one. But the videos did the trick. I finally had the proof I needed, and he was escorted away from my classroom and the school."

"Did you ever hear from him again?"

"No."

"Do you recognize the names Karen and Todd Beck?"

She shook her head again.

Lizzy couldn't hide her disappointment. She'd come here in hopes that this woman could tell her where Robert Beck was now. "Karen and Todd Beck were the people who took Robert in next. In fact, they adopted Robert."

Mrs. Trumble continued to shake her head, saddened. Saddened for Robert or saddened for the couple who took him in, Lizzy wasn't sure.

"They were embalmers," Lizzy went on, "and they pleaded guilty to stuffing two corpses with dead pine sawyer beetles."

The woman shut her eyes. Tears slid down both sides of her face.

"What is it?" Lizzy asked.

"It was him all along."

"Who?"

"Every year for the past ten years, two dead beetles arrive at my house—either by mail or left on my doorstep. I always wondered if it was him."

CHAPTER 29

I carried it too far, that's for sure.
—Jeffrey Dahmer

Sacramento
Saturday, June 9, 2012

Hayley glanced at her phone. They had been at the woman's house for thirty minutes and she had told them absolutely nothing. They didn't have time for this. She bolted to her feet and said, "We need to go, Jessica. People's lives are in danger and we're getting nowhere."

"Well, why did you have us come here in the first place?" Jessica asked.

"Jimmy was at the house in Lincoln, and Lizzy was talking to the teacher in hopes of finding out what happened to Robert Beck. We had to do something. Come on. Let's go."

As Jessica glanced at Claire Schultz, she reached over and patted the top of the woman's hand. "Don't worry. Everything is going to be OK."

"Nothing is going to be OK," Hayley cut in, clearly frustrated. "John Robinson might have killed Eli Simpson's sister, but we'll never know for sure unless people like her stand up to these criminals and tell the truth."

"Don't be rude," Jessica said.

Hayley narrowed her eyes. "She knows what happened the night Eli Simpson's sister disappeared, and yet for some reason she refuses to help. I don't get it."

The woman turned so that her gaze met Hayley's straight on. Her old hands with their paper-thin skin were shaking as she removed her scarf. She reached for the collar of her blouse, yanked the fabric downward, and revealed a red keloid scar that made a twelve-inch winding path over her collarbone and shoulder. "This is what the monster did to me and what he threatened to do again if I talked."

Jessica gasped.

The woman lifted her pant leg, revealing another jagged scar, severely red and puffy, more recent than the other.

"The woman John Robinson brought home that night was trying to get away," Claire said indignantly. "I saw everything through my kitchen window. The young woman who was with him climbed into his car to get away from him, then locked the doors. Nobody else was around. No men surrounding the car, as John Robinson told the police. He's delusional. He believed the woman loved him and wanted to marry him, but according to her brother, Eli, none of that's true. To this day John Robinson talks about Rochelle as if they were a couple in love."

"He did that to you?" Jessica asked.

The woman pointed a shaky finger at Hayley, still unable to look away from her. "Oh, this is nothing. He visits whenever he can just to make sure I'm staying quiet."

Hayley shifted her weight from one foot to the other. "Why didn't you leave?"

"I would have moved from this godforsaken neighborhood years ago if I had the money. But nobody would buy this house.

I never married. I don't have a husband or kids. This house is all I have."

"You have to come with us," Jessica said. "The police will protect you."

"The police don't care. The murderer down the street has convinced them that he's the only one who's *not* crazy. John Robinson is a decent talker. He could convince a brain-surgery patient to skip the anesthesia. He's all talk, but his strong conviction and superior belief in his make-believe stories are hard to challenge. I could talk about what I saw until I was blue and it wouldn't do anyone any good. But there you have it. He's the devil. He's egotistical, arrogant, and pure evil. He was the one who put a fist through the window of his car that night. He choked the girl until she passed out and then he carried her into his house."

"What did you do?" Hayley asked.

"I grabbed my cane and I went to the house. I knocked on his door and I could hear her screams. He didn't answer the door. He obviously didn't care, so I ran home. Before I could grab the phone, I tripped and hit my head on the tile floor. It was all over after that. Days went by before the UPS man found me and called 911. I was in a coma for weeks, and it was weeks after that before I was brought home. Sooner rather than later, John Robinson began to pay me regular visits. I thought he was an angel sent from above. He brought me flowers and groceries and even made me home-cooked meals. But then the memories began to return and I made the mistake of confiding in my new friend. After that, he still visited every week, but only to make certain that I would remain quiet. His methods were quite effective."

"And nobody has seen the girl since that night?"

"She could be buried in his yard, for all I know. John Robinson is a beast. I don't want to know what he did with the poor girl."

When Jessica pulled her phone from her pocket, the business card she'd seen earlier fell out. She picked up the card and was about to make a call, when she read the name scribbled on the back again. "Belle Gunness," she said aloud, followed by, "Shit."

"What is it?" Hayley asked.

"John Robinson, Dennis Nilsen, and Belle Gunness. I know where I've heard their names. I learned about all three of these people during my last behavioral class."

"Spit it out," Hayley said. "Who are they?"

"They're all serial killers."

Hayley went to the window and looked down the street toward John Robinson's house. "Jared could be in there."

"John Robinson could be a man of many names, including Robert Beck, the adopted son of the embalmers," Jessica said. "I'm calling Lizzy."

Sacramento
Saturday, June 9, 2012

Lizzy left Mrs. Trumble and climbed into her car at the same moment her phone rang. She picked up the call.

"He is going to die. You understand that, don't you?"

Lizzy drew in a breath.

"You don't catch on quickly, do you?"

"Call me slow," she said. "So you're a serial-killer wannabe, is that it?"

"I'm God."

"Give me a break. You're not even Satan's cousin. You can't even find your own victims. You have to use someone else's leftovers," she said, referring to herself.

"I have something I believe you might want."

"And what would that be?"

"I believe his initials are J.S."

She closed her eyes but said nothing, praying Jared was still alive.

"No smart-ass response?"

"Fuck you."

He laughed. "Much better."

"Oh, good, because I aim only to please you."

"You are a gritty little bitch, aren't you?"

"Oh, stop, you're making me blush. Since I have you on the phone," Lizzy added, "what's with the beetle fetish?"

"I don't know what you're talking about."

She didn't believe that for a minute. "If you're so sure of yourself, so confident that you can kidnap an FBI agent and not get caught, then hand him the phone and let me talk to him."

"Because I'm a nice guy, I'll let you say your goodbyes. Because this is it, Lizzy Gardner. You and your boyfriend are finished, kaput, it's over. You had your one chance at true love and you blew it, sister. How does it feel to recognize that you could have had it all, but you were too self-involved, worried about your own silly problems? How does it feel to know that you'll spend the rest of your life all alone?"

"You're an ass."

"I'm not the one who took my life for granted. I really don't think you understand the gravity of your situation. This will be the last time you're ever going to hear his voice. This is your last chance to tell him how you feel."

She could hear some shuffling before she heard Jared's voice. "Lizzy, are you there?"

"Jared," she said, her gut twisting. "Where are you?"

"Absolutely no idea. Kassie Scott is here, though, and she needs medical attention. I want you to keep that in mind as you work with Jimmy."

"I'll tell Jimmy. He's searching a house in Lincoln."

"Not that far," Jared said.

"Sacramento?" she asked. They both knew the drill. There was no time for heartfelt sentiments. Get out as much information as quickly as possible.

"Yes."

"Can the phone be traced?"

"Disposable."

"Is there anything you can tell me about him? Anything to help us figure out who he is?"

"Basement. Two cages. Reminds me of a kennel. He likes to play dress-up."

"Hand over the phone or the woman gets cut. Now!"

Lizzy heard a woman cry out.

"I think we're done here," the killer told Lizzy. "You had your chance to say goodbye."

"Let Kassie go," Lizzy pleaded. "If she needs medical attention, the last thing you need is another murder on your list of offenses."

"My, my, you do sound a lot like your boyfriend."

"Why are you doing this? What's the endgame?"

He chuckled at that. "Endgame?"

"Yeah, what do you get out of this? What's in it for you?"

"Are you fucking kidding me? This is it! Talking to you and having long thoughtful chats with a child psychologist." She could hear him breathing heavily before he added, "I have an FBI agent sitting in a cage...and you're asking me what's in it for me? This is a fucking thrill! I feel like I'm riding one of those state-of-the-art roller coaster rides with all those amazing g-forces and vertical loops. But you know what, sweetheart, you're right, there is an endgame, and the ultimate orgasmic thrill involves you, Lizzy. I want to see your face when you find your boyfriend's head on a pole on Highway 80. But first, before I kill him, I want Mr. Shayne to watch me closely as I deal with Kassie. I want your boyfriend to see firsthand how a dark mind really works."

After the killer disconnected their call, Lizzy's cell rang again. It was Jessica. "What's going on?" Lizzy asked, unwilling to allow herself time to fall apart.

"We have a connection: John Robinson, Dennis Nilsen, and Belle Gunness. All three are names belonging to serial killers. I believe they're all the same person, including Robert Beck."

Lizzy let the news sink in. Robert Beck was a bad seed. He went from foster home to foster home until he was finally adopted by Karen and Todd Beck. Where were Karen and Todd Beck now? she wondered. Was their son, Robert, the one responsible for stuffing the corpses with dead beetles? Did they love him so much that they had been willing to take the fall for their son's actions?

"Lizzy, are you there?"

"I'm here."

"Hayley and I are with John Robinson's neighbor Claire Schultz. She told us everything. Eli Simpson was right. Not only was John Robinson with Eli's sister, Rochelle, the night she disappeared, but, according to Claire, the man put his fist through the car window, choked her until she passed out, and then carried her into his home. She said that nobody else was involved. The story he told the police was one big lie."

"Why didn't Claire go to the police?"

"Because John Robinson has been torturing her and threatening her. She has the scars to prove it. It's awful, Lizzy."

"I need you to call the police. I'll call Jimmy and tell him what's going on."

"Hayley already called," Jessica answered. "They're on their way."

CHAPTER 30

Even when she was dead, she was still bitching at me.
I couldn't get her to shut up!
—Edmund Kemper

Saturday, June 9, 2012

Jared watched the Lovebird Killer ready a table—a modern-day stretcher/gurney that an EMT might use to get a patient to the ambulance. It was equipped with a device that would raise and lower the table. There were also wheels, making it easy for him to move the table from one end of the room to the other. Next, he set up a surgical tray and proceeded to methodically prepare his tools. For a moment he appeared deep in thought as he examined an assortment of scalpels.

Holding a scalpel in the air, he said, "I prefer the rounded number ten blade for making the first cut into the skin." He used a cloth to wipe his favorite scalpel, then held up a retractor used to hold open parts of the body and examined it closely.

Jared glanced at Kassie.

Once again, the killer was hoping for a reaction and yet he wasn't getting one from either of them.

"A dull blade leaves a jagged scar. Not pretty."

Jared watched him closely.

"I bet you're dying to know what I'm going to do with all of this."

"Nope," Jared said. "Not interested."

The man smirked. "It's not for you, if that makes you feel any better."

"It doesn't."

The man smiled as if he already knew what Jared would say. He gently placed a jar on the surgical tray next to the scalpel, the same sort of jar sitting next to the television set—the one with the semipreserved heart inside.

"Was your father a doctor?" Jared asked.

"I have no idea who or what my father was."

"Oh, come on. You must have heard something," Jared prodded. "Where was your father from?"

He picked up the scalpel that he'd already cleaned and wiped it with the cloth again, more vigorously than before.

"Was he a doctor, a mayor, or maybe the town drunk?"

His hands shook slightly as he held the sharp tip toward Jared like he might come forward and enter the cage to finish him off. More than anything, Jared hoped that he would try. He wanted nothing more than to get his hands on the man and take him down.

In the blink of an eye, though, the killer's facial expression changed from outrage to utter calmness. "I get what you're trying to do. Very good. You almost had me for a minute there."

"I'm not trying to do anything," Jared said. "I'm only interested to learn what makes someone like you tick."

"You may be an agent, but you're a profiler at heart, aren't you, Jared Shayne? You like to open up the minds of people like me and dig around, hoping to find something new to throw into your bag of tricks so maybe the next time you're searching for a killer, you might save a life. You're wasting your time. I won't be able to help you, since you'll be as dead as Kassie when I'm done, but I understand your need to prod and analyze."

He left his tools and focused his attention on setting up a digital camcorder, making sure he inserted a new memory card. His actions seemed robotic. Clearly, he'd done this many times before.

After he finished setting up the camera, he said, "Being a killer is like being in love."

"How so?" Jared asked.

"You can't make another person love you, nor can you force yourself to fall in love with someone. Either it is or it isn't. It's the same way with killing. People like me," he said, picking up the scalpel again and brushing the blade across his forearm, "don't suddenly decide to kill one day." Blood dripped slowly down his arm. He smiled. "Either we're born killers or we're not."

He put the scalpel down and fiddled with another tool, making sure it was in working order. Then he looked at Jared. "You're shaking your head. Why is that?"

"Nothing is that simple."

"I respectfully disagree."

"Many killers are made," Jared said, "sculpted by society, the by-product of their parents, relatives, friends, and the life they've been dealt."

"Not in my case."

"How so?"

"I grew up with a loving mother. She doted on me. I was her everything. I was her sunshine and she was mine. She spent time with me, taught me everything she knew, and made sure to tuck me into bed every single night."

Kassie snorted.

Jared ignored her, hoping the man would do the same.

"What is it, Kassie? You have something you want to add to the conversation?"

"You're clearly delusional."

"Ahh, I see. You think you know me, don't you? Think you've seen it all before? Is that what you're thinking, little Miss Child Psychologist?"

"That's right, asshole. You are nothing new. Same old, same old," she said with an exaggerated yawn. "If I had a dollar for every screwed-up kid that sat in my office, looked me right in the eye, and told me his childhood was the best ever, I would have retired years ago."

"Are you saying I'm a liar?" He set down the scalpel, his face a maze of angry lines as he walked forward and wrapped his long pale fingers around the steel bars of Kassie's cage. "Are you saying that my mother was a selfish whore who didn't know I existed—a woman who cared more about feeding food scraps to the pigs than caring for her only son? A woman who was afraid of me because I reminded her of her attacker—her rapist, my father?"

"I don't think that's what she means at all," Jared cut in.

"That's exactly what I'm saying," Kassie said, her voice uncaring and flat, bordering on lifeless.

Clearly she'd been overpowered by defeat, Jared thought, and had already prepared herself for whatever the lunatic had planned for her, including a quick death to end it all.

"How many people have you killed?" Jared asked, hoping to get his attention away from Kassie.

"Not nearly enough," he said, rattling Kassie's cage, but getting no response from the woman inside.

"Are you responsible for the deaths of Charles and Maureen Baker?"

"Of course," he said with a smile, the deep lines in his face softening. "Charles didn't want anything to do with me, but like so many foolish men, there wasn't anything he wouldn't do for Maureen." He sighed. "Love can be so bittersweet."

"What about the Daltons?" Jared asked.

He went to his desk and Jared watched him select a CD from a box. As Roy Orbison's "Only the Lonely" played, he returned to his table and hovered over his tools again. He mouthed the words to the song, singing along with Roy Orbison as he lifted a knife and once again pointed the sharp tip at Jared. "The Daltons," he said, loud enough to be heard over the music. "Those two were tricky. They both had me fooled, but in the end they weren't worth all the trouble I went to. Michael was only in love with himself, but he never would have killed his wife—didn't have the balls for that. Your girlfriend was the only one who seemed to see the big picture. Why is that? All of your big FBI meetings…all of those supposedly brilliant minds in one room, but nobody can put two and two together except for one very scared lost soul." He smiled, his eyes wide and demented. "She's a keeper, that one. After you're out of the way, she'll be all mine. My sweet Lizzy was curious to know what my endgame was. That's it," he said, his wide grin revealing two rows of neglected teeth.

"What about the love of your life?" Jared asked, referring to the woman in the chair, who hadn't moved since his arrival. Jared had no idea if there was a human being or a blow-up doll beneath all the clothes and accessories.

"She'll get over it. She understands that, in the end, I always come back to her."

"How long has your lover over there been dead?" Kassie asked.

He snickered. "She's more alive than you'll ever be."

"Just another delusion," Kassie said with a sigh. "You loved her to death, didn't you? The only way you could keep her at your side was to kill her, dress her up, and play house." She let out a derisive laugh. "Even after she was dead, you had to tie her to the chair to keep her with you. So sad."

That was the proverbial last straw. The man went ballistic. He fished inside his front pocket and pulled out the key to Kassie's cage. There was no hesitation as he unlocked her cage door and dragged Kassie to the table he'd been carefully setting up.

Jared knew Kassie wouldn't be able to fight the man, and she didn't. She had nothing left. The infection from her wounds had caused her body to become feverish and wracked with chills.

"Let her be," Jared said. "Don't do this."

But the man had already strapped her to the table and then raised the gurney to a workable height. He picked up the same scalpel he'd used to cut his arm and didn't waste any time getting started.

Sacramento
Saturday, June 9, 2012

Lizzy pulled up to the curb on Bunker Street. There were police cars and unmarked sedans lining both sides of the street. The media vans had just arrived. She kept hoping her phone would ring again and she would hear Jared's voice. She wanted another chance to tell him she loved him. She wiped her eyes, angry at the world. She had to stay strong. No time for tears. They would find Jared. They had to.

She had talked to Jimmy a few minutes ago. His warrant had arrived and he and his men were finally inside the Lincoln house.

Still no sign of Jared or Kassie Scott, but they did find the well-preserved and embalmed bodies belonging to Todd and Karen Beck. Inside another barnlike building on the edge of their property, they found an old limousine with two dead bodies that consisted mostly of bone and hair, bodies they believed belonged to Maureen and Charles Baker.

Lizzy opened her car door, but before she could exit, Jessica hurried over—her eyes puffy and bloodshot.

Lizzy's heart sank as she prepared herself for the worst. "What did they find?"

"Jared's not inside the home."

Lizzy's phone rang. She opened her cell and held it to her ear, disappointed when she heard Maria Trumble's voice instead of Jared's.

"There were a few things I remembered about Robert."

"What?"

"Every Wednesday, I have the kids in my class write about something or someone important in their lives. It's a task I've had my kids do since I began teaching thirty years ago. Robert always wrote about his biological mother, who disappeared when he was young. Her name was Lily. I think that's why he was always fascinated with flowers. Every so often, Robert would come to school dressed up as a female. I'm not certain, but I think many of the clothes he used to wear belonged to an older woman. In fact, I always figured the clothes must have belonged to his dead mother."

Lizzy thanked her and then hung up the phone.

Flowers.

A man dressed as a woman.

She looked at Jessica and said, "Lily's Flower Shop. That's it!"

"What are you talking about?" Jessica asked. "Who was that?"

"I don't have time to explain. I'll call Jimmy on my way. I need you to tell Lieutenant Greer that I'm headed for Lily's Flower Shop downtown. Tell him to send backup. Now."

Lizzy shut her door and took off, leaving screech marks on the pavement.

"Where is she going?" Hayley asked as she ran across the street.

"She wants me to tell Lieutenant Greer that she's going to Lily's Flower Shop and to send backup."

"Come on," Hayley said. "We've got to follow her. She can't do this alone."

"Can't do what alone? What about the lieutenant?"

Hayley was already jumping into the passenger seat of Jessica's red Volvo. "I'll call Greer on our way. Come on, Jessica. Hurry up. We don't want to lose her."

Sacramento
Saturday, June 9, 2012

Lizzy parked at the curb in front of Lily's Flower Shop, turned off the engine, and jumped out. She ran to the front entrance, but the door was locked. Peering through the glass, she could see the front counter where she'd talked to Jane, the owner, when she was here last. Jane had been dressed up as a woman, but she was a man. She was Robert Beck, Lizzy was sure of it. Eli had said that John Robinson worked at a shop downtown, but Lizzy hadn't thought to ask for more details because she'd had no reason to believe John Robinson was the Lovebird Killer. She'd also been overwhelmed with too much going on at once. But at the moment, she had clarity. John Robinson was a man of many names. He had tortured Claire Schultz into silence. No doubt, he had killed Eli's sister and how many others?

She ran to the rear of the store, but the storage area where trucks made deliveries was closed off by a high metal gate topped off with circular barbed wire. A lot of security for a flower shop. She rushed back to the entry door, gun in hand, ready to fire at the lock, when she heard Hayley yell, "Stop."

While Hayley pulled out a tool and worked the lock, Lizzy looked toward the street. "Where's Jessica?"

"She's in the car, talking to Greer."

"Why isn't the alarm on your ankle monitor beeping?"

"It's a long story," Hayley said right before they heard a *click* and the door came open.

Without waiting for an explanation, Lizzy ran inside the building. "Stay near the front of the store," she ordered. "I'm going to take a look around."

Lizzy held her gun in front of her as she took slow, methodical steps. The front room was empty. The back room was covered with boxes: some empty, many filled with vases and dried flowers used in the arrangements. The sweet smell of tuberoses contrasted greatly with the deadly games the owner of the shop played on a daily basis. There were two small desks. She glanced under both, and then opened drawers and cupboards lining the walls. She came up empty.

After a moment, she stopped and listened.

Hayley walked into the room and pointed to the five-by-six wool carpet in the middle of the room. Lizzy pulled at a corner of the carpet, but it wouldn't budge. The carpet was stuck to the floor, but she heard something click beneath the rug. "Help me out here," she told Hayley. Together they pulled as hard as they could and ended up opening a trapdoor—the entrance to the bowels of Hell, no doubt.

Was Jared down there? Was she too late?

Music blared from inside the hole. Lizzy looked at Hayley. "I want you to stay here. I mean it, Hayley."

Hayley nodded.

"Do you have something to protect yourself with?" Lizzy asked next.

"Do bears shit in the woods?"

Lizzy headed down the steep wooden stairs leading to a concrete floor below. The smell of antiseptic was overwhelming, immediately overpowering her senses. She didn't bother looking at Hayley; she just headed downward, unafraid, determined to find Jared before it was too late.

Saturday, June 9, 2012

Blood pumped faster through Jared's veins as he watched the killer slice through Kassie Scott. The worst part was that there was nothing he could do about it. The lunatic was right. Nothing Jared had done in his life as an agent so far had prepared him for this moment. Like many agents, he'd spent hours sitting across the table from a killer, looking into the eyes of a madman as the unsub rambled on, gleefully recalling one horrific act after another—no remorse, no shame—retelling his stories for the sheer pleasure of being able to relive the killing within the ears of the listener.

For years, Jared had thought he understood what Lizzy must have felt when she talked about being beaten down by flashbacks of when she was held captive by a killer and forced to watch young girls being tortured. Now he realized he hadn't understood at all.

For the first time since he'd been dragged into the madman's basement, he felt a powerful rage building within.

So far, Kassie had been cut open in three different places. The killer had engraved the outline of a heart in her chest, deep enough to draw blood, but not deep enough to cause her to bleed to death. It was clear he took his surgical procedures seriously, as if each cut were an art form. One thing was certain: he had succeeded in getting Kassie's adrenaline going. Her chest rose and fell with each breath. Every time she asked the madman to kill her and be done with it, he seemed to become calmer and more composed. While the man worked on Kassie, Jared continued to check every inch of the cage. He crawled to the top and rattled every corner, making the killer laugh every time he did so.

Ignoring Jared for a while, the man talked to Kassie instead. "I heard you talking on the phone when I was hiding out in your closet, waiting for you to enter your bedroom. I believe you said you had a surprise for your husband. Tell me your secret, Kassie dear, or I'm going to cut you open and see it for myself."

"I have no idea what you're talking about," she said, her voice quivering.

He calmly unscrewed the lid from the jar. "Don't worry if you pass out during the surgical procedure. When you wake up, your baby will be preserved in a jar. I'll make sure Drew gets—"

"I'm pregnant," she said as if her declaration might save her baby. "Don't hurt my baby. Please."

"You forgot to turn on the video," Jared blurted, finally able to breathe when the man left Kassie's side long enough to check.

"Nice try," he said, smiling at Jared, knowing he'd been tricked. He returned to the table and put the scalpel to her stomach. "Don't worry," he told Kassie. "Your baby won't feel a thing."

Behind the killer, Jared saw movement. Stunned to see Lizzy making her way down the stairs, he threw his body into the front of the cage, over and over, screaming at the top of his lungs, anything to stop the man from looking over his shoulder.

Lizzy didn't try to make sense of what she was seeing: Jared screaming and Roy Orbison's voice singing "Only the Lonely." She knew crazy and this was it. The moment both feet were firmly on the concrete floor, she kept a good distance away from the man in the lab coat and raised her gun. "Drop the knife, Robert. It's over."

He whirled around, the scalpel firmly in his grip as he grinned from ear to ear. "You found me. Spiderman was right about you. You *are* full of surprises."

She recognized him at once. Not only was he the owner of the flower shop, the man dressed up as Jane, he was also her attacker in the park. "Drop the knife or I'll shoot."

He hardly flinched. Just kept smiling, a wild fanatical look in his eyes. "I should have taken care of you while I had the chance."

"Yeah, that's what they all say. Drop the knife."

"You won't shoot because you can't."

She'd been practicing at the shooting range for years. She knew all about vertical alignment. She had no reason to twist at the waist or the knees. Hitting her target would not require a lot of effort, especially at such close range.

Disregarding her completely, Robert Beck returned to his work, intent on finishing whatever it was he'd started.

Lizzy squeezed the trigger. The first shot hit his left shoulder.

He kept on working.

The next bullet lodged into his upper thigh and the third bullet slammed into the back of his knee, the sound of the gunshots echoing off the walls.

He crumpled to the ground, faceup, his eyes wide with astonishment as if he still didn't believe she'd dared shoot him.

"This was all a game to you," she said, keeping her gun aimed at his heart. "You thought you could just keep pissing me off and I wouldn't find you?"

She heard the sounds of sirens getting closer. Thank God, because she had no idea if the woman on the table was dead or alive. There were no gaping wounds, just odd outlines and areas that had been cut and sewn up, green pus seeping from a wound on her collarbone, and blood everywhere.

Lizzy's gaze fell on the woman in the chair. Keeping the gun aimed at Robert Beck, she moved toward the woman and lifted her hat. She recognized her face at once and sucked in a breath at the horrid sight of her. "Rochelle Simpson. That police report you filed," she said to Robert, "was all lies."

"It was the truth," Robert said.

Lizzy shook her head at him. "Claire Schultz saw you break the car window, choke Rochelle, and then carry her into your house. She heard Rochelle's screams. There was nobody else in the vicinity. You killed the one woman who cared about you."

He remained silent.

"You preserved her body. Why?"

He picked up the scalpel from the floor nearby and began to slowly cut into his chest, starting at the point just beneath his throat and working his way downward, cutting straight and deep. "You wouldn't understand," he said, his gaze focused on the blood seeping out of his body as he sliced through his skin. "I was lonely."

Blood oozed from his gaping wound.

Lizzy did nothing to stop him.

Robert looked at Jared. "Do you want to know why I finally killed my mother?"

Jared didn't say a word, didn't flinch.

"She didn't love me. She never loved me," Robert said as his hand, along with the scalpel, fell to the concrete floor with a *clank*.

Lizzy looked from Jared to the lock on the door to his cage. "Where's the key?"

"In his front pant pocket."

She kicked the scalpel out of the way, and it skidded through a puddle of blood. Kneeling at Robert's side, she reached deep into his pocket and pulled out the keys. Robert Beck's eyes were wide open, but he was dead.

Footsteps sounded overhead—her backup had arrived.

She stood and headed for the cage as one thought played in her mind: Jared was alive.

"I love you," she said loudly enough for him to hear her over the music.

CHAPTER 31

I saw so many boys whipped, it took root in my head.
—Albert Fish

Antelope
Sunday, June 10, 2012

Nobody had gotten any sleep in more than twenty-four hours, but Jessica was done being patient. With or without Lizzy or Jared, or Hayley, for that matter, she was going to the construction site. She wouldn't be able to sleep until she searched the property. She was done with the lies and the hidden agendas. She was done with the whole private-eye thing. She had no idea who Magnus Vitalis was, but damn it all, she was going to find him once and for all and make sure he was alive and well.

She had given Lizzy her notice. She was quitting, which made things easier for Lizzy since it turned out she had planned to fire her on Monday for her own good. Not only was Jessica quitting her job, she was giving up her apartment after living in it for less than a month, more determined than ever to return to school and get her degree in criminology. She knew what she wanted out of life, and she was going for it.

She would move in with her mom. She'd already called her brother in New Jersey and chewed him out for abandoning her. He was moving home, too, and together they would help their mother pull herself together; they would be a family again.

Although she'd threatened to go to the construction site alone, there was no need. Jared used his contacts along with his clout to have the garage and patio at the construction site jackhammered. If no bodies were found, he would even cover the costs of hiring the men himself.

The noise was deafening as Jessica impatiently stood in the driveway and watched the men work. She couldn't stand the wait, the not knowing. It was all too much for her, so she headed for the backyard.

When the jackhammering finally stopped, she heard a noise coming from the Dumpster nearby. She tried to lift the top, but it was padlocked. There was more pounding after she tried to lift the lid. Someone was definitely inside. She ran to the front of the house and saw Jared and the men he'd hired looking through the bags they had dug up. She could smell the rotted bodies from where she stood. Frantically, she caught Jared's attention and pointed to the backyard. He followed her to the Dumpster.

It didn't take long for the men to cut off the padlock and open the Dumpster.

There was a man inside. He stood up. He'd lost a lot of weight and he was covered in grime, but it was him: Magnus Vitalis in the flesh.

With Jared's gun pointed at him, he appeared weak and malnourished as he flashed a badge of his own and talked fast.

Jessica couldn't believe what she was seeing or hearing. Magnus was an undercover drug enforcement officer working the Dominic Povo case.

After Jared pulled him from the Dumpster and gave him water, Magnus shook Jared's hand and then looked at Jessica and said, "What took you so long?"

She frowned and pointed to her chest. "Me?"

"Yeah, you. I thought you liked me."

"I don't know what gave you that idea." After a short pause, Jessica smiled and he put an arm around her shoulder, using her for support as she walked him to a nearby chair.

He was weak and his legs were wobbly. He smelled like rotten tomatoes and sewage, but for some reason she didn't mind. After he took a seat, someone handed him another water bottle.

"What happened?" Jessica asked him.

"I've been working undercover, watching Povo for months," he said between gulps of water. "He's a major distributor of meth in the area. His men thought they killed me and left me for dead. Food scraps and half-filled soda cans kept me alive. But I owe you, Kat Sylvester."

She rolled her eyes. "It's Jessica," she reminded him.

"Yeah, I know."

Sacramento
Sunday, June 10, 2012

It didn't matter that Stacey Whitmore had gotten four hours of sleep in the past forty-eight; she looked and felt better than ever in her royal-blue fitted suit with gold buttons. Every hair was in its place, her makeup flawless, her eyes wide and alert as she took a seat behind the anchor desk and got ready to report the nightly news.

Five, four, three, two, one. A wave of the finger from the set director, and the teleprompter began rolling.

"It has been confirmed that Robert Beck, a man of many names, including the Lovebird Killer, is dead. Although he was shot three times, his death was caused by a self-inflicted wound. We've been told that Lizzy Gardner had a hand in leading the FBI to his hideout, where two people were being held captive. A woman, whose name will not be released until relatives have been notified, is in critical condition at Sutter Medical Center in Sacramento.

"The Lovebird Killer's hideout has been described as a windowless basement. It's a cold, dank place where he performed surgical procedures on his victims. It appears the Lovebird Killer embalmed and preserved some of his victims for years. At this time, the FBI has confirmed that Robert Beck is responsible for at least eleven deaths, including those of his adoptive parents, Todd and Karen Beck. A full list of the victims' names will be released after families have been notified.

"In light of new evidence discovered at the site, Michael Dalton was freed this afternoon, exonerated by DNA that was found at the killer's hideout—evidence connecting Robert Beck to Jennifer Dalton's murder."

Stacey continued to smile at the monitor, which was easy to do under the circumstances. Although she never wished Jennifer any harm, she wished she could have been at the prison to see Michael's release. She had no idea where the future would lead her and Michael, but she had already called her lawyer to start divorce proceedings, something she should have done long ago.

The set director gave her the sign that they were off the air. Her smile remained. That was it. She was free to go.

Sacramento
Sunday, June 10, 2012

Eli Simpson shut off the television set and then looked over at Lizzy, who had been sitting in his living room for the past thirty minutes, watching the news with him.

"So, that's it?" he asked after the news ended.

She nodded. "That's it."

He scratched his head. "The police believed that lunatic over me?"

Lizzy sighed, knowing that Eli Simpson's temper probably hadn't helped matters.

"Rochelle's funeral is scheduled for Thursday," he said after a short bout of silence. "It'll be a few family members, along with a couple of Rochelle's friends who stayed in touch. You're welcome to come."

"I'll be there."

"So, this delusional-disorder thing…it's a real disease?"

She nodded again. "I saw the reports from Robert's childhood therapists. It's an uncommon psychiatric condition. The people who have it hold a persistent belief in their reenactment of life events, and they will act out with hostility, if need be, fighting those who try to disprove their 'stories.' Now that he's dead, more and more witnesses are coming forward to disprove his stories."

"Where was his father while he was growing up?"

"His mother was raped," Lizzy told him. "She moved to California to raise her son on a farm she inherited. But everything about Robert reminded her of the man who attacked her. Relatives are saying she was unable to give Robert the love he craved because she was afraid of her own son. Apparently, when Robert was eleven, she discovered he was killing farm animals and burying them in the barn. She confronted him, and within days of her findings, she disappeared, never to be seen again."

"I would hope that they're going to reopen the case of her disappearance."

"It's in the works. Excavation at the farm begins next week."

Eli disappeared for a moment before returning with her digital camera. "Here you go. Never did get any pictures, so I guess you don't owe me anything after all."

She stood, took the camera from him, and smiled. Peering into his eyes, she said, "I'm sorry about your sister. I'm also sorry nobody believed you."

"You believed me." His eyes watered. "You, Lizzy Gardner, were the only one."

She offered him a handshake, but he bent forward and gave her a hug instead.

Sacramento
Sunday, June 10, 2012

As soon as Lizzy left Eli's house, she headed for Sutter Medical and called her sister on the way there. Cathy answered on the second ring.

"I'm sorry," Lizzy blurted, wishing she could take her sister in her arms and hold her close.

There was no response, but she knew Cathy was still on the line because she could hear her breathing. "You're not going to talk to me."

"I don't want to fight with you anymore," Cathy said.

"I don't want to fight anymore either. If Richard is the man you love, the man you want in your life, then I'm all for it. The *only* thing that matters is that you're happy."

"I appreciate that," Cathy said. "There's someone standing right here by my side who is eager to talk to you."

Lizzy smiled. "Put her on the phone."

"Hi, Lizzy!"

"Is this my favorite niece?"

"I passed the test. I have my license. The instructor said I was one of the best drivers he'd ever had the pleasure of passing."

"That doesn't surprise me one bit. I bet your mom is thrilled."

Brittany laughed because they both knew that was *not* the case. "Can you and Jared come over for dinner next weekend?"

"What does your mom think about that?"

"Here, she wants to talk to you again."

"I love you, Britt."

"I love you, too, Lizzy."

"Go get changed," Lizzy heard her sister tell Brittany, "and we'll head out in ten minutes.

"OK, I'm here," Cathy told Lizzy. "We're going shopping."

"Fun."

Cathy cleared her throat. "I saw the news. You've been through a lot these past few days."

"I'm just glad it's all over and Jared is safe."

"Me, too. So what about dinner? Can you two come to the house next Friday?"

"We'd love to. Is it OK if we bring Hayley?"

"Brittany would love that. I'd like to see her, too. We'll look forward to seeing you all."

"See you then." As soon as Lizzy hit the Off button on the console, she received a call from Adele Hampton's biological mother.

The woman was frantic. Her husband was going to be sworn into office soon and she desperately wanted her long-lost daughter to be at her side. Her husband's campaign was losing steam and he was lagging behind in the polls.

Hayley and Jessica had already given Lizzy the scoop, and that was the story Lizzy relayed to the woman on the phone. The truth: Adele had no interest in meeting her mother.

As the woman cursed up a storm, Lizzy hit the Mute button.

Fifteen minutes later, Lizzy did her best to ignore the smell of antiseptic as she walked down the glistening white corridor of the hospital. Jared, along with a couple of Kassie Scott's family members, stood silently inside Kassie's room, waiting for her to wake up.

Jared made introductions and they all hugged Lizzy as if she were part of the family. She was glad to find out that Kassie and the baby would pull through. If all went well, their baby would be born in another seven months. Kassie's husband, Drew Scott, was still in custody for disobeying federal agents, but they all had high hopes that he would be freed before the end of the week.

Lizzy's phone vibrated. She excused herself and moved into the hallway. It was Jessica; she was concerned about Hayley's mom, who had left the women's shelter. Jessica was worried that Hayley might seek out Brian and do something she might later regret, something that might get her into trouble.

Since nobody could sleep last night, Lizzy and Jared had had a heart-to-heart talk with Hayley. Feeling good about how far Hayley had come in such a short time, Lizzy told Jessica not to worry. She also told her she would call her after she and Jared returned to the house.

Because of Hayley's help with the Lovebird Killer case, the judge had already told Jimmy Martin that he would grant Hayley leniency. For now, at least, she wouldn't have to wear the ankle monitor. Hayley had a lot of people rooting for her, including Jimmy Martin, Jared Shayne, and now a judicial court judge.

Right after Lizzy hung up with Jessica, Jared joined her in the hallway. Kassie was awake, and he wanted to give her and her family time alone.

Lizzy filled him in on what was happening with Hayley, and they agreed it would be a good idea to stop by Hayley's mom's house on their way home. As she gazed at Jared, no words could explain how good it was to have him standing before her. It was difficult to fathom that she'd come so close to losing him. "So," Lizzy said as she took Jared's hand in hers, "are you going to marry me, or not?"

"The answer is still no," he said. "You've hardly slept in three days. You're riding the adrenaline wave. You're in euphoria mode."

"That's the most ridiculous thing I've ever heard."

"We've waited this long. Ask me in another week."

"I'll have to think about it. What if I meet a guy next week who can do twenty skips with a stone instead of a measly fifteen?"

Before he could answer, a woman who looked a lot like Kassie stuck her head out the door and waved her arm to get their attention. "Do you mind coming back inside for a moment? Kassie wants to thank you both for everything."

Hand in hand, Jared and Lizzy returned to Kassie's room. Everyone was smiling. It was turning out to be a good day.

CHAPTER 32

When this monster entered my brain, I will never know,
but it is here to stay. How does one cure himself? I can't stop it,
the monster goes on, and hurts me as well as society.
Maybe you can stop him. I can't.
—Dennis Rader

Sacramento
Sunday, June 10, 2012

It was already dark when Hayley slid off the back of Tommy's
bike and asked him to wait there. She didn't like the ache she felt
inside—like sharp teeth gnawing at her gut.

Why did Mom leave the shelter? She'd been doing so well.

Brian had something to do with her mom's sudden disappearance, she was sure of it.

And she had a bad feeling about being at the house where
she'd grown up. Mom still wasn't answering her phone. Hayley
and Tommy had just left the shelter. A woman on staff had told
them that her mom had left two days ago. She'd left willingly with
a man. No description. Just a man.

Hayley took her time walking to the front door, listening to
the sounds as she went: rustling movements in a dead bush to her

right, probably a lizard. The croaking of frogs could be heard in the distance. The place was a mess, and even the recent rains had been unable to wash away the moldy smells of decay and neglect. She couldn't imagine what Jessica must have been thinking when she'd visited.

The last time Hayley had been here was almost a year ago. The door had graffiti scribbled across it: STAY OUT was the message painted in large black letters across the middle of the door.

Good advice.

Her fingers settled over the ugly brass handle. She pushed down on the latch and the door came easily open. Maybe somebody was expecting her.

As she stepped inside, the first breath she took made her feel weak in the knees. The stench was overpowering, nearly unbearable, way worse than she remembered. Trash was everywhere. She couldn't take a step without causing a rat to scurry out of its private home made of pieces of cardboard, cans, and food scraps.

She waded through waste and rubbish to get to the kitchen. She wasn't ready to call out her mom's name. Instead, she hoped and prayed that her mom had not returned, and never would return, to this dump. The kitchen counters had been used as an ashtray. Cigarette butts covered the old Formica top—black holes burned into every square inch. A leaky faucet was the only sound in the whole damn place. Above the sink filled high with dirty, moldy dishes was a cracked window. The backyard was covered with old tires and lots of broken plastic chairs.

Hayley's gaze settled on the rusty old swing set. It was tilted to one side, but all she saw was a beautiful young woman pushing her only daughter on the swing. They both had grins on their faces. The sun was shining. The air was fresh.

Looking around the kitchen with new eyes, Hayley saw her mom coming toward her. She looked happy as she carried a small plate with a cupcake topped off with six candles, the tiny flames flickering. Together, they made a wish and then blew, laughing together when one candle still burned bright, refusing to dim.

She turned toward the sound of another rat scurrying across the floor. She thought of Tommy waiting outside for her. He had become such an important part of her life in such a short amount of time. He was someone she could call her friend. Someone she could confide in.

Eager to check the house and get out, she quickened her pace as she made her way down the hallway. Her mom's bed had been slept in; dirty sheets and stained pillows were crumpled in a pile. Nobody appeared to be inside the bathroom. The yellowed curtain across the bathtub was pulled shut. Hayley took a fistful of plastic and yanked the curtain open.

She exhaled after she saw that it was empty.

Exiting the bedroom, she turned left and continued down the hallway. Two more doors to go through and she would be done. Her old bedroom was to the right and the garage door was straight ahead at the end of the hallway. With her hand on the doorknob leading to her bedroom, she realized she really didn't want to go inside. She wished more than anything that the whole damn house had burned down years ago. That might have solved a lot of problems.

She turned the knob, knowing it had to be done. The putrid smell of rotted eggs and human stink made her gag.

There *was* a Hell and she was looking at it.

Her old desk was still there, pushed against the wall to her left. Dirty, chipped plates were stacked high in the middle of the desk. Even from the doorway where she stood, she could see maggots making a feast of an ancient meal. The floor was littered with empty soup cans and beer bottles. *One hundred bottles of beer on the wall, one hundred bottles of beer, you take one down, you pass it around, ninety-nine bottles of beer on the wall.* That was only one of many songs Brian would sing when he finished off a bottle of beer. There was such an eclectic mix of things inside the room that she really didn't know where to look first.

Probably best if she didn't linger here too long.

The closet door, an old wooden slider, was closed. A strong sense of foreboding fell over her. *Leave. Get out while you can.* But she already knew that she couldn't leave without making sure there was nothing inside the closet. Her phone vibrated in her pocket. She ignored it and continued to walk across a sea of old clothes. Bottles and cans clinked together as she went. Cigarette butts, a mountain of them, decorated the corner of the room.

Before she looked inside the closet, she sank down to her knees and took a quick glance under the bed. Again, she took another relieved breath, filling her lungs with mold. Nothing under the bed except more trash. Glad to have that over with, she pushed herself to her feet. Next, she reached for the rough hole in the wood that served as a makeshift handle to open and close the closet door. The wood door creaked and squeaked in protest, but it came open. No clothes hung from a warped wooden post. There was one shelf, though, and way in the back, she saw a shoe-box. She reached for it and opened the lid. The first thing she saw was her mom smiling back at her.

The entire box was filled with old pictures.

All sorts of pictures: wonderfully happy pictures of her and her mom on the swing, eating cupcakes, dancing and hugging.

All of those memories that had flashed in her mind while she stood in the kitchen.

Who took all of these pictures? she wondered as she shuffled through the pile. Faster and faster, one picture after another, she flipped through the memories. And there it was on the very bottom. A distant memory preserved on paper, but not a memory inside her head. Who was that man? Her father? Could it be?

With the box under one arm and the picture in her right hand, she walked out of her bedroom, down the hallway, and back to her mom's bedroom. Standing in front of the mirror in her mother's bathroom, she held the picture next to her face and gazed into the mirror.

Two peas in a pod.

It was him—her father. She looked just like him: dark hair, seminormal-looking nose except for the little dent in the tip. Their eyes were the same, too. *What was his name?* She turned the picture over. No date. No name scribbled on the back.

Can't have everything.

In the photo she stood in between her parents. She was smiling. Her father was smiling, too, but her mom was looking up at him, love beaming from her eyes.

What happened? What went wrong? So close to having it all.

Her phone vibrated again and this time she picked it up. It was Tommy.

"Are you OK?" he asked.

"I'll be a few more minutes."

She hung up the phone, and then slid the photo she'd been looking at into her back pocket. Clutching the box as if it were some sort of lifeline, she headed for the garage.

No longer feeling the same trepidation she'd felt when she'd walked into the house fifteen minutes ago, she opened the garage door.

"No."

The box dropped from her hands. Pictures scattered. A couple of the photos fluttered to her feet.

Hayley didn't blink.

No matter how hard she tried, she couldn't look away from those eyes. Wide-open eyes. Not the loving smiling eyes she'd just seen in the photo, but dead lifeless eyes. Mom was on her back, her head propped up on enough debris that it appeared she was looking right at Hayley.

Brian had said he would use the axe from the shed to cut off her mom's head. Instead, the axe was embedded in the top of her skull, the wood handle sticking straight out to the right, the weight of it pulling her head as if she were curious about why Hayley hadn't come sooner. Mom was wearing her pink nightgown, the same gown she'd been wearing for too many years. Only it wasn't pink any longer. It was red—blood red.

Walking toward her, Hayley sank to her knees and took hold of her mom's cold hand, entwining their fingers, clutching tightly, willing her mom back to life, praying this moment was not real and instead just a figment of her wildly fucked-up imagination.

Hayley wasn't sure how long she lay there, but when the tears stopped, she looked up and saw her reflection in the broken mirror across the way. Her arms were wrapped around her mom's bloody corpse.

Mom was gone.

Forever.

She curled up close and rested her head on her mom's cold, hard chest, all the while staring at the bright red eyes in the mirror looking back at her. She recognized those eyes; they were *her* eyes. It was over now, Hayley realized. It was all over and the demon inside of her had won.

Fuck hope.

Fuck optimism.

Fuck you all.

ACKNOWLEDGMENTS

My deepest appreciation goes to my editor, Alan Turkus, for believing in me and my stories. I would like to thank Alison Dasho for working so hard to help make *A Dark Mind* a better book. Many thanks to my beta readers: Janet, Joey, Brittany, and Joe. I want to thank Zoey Winters of Granite Bay for using her wicked imagination to help brainstorm my Lizzy Gardner series. I am forever grateful to Sandy Scrivano for reading *Abducted* and telling me I had a best seller on my hands, and then pushing me to publish it. And to Sam Johnston, thank you for being my number one fan!

ABOUT THE AUTHOR

Photograph by Morgan Ragan, 2012

T.R. Ragan grew up in a family of five girls in Lafayette, California. She is an avid traveler whose wanderings have carried her to Ireland, the Netherlands, China, Thailand, and Nepal, where she narrowly survived being chased by a killer elephant. Before devoting herself to writing fiction, she worked as a legal secretary for a large corporation. She is the author of *Abducted* and *Dead Weight*, the first books in the Lizzy Gardner series. Writing under the name Theresa Ragan, she is also the author of *Return of the Rose*, *A Knight in Central Park*, *Taming Mad Max*, *Finding Kate Huntley*, and *Having My Baby*. She and her family live in Sacramento.

Improving
Your
Study
Skills